"Bodies here." Jakob's voice ⸺ think I've found the crew . . ⸺ Saints—"

There was a snarling, and ⸺ went out and in the blackness ⸺ into a fury. The skipper glimpsed the yellow gleam of an eye, like a ravening fire far off on a pitch-black night. His lips formed Jakob's name but no sound came out; his tongue had turned to sand. He backed away and bumped into a crate.

Run, some part of his mind shrieked at him, but his marrow had become like granite within his very bones.

Then the thing was swarming up the companion towards him, and he had not even the time to mouth a prayer before it was rending his flesh, and the yellow eyes were witness to his soul's flight.

Praise for the *Monarchies of God* novels:

"An action-packed, fast-paced fantasy adventure."
—SF Site (naming Book Four of the
Monarchies of God one of the Ten Best Books of the Year)

"Impressive for its human insights, its unusual take on the use of magic and its fine blending of historical elements with sheer invention."
—*Locus*

Coming next month:

THE HERETIC KINGS

THE MONARCHIES OF GOD, BOOK TWO

HAWKWOOD'S
VOYAGE

BOOK ONE OF THE MONARCHIES OF GOD

PAUL KEARNEY

ACE BOOKS, NEW YORK

HAWKWOOD'S VOYAGE

An Ace Book / published by arrangement with
Orion Publishing Group

PRINTING HISTORY
Victor Gollancz edition / 1995
Vista mass-market edition / 1996
Ace mass-market edition / January 2002

Visit our website at
www.penguinputnam.com
Check out the ACE Science Fiction & Fantasy newsletter!

ISBN: 0-441-00903-4

ACE®
Ace Books are published by The Berkley Publishing Group,
a division of Penguin Putnam Inc.,
375 Hudson Street, New York, New York 10014.
ACE and the "A" design
are trademarks belonging to Penguin Putnam Inc.

PRINTED IN THE UNITED STATES OF AMERICA

10 9 8 7 6 5 4 3 2 1

For the Museum Road bunch:
John, Dave, Sharon, Felix, and Helen;
and for Dr. Marie Cahir,
partner in everything.

They that go down to the sea in ships,
that do business in great waters;
these see the works of the Lord, and
his wonders in the deep.

Psalm 107:23-24

PROLOGUE
YEAR OF THE SAINT 422

A ship of the dead, it coasted in on the northwest breeze, topsails still set but the yards braced for a long-lost wind on the open ocean. The yawlsmen sighted it first, on the eve of St. Beynac's Day. It was heeling heavily, even on the slight swell, and what was left of its canvas shuddered and flapped when the breeze fell.

It was a day of perfect blueness—sea and sky vast, even reflections of one another. A few gulls flapped expectantly round the silver-filled nets the yawl crews were hauling in hand over fist, and a school of gleaming oyvips were sporting off to port: an unlucky omen. Within each, it was said, howled the soul of a drowned man. But the wind was kind, and the shoal was large—it could be seen as a broad shadow under the hull, twinkling now and then with the bright flank of a twisting fish—and the fishermen had been here since the forenoon watch, filling their nets with the sea's uncertain bounty, the dark line of the Hebrionese coast a mere guess off behind their right shoulders.

The skipper of one yawl shaded his eyes, paused and peered out to sea, blue stone glinting out from rippled leather, his chin bristling with hairs as pale as those on the stem of a nettle.

Water shadow writhed luminously in the hollows of his eye-sockets.

"There's a sight," he muttered.

"What is it, Fader?"

"A carrack, lad, a high-seas ship by the looks of her. But the canvas is hanging in strips off her yards—there's a brace flying free. And she's made a ton of water, if I'm any judge. She's taken a pounding, all right. And what of the crew? Un-handy lubbers."

"Maybe they're dead, or wore out," his son said eagerly.

"Maybe. Or maybe sick of the plague as I hears ravages them eastern lands. The curse o' God on unbelievers."

The other men in the yawl paused at that, staring darkly out at the oncoming vessel. The wind veered a point—they felt it shift out of one eye—and the strange ship lost way. She was hull up, her battered masts black against that uncertain band of horizon that is either sea or sky. Water dripped from the men's hands; the fish flapped feebly in the nets, forgotten and dying. Droplets of sweat gathered on noses and stung their eyes: salt in everything, even the body's own water. They looked at their skipper.

"It's salvage, if the crew's all dead," one man said.

"It's an unlucky ship that coasts in from the empty west and no sign of life aboard," another muttered. "There's naught out there but a thousandscore leagues of unsailed sea, and beyond that the very rim of the earth."

"There may be men alive aboard her in need of help," the skipper said sternly. His son gazed at him with round eyes. For a moment, the stares of all his crew were fixed on his face. He felt them like he did the warmth of the sun, but his seamed visage revealed nothing as he made his decision.

"We'll close with her. Jakob, set the forecourse, brace her round. Gorm, get these nets in and hail the other boats. They should stay. There's a good shoal here, too good to let by."

The crew leapt to their tasks, some sullen, some excited. The yawl was two-masted, the mizzen stepped abaft the rudder head. She would have to beat into the landward breeze to board the carrack. Men on the other boats paused in the haul-ing of their catch to watch as the yawl closed on her goal. The bigger vessel was broadside on to the swell, listing to starboard as the waves broke on her windward side. As the yawl drew close, her crew broke out sweeps and strained at the heavy oars whilst the skipper and a few others stood poised on the gunwale, ready to make the perilous leap on to the side of the carrack.

She towered darkly above them now, a looming giant, her running rigging flying free, the lateen yard on her mizzen a mere stump and the thick wales that lined her side smashed and splintered as though she had squeezed through a narrow place. There was no sign of life, no reply to the skipper's hail. Surreptitiously, men at the sweeps paused in their labour to make the Sign of the Saint at their breasts.

The skipper leapt, grunted at the impact as he hit the carrack's side, hauled himself over her rail and stood panting. The others followed, two with their dirks in their teeth as if they expected to fight their way aboard. And then the yawl drew off, her mate putting her about on the port tack. She would heave to, keep the wind on her weather bow and ride out the breeze. The skipper waved at her as she eased away.

The carrack was wallowing low in the water and the wind was working on her high fore- and sterncastles. There was no sound but the hiss and lap of the sea, the creak of wood and rigging, the thump of a staved cask that rolled back and forth in the scuppers. The skipper raised his head as he caught the whiff of corruption. He met the knowing gaze of old Jakob. They nodded at each other. There was death aboard, corpses rotting somewhere.

"The Blessed Ramusio preserve us, let it not be the plague," one man said hoarsely, and the skipper scowled.

"Hold your tongue, Kresten. You and Daniel see what you can do to put her before the wind. It's my belief her seams are working in this swell. We'll see if we can't get her into Abrusio before she spews her oakum and sinks her bow."

"You're going to bring her in?" Jakob asked.

"If I can. We'll have to look below though, see if she's anywhere near settling." The roll of the ship made him lurch a little. "Wind's picking up. That's all to the good if we can get her head round. Come, Jakob."

He pushed open one of the doors in the sterncastle and entered the darkness beyond. The bright blue day was cut off. He could hear Jakob padding barefoot and breathing heavily behind him in the sudden gloom. He stopped. The ship heaved like a dying thing under his feet—that smell of putrefaction, stronger now, rising even over the familiar sea smells of salt and tar and hemp. He gagged as his hands, groping, found another door.

"Sweet Saint!" he breathed, and pushed it open.

Sunlight, bright and blazing, flooding through shattered stern windows. A wide cabin, a long table, the gleam of falchions crossed on a bulkhead, and a dead man sitting watching him.

The skipper made himself move forward.

There was water underfoot, sloshing about with the heave of the ship. It looked as though a following sea had swamped the windows; at the forward end of the cabin was a tangle of clothing, weapons, charts, and a small brassbound chest, much battered. But the dead man sat upright in his chair with his back to the stern windows and the brown skin stretched tight as parchment over the lines of his skull. His hands were shrunken claws. The rats had gnawed him. His chair was fixed in wooden runners to the deck, and he was tied into the chair by line after line of sodden cordage. It looked as though he had bound himself; the arms were free. A tattered scrap of paper was clenched in one decaying fist.

"Jakob, what is this we see?"

"I know not, Captain. There has been devilry at work in this ship. This man was the master—see the charts?—and there is a broken cross-staff here too. But what happened to him that he did this?"

"There is no explaining it—not yet. We must go below. See if you can find a lantern here, or a candle. I must have a look at her hold."

"The hold?" The old man sounded doubtful.

"Yes, Jakob. We must see how fast she is making water, and what her cargo is."

The light left the windows and the motion of the ship grew easier as the men on deck put her before the wind. Jakob and his captain gave a last look at the dead master and his skull face, and left. Neither told the other what he was thinking: the dead man had ended his tenure of the world with his face distorted by terror.

●   ●   ●

BRIGHT sunlight again, the clean spray of the sea. The other boarders were busy with the lifts and braces, moving yards far heavier than they were used to. The skipper barked a few orders. They would need canvas and fresh cordage. The mainmast shrouds were ripped to shreds on the port side; a wonder she had not rolled out the mast.

"No storm ever did this to a ship," Jakob said, and ran his horny hands along the ship's rail. The wood was torn, punctured. Bitten, the skipper thought, and he felt a cold worm of fear coil in his stomach.

But he shut his face to Jakob's look of enquiry.

"We are mariners, not philosophers. Our task is to make the ship swim. Now are you coming with me or shall I ask one of the youngsters?"

They had sailed the Hebrionese coast for more than twoscore years together, weathered more storms than they could remember, hauled in a million fish. Jakob nodded mutely, anger burning away his fear.

The tarpaulins over the hatchways were flapping and torn. It was dark there, in the very bowels of the ship, and they lowered themselves down with care. One of the others had found and lit a lantern. It was passed down into the dark and by its beam they found themselves surrounded by crates, casks and sacks. There was a musty smell in the air, and again the faint stink of corruption. They could hear the swirl and gurgle of water deeper in the hold, the rolling rumble of loose cargo, the creak of the ship's overworked hull. The stink of the bilge, usually overpowering in a large ship, had been overwhelmed by incoming seawater.

They made their slow way along an avenue between the cargo, the lantern beam swinging shadows in chaotic directions. They found the remains of rats half eaten, but none alive. And there was no sign of the crew. The master in his cabin above might have been piloting the ship alone and unaided until his death.

Another hatch, and a companion ladder leading down, deep into utter blackness. The ship creaked and groaned under their feet. They could no longer hear the voices of their shipmates above, in that other world of salt air and spray. There was only this hole opening on nothingness, and beyond the wooden walls that surrounded them nothing but the drowning sea.

"Water down there, deep enough too," Jakob said, lowering the lantern through the hatch. "I see it moving, but there's no spume. If it's a leak, it's slow."

They paused, peering down into a place neither of them wanted to see. But they were mariners, as the skipper had said, and no man bred to the sea could stand idle and watch a ship die.

The skipper made as if to start down, but Jakob stopped him with an odd smile and went first, the breath rattling audibly in his throat. The skipper saw the light break and splinter on multifaceted water, things bobbing in it, a splash amid the chiaroscuro of shadow and flame.

"Bodies here." Jakob's voice came up, distorted, far away. "I think I've found the crew. Oh sweet God, his blessed Saints—"

There was a snarling, and Jakob screamed. The lantern went out and in the blackness something thrashed the water into a fury. The skipper glimpsed the yellow gleam of an eye, like a ravening fire far off on a pitch-dark night. His lips formed Jakob's name but no sound came out; his tongue had turned to sand. He backed away and bumped into the sharp corner of a crate. *Run*, some part of his mind shrieked at him, but his marrow had become like granite within his very bones.

Then the thing was swarming up the companion towards him, and he had not even the time to mouth a prayer before it was rending his flesh, and the yellow eyes were witness to his soul's flight.

PART ONE

THE FALL OF AEKIR

ONE

T HE City of God was burning . . .
    Long plumes of fire sailed up from the streets like wind-coiled banners, detaching to consume themselves and become lost in the grim thunderheads of impenetrable smoke that low-ered above the flames. For miles along the Ostian river the city burned and the buildings crumbled, their collapse lost in the all-encompassing roar of the fire. Even the continuing noise of battle by the western gates, where the rearguard was still fighting, was swallowed up by the bellowing inferno.

The cathedral of Carcasson, greatest in the world, stood stark and black against the flames, a solitary sentinel horned with steeples, nippled with domes. The massive granite shrugged off the heat but the lead on the roof was melting in rivulets and the timber beams were blazing all along their length. The bodies of priests littered the steps; the Blessed Ramusio gazed down sorrowfully with a horde of the lesser saints in attendance, their eyes cracking open, the bronze staffs they held buckling in the inferno. Here and there a gargoyle, outlined in scarlet, grinned malevolently down.

The palace of the High Pontiff was full of looting troops. The Merduks had ripped down tapestries, hacked apart relics for the precious stones that adorned them, and now they were drinking wine out of the Holy Vessels whilst they waited their turn with captured women. Truly, Ahrimuz had been good to them today.

Further westwards within the city, the streets were clogged with fleeing people and the troops who had been stationed here to guard them. Hundreds were trampled underfoot in the panic, children abandoned, the old and slow kicked aside. More than once a collapsing house would bury a score of them in a fury of blazing masonry, but the rest would spare hardly a glance. Westwards they forged, west towards the gates still held by Ramusian troops, the last remnant of John Mogen's Torunnans, once the most feared soldiers in all the west. These were a desperate rabble now, their valour bled away by the siege and the six assaults which had preceded the last. And John Mogen was dead. Even now, the Merduks were crucifying his body above the eastern gate where he had fallen, cursing them to the last.

The Merduks poured through the city like a tide of cockroaches, glinting and barbed in the light of the fires, their faces shining, sword arms bloody to the elbows. It had been a long siege and a good fight, and at last the greatest city of the west was theirs for the taking. Shahr Baraz had promised to let them loose once the city had fallen and they were intent on plunder. It was not they who were burning the city, but the retreating western troops. Sibastion Lejer, lieutenant of Mogen, had sworn to let not one building fall intact into the hands of the heathens and he and a remnant of men still under orders were methodically burning the palaces and arsenals, the storehouses and pleasure theatres and churches of Aekir, and slaughtering anyone, Merduk or Ramusian, who tried to stop them.

CORFE watched the tall curtains of flame shift against the darkened sky. The smoke of the burning had brought about a premature twilight, the end of a long day for the defenders of Aekir; for many thousands, the last day.

He was on a flat rooftop, apart from the maelstrom of screaming people below. The sound of them carried up in a solid wave. Fear, anger, desperation. It was as though Aekir itself were screaming, the tormented city in the midst of its death throes, the fire incinerating its vitals. The smoke stung

Corfe's eyes and he wiped them clear. He could feel ashes settling on his brow like a black snow.

A tatterdemalion figure, no longer the dapper ensign, he was scorched, ragged and bloodied. He had cast aside his half-armour in the flight from the walls, and wore only his doublet and the heavy sabre that was the mark of Mogen's men. He was short, lithe, deep-eyed. In his gaze alternated murder and despair.

His wife was somewhere down there, enjoying the attentions of the Merduks or trampled underfoot in some cobbled alley, or a burnt corpse in the wreck of a house.

He wiped his eyes again. Damn smoke.

"Aekir cannot fall," Mogen had told them. *"It is impregnable, and the men on its walls are the best soldiers in the world. But that is not all. It is the Holy City of God, first home of the Blessed Ramusio. It cannot fall."* And they had cheered.

A quarter of a million Merduks had proved otherwise.

The soldier in him wondered briefly how many of the garrison had or would escape. Mogen's bodyguards had fought to the death after he had gone down, and that had started the flight. Thirty-five thousand men had garrisoned Aekir. If a tenth of them made it through to the Ormann line they would be lucky.

"I can't leave you, Corfe. You are my life. My place is here." So she had said with that heartbreakingly lopsided smile of hers, the hair as dark as a raven's feather across her face. And he, fool, fool, fool, had listened to her, and to John Mogen.

Impossible to find her. Their home, such as it was, had been in the shadow of the eastern bastion, the first place to fall. He had tried to get through three times before giving up. No man lived there now who did not worship Ahrimuz, and the women who survived were already being rounded up. Handmaidens of Ahrimuz they would become, inmates of the Merduk field brothels.

Damned stupid bitch. He had told her a hundred times to move, to get out before the siege lines began to cut the city off.

He looked out to the west. The crowds pulsed that way like sluggish blood in the arteries of a felled giant. It was rumoured that the Ormann road was still open all the way to the River

Searil, where the Torunnans had built their second fortified
line in twenty years. The Merduks had left that one slim way
out deliberately, it was said, to tempt the garrison into evacuation. The population would be choking it up for twenty
leagues. Corfe had seen it before, in the score of battles that
had followed after the Merduks had first crossed the Jafrar
Mountains.

Was she dead? He would never know. Oh, Heria.

His sword arm ached. He had never before been a part of
such slaughter. It seemed to him that he had been fighting for
ever, and yet the siege had lasted only three months. It had
not, in fact, been a siege as *The Military Manual* knew one.
The Merduks had isolated Aekir and then had commenced to
pound it into the ground. There had been no attempt to starve
the city into submission. They had merely kept on attacking
with reckless abandon, losing five men for every defender who
fell, until the final assault this morning. It had been pure sav-
agery on the walls, a to and fro of carnage, until the critical
moment had been reached, the cup finally brimming over and
the Torunnans had begun the trickle off the ramparts which
had turned into a rout. Old John had roared at them, before a
Merduk scimitar cut him down. There had been near panic
after that. No thought of a second line, a fighting retreat. The
bitter tension of the siege, the multiple assaults, had left them
too worn, as brittle as a rust-eaten blade. The memory made
Corfe ashamed. Aekir's walls had not even been breached;
they had simply been abandoned.

Was that why he had paused, was standing here now like
some spectator at an apocalypse? To make up for his flight,
perhaps.

Or to lose himself in it. *My wife. Down there somewhere,
alive or dead.*

Rumbling booms, concussions that shook the smoke-thick
air. Sibastion was touching off the magazines. Crackles of arquebus fire. Someone was making a stand. Let them. It was
time to abandon the city, and those he had loved here. Those
fools who chose to fight on would leave their corpses in its
gutters.

Corfe started down off the roof, wiping his eyes angrily. He
probed the stairway before him with his sabre like a blind man
tapping his stick.

It was suffocatingly hot as he came out on the street, and the acrid air made his throat ache. The raw sound of the crowds hit him like a moving wall, and then he was in amongst them, being carried along like a swimmer lost in a millrace. They stank of terror and ashes and their faces seemed hardly human to him in the hellish light. He could see unconscious men and women being held upright by the closeness of the throng, small children crawling upon the serried heads as though they were a carpet. Men were being crushed at the edges of the street as they were smeared along the sides of the confining walls. He could feel the bodies of others under his feet as he was propelled along. His heel slid on the face of a child. The sabre was lost, levered out of his hand in the press. He tilted his face to the shrouded sky, the flaming buildings, and fought for his share of the reeking air.

Lord God, he thought, I am in hell.

AURUNGZEB the Golden, third Sultan of Ostrabar, was dallying with the pert breasts of his latest concubine when a eunuch paddled through the curtains at the end of the chamber and bowed deeply, his bald pate shining in the light of the lamps.

"Highness."

Aurungzeb glared, his black eyes boring into the temerarious intruder, who remained bowed and trembling.

"What is it?"

"A messenger, Highness, from Shahr Baraz before Aekir. He says he has news from the army that will not wait."

"Oh, won't it?" Aurungzeb leapt up, hurling aside his pouting companion. "Am I at the beck and call, then, of every hairless eunuch and private soldier in the palace?" He kicked the eunuch sprawling. The glabrous face twisted silently.

Aurungzeb paused. "From the army, you say? Is it good news or bad? Is the siege broken? Has that dog Mogen routed my troops?"

The eunuch hauled himself to his hands and knees and wheezed at the fantastically coloured carpet. "He would not say, Highness. He will only relay the news to you personally. I told him this was very irregular but—" Another kick silenced him again.

"Send him in, and if he has bad news then I'll make a eunuch of him too."

A jerk of his head sent the concubine scurrying into the corner. From a jewelled chest the Sultan took a plain dagger with a worn hilt. It had seen much use, but had been put away as though it were something hugely precious. Aurungzeb tucked it into his waist sash, then clapped his hands.

The messenger was a Kolchuk, a race the Merduks had long ago conquered in their march west. The Kolchuks ate reindeer and made love to their sisters. Moreover, this man stood tall before Aurungzeb despite the hissings of the eunuch. He had somehow bypassed the Vizier and the Chamberlain of the Harem to come this far. It must be news indeed. If it was bad tidings Aurungzeb would make him less tall by a head.

"Well?"

The man had the unknowable eyes of the Kolchuks; flat stones behind slits in his expressionless face. But there was something of a glow about him, despite the fact that he swayed slightly as he stood. He smelt of dust and lathered horse, and Aurungzeb noticed with interest that there was a gout of dried blood blackening the gut of his armour.

Now the man did fall to one knee, but his face remained tilted upwards, shining.

"The compliments of Shahr Baraz, Commander in Chief of the Second Army of Ostrabar, Highness. He begs leave to report that, should it please your excellency, he has taken possession of the infidel city of Aekir and is even now cleansing it of the last of the western rabble. The army is at your disposal."

Aekir has fallen.

The Vizier burst in followed by a pair of tulwar-wielding guards. He shouted something, and they grasped the kneeling Kolchuk by the shoulders. But Aurungzeb held up a hand.

"Aekir has fallen?"

The Kolchuk nodded, and for a second the inscrutable soldier and the silk-clad Sultan smiled at each other, men sharing a triumph only they could appreciate. Then Aurungzeb pursed his lips. It would not do to press the man for information; that would smack of eagerness, even gracelessness.

"Akran," he barked at his glowering, uncertain Vizier.

"Quarter this man in the palace. See that he is fed, bathed, and has whatever he wishes."

"But Highness, a common soldier—"

"Do it, Akran. This common soldier could have been an assassin, but you let him slip past you into the very harem. Had it not been for Serrim"—here the eunuch coloured and simpered—"I would have been taken totally by surprise. I thought my father had taught you better, Akran."

The Vizier looked bent and old. The guards shifted uneasily, contaminated with his guilt.

"Now go, all of you. No, wait. Your name, soldier. What is it and with whom do you serve?"

The Kolchuk gazed at him, remote once more. "I am Harafeng, Lord. I am one of the Shahr's bodyguard."

Aurungzeb raised an eyebrow. "Then, Harafeng, when you have eaten and washed, the Vizier will bring you back to me and we will discuss the fall of Aekir. You have my leave to go, all of you."

The Kolchuk nodded curtly, which made Akran splutter with indignation, but Aurungzeb smiled. As soon as he was alone in the chamber his smile turned into a grin which split his beard, and it was possible to see the general of men that he had briefly been in his youth.

Aekir has fallen.

Ostrabar was counted third in might of the Seven Sultanates, coming after Hardukh and ancient Nalbeni, but this feat of arms, this glorious victory, would propel it into the first rank of the Merduk sultanates, and Aurungzeb at its head. Centuries hence they would talk of the sultan who had taken the holiest and most populous city of the Ramusians, who had broken the army of John Mogen.

The way lay open to Torunn itself now; there remained only the line of the River Searil and the fortress of Ormann Dyke. Once they fell there was no line of defence until the Cimbric Mountains, four hundred miles further west.

"Ahrimuz, all praise to thee!" the Sultan whispered through his grin, and then said sharply, "Gheg."

A homunculus sidled from behind one of the embroidered curtains, flapped its leathery little wings and perched on a nearby table.

"Gheg," it said in a tiny, dry voice, its face a picture in cunning malevolence.

"I wish to speak to your keeper, Gheg. Summon him for me."

The homunculus, no larger than a pigeon, yawned, showing white needle-teeth in a red mouth. One clawed hand scratched its crotch negligently.

"Gheg hungry," it said, disgruntled.

Aurungzeb's nostrils flared. "You were fed last night, as fine a babe as you could wish. Now get me your keeper, hell-spawn."

The homunculus glowered at him, then shrugged its tiny shoulders. "Gheg tired. Head hurts."

"Do as I say or I'll spit you like a quail."

The homunculus smiled: a hideous sight. Then a different light came into its glowing eyes. In a deep, human tone it said, "I am here, Sultan."

"Your pet is somewhat sullen of late, Orkh—one of the reasons I use him so seldom nowadays."

"My apologies, Highness. He is getting old. I shall consign him to the jar soon and send you a new one . . . What is your wish?"

"Where are you?" It was odd to hear petulance from such a big, hirsute figure.

"It is no matter. I am close enough. Have you a boon you would ask of me?"

Aurungzeb struggled visibly to control his temper.

"I would have you look south, to Aekir. Tell me what transpires there. I have had news. I wish to see it substantiated."

"Of course." There was a pause. "I see Carcasson afire. I see siege towers along the inner walls. There is a great burning, the howls of Ramusians. I congratulate you, Highness. Your troops run amok through the city."

"Shahr Baraz. What of him?"

Another moment's silence. When the voice came again it held mild surprise.

"He views the crucified body of John Mogen. He weeps, Sultan. In the midst of victory, he weeps."

"He is of the old *Hraib*. He mourns his enemy, the romantic fool. The city burns, you say?"

"Yes. The streets are crawling with unbelievers. They fire the city as they go."

"That will be Lejer, the dastard. He will leave us nothing but ashes. A curse on him and his children. I'll have him crucified, if he is taken. Is the Ormann road open?"

The homunculus had come out in beads of shining sweat. It trembled and its wing tips drooped. The voice which came out of it did not change, however.

"Yes, Highness. It is clogged with carts and bodies, a veritable migration. The House of Ostrabar reigns supreme."

Eighty years before the House of Ostrabar had consisted solely of Aurungzeb's grandfather and a trio of hardy concubines. Generalship, not lineage, had reared it up out of the eastern steppes. If the Ostrabars could not win battles themselves, they hired someone who could. Hence Shahr Baraz, who had been Khedive to Aurungzeb's father. Aurungzeb had commanded troops competently in his youth, but he could not inspire them in the same way. It was a lack he had never ceased to resent. Shahr Baraz, though originally an outsider, a nomad chief from far Kambaksk, had served three generations of Ostrabars honestly and ably. He was now in his eighties, a terrible old man much given to prayer and poetry. It was well that Aekir had fallen when it did; Shahr Baraz's long life was near its close, and with it would go the last link between the Sultans and the horse-borne chieftains of the steppes who had preceded them.

Shahr Baraz had recommended that the Ormann road be left open. The influx of refugees would weaken and demoralize the men who manned the line of the Searil river, he said. Aurungzeb had wondered if some outdated chivalry had had a hand in the decision also. No matter.

"Tell the—" he began, and stopped. The homunculus was melting before his eyes, glaring at him reproachfully as it bubbled into a foul-smelling pool.

"Orkh! Tell the Khedive to push on to the Searil!"

The homunculus' mouth moved but made no sound. It dissolved, steaming and reeking. In the nauseous puddle it became it was possible to make out the decaying foetus of a child, the wing-bones of a bird, the tail of a lizard. Aurungzeb gagged and clapped his hands for the eunuchs. Gheg had outlived its usefulness, but no doubt Orkh would send him another of the creatures soon. He had other messengers—not so swift, perhaps, but just as sure.

Aekir has fallen.

He began to laugh.

TWO

"SWEET God!" Hawkwood said. "What is happening?"

"Vast heaving there!" the boatswain roared, eyeing a flapping sail. "Brace round that foretopsail, you God-damned eunuchs. Where do you think you are, a two-copper curiosity show?"

The *Grace of God*, a square-rigged caravel, slid quietly into Abrusio at six bells in the forenoon watch, the water a calm blue shimmer along her sides dotted with the filth of the port. Where the sun struck the sea there was a white glitter, painful to look at. A faint north-west breeze—the Hebrionese trade—enabled her to waft in like a swan, with hardly a rope to be touched by the staring crew despite the outrage of the boatswain.

Abrusio. They had heard the bells of its cathedral all through the last two turns of the glass, a ghostly echo of piety drifting out to sea.

Abrusio, capital of Hebrion and greatest port of the Five Kingdoms. It was a beautiful sight to behold when coming home from even a short coasting voyage such as the *Grace*'s crew had just completed; an uneasy cruise along the Macassar coast, haggling with the Sea-Rovers over tolls, one hand to their dirks and the slow-match burning alongside the culverins

all the while. But profitable, despite the heat, the flies, the pitch
melting in the seams and the marauding river lizards. Despite
the feast drums at night along the bonfire-studded coast and
the lateen-winged feluccas with their cargoes of grinning corsairs. Safe in the hold were three tons of ivory from the skel-
etons of great marmorills, and fragrant Limian spice by the
hundredweight. And they had lost only one man, a clumsy
first-voyager who had leaned too far out over the rail as a
shallowshark passed by.

Now they were back among the Monarchies of God, where
men made the Sign of the Saint over their viands and the
Blessed Ramusio's likeness stared down upon every cross-
roads and market place.

Abrusio was home port for almost half of them, and contained the shipyard where the *Grace*'s keel had been laid down
thirty years before.

Two things struck the seaward observer about Abrusio: the
forest and the mountain.

The forest sprouted out of the glassy bay below the city, a
vast tangle of masts and spars and yards, like the limbs of a
leafless wood, perfect in their geometry, interconnected with
a million rigging lines. Vessels of every nationality, tonnage,
rig, complement and calling were anchored in the bay of Abrusio by the hundred, from coastal hoys and yawls with their
decks asprawl with nets and shining fish to ocean-going carracks bedecked with proud pennants. And the Navy of Hebrion
had its yards here also, so there were tall war-carracks, galleys
and galleasses by the score, the wink of breastplate and helmet
on quarterdecks and poops, the slow flap of the heavy Royal
standards on mainmasts, the pendants of admirals on mizzens.

Two more things about this floating forest, this waterborne
city: the noise and the smell. There were hoys offloading their
catches, merchantmen at the quays with their hatches open and
gangs hauling on tackles to bring forth from their bellies the
very life's blood of trade. Wool from Almark, amber from
Forlassen, furs from Fimbria, iron from Astarac, timber from
the tall woods of Gabrion, best in the world for the building
of ships. The men that worked the vessels of the port and the
countless waggons on the wharves set up a rumbling murmur
of sound, a clatter, a squeal of trucks, a creak of wood and

hemp that carried for half a mile out to sea, the very essence of a living port.

And they stank. Further out to sea on such a still day drifted the smell of unwashed humanity in its tens of thousands, of fish rotting in the burnished sunlight, of offal tossed into the water to be quarrelled over by hordes of gulls, of pitch from the shipyards, ammonia from the tanneries; and underlying it all a heady mixture, like a glimpse of foreign lands, a concoction of spices and new timber, salt air and seaweed, an elixir of the sea.

That was the bay. The mountain, also, was not what it seemed. From afar it looked to be a blend of dust and ochre stone, pyramidal in shape, hazed with blue smoke. Closer inshore an approaching mariner would see that a hill reared up from the teeming waterfront and built upon it, row upon row, street upon narrow, crowded street, was the city itself, the house walls whitewashed and thick with dust, the roofs of faded red clay from the inland tile works of Feramuno. Here and there a church thrust head and lofty shoulders above the throng of humbler dwellings, its spire a spike reaching for blue, unclouded heaven. And here and there was the stone-built massiveness of a prosperous merchant's house—for Abrusio was a city of merchants as well as of mariners. Indeed, some said that a Hebrian must be one of three things at birth: a mariner, a merchant or a monk.

Towards the summit of the low hill, making it higher than it truly was and giving it the aspect of a steep-sided mountain, was the citadel and palace of the King, Abeleyn IV, monarch of Hebrion and Imerdon, admiral of half a thousand ships.

The dark granite walls of his fortress-palace had been reared up by Fimbrian artificers four centuries before, and over their high walls could be glimpsed the tallest of the King's cypresses, the jewels of his pleasure gardens. (A fifth of the city's water consumption, it was rumoured, went on keeping those gardens green.) They had been planted by the King's forebears when the first Hebrion shrugged off the decaying Fimbrian yoke. They flickered now in the awful heat, and the palace swam like a mirage of the Calmari desert.

Beside the King's palace and pleasure gardens the monastery of the Inceptine Order shimmered also. So-called because they were the first religious order founded after the visions of the Blessed Ramusio brought light to the darkness of the idol-worshipping west (indeed, some would have folk believe that Ramusio himself founded them), the Inceptines were the religious watchdogs of the Ramusian kingdoms.

Palace and monastery, they frowned down together over the sprawling, stinking, vibrant city of Abrusio. A quarter of a million souls toiled and bargained and revelled beneath them, natives of the greatest port in the known world.

"SWEET God," Richard Hawkwood had said. "What is happening?"

He had reason to speculate, for over the upper half of Abrusio a black smoke hung in the limpid air, and a worse stink was wafting over the crowded port towards his ship. Burning flesh. The gibbets of the Inceptines were crowded with stick-like shapes and a pall of scorched meat hung sickeningly far out to sea, more greasy and unclean than the foulest odour of the sewers.

"They're sending heretics to the pyre," the boatswain said, disgusted and awed. "God's Ravens are at it again. The Saints preserve us!"

Old Julius, the first mate, an easterner with a face as black as pitch, looked at his captain with wide eyes, his dusky countenance almost grey. Then he bent over the rail and hailed a bumboat close by, packed to the gills with fruit, its pilot a broad hideous fellow who lacked an eye.

"Ho! What's in the air, friend? We're back from a month-long cruise down in the Rovers' kingdoms and our tongues are hanging out for news."

"What's in the air? Cannot your nostrils take in the stink of it? Four days it's been hanging over the city, honest old Abrusio. We're a haven of sorcerers and unbelievers it seems, every one of them in the pay of the sultans. God's Ravens are ridding us of them, in their kindness." He spat over the gunwale into water becoming thick with the detritus of the port. "And I'd watch where you go with that dark face, friend. But wait—you've been out a month, you say. Have you heard the news from the east? Surely to God you know?"

"Know what, fellow?" Julius cried out impatiently.

The bumboat was being left behind. Already it was half a

cable abaft the port beam. The one-eyed man turned to shout:
"We are lost, my friends! Aekir has fallen!"

T HE port captain was waiting for them as one of Abrusio's
    tugs, her crew straining at the oars, towed them to a free
wharf. The breeze had failed entirely and the brassy heat beat
down unrelentingly on the maze of ships and men and docks,
shortening tempers and loosening rigging. And all the while
the slick stench of the pyres hung in the air.

Once the dock-hands had moored them to bollards fore and
aft, Hawkwood collected his papers and stepped ashore first,
reeling as his sea-accustomed legs hit the unyielding stone of
the wharf. Julius and Velasca, the boatswain, would see that
the offloading was conducted correctly. The men would be
paid and no doubt would scatter throughout the city seeking
sailors' pleasures, though they would find little pleasure tonight, Hawkwood thought. The city was busying along at
something like its normal, frenetic pace, but it seemed subdued. He could see sullen looks, even open fear on the faces
of the dock-hands who stood ready to help with the offloading;
and they regarded the *Grace*'s crew, at least half of whom
were foreigners out of one port or another, with some suspicion. Hawkwood felt the heat, the bustle and the uneasiness
working him up into a black mood, which was strange considering that only hours before he had been looking forward
to the voyage's end. He shook hands with Galliardo Ponera,
the port captain whom he knew well, and the two fell into step
as they wove their way to the port offices.

"Ricardo," the port captain said hurriedly, "I must tell
you—"

"I know, lord God I know! Aekir has fallen at last and the
Ravens are seeking scapegoats, hence the stink." The "Inceptines' incense" it was sometimes called, that bleary reek which
marked the end of heretics.

"No, it is not that. It is the orders of the Prelate. I could do
nothing—the King himself can do nothing."

"What are you prattling about, Galliardo?" The port captain
was a short man, like Hawkwood himself, and once a fine
seaman. A native of the Hebrionese, his skin was burnt as dark
as mahogany, making for brilliant smiles. But he was not smiling now.

"You have returned from Macassar, the Malacar Islands?"

"So?"

"There is a new law, an emergency measure the Inceptines have badgered the King into drawing up. I would have got you word, warned you to divert to another port—"

But Hawkwood had halted in his tracks. Marching down the wharf towards them was a demi-tercio of Hebriate Marines, and at their head a brother of the Inceptines in rich black, the "A" sign that was the symbol of the Saint swinging from a golden chain at his breast, glinting painfully in the sun. He was youngish, apoplectic-looking in his heavy robes and the blaring heat, but his face was shining with self-importance. He halted before Hawkwood and Galliardo and the marines crashed to attention behind him. Hawkwood pitied them in their armour. Their sergeant met his eyes and raised his own a fraction towards heaven. Hawkwood smiled despite himself, then bowed and kissed the brother's hand, as was expected.

"What can we do for you, Brother?" he asked brightly, though his heart was sinking fast.

"I am on God's business," the brother said. Sweat dripped from his nose. "It is my duty to inform you, Captain, that in his infinite wisdom the Prelate of Hebrion has come to a painful but necessary decision under God, to whit, foreigners who are not of the Five Ramusian Kingdoms of the West, or of states in vasselage to the above, are to be denied entry to their kingdoms, lest they with their unholy beliefs contaminate still further the sorry souls of our peoples and bring further calamities upon their heads."

Hawkwood stood rigid with anger, but the brother went on in a rushed monotone, as if he had said the words many times before:

"I am therefore bound to search your ship, and on finding any persons on board who come under the writ of the Prelate, am to escort them from this place to a place of security, there to retain them until our spiritual guides at the head of the august order of which I am a minuscule part have decided what is to be their fate." The brother wiped his brow and appeared slightly relieved.

Hawkwood spat with feeling over the side of the wharf into the oily water. The Inceptine did not seem offended. Sailors, soldiers and others of the lower orders often expressed themselves similarly.

"So if you will stand aside, Captain . . ."

Hawkwood drew himself up. He was not tall—the brother topped him by half a head—but he was as broad as a door with the arms of a longshoreman. Something cold in the sea-grey of his eyes halted the Inceptine in his tracks.

Behind the cleric the marines broiled silently.

"I am Gabrionese, Brother," Hawkwood said in a quiet voice.

"I have been made aware of that. Special dispensation has been granted to your countrymen in recognition of their gallant efforts at Azbakir. You need not worry, Captain. You are exempt."

Hawkwood felt Galliardo's hand on his arm.

"What I am saying, *Brother*, is that many of my crew, though not of the kingdoms or even of the no-doubt-worthy vassal states of the kings, are fine seamen, honest citizens, and worthy comrades. Some of them I have sailed with all my life, and one even took part in the battle of which you speak, a battle which saved southern Normann a from the Sea-Merduks."

He spoke hotly, thinking with rage of Julius Albak, a secret worshipper of Ahrimuz but who as a boy, a mere child out of Ridawan, had stood on the deck of a Gabrionese war-carrack as three Merduk galleys rammed and boarded, one after the other. That was at Azbakir. The Gabrionese, consummate seamen but proud, wilful and stubborn, had stood alone that day and turned aside the fleets of the Sea-Merduks off the Calmaric coast as they sought to invade southern Astarac and Candelaria, the soft underbelly of the west.

"What were you at the time of Azbakir, Brother? A seed in your father's loins? Or were you out in the world and still shitting yellow?"

The Inceptine flushed dark, and behind him Hawkwood saw the marine sergeant's face struggling to maintain a wooden blankness.

"I should have expected no more from a Gabrionese corsair. Your time will come, Captain, and that of all your stiff-necked countrymen. Now stand aside or you will share the fate of the unbelievers in our midst a little early."

And when Hawkwood did not move: "Sergeant, shift me this impious dog!"

The sergeant hesitated. He met Hawkwood's eyes for a second. It was almost as if they had made an agreement on something. Hawkwood stood aside, hand on dirk.

"Were it not for your calling, Priest, I would spit you like the black, liverless fowl you are," he said, his voice icy as spindrift off the northern sea.

The Inceptine quailed. "Sergeant!" he screeched.

The marine moved forward purposefully, but Hawkwood let him and his fellows clank past him towards his ship, closely followed by the cleric. The brother turned once they were past.

"I know your name, Gabrionese. The Prelate will soon know it also, I promise you."

"Flap away, Raven," Hawkwood jeered, but Galliardo pulled him along.

"For the Saint's sake, Ricardo, come away. We can do nothing here but make things worse. Do you want to end up on a gibbet?"

Hawkwood moved stiffly, a sea creature out of its element. The blood had filled his face.

"Come to my offices. We will discuss this. Maybe we can do something."

The marines were boarding the *Grace*. Hawkwood could hear the official drone of the Inceptine's voice again.

Then there was a splash, and one of the crew had leapt over the side and was swimming with no visible destination in mind. The Inceptine shouted and Hawkwood, as if in a nightmare, saw a marine level his arquebus.

A sharp report that seemed to stun the port into silence for a moment, a heavy globe of smoke that obscured the ship's rail, and then the man was no longer swimming but was a dead, bobbing thing in the filthy water.

"Holy God!" Galliardo said, shocked, staring. Around the wharves work ceased as men paused to look on. The marine sergeant's voice could be heard bellowing angrily.

"May God curse them," Hawkwood said slowly, his voice thick with grief and hatred. "May He curse all black-robed Ravens that practice such foulness in His name."

The dead man had been Julius Albak.

Galliardo pulled him away by main strength, the sweat pulsing down his dark face in shining beads. Hawkwood let himself be dragged from the wharf, but stumbled like an old man, his eyes blind with tears.

ABELEYN IV, King of Hebrion, was not happy either. Though he knelt in the required manner to kiss the Prelate's ring, there was a stiffness, a certain reluctance about his gesture that betrayed his feelings. The Prelate laid a hand on his dark circleted head.

"You wish to speak to me, my son."

Abeleyn was a proud young man in the prime of life. More, he was a king, one of the Five Kings of the West; and yet this old man never failed to treat him like an erring, wilful but ultimately amiable child. And it never failed to irritate him.

"Yes, Holy Father." He straightened. They were in the Prelate's own apartments. High, massive stone walls and the vaulted ceiling kept out the worst of the heat. Far off Abeleyn could hear the brothers singing Prime, preparing for their midday meal. He had misjudged the timing of his visit: the Prelate would be impatient for his lunch, no doubt. Well, let him be.

Tapestries depicting scenes from the life of the Blessed Ramusio relieved the austere grandeur of the chamber. There was good carpet underfoot, sweet oil burning in censers, the glint of gold in the hanging lamps, a tickle of incense in the nostrils. On either side of the Prelate an Inceptine sat on a velvet-covered stool. One had pen and parchment, for all conversations were recorded here. Behind him Abeleyn could hear the boots of his bodyguards clumping softly as they knelt also. Their swords had been left at the door: not even a king came armed into the Prelate's presence. Since Aekir, and the disappearance of the High Pontiff in the wreck of the city's fall, the five Prelates of the Kingdoms were God's direct representatives on earth. Abeleyn's mouth twitched. It was rumoured that the High Pontiff, Macrobius IV, had wished to leave Aekir early on in the siege to preserve the Holy Person, but John Mogen and his Torunnans had convinced him otherwise, saying that for the Pontiff to flee the city would be to acknowledge defeat. It was said that Macrobius had had to be locked in a storeroom of his own palace to convince him.

Abeleyn's mood soured. The west would need men like Mo-

gen in the times to come. He had been worth half a dozen
kings.

As Abeleyn rose a low stool was brought for him, and he
sat at the Prelate's feet, for all the world like an apprentice at
the foot of his master. Abeleyn swallowed anger and made his
voice as even as silk.

"We have spoken about this edict concerning the heretics
and foreigners of the city, and we have agreed that it is necessary to root out the disloyal, the unbelieving, the treacherous . . ."

The Prelate inclined his head, smiling graciously. With his
large nose and keen eyes he looked like a liver-spotted eagle
nodding on a perch.

". . . but, Father, I noticed you have included in the wording
of the edict the cantrimers, the mindrhymers, the petty
Dweomer-users of the kingdom—the folk who possess any
kind of theurgical ability. Already my soldiers, under the lead-
ership of your brothers, are rounding up these people. What
for? Surely you cannot mean to consign them to the flames?"

The Prelate continued to smile. "Oh, but I do, my son."

Abeleyn's mouth became a scar in his face, as though a
bitter fruit had been placed therein.

"But that would mean hunting out every oldwife who cures
warts, every herbalist who spells his wares, every—"

"Sorcery is sorcery, my son. All theurgy comes from the
same source. The Evil One." The Prelate was like a saintly
tutor humouring a dull-witted pupil. One of Abeleyn's bodyguards stirred angrily, but a glance from one of the Inceptines
quelled him.

"Father, in doing this you could send thousands to the pyre,
even members of my own court. Golophin the Mage, one of
my own advisers—"

"God's work is never easy. We live in trialling times, as
you should know better than anyone, my lord King."

Abeleyn, interrupted twice in as many minutes, struggled to
keep his voice from rising. He felt an urge to pick up the
Prelate and dash his brains out against a convenient wall.

He smiled in his turn. "But surely you must at least recognize the practical difficulties involved in fulfilling such an
edict, especially at a time like this. The Torunnans are crying
out for reinforcements to halt the Merduk push and hold the

Searil line. I am not sure"—here Abeleyn's smile took on a particular sweetness—"I am not sure I can spare you the men to carry out your edict."

The Prelate beamed back. "Your concern does you credit, my son. I know that the temporal cares of the moment lie heavy on your shoulders, but do not fear. God's will shall be done. I have asked for a contingent of the Knights Militant to be dispatched from the home of our order at Charibon. They will relieve you somewhat of the burden you bear. Your soldiers will be freed for service elsewhere, in the defence of the Ramusian kingdoms and the True Faith."

Abeleyn went white, and at his look even the Prelate seemed to shrink.

"I do what I can for the good of the kingdom, my lord King."

"Indeed." The Prelate was playing for higher stakes than Abeleyn had thought. Whilst his own soldiers were off on the frontier helping the Torunnans, the Knights Militant—the military arm of the Church—would have free rein in Abrusio. His spies should have informed him of this before today, but it was notoriously difficult to eavesdrop on the doings of the Inceptines. They were as tightly knit as chainmail. Abeleyn beat down the simmering fury and chose his words with care.

"Far be it for me, Father, to point out to you, one of the lords of the Church, what may or may not be necessary or desirable in God's eyes. But I do feel bound to say that your edict—*our* edict—has not been well received among the populace. Abrusio, as you are well aware, is a port, the most important in the west. It survives on trade, trade with other kingdoms, other nations and other peoples. Therefore in the way of things a certain number of foreigners filter through and make lives for themselves here in Hebrion. And there are Hebrians living in a dozen other countries of Normannia—even in Calmar and distant Ridawan."

The Prelate said nothing. His eyes were like two sea-polished shards of jet. Abeleyn ground on.

"Trade lives on goodwill, on accommodation, and on compromise. It has been represented to me that this latest edict could do much towards strangling our trade with the southern kingdoms and the city-states of the Levangore—Merduk lands, yes, but they have not lifted a finger against us since Azbakir, forty years ago, and their galleys help us keep the Malacar Straits free of the corsairs."

"My son," the Prelate said, his smile as warm as flint, "it grieves me to hear you speak thus, as though your concerns were those of a common merchant rather than those of a Ramusian king."

There was a sudden, dead silence in the chamber. The scribe's quill described an inky screech across his parchment. No one spoke thus to a king in his own kingdom.

"It is unfortunate," Abeleyn said into the hush, "but I feel I cannot send to Torunna the reinforcements which are so needed there. I feel, Holy Father, that the True Faith can be safeguarded here by my men as well as on the frontier. As you have so ably made clear to me, threats to the crown can come from any quarter, within and without its borders. I think it prudent that my troops continue their work in conjunction with the Church here, in Abrusio; and though you have not, in your graciousness, rebuked me, I feel I have not taken a responsible enough role in these matters until now. Henceforth the lists of the suspects, the heretics, the foreigners—and the sorcerers, of course—will be brought to me so that I may confirm them. I will then pass them on to you. As you say, these are trialling times. It grieves me to think that a man of your piety and advanced years should have the twilight of his life disturbed by such distasteful matters. I will endeavour to lift some of your burden. It is the least I can do."

The Prelate, a vigorous man in his fifties, inclined his head, but not before Abeleyn had glimpsed the fire in his cold eyes. They had both revealed their weapons, had put their pieces on the board and shifted them in the opening moves. Now the real negotiations would have to begin, the haggling for advantage that men called diplomacy. And Abeleyn had the upper hand. The Prelate had revealed his strategy too soon.

So I must debate with this old man, Abeleyn thought darkly, manoeuvre for advantage in my own kingdom. And the Torunnans; they will have to stand alone for a while longer because this grasping cleric chooses to see how far he can flex his muscles with me.

THREE

BARDOLIN'S imp was restless. It was the heat. The little creature darted from inkwell to table lantern, its green tongue lolling. Finally it collapsed in a heap atop the parchment the wizard had been working on and scratched behind one hairy ear with the nub of an old quill, covering itself with ink.

Bardolin chuckled and lifted it gently up to the shelf. Then he smoothed the parchment and continued to write.

The Prelate of Abrusio is not, of course, an evil man, but he is an ambitious one, and with the fall of Macrobius there is a certain hiatus. All five of the Prelates will be watching events along the Searil with an interest that goes beyond the mere outcome of siege and battle. Will Macrobius surface again? That is the question. It is rumoured that eight thousand of the Knights Militant have already been set aside for policing duties within the borders of the five Kingdoms. Eight thousand! And yet they are to send only five thousand to the Searil defences. This is a war within a war. These holy men will see the Merduk at their altars ere they will lift a finger to help

*another of their rank. It is the Inceptine disease, this
empire-building. It may yet bring the west to its knees.*

He paused. It was late, and the stars were hanging bright
and heavy over the humid, sleeping city. Now and then he
would catch the cry of a night watchman or one of the city
patrol. A dog barked and there was the sudden splurge of
laughter from some revellers leaving an all-night tavern. The
offshore breeze had not yet picked up, and the reek of the
burning hung over the city like a shroud.

*I tell you, Saffarac: leave Cartigella while there is time.
This madness will spread, I am sure of it. Today it is
Hebrion, tomorrow it will be Astarac. These holy men
will not be happy until they have burnt half the west in
their zeal to outdo one another in piety. A city is not a
safe place to be.*

Again, he stopped. Would it revert to the way it had been
in the beginning? The Dweomer-folk reduced to petty oldwi-
fery, the doctoring of dry cows in some mountain village.
There would be a welcome in such a place, at least. The
country-folk understood these things better. Some of them still
worshipped the Horned One in nights of moon up in the Hebros.

He dipped his quill in the inkwell but the pen remained
unmoving in his fingers. A drop of ink slipped down the nib
and drip, dripped on to the parchment, like a raven tear. The
imp watched Bardolin from its shelf, chirruping quietly to itself. It could sense his grief.

He knuckled his bloodshot eyes, grimaced at the blotted
page, and then wrote on.

*They took away my apprentice today. I have made pro-
tests, enquiries, even bribes; but nothing will answer.
The Inceptines have begun to whip up fear, and with the
news from the east that is no hard task. When it started,
the soldiers would sometimes look the other way: now
they also have the sniff of fanaticism about them. It is
rumoured, though, that King Abeleyn disapproves of the
scale of the purge and keeps the Prelate from even*

*worse excesses. They burned forty today, and they hold
half a thousand in the catacombs for want of space in
the palace cells. God forgive them.*

He halted a third time. He could write no more, but it would
have to be finished tonight for there might not be time in the
morning. He sighed and continued.

*You are high in the councils of King Mark. I beg you,
Saffarac, use your influence with him. This hysteria must
be halted before it sweeps all the Ramusian states. But
if you see no hope, you must get some of our folk out.
Gabrion will take them, I am sure, and if not Gabrion
then the Sea-Merduks.*

*Desperate times, to suggest such remedies. Take care,
my friend. May God's light shine ever on your path.*

He signed and sealed the letter, and his eyes stung with
tiredness. He felt worn and old. A dispatch-runner would take
it on the morning tide, if this calm lifted and the north-west
breeze struck up again.

His imp was asleep. He smiled at the little creature, the last
in a long line of familiars. They would come for him tomorrow
as they had come today for young Orquil, his apprentice. A
promising lad, he had been, already at home in cantrimy and
beginning to learn the way of mindrhyming, perhaps the least
understood of the Seven Disciplines.

He knew why they had not taken him today.

Bardolin had been a soldier once upon a time. He had served
with one of the tercios which currently garrisoned Abrusio and
he knew their commanding officer well. His . . . abilities had
begun to manifest themselves on a campaign against bandits
in the Hebros. They had saved lives. The ensign had recommended him for promotion, but he had left to study thauma-
turgics under Golophin, a great name, even then.

That had been thirty years ago, but Bardolin still had the
carriage of a soldier. He kept his hair brutally short and his
broken nose gave him the appearance of a prize fighter. He
did not look like a wizard, a master of at least four of the
Realms of Dweomer. He looked more like the hard-bitten sergeant of arquebusiers that he had once been, the tell-tale scars

at his temples speaking of long years wearing the iron helmet
of the Hebriate soldiery.

That's why they left me, he thought. But they'll be back
tomorrow, no doubt, with one of the Ravens prodding them
on.

A distant tumult outside. A rattle of hard voices, feet spat-
tering on the cobbles.

Had they come for him already?

He stood up. The imp sprang awake, its eyes glowing.

The feet pattered past, the shouts faded. Bardolin relaxed,
chiding himself for his hammering heart.

An arquebus shot. It ripped the night quiet apart. Another,
and then a ragged volley. There was a huge animal howling,
and men began to scream.

Bardolin leapt to the window.

Dark streets, the sliver of a moon shining faintly off cobbles.
Here and there a yellow light flickering. If he leaned out far
enough he could see the glitter of moonlight on the Western
Sea. Abrusio slept like a tired old libertine made weary by his
excesses.

Where, then?

"Go, my friend; be my eyes for me."

The imp's eyes dulled. The useless wings on its back
flapped feebly. It darted out of the window and appeared to
leap into empty space, though the air was so warm and thick
it seemed a different element, capable of buoying the tiny body
up like a leaf.

Now, yes. Bardolin was seeing in the spectrum of the imp's
vision. A lantern at a window was a green flare, too bright to
look at. A rat made a small luminosity and the imp changed
its swift scamper in pursuit, but Bardolin held it to his will
again, reproved it gently and sent it on its way.

A leap between two roofs, an unbelievably quick series of
gymnastic movements and the imp was in the street scurrying
along in the gutter, ignoring the rats now. There was a confused glow up ahead, green figures dancing. But one towered
over the rest, and shone as brightly as a bonfire. The heat from
it was a palpable thing on the imp's clammy skin.

A shifter cornered by the city patrol! And it was already
badly wounded. Bardolin noted the three corpses which lay in
fragments around the street. The shifter was giving a good

account of itself, but that last volley had caught it at point-blank range and even its immense vitality was waning. The lead balls had ripped through the great chest and out of the muscles of the back. Already the wounds were repairing themselves, but the arquebusiers were reloading with panicked haste, not daring to go near the dying creature. The darkened street was sickening with the reek of gore and slow-match and powder smoke.

"Damn you all," the shifter said clearly, despite its beast's mouth. "You and all black-robed carrion. You have no right—"

A bang. One fellow, reloading faster than the rest, fired his weapon at the huge, long-eared skull. The shifter's head bounced back to hit the wall behind it. The jaws opened, roaring, and the black tongue lolled wetly.

Others fired. Bardolin's imp whimpered but remained at its station, impelled by its master's will. It shut its sensitive eyes to the flashes of the volley, poked tiny fingers in its ears and cowered appalled as the patrol fired ball after ball into the massive beast. Pieces of flesh, dark-furred, were blasted off to litter the cobbles. One of the luminous yellow eyes went dark.

People began coming out of their houses. The entire district was waking to what sounded like a small battle being fought in their midst. Lantern light spilled out in pools and wands on the cobbles. The stouter-hearted ventured close to the inferno of noise and light that was the firing patrol, saw what they were aiming at and hurried back into their homes, barring their doors.

The noise stopped. The street was an opaque fog of powder smoke and the patrolmen shouted to one another reassuringly in the midst of it. They had used all their charges, but the beast was dead—sure to be after having thirty rounds blasted into it.

"Ho, Harlan, where are you? Can't see a thing in this powder brew!"

"I claim its paw, Ellon. It's the biggest I've ever seen."

"Where in the name of the Saint *is* it?"

There was a silence, heavy with fear. The powder smoke refused to clear; in fact if anything it was growing thicker by the moment. The arquebusiers blundered around, terrified, sure

that the shifter had somehow called up a fog and was still alive
in the midst of it, biding its time.

"Sorcery!" one wailed. "The beast lives! It'll be at our
throats in a moment. This is no gunpowder smoke!"

Their sergeant tried to rally them, but they made off, some
dropping their weapons, seeking only to get away from the
unnatural smoke. They scattered, shouting, whilst the folk who
lived on the street shuttered their windows despite the heat of
the night and knelt behind locked doors, quaking.

*S*LOWLY, *my little comrade, slowly. Look into him. Can
you see the heat? Is that the radiance of his heart, beating
yet? Yes! See how the bright bloodlines clot and heal themselves, the darker holes knit together and close. And there is
the eye rebuilding itself, pushing out again like an air-filled
bladder.*

Bardolin was trembling with strain. Casting was difficult
enough at the best of times without having to relay it through
his familiar. And now the creature was edging out of his control, like a tool slipping in sweat-blurred hands. It wanted to
come home to its safe, quiet shelf, but Bardolin was making
it approach the great body that lay seemingly inert on the
ground with its blood a thick sticky pool around it.

A hairy piece of meat slithered across the stones and reat-
tached itself to the shifter.

Bardolin was lucky in the powder smoke. All he had had
to do was thicken it, and the still, humid air of the night had
done the rest. But now he was attempting something more
difficult. Mindrhyming, through the minute skull of the imp.
The familiar acted as a buffer, a cut-off, but a frail one. Its
heart would fail if it suffered much more stress this night, but
there was not much time. The fog was thinning, and the patrol
would soon return with reinforcements.

Shifter, can you hear me? Are you listening?

*Pain agony light blooming in my skull the muzzles pointing
at me rend them tear them drink sweet blood dying. Dying.*

*Shifter! Listen to me. I am a friend. Look at me. See the imp
before you.*

The yellow eyes blazed, shot with blood.

"I see you. Whose are you?"

The imp spoke with its master's voice, quivering with relief.

Its brain was near overload. "Bardolin. I am the mage Bardolin. Follow the imp and it will lead you to me."

The huge muzzle worked. The words came out as a growl. "Why should you help me?"

"We are brothers, Shifter. They are after us all."

The shifter raised its blood-mired head off the cobbles and seemed to sigh. "You have the right of it there. Lead on, then, but go slow—and no crevices or cracks. I am no imp that can crawl through keyholes."

They moved out, the imp scampering ahead, its eyes two green lights shining in the dark, the shifter a hulking, shattered shape behind it. After them the cadenced step of the city patrol came echoing up the street.

THE imp was barely conscious by the time it returned, and Bardolin immediately popped it into a rejuvenating jar. The shifter entered the room warily, the candlelight shining on the broken places in its body that had not yet mended. Its heat was overwhelming; a by-product of the sorcery which kept its form stable. Hunched with pain though it was, it towered over Bardolin like some black, spiked monolith, the saffron-bright eyes slitted like a cat's. Its horn-like ears scraped the ceiling.

"I thirst."

The mage nodded and sank a gourd dipper in the pail he had prepared. The shifter took it and drank greedily, water running down the fur of the bull-thick neck. Then it slumped to the floor.

"Can you shift back yet?" Bardolin asked.

The creature shook its great head. "My injuries would kill me. I must remain in this form until they are healed . . . I am called Tabard, Griella Tabard. I thank you for my life."

Bardolin waved a hand. "They took away my apprentice today. Tomorrow they will take away me. I have brought you a momentary respite, no more."

"Nevertheless I am in your debt. I will kill them tomorrow when they come for you, hold them off so you may escape."

"Escape? To where? The soldiery have Abrusio sealed off tighter than a virago's bustle. There is no escape for the likes of us, my friend."

"Then why did you aid me?"

Bardolin shrugged. "I do not like wanton slaughter."

The shifter laughed, a hideous sound in the beast's mouth. "You say that to the likes of me, a sufferer of the black disease? Wanton slaughter is half my nature." The creature sounded bitter.

"And yet, you do not kill me."

"I . . . I would not harm a friend. Like a fool I came down out of the Hebros, seeking a cure for my affliction, and arrived here in the midst of a purge. I killed my father, Mage."

"Why?"

"We are a simple folk, we mountain dwellers. He tried to force me."

Bardolin was puzzled, and the beast laughed again. "No matter. You will understand in the morning maybe. For now, I am hurt and weary. I would sleep here if you'll let me."

"For tonight you will be my guest. Is there anything I can do for your hurts?"

"No. They heal themselves. It takes a lot to kill a full-blooded shape-shifter, though no doubt your magicks could do so in a trice. Those stinking militia thought to use me for their sport, and before I could stop myself the change was upon me. Then the hue and cry began. Six of them at least I slew. I was fortunate. Some of them have taken to using iron balls in their arquebuses. That would have been my end."

Bardolin nodded. Iron and silver were the only things which disrupted the magical regenerative powers of a shifter. Golophin had presented a paper on the subject to the Mages' Guild only the year before, little knowing it would soon be put to use.

Bardolin yawned. His imp stared dreamily at him from the liquid depths of its jar. He tapped the glass, and the little mouth smiled vaguely. It would be recovered in the morning. Some mages, it was rumoured, had bigger jars made for themselves to rejuvenate their ailing bodies, but there was the cautionary tale of the treacherous apprentice who had not followed instructions and had left his master in the jar to smile dreamily for all eternity.

"I'm for bed," he told his monstrous guest. "You are safe here tonight; the imp made sure you were not followed. But it will be dawn in less than four hours. If you wish to make good your escape before then you are welcome."

"I will be here when you wake," the shifter insisted.

"If you will. The soldiers usually come midmorning, after a hearty breakfast and a tot of rum."

The shifter grinned horribly. "They will have need of their rum if they are to take us."

Us? Bardolin thought. But his bed was calling him. Perhaps tomorrow night he would be sharing a pallet of bare stone with Orquil in the catacombs.

"Goodnight, then." He tottered off to bed, an old man in need of rest. The Dweomer always did that to him, and working through the imp had been doubly exhausting.

HE woke up, though, in the dark hour before the dawn with a name going through his head.

Griella?

And when he crept downstairs, instead of the monstrous, bloodied beast, he saw sleeping on his floor the pale shape of a nude young woman.

FOUR

THE fire was brightening as evening drew on. The storm had blown itself out and the sky was a washed-out blue with rags of sunset-tinted clouds scudding off along the darkening horizon. Northward the Thurian Mountains loomed, dark and tall, and to the south-east the sunset was rivalled by another red glow that gave way to a black smoke cloud like the thunderhead of an approaching tempest. Aekir, still ablaze even now.

Closer by a constellation of winking lights littered the earth for as far as a tired man might care to look. The campfires of a defeated army, and the multitude of refugees that clung to it. A teeming throng, enough to populate half a dozen minor cities, sat under the light of the first stars and the waning moon, cooking what food they had gleaned from the famished countryside, or sitting blank-eyed with their stares anchored in the flames.

As Corfe was sitting.

Perhaps a dozen of them squatted round the wind-ruffled campfire, their faces black with soot and filth and encrusted blood. Aekir was ten leagues back, but the red glimmer of its dying had followed them for the past five days. It would follow them for ever, Corfe thought, fastening on their minds like a succubus.

Heria.

He poked at the blackened turnips in the fire with a stick and finally managed to lever one out of the ashes. The others at the fire eyed it hungrily, but knew better than to ask for some. They knew enough not to cross this silent soldier of Mogen's.

Corfe did not wince as the turnip burnt his fingers. He wiped off the ash and then ate mechanically. A sabre lay in its scabbard at his side. He had taken it off a dead trooper to replace the one he had lost in the flight from the city. It and his tattered uniform commanded respect from his fellow fugitives. There were men who went about the displaced horde in ragamuffin bands, killing for food and gold and horses, anything which would speed their journey west, to safety. Corfe had slain four of them, appropriating their meagre spoils for himself. Thus he was the richer by three turnips.

Merduk cavalry had shadowed the mass of moving people ever since they had left Aekir's flaming gates, but had not closed. They were monitoring the progress of the fleeing hordes, channelling them along the Searil road like so many sheep. Leagues to the rear, it was said, Sibastion Lejer and eight thousand of the surviving garrison were fighting a hopeless rearguard battle against twelve times their number. The Merduk would let the noncombatants escape, it seemed, but not what was left of the Torunnan army.

Which makes me an absconder, a deserter, Corfe thought calmly. I should be back there dying with the others, making an end worth a song.

The thought raised a sneer on his face. He bit into the wood-hard turnip.

Children crying in the gathering darkness, a woman keening softly nearby. Corfe wondered what they would find when they got to the Searil line, and shook his head when he considered the enormity of the task awaiting its defenders. Like as not the Merduk would strike when the confusion of the refugee influx was at its height. That was why Lejer and his men were making their stand, to buy time for the Searil forces.

And what will I do when I reach the river? he wondered. Offer my services to the nearest tercio?

No. He would trek on west. Torunna was done for. Best to keep going, across the Cimbric Mountains, perhaps, and into Perigraine. Or even further west, to Fimbria. He could sell his services to the highest bidder. All the kingdoms were crying out for fighting men these days, even men who had run with their tails between their legs.

That would be giving up any dream of ever finding his wife again.

She is dead, Corfe, an empty-eyed corpse in a gutter of Aekir.

He prayed it was so.

There was a commotion in the firelit gloom, movement. His hand strayed to his sabre as a long line of mounted shapes came looming up. Cavalry, all light and shadow as they wound through the dotted campfires. People raised hands to them as they passed. It was a half-troop heading east, joining Lejer's embattled command, no doubt. They would have a devil of a time fighting their way through the Merduk screen.

Something in Corfe stirred. He wanted momentarily to be riding east with them, seeking a hero's oblivion. But the feeling passed as quickly as the shadowed horsemen. He gnawed on his turnip and glared at those who peered too closely at his tattered livery. Let the fools ride east. There was nothing there but death or slavery and the burning ruins of an empty city.

"THERE is a rutter, a chart-book, that will confirm the man's story," Murad told the King.

"Rutters can be forged," Abeleyn said.

"Not this one, Majesty. It is over a century old, and most of it details the everyday passages of an everyday oceangoer. It contains bearings and soundings, moon changes and tides for half a hundred ports from Rovenan of the corsairs to Skarma Sound in far Hardukh, or Ferdiac as it was known then. It is authentic."

The King grunted noncommittally. They were seated on a wooden bench in his pleasure garden, but even this high above the city it was possible to catch the reek of the pyre. The sun beat down relentlessly, but they were in the dappled shade of a stand of mighty cypresses. Acacia and juniper made a curtain about them. The grass was green and short, a lawn tended by a small army of gardeners and nourished with a stupefying volume of water diverted from the city aqueducts.

Abeleyn popped an olive into his mouth, sipped his cold wine and turned the crackling pages of the old chart-book with delicate care.

"So this western voyage is authentic also, this landfall made in the uttermost west?"

"I believe so."

"Let us say you are right, cousin. What would you have me do about it?"

Murad smiled. His smile was humourless, wry. It twisted his narrow face into an expression of knowing ruefulness.

"Why, help me outfit a voyage to test its veracity."

Abeleyn slammed the ancient book shut, sending little flakes of powder-dry paper into the air. He set one long-fingered hand atop the salt-stained cover. Sweat beaded his temples, coiling his dark hair into tiny, dripping tails.

"Do you know, cousin, what kind of a week I've had?"

"I—"

"First I have this God-cursed—may the Saints forgive me— holy Prelate with his putrefactive intrigues in search of more authority; I have the worthy merchants of the city crying on my shoulder about his—no, *our*—edict's resultant damage to trade; then I have old Golophin avoiding me—and who can blame him?—just at the time when I need his counsel most; I have this blasted burning every God-given hour of the day in the one month of the year when the trade wind has fallen, so that we wallow in it like peasants in a chimneyless hut; and finally I have the Torunnan king screaming for troops at the one time when I cannot afford to give them to him—so up in more smoke goes the Torunnan monopoly trade. And now you say I should outfit an expedition into the unknown, presumably so that I may rid myself of the burden of a few good ships and the crack-brained notions of a sunstruck kinsman."

Murad sipped wine. "I did not say that you should provide the ships, Majesty."

"Oh, they'll spring out of the yards fully rigged, will they?"

"I could, with your authority, commandeer some civilian ships—four would suffice—and command them as your vice-roy. A detachment of marines is all I would have to ask you for, and I would have volunteers aplenty from my own tercio."

"And supplies, provisions, equipment?"

"There is any amount of that locked up in warehouses all along the wharves—the confiscated property of arrested merchants and captains. And I know for a fact that I could crew half a flotilla from the foreign seamen currently languishing in the palace catacombs."

Abeleyn was silent. He stared at his kinsman closely.

"You come here with some interesting notions under your scalp along with the tomfoolery, cousin," he said at last. "Maybe you will overreach yourself yet."

Murad's pale countenance became a shade whiter. He was a long, lean nobleman with lank dark hair and a nose any peregrine would have been proud of. The eyes suited the nose: grey as a fish's flank, and with something of the same brightness when they caught the light. One cheek was ridged with a long scar, the legacy of a fight with one of the corsairs. It was a surpassingly ugly, even sinister face, and yet Murad had never lacked the companionship of the fairer sex. There was a magnetic quality about him that drew them like moths to a candle flame until, burnt, they limped away again. Several of their outraged husbands, fathers and brothers had challenged Murad to duels. None had survived.

"Tell me again how you came by this document," Abeleyn said softly.

Murad sighed. "One of my new recruits was telling tall tales. His family were inshore fishermen, and his great-grandfather had a story of a crewless ship that came up out of the west one day when he and his father were out on the herrin run. His father boarded with three others, but a shifter was on board, the only thing living, and it killed them. The ship—it was a high-seas carrack bound out of Abrusio half a year before—was settling slowly and the yawlsmen drew off. But the shifter jumped overboard and swam for shore. They reboarded to collect their dead and the boy, as he was then, found the rutter in the stern cabin along with the corpse of the master and took it as a sort of were-gild for his father's life."

"How old is this man?" Abeleyn demanded.

Murad shifted uncomfortably. "He died some fifteen years ago. This is a tale kept by the family."

"The mutterings of an old man garbled by the passage of time and the exaggerations of peasant storytelling."

"The rutter bears the story out, Majesty," Murad protested.

"The Western Continent exists, and what is more the voyage there is practicable."

Abeleyn bent his head in thought. His thick, curly hair was hardly touched by grey as yet. A young king fighting against encroachments on his authority from the Church, the guilds, other monarchs. His father had had no such problems, but then his father had not lived to see the fall of Aekir.

We live in trialling times, he thought, and smiled unpleasantly.

"I do not have the time to pore over an ancient rutter, Murad. I will take what you have told me on trust. How many ships did you say you would need?"

The scarred nobleman's face blazed with triumph, but he kept his voice casual.

"As I said, four, maybe five. Enough men and stores to start a viable colony."

Abeleyn's head snapped up. "A colony, sanctioned by the Hebriate crown, must needs have someone of sufficient rank to be its governor. Who do you have in mind, cousin?"

Murad coloured. "I thought . . . it had occurred to me that—"

Abeleyn grinned and raised a hand. "You are the King's cousin. That is rank enough." His grin faded swiftly. "I cannot, however, let you commandeer the ships of those who have been caught up in these heresy trials. Men would say that I was profiting from them, and some of the odium that the Prelate is unfortunately collecting for himself would be dumped at my door. A king must not be *seen* to benefit from the misfortune of his subjects."

Murad caught the slight emphasis and watched his monarch narrowly.

"However, what stores and cordage and spare yards and provisions and suchlike that are currently piling up in the warehouses might conceivably be moved elsewhere, for the sake of storage, you understand. These things, Murad, would not be missed. Ships are a different thing. We Hebrionese have a sentimental attachment to them. For their masters they are like wives. I know of your reputation in the wife-netting field, but if this is to be a crown-sponsored expedition it must start off on a wholesome note. Do you understand me?"

"Perfectly, Majesty."

"Excellent. No ships, then, will be confiscated, but I will give you a letter of Royal credit for the purpose of hiring out and outfitting two ships."

"Two ships! But Majesty—"

"Kings do not relish being interrupted, Murad. As I have said, two ships, both out of Abrusio, and they must be ships whose masters have lately lost a large number of crewmen to the Inceptines. You will represent to their masters that they will regain their full crews for the voyage, which, if they undertake it, will be considered a form of amnesty. If they choose not to avail themselves of the crown's generosity then you must make it clear that they are liable to be investigated for having so many heretics and foreigners in their complement in the first place."

Murad began to grin.

"The letters of credit, I take it, Majesty, will be redeemed on the safe return of the ships to Abrusio."

The King inclined his head. "Even so. I will also let you take a demi-tercio of marines from your own command and will confer on you the governorship—under certain conditions—of whatever colony you choose to set up in this Western Continent. But to set up a colony you will need colonists."

Here the King looked so pleased with himself that Murad became wary.

"I will find you colonists, never fear," the King continued. "I have a body of people in mind at this very moment. Is all this agreeable to you, cousin? Are you still willing to undertake the expedition?"

"I will, of course, be able to vet the potential colonists for myself."

"You will not," Abeleyn said sharply. And in a softer tone: "You will be far too busy to interview each and every passenger. My people will look after that end of things."

Murad nodded. His wings had been well and truly clipped. Instead of a small fleet sailing out under his command to set up an almost independent fiefdom, he would be transporting a horde of undesirables into the unknown in two—*two*—crowded vessels.

"I beseech you, majesty, let me have more ships. If the colony is to succeed—"

"We do not yet know for sure if there is land for the colony to be founded upon," the King said. "I will not hazard more than I have to on what is to all intents a doubtful scheme. It is only my affection for you and trust in your abilities, cousin, that prompts me to do anything."

Murad bowed. That, he told himself, and the fact that my idea can be worked into your own plans.

But he had to admire Abeleyn. Only five years on the throne, and the Hebrian monarch had already established himself as one of the most formidable of the western rulers.

I must work with what I am given, Murad thought, and be grateful for it.

Abeleyn poured out more wine for them both. It was losing its chill, even in the shade of the cypresses.

"Come, cousin, you must see that we all act under certain constraints, even those of us who are kings. The world is a place of compromise. Unless, of course, you happen to be an Inceptine."

They laughed together, and clinked glasses. Murad could see a trio of Royal secretaries hovering in the trees, their arms full of papers, inkwells hanging from their buttonholes. Abeleyn followed his gaze, and sighed.

"Damned paperwork follows me everywhere. You know, Murad, I almost wish I were coming with you, leaving the cares of a kingdom behind. I remember my voyage on the *Blithe Spirit* when I was a prince, a snotty-nosed youngster full of himself. The first time I felt the blow of a rope's end I wanted the boatswain hung, drawn and quartered." He took a gulp of wine. "Those were the days, following the coast round to the easternmost of the Hebrionese, and then across the Fimbrian Gulf to Narbosk. There is something about the sea that is in our blood, we Hebrians. Maybe we do not have veritable saltwater running in our veins like the Gabrionese, but the tilt of a deck under our feet is always in the manner of a homecoming."

He stared into his wine.

"I will see this land the greatest seapower on the earth ere I die, Murad—if I am spared, and if grasping clerics do not finish me before my time."

"Your reign will be a long and glorious one, Majesty. People will look back on it in later years and wonder what men were like who lived then, what giants they were."

The king looked up and laughed, seeming like a boy as he threw back his head. "I put on my breeches one leg at a time the same as everyone else, kinsman. No, it is the glow of history, the mist of the intervening years that confers glory on a man. It may be that I will be remembered solely because the Holy City fell in my reign, and my troops stayed home chasing witches instead of joining the defence of the west. Posterity is a fickle thing. Look at my father."

Murad said nothing. Bleyn II had been a tyrannical ruler and a fanatically pious man. It was rumoured that the current purge had been first suggested by him a dozen years before, but the old Mage Golophin had talked him out of it. Now the Inceptines were portraying him as the ideal of a saintly king, and his son was described in a hundred pulpits as a wild young man, good-hearted but wayward and totally lacking in respect for the representatives of the Blessed Saint on earth. Relations between crown and Church did not seem destined to improve.

And yet the navy and the army worshipped Abeleyn, and in the pikes of the soldiers and the culverins of the ships rested the power behind the throne. So the Inceptines trod warily, and hastened to bring their own swords, the Knights Militant, into the city.

"I have heard that none of the Aekir garrison escaped," Murad said sombrely, following his own train of thought. "Thirty-five thousand men."

"You heard wrong," the King told him. "Sibastion Lejer brought almost ten thousand men out of the city and is fighting a rearguard action on the Searil road."

Murad wanted to ask his king how he knew, how news travelled so swiftly over seven hundred leagues, but stopped himself. Golophin would have his ways and means. But if Golophin was avoiding Abeleyn . . .

"Duty calls," Abeleyn said. "I must meet another delegation from the guilds this afternoon. Thanks to you, Murad, I may have a crumb of comfort for the Thaumaturgists' Guild. Golophin may even begin talking to me again. Just as well. There is the Conclave of Kings to prepare for in a month's time."

"Is it still going ahead?" Murad asked, surprised.

"Now more than ever. Lofantyr of Torunn will be shrieking for more troops, of course, and Skarpathin of Finnmark will be convinced that the next blow is to fall upon him. I foresee a trying time, especially as the Synod meets a short while before, so we will have their worthy resolutions to debate also. I tell you, Murad, you are lucky in only having to worry about a hazardous voyage into the unknown. The shoals between palaces are more difficult to navigate."

Murad rose, and bowed deeply. "With your permission I will leave you to your navigating, Majesty."

As he left the shade of the cypresses the punishing sunlight bore down on him, and he saw the cluster of secretaries gather round their monarch like flies feeding off a corpse. The image was an unlucky one, and Murad banished it from his mind. He would have his ships, and his men, and he would have his city in the west.

He had not told the King that there was a log accompanying the rutter which detailed that voyage to the west of a century ago, and he was glad that he had kept the knowledge to himself. If the King had read the tattered pages he would most likely have found nothing. Murad himself had had a hard time deciphering the scrawled writing and stained parchment of the document, and the entries were hard to find—but they were there.

They referred to the very first expedition to the west, three centuries before the master of the *Faulcon* had made his ill-fated voyage. It was a venture that had ended, as far as Murad could make out, in slaughter and madness.

But that had been a long time ago. Such things became garbled and fantastic with every passing year. There would be nothing in the west that Hebrian arquebuses and pikes could not face down.

Time enough to worry about such things when the fabled Western Continent was looming off his bow with its secrets, its dangers and its unknown riches. It would be too late then for anyone to turn back.

FIVE

RICHARD Hawkwood opened the ornate grille that enclosed the balcony and stood naked, sipping his wine. There was no breeze. It was unheard of for the Hebrian trade to fail so early in the year. He could look down the steep, teeming roofs to the harbour and see the Outer Roads crowded with caravels and carracks, galeots and luggers, all harbour-bound by lack of wind. The only seamen doing a good trade were the masters of oar-powered galleys and galleasses, the swift dispatch runners of the crown who would sometimes condescend to transport compact cargoes for a small fortune.

He could see the *Grace* in the inner yards, still being refitted. Seaworms had riddled her hull in the voyage to the Malacars and she was having her outer planking replaced. Somewhat further out was his other ship, a tall carrack named the *Gabrian Osprey*. She had crawled in two days ago, labouring under sweeps, and was now at anchor waiting for a free berth. Her crew were being kept under hatches until Hawkwood could devise some way of slipping them past the Inceptines. A longboat perhaps, at night. Or he could hire a smack to stand off and let them swim out to it. No, that would never do.

He rubbed his forehead wearily. His torso shone with sweat

and the stink of the pyres seemed to grease it like some foul second skin. He closed the grille as a woman's voice said: "Richard, are you coming back to bed?"

"A moment."

But she had risen, a sheet draped about her shoulders, and was padding over the cool marble floor toward him. Her arms encircled him from behind and he felt the heat of her through the crumpled linen.

"My poor captain who has so much to occupy his mind. Are you thinking of Julius?"

"No." Julius Albak's body had been retrieved and burnt by the Inceptines. There was no family to speak of, save the sea-going one that was Richard's crew. A dozen of them were in chains in the catacombs awaiting a hearing. No, Julius Albak had gone to the long rest at last. There was nothing more to be done about that.

The woman's hand drifted down to caress his manhood but he was unresponsive.

"I'm not in the mood, Jem."

"I noticed. Usually when you return from a voyage we never even make it as far as the bed."

"I have a lot on my mind. I'm sorry."

She left him and went back to the bed and the tall decanter that stood beside it. The room was quite cool, thick-walled, faced with marble and white-painted plaster. The ceiling rose up far beyond Hawkwood's head to be lost in a maze of arches and buttresses of dark cedar. The enclosed balcony stretched along the whole of one wall, and the bed occupied another. There were elegant chairs, a dressing table, hangings heavy with gilt. Over all were thrown a pretty tumble of women's clothes and head-dresses. High in a corner a tiny monkey stared down from a golden cage with wide, unblinking eyes. Richard had brought it to her from far Calmar half a dozen years ago.

The sound of the city drifted in as a distant surf of noise. This far up the hill one was removed from the narrow filth of the streets, the shocking heat, the stinking open sewers, the noisy vitality of Abrusio. This was how the nobility lived.

"Have you seen your wife yet?" Jemilla asked him tartly, and he winced.

"No. You know I haven't."

"You've been back three days, Richard. Shouldn't you pay her a visit, at least for form's sake?"

He turned to look at her. Whereas his body was burnt a deep brown by sun and wind and seaspray, hers was as white as alabaster, which made the heavy mane of dark hair all the more striking. Her eyes were as black and bright as pitch bubbles on a tropic-heated deck, wonderfully mobile brows arching over them like two black birds rising and falling in tune with her moods. She was a passionate, almost a savage lover, and he often came away from her covered with scratches and bites. And yet he had seen her on her way to the palace in a barouche, hair coiled on her head, robes stiff with brocade, a linen ruff encircling her face making it seem that of a porcelain doll.

She had other lovers: noble, or humble like himself. He could not expect her to be faithful, she always protested, when he was away two-thirds of the year. But she was careful. A virtuous noble widow she appeared to be, and was believed to be by most people at court, but the servants knew differently, as did Hawkwood. He had procured a misbirth for her not two years ago—at her insistence. An oldwife in the lower city had done it in a cramped little back room. She would never tell him if the child had been his or not. Perhaps she did not know herself. He thought about it sometimes.

"My wife understands that I have many things to clear up when I finish a voyage," he said coldly.

She laughed, water rippling in a silver ewer, and reached out a slender hand. "Oh, don't be so stiff and proper, Richard. Come here to me. You look like a mahogany statue."

He joined her on the bed.

"It is Julius and your crew, I know. I have tried, Richard. There is nothing anyone can do, perhaps not even Abeleyn himself. He is not happy about it either."

"He discusses policy with you, then, as you lie together."

She flushed. "I don't know what you mean."

"Only that you should be more careful, Jem. I've been back three days, but already I know who the King's new bedfellow is."

One eyebrow soared up her forehead disdainfully. "Rumour and truth have a large gap between them."

"The King does not like his lovers to bruit his affairs in

public. He has made a policy of bachelorhood. If you are not careful you may wake up one morning aboard a Merduk slave transport."

"Do you presume to tell me how to regulate my affairs, Captain? I suppose your voyaging from one louse-ridden port to another makes you qualified to discuss the doings at court."

He turned away. She loved throwing his humble birth in his face. Perhaps it gave their lovemaking an added spice for her. And yet they were as close as lovers ever got. Sometimes they argued as though they were married.

He finished his wine and stood up. "I must go. You are right. I should visit Estrella."

"No!" She pulled him back down on the bed, eyes blazing. He had to smile. For all her bedhopping, she was still jealous if he went to someone else.

"Stay, Richard. We have things to talk about."

"Such as?"

"Well . . . news. Don't you wish to catch up on what has happened since you left?"

"I know what has been happening, and so does my crew."

"Oh, that silly edict. Everyone knows that the Prelate put Abeleyn up to it. The King is not the sort to think up a thing like that, though his father was. No, Abeleyn is more one of your sort. A soldier's man, the sailor's darling. He and the Prelate have had a contretemps, and all Abrusio is on the side of the King, except those whose wits are addled by religion, may God forgive me." She made the Sign of the Saint against her bare breasts. For some reason Hawkwood found the gesture arousing.

"The Prelate is on his way to the Synod in Charibon, and do you know, the moment he was out of the city gates the burnings lessened? Two days ago they were consuming forty unfortunates every afternoon. Today six were sent to the pyre. Abeleyn has his officers accompanying the Inceptines on their rounds and the lists go straight to him. Just as well. My maid was becoming hysterical. She's from Nalbeni."

Hawkwood stroked her smooth thigh. "I know."

"And Golophin. Some say he has organized a kind of underground escape route for the Dweomer-folk of the city. He's never at court any more. The King went in person to the old bird's tower to seek him out, but the door was barred! To the

King! Abeleyn's father would have had the place razed to the
ground, but not our young monarch. He's biding his time."

Hawkwood's fingers were caressing the curly hair at the
crux of her legs, but she appeared not to notice.

"And the streets are a terror at night. There are shifters
abroad, seeking revenge for the execution of their kinfolk.
Only last night one of them slaughtered a dozen of the city
patrol and then slipped away . . ." She moaned as Hawkwood's
fingers worked on her.

"Murad has been stalking around the palace with a smug
grin on his face. I don't like him . . . Oh, Richard!"

She lay back on the bed with her legs asprawl and began
to touch herself where he had been touching her. Hawkwood
watched her with the fascination of the mouse eyeing the cat.

"Is this not better than the rump of some cabin boy?" she
asked.

Hawkwood became very still, and she smiled teasingly. "Oh
come on, Richard. I know what pressures are on you seamen
on a long voyage, with never a woman aboard to relieve your
. . . stress. Everyone knows what you get up to. In the hold,
perhaps, in a dark corner with the rats skipping round you?
Does the boy squeal, Richard, as you take him? My fine Captain, were you even taken yourself by some hairy master's
mate when you first began your voyaging?"

As she saw his face flood with anger she laughed her tin-
kling laugh and worked ever more busily on herself.

"Will you deny it to my face? Will you say it's not true? I
can read it in your eyes, Richard. Is that why you have been
unable to please me on this return? Are you pining after some
smooth-chinned boy with lice in his hair?"

He set his hand about her white throat. His skin looked as
dark as leather against hers. As his fingers tightened, hers became busier. Her back arched slightly.

"Am I not enough for you?" she moaned. "Or am I too much
for you?"

With one swift movement he spun her on her stomach. The
blood of fury and shame and arousal was beating a rigid tattoo
in his every vein. He set his weight atop her, crushing her into
the bed. She cried out, flailing behind her with her arms. He
caught the thin wrists and imprisoned them.

She screamed into the pillow and bit the linen fiercely as

he forced inside her. It did not take long. He withdrew, feeling sickened and exultant at the same time.

She rolled on to her back. Her body was mottled with the rush of blood. Her wrists were red. She bruised so easily, he thought. He could not meet her eyes.

"Poor Richard. So easily goaded, so easily outraged." She extended a hand and pulled him down beside her.

He was baffled, confused. "Why do you say such things?"

She stroked his face. "You are an odd mix, my love. Sometimes as unapproachable as a closed oak door, sometimes all your nerves in the open, to be played on like the strings of a lute."

"I'm sorry, Jem."

"Oh, don't be absurd, Richard. Don't you know that you never do anything unless I want you to?"

ELSEWHERE in Abrusio, the day passed and the soldiers did not come. The girl Griella, who had been a beast, dressed herself in some of Bardolin's cast-off robes and sat at his table looking absurdly young and vulnerable.

They sipped cellar-cool water and ate bread with olives and a bowl of pistachios, which she loved. The imp stirred restlessly and watched them from its jar; it was almost recovered from its ordeal of the night before.

Why had they not come? Bardolin did not know; but instead of relieving him, their non-appearance made him more uneasy and this was compounded by the face of the slim young girl sitting across the table from him, swinging her bare feet as she ate.

She had a peasant face, which was to say it was browned and freckled by hours and days out in the sun. Her hair was cut short and it gave back a bronze tint to the sunlight, as though some smith had hammered it out on his anvil that morning. Her eyes were as brown as the neck of a thrush and her skin where the ingrained dust had been washed off had a tawny bloom. She was not more than fifteen years old.

Bardolin had helped her wash the clotted blood from her hands and mouth.

After lunch they sat by the great window in the wall of Bardolin's tower that looked out to the west, down over the city to the sea and the crowded harbour with its tangle of

masts. Out on the horizon ships were becalmed by the fallen
trade. Their boats were hauling them in, oarstroke by agonizing oarstroke under the torrid examination of the sun.

"Can you see them?" Griella asked him. "I've heard that
wizards can look further than any other men, can even watch
the flames that flicker in the bosoms of the stars."

"I could cast a farseeing cantrip. With my own eyes I would
not be much good to you, I am afraid."

She digested this. "When I am a beast, I can see the light
of men's hearts in their breasts. I can see the heat of their eyes
and bowels in the dark, and I can smell the fear that comes
out of them. But I cannot see their faces, whether they are
afraid or brave, surprised or astonished. They are no longer
men then. That is the way the beast thinks when I am inside
it instead of it being inside me." She looked at her fingers,
clean now, the nails bitten down to the quick.

"I can feel their life give out under my hands, and it is a
joyous thing. It does not matter whether they are my enemies
or not."

"Not everyone is your enemy, child."

"Oh, I know. But I do not know of anyone who is my *friend*.
Except you, of course." She smiled so brightly at him that he
felt both touched and disturbed.

"Why did they not come?" she asked. "You said they would
try to take you away today."

"I don't know." He would have liked to send the imp out
into the city to nose around, but he doubted if it were up to
that yet. And with Griella here, he did not like to go out himself. Though he had barely admitted it even to himself, he
knew he would not let her slaughter any more men, even those
who were taking the pair of them to their deaths. If the soldiers
came he would smite her with a spell of unconsciousness.
They might even leave her alone, believing her to be just another street urchin. If she changed into her beast form again,
she would surely be killed.

"No, don't touch that."

She was tapping the imp's jar and exchanging grins with
the little creature.

"Why not? I think it likes me."

"Nothing must disturb it when it is rejuvenating, else it

might metamorphose into something different to what it should be."

"I don't understand. Explain."

"The liquid in the jar is Ur-blood, a thaumaturgical fluid. It is the basis for many experiments, and is difficult to create. But once it has been made, it is . . . malleable. I can adjust it to the needs of the moment. At the moment it is a balm for the tiredness of the imp, like wet plaster being pasted over the cracks in the façade of a house. The imp was grown out of Ur-blood, helped along by various spells and the power of my own mind."

"Can you grow me one? What a pet it would make!"

Bardolin smiled. "They take months to grow, and the procedure is exhausting, consuming some of the essence of the caster himself. If the imp dies, some of me dies also. There are quicker ways of breeding familiars, but they are abhorrent and the creatures thus engendered, called *homunculi*, are wayward and difficult to control. And their appetites are foul."

"I thought that a true mage would be able to whistle up anything he pleased in a trice."

"The Dweomer is not like that. It extracts a price for every gift it gives. Nothing is had for nothing."

"You sound like a philosopher, one of those old men who hold forth in Speakers' Square."

"There is a philosophy, or rather a law, to the Dweomer. When I was an apprentice I did not learn a single cantrip for the first eight months, though my powers had already manifested themselves. I was put to learning the ethics of spellweaving."

"Ethics!" She seemed annoyed. "I partake of this Dweomer also, do I not?"

"Yes. Shape-shifting is one of the Seven Disciplines, though perhaps the least understood."

She brightened. "Could I become a mage, then?"

"To be a mage you must master four of the Seven, and shape-shifters are rarely able to master any discipline other than shifting. There was a debate in the Guild some years ago which contended that shifting was not a discipline at all but a deviancy, a disease as the common folk believe. The motion failed. You and I both have magic in our blood, child."

"The black disease, they call it, or sometimes just 'The

Change', Griella said quietly. Her eyes were huge and dark.

"Yes, but despite the superstitions it is not infectious. And it can be controlled, made into a true discipline."

She shook her head. Her eyes had filled with tears.

"Nothing can control it," she whispered.

He set a hand on her shoulder. "I can help you control it, if you'll let me."

She buried her head in his barrel-like chest.

Someone hammered on the door downstairs.

Her head snapped up. "They're here! They've come for you!"

Under his appalled stare, her eyes flooded with yellow light and the pupils became elongated, cat-like slits. He felt her slight body shift and change under his hands. A beast's growl issued from her throat.

While she is changing. Before it is too late.

He had had the construction of the spell memorized all morning. Now it left him like a swift exhalation of breath and swooped into her.

There was a savage conflict as the birthing beast fought him and the girl writhed, agonized, caught between two forms. But he beat the thing down. It retreated and underneath it he could sense her mind—human, unharmed, but utterly alien. The revelation shocked him. He had never looked into the soul of a shifter before. In the split second before the spell took hold he saw the beast spliced to the girl in an unholy marriage, each feeding off the other. Then she was limp in his arms, breathing easily. He shuddered. The beast had been strong, even in the moment of its birthing. He knew that if it ever became fully formed he would not be able to control it. He would have to destroy it.

Sweat was rolling down into his eyes. He set the girl down, still trembling.

"Prettily done, my friend," a voice said.

Standing in the room's doorway was a tall old man who looked as thin as a tinker's purse. His doublet, though expensive, hung on him like a sack and his broad-brimmed hat was wider than his shoulders. Behind him a frightened-looking young man bobbed up and down, crushing his own hat between his hands.

"Master," said Bardolin, a swell of relief rushing through him.

Golophin took his arm. "I must apologize for the rowdiness of our entrance. Blame young Pherio here. He does not like me walking the streets in these times, and he sees an Inceptine on every corner. Pherio, the girl."

The young man stared at Griella as though she were a species of particularly poisonous snake. "Master?"

"Put her on a couch somewhere, Pherio. You need not worry. She will not rip your head off. And hunt up some wine—no, Fimbrian brandy. Bardolin always has a stock in his cellar. Run now."

The boy staggered off carrying Griella. Golophin helped Bardolin into a chair.

"Well, Bard, what's this? Consorting with nubile young shifters, eh?"

Bardolin held up a hand. "No jokes if you please, Golophin. It was too close, and it has wearied me."

"Worth a paper in the Guild's records, I think. If this is in the nature of research, Bard, then you are certainly on the cutting edge." He chuckled and swept off his preposterous hat, revealing a scalp as bald as an egg.

"We were expecting soldiers with an Inceptine at their head," said Bardolin.

"Ah." Golophin's bright humour darkened.

"They took Orquil away yesterday. I had thought today they would take me."

When Pherio came back with the brandy Golophin poured two glasses and he and his one-time apprentice drank together.

"You bring me to the reason for my visit, Bard: these atrocities that the Inceptines practice in the name of piety."

"What about them? In the name of the Saints, Golophin, they can't be after *you*. You've been the adviser to three kings. You had Abeleyn sitting on your knee when he was too young to wipe his own arse—"

"Which is why I am the one man the Prelate *must* bring down. Without me the King has no disinterested advisers— nor any who can tell him what is going on halfway across the world at the drop of a hat, I might add. Abeleyn knows this too, as I hoped he would. With the Prelate on his way to the Synod at Charibon he has a breathing space. Already the burnings have abated, which is why you are here today, my friend. Only the hopelessly heretical are going to the pyre at the moment, but the catacombs are still filling. By the time the Prelate returns there will be thousands there awaiting his pleasure, and if the Synod approves his actions here then there will be nothing Abeleyn can do, unless he wants to be excommunicated. Worse, the Prelate of Abrusio will no doubt try to persuade the other Prelates of the Kingdoms to instigate similar purges in their own vicariates."

"I have already written to Saffarac in Cartigella, warning him."

"So have I. He can speak to King Mark. But there is another thing. Macrobius has not reappeared. He must be dead, so they will have to elect a new High Pontiff, a man who shows by his actions that he is not afraid to incur the ill-will of kings in the struggle to fulfill God's plans, a man who has the good of the Kingdoms at heart, who is willing to purify them with the fire."

"Holy Saints! You're not telling me that maniac of ours has a chance?"

"More than a chance. The damned fool cannot see further than his own crooked nose. He will bring down the west, Bard, if he has his way."

"Surely the other Prelates will see this also."

"Of course they will, but what can they say? They are each striving to outdo one another in zealousness. None of them will dare denounce our Prelate's actions in common-sense terms. He might face excommunication himself. There is a hysteria abroad with the fall of Aekir. The Church is like an old woman who's had her purse snatched. She longs to strike out, to convince herself that she is still all of a piece. And do not forget that almost twelve thousand of the Knights Militant went up in smoke along with the Holy City, so the Church's secular arm is crippled also. These clerics are afraid that their privileges are going to be swept away in the aftermath of the disaster in the east, so they make the first move to remind the monarchies that they are a force to be reckoned with. Oh, the other Prelates will jump at the chance to do something, I assure you."

"So where does that leave us, the Dweomer-folk?" Bardolin asked.

"In the shit, Bard. But here in Abrusio at least there is a slim ray of hope. I talked with Abeleyn last night. Officially we never see one another these days, but we have our ways and means. He has intimated that there may be an escape route for some of our folk. He is hiring ships to transport a few fortunates away from these shores to a safe place."

"Where?"

"He would not tell me. I have to trust him, he says, the whelp. But he does not want our sort fleeing wholesale into the hands of the Merduk, as you can imagine."

"Gabrion?" Bardolin said doubtfully. "Narbosk maybe? Not the Hardian Provinces, surely. Where else is there that is not under the thumb of the Church?"

"I don't know, I tell you. But I believe him. He is twice the man his father was. What I am saying, Bard, is would you be willing to take ship in one of these vessels?"

Bardolin sipped his brandy. "Have you put this to the Guild?"

"No. The news would be out on the streets in half an hour. I am approaching people I trust, personally."

"And what about the rest? Is it just we mages who are to be offered this way out, Golophin? What about the humbler of our folk, the herbalists, the oldwives—even shifters like poor Griella there? Have they a choice?"

"I must do what I can, Bard. I will not be going. I stay here to save as many of them as I can. Abeleyn will hide me, if it comes to that, and there are others of the nobility with sons and daughters in training with the Guild who are, naturally, sympathetic to our cause. It may be that we will be able to evacuate a shipload from time to time and sail them out to whatever bucolic utopia you will have carved out of the wilderness. This thing will blow over once the true extent of the Merduk threat is realized." He paused. "After Ormann Dyke falls there will be less of this nonsense. The clerics will be brushed aside, and the soldiers will come into their own. We have only to ride out the storm."

"After Ormann Dyke falls? What makes you think it will? Golophin, that would be a disaster to rival the taking of Aekir."

"There is little hope that it will stand," Golophin said firmly. "Lejer's men were overwhelmed this morning, and soon the Searil line will be fatally disorganized by the refugees streaming west. Shahr Baraz's army will surely move once more."

"You're positive?"

Golophin smiled. "You have your imp, I have my gyrfalcon. I can see the earth spread out beneath me. The mobs of fugitives on the western roads, the blackened ruins of Aekir, the lines of Ramusian slaves trekking north under the lash, may God help them. And I can see the columns of Merduk heavy cavalry fanning out from where Lejer's men fought their last stand. I can see Shahr Baraz, a magnificent old man with the soul of a poet. I would like to talk to him some day. He has served kings as I have."

Golophin rubbed his eyes. "Abeleyn knows this. It has helped convince him. I will not be going with him to the Conclave of Kings next month, though. I am needed here, and I must be discreet these days. It will be Abeleyn's job to try and convince the other monarchs of the knife-edge we teeter on. It may be that he will even save the dyke; who knows?"

He stood up and retrieved his hat. "What about it, Bardolin? Will you take ship? Your little shifter can come along if you've a mind to continue your research, but I can do nothing for poor Orquil, I'm afraid. He must make his peace with God."

Bardolin looked around at the rooms which had been his home for twenty years. He missed the breezy exuberance of young Orquil, and it was a shattering blow to realize the boy was beyond saving. The knowledge left him feeling very old, obsolete. But even his battered old nose could sniff the hint of burning flesh that hung on the air. The city would be a long time getting free of it. And Bardolin was sick of it.

He raised his glass.

"To foreign shores," he said.

SIX

A terrace shaded by a canopy of stickreed stems, the earthen water jars hanging from every corner to add some moisture to the arid air. In the shade the heat was bearable, and Hawkwood had his hands about a flagon of cold beer as though he were warming them.

The quayside tavern was busy both inside and out. It was an up-market sort of place, not a sailor's haunt, more the kind of place a landsman would imagine a sailor to frequent. Periodically men watered the street in front of the tables so that patrons would not be sullied by the rising dust as the waggons and carts and mules and oxen and peasants and sailors and soldiers sauntered past.

But the beer was good, straight up from a cold subterranean taproom below the street, and there was a fine view of the harbour. Hawkwood could just pick out the tall mainmast of the *Osprey*, berthed at long last, her hatches open and men hauling on tackles to bring the precious cargo out into the white sunlight. Galliardo had assured him that the Inceptines no longer came down to the wharves to check the ship crews for foreigners. Things had relaxed somewhat, but Hawkwood had still left orders that none of the *Osprey*'s crew who were not native-born Hebrionese were to be allowed ashore. The

men had not protested: news of Julius Albak's fate had raced
through the port like fire. Yawlsmen on the herrin run reported
that Abrusio-bound ships were diverting to Cherrieros and
even Pontifidad. The madness could not last. If it did, trade
would be ruined.

Hawkwood sipped his beer and picked at his bread. He
could hardly hear himself think with the noise of the tavern
and the wharves surrounding it. He wished the wind would
pick up. He felt almost marooned by the unmoving air, though
many a time he had cursed the Hebrian trade as it blew in his
teeth and he beat up into it, tack upon tack, trying to clear the
headland beyond the harbour.

He must promote himself a new first mate, take on more
hands. Would Billerand relish promotion?

For some reason he thought of his wife, delicate little Estrella. He had been back five days and still he had not been
home. He hated her tears, her hysterics, her protestations of
love. She was like some nervous little bird when he was
around, forever darting about and cocking one eye to look at
him for approval. It drove him mad. He would far rather be
clawed and abused by that high-born bitch, Jemilla.

I love Jemilla, a whisper inside him said, but he hunted the
thought quickly out of his mind.

A nobleman on a black destrier clove a path down the
crowded street like a crag breaking a wave. He was thin to the
point of emaciation, and he wore sable riding leathers, even in
the heat. His face was long, narrow, marred by a badly puckered scar, and his hair hung in sweaty strings to his shoulders.
A basket-hilted rapier was scabbarded by his side. He reined
in and dismounted as the keeper of the tavern rushed out,
clucking solicitously and brushing the dust from his shoulders.
He batted the man from him, caressed the destrier's muzzle as
a liveryman led it away, and then stalked over to Hawkwood's
table, his spurs jingling. Hawkwood rose.

"My lord Murad of Galiapeno. You are late."

Murad said nothing, but sat and slapped dust from his thighs
with a doeskin gauntlet. The tavern keeper set a decanter of
wine and two glasses on the table, and bowed as he retreated.
Hawkwood chuckled.

"Something amuses you?" Murad asked, pouring the wine.
He somehow managed to give an aura of world-weary con-

tempt that immediately set Hawkwood's teeth on edge.

"You said you wanted this meeting to be discreet."

"That does not mean we must tryst in some stinking pot-house. Do not worry, Captain; the people I must be discreet for would never come so far down into the city."

Hawkwood sampled the wine. It was a Gaderian red, one of the finest he had ever tasted, and yet when Murad sipped his he grimaced as though it were vinegar.

"You said in your missive that you might have need of my ships. Do you have a cargo you wish to transport?"

Murad smiled. His lips were as thin as blood-starved leeches. "A cargo. Yes, I suppose so. I wish to commission you, Captain, and both your vessels, to undertake a voyage with myself and several others as passengers."

"To where?"

"West."

"The Hebrionese, the Brenn Isles?" Hawkwood was puzzled. Hebrion was the westernmost kingdom in the world.

"No." Murad's voice lowered suddenly, became almost conspiratorial.

"I mean to sail across the Western Ocean, to a continent that exists on the other side."

Hawkwood blinked for a moment, and finally found his voice. "There is no such continent."

"And if I were to tell you that you are mistaken, and that I know where it lies and how to get there?"

Hawkwood hesitated. His first impulse was to tell this nobleman that he was either a liar or a fool—or both—but something in the man's manner stopped him.

"I would need convincing."

Murad leaned back, satisfied. "Of course you would. No sane captain would risk his ships on a foolhardy venture without some manner of surety." He leaned forward again until Hawkwood could smell the wine and garlic on his breath.

"I have the rutter of a ship which accomplished the voyage to the west and returned safely. I can tell you, Captain, that the crossing of the Western Ocean took this vessel some two and a half months, with favourable winds, and that it was bound out of this very port. One has but to keep on a certain latitude for some twelve hundred leagues, and the same landfall can be made."

"I have never heard of this ship, or this voyage," said Hawkwood, "and my family has been at sea for five generations. Why is this discovery not better known?"

"The master died soon after the return voyage, and the voyage itself took place a century ago. The Hebrian crown has kept the information to itself until now, for reasons of state, you understand. But the time is ripe at last for this information to be exploited."

"The crown, you say. Then the King himself is behind this?"

"I am the King's kinsman. I speak for him in this also."

A crown-sponsored voyage. Hawkwood experienced mixed feelings. The Hebrian crown had sponsored several expeditions down the years, and the captains of some had become rich, even ennobled as a result. But many others had lost their ships, their lives and their reputations.

"How do I know you come from the King?" he asked at last.

Wordlessly, Murad reached into his belt pouch and produced two rolls of parchment weighed down with heavy seals. Hawkwood unrolled them with sweating hands. One was a Royal letter of credit for the hiring and provisioning of two ships of between eighty and two hundred tons, and the other was a letter of authorization conferring upon Lord Murad of Galiapeno the governorship of the new colony to be founded in the west with the powers of viceroy. A list of conditions followed. Hawkwood let the parchments spring back in on themselves.

"They seem genuine enough." In truth, he was shocked. He felt as though he were cruising in through shoaling water without a leadsman in the bows.

"Why me?" he asked. "There are many captains in Abrusio, and the crown owns many ships. Why hire a small independent who is not even Hebrionese?"

"You fulfill certain . . . conditions. I want two ships owned by the same man; that way it is easier to keep a track of things. You are a skilled seaman, not afraid to sail the lonelier sea lanes beyond sight of land. It is amazing, the number of so-called sea captains who do not feel comfortable unless they have a coastline within spitting distance of their hull."

"And?"

"And, I have something you want."

"What?"

"Your crew, Hawkwood, those men of yours currently interned in the catacombs. Take on this commission and they will be returned to you the same day."

Hawkwood met the cold eyes and scimitar smile, and knew he was being manipulated by the same forces which governed kingdoms.

"What if I refuse the commission?"

Murad's smile did not waver. "Six of them are marked down for the pyre tomorrow. I would be sorry to see such worthy men go to the flames."

"It may be that I value my own skin over theirs," Hawkwood blustered.

"There is that, of course. But there is also the fact that certain captains with a large proportion of foreigners and heretics in their crew are open to investigation themselves, especially since some of those captains are not even Hebrionese to begin with."

So there it was: the sword hanging over his head. He had expected something like this from the moment he had seen the Royal letters. He uncurled his fist from around the wine glass lest it break.

"Come now, Captain, think about what is being offered you. The lives of your crew, a chance to make history, to join the ranks of the great in this world. The riches of a new world beyond the bend of the seas."

"What concessions can I expect, always assuming that this venture works out as you have planned it?"

Murad watched him for a moment, gauging.

"The man who sails me to my governorship can expect certain prerequisites. Monopolies, Captain. If you wish, the only ships which sail from our new colony will be constructed in your yards. A modest tariff on incoming and outgoing cargoes will finance whatever ambitions you have. There may"—and here Murad could not stop himself from sneering—"even be a title in it for you. Think of passing that down to your sons."

Estrella was barren. There would never be any sons for Hawkwood. He wondered if Murad somehow knew that, and felt like flinging his glass in the sneering aristocrat's face.

Yet again the agonized question: had it been his child that Jemilla had aborted?

Hawkwood stood up. He felt soiled and filthy. He wanted a living deck under his feet, a sea wind in his hair.

"I will think over your proposition."

Murad looked surprised, then shrugged. "As you will. But do not take too long, Captain. I must know by tomorrow morning if your men are to be spared their ordeal."

"I will think over your proposition," Hawkwood repeated. He tossed some small, greasy coins on the table and then walked away, losing himself in the lifestream of the port. He was going to find some stinking pothouse and drink himself into oblivion, and in the morning he would send word to this aristocratic serpent accepting his offer.

"THAT, lord, was the Street of the Silversmiths. Already our men have recovered half a ton of the metal, melted by the heat of the burning. It is the only thing which survived."

The horses of the entourage picked their way gingerly in between the broken masonry, the charred wood—some beams still had tiny flames licking at them—and the scattered bricks. The corpses had been hauled from their path and the way cleared a little, but Shahr Baraz could see objects which seemed to be thick lengths of burnt logs inside the ruins on either side. Bodies, immolated until they were nothing but the stumps of torsos. They had been so thoroughly burned that they presented no threat of disease. The reek of ash and smoke was the only smell in the air. Shahr Baraz nodded approvingly. The clean-up crews had done their work well.

For as far as the eye could see the desolation extended. The shells of buildings towered in abject ruin, burnt black, gutted, half fallen. Their remains were as bare as gravestones, the foundations buried in rubble, like black crags standing in the breakers of a grey sea. Aekir had become a ghostly place. Already it seemed like a monument, the ruin of a long-dead civilization.

Jaffan was jovially pointing out other landmarks gleaned from books and maps. Even the more stolid of his staff, Shahr Baraz thought, seemed a bit drunk, as though the victory were a potent spirit still singing in the blood five days after the event. The enormity of the thing they had achieved had been slow in sinking home in the aftermath of reorganization and the crushing of the last resistance. Now, as they rode unhindered through what had been the greatest and holiest city of the unbelievers in the world, they were at last savouring the taste of triumph.

For Shahr Baraz, the triumph had a bitter aftertaste. Aekir had been burned to the ground. The day after the city's fall, he had been forced to order its evacuation by all troops and let the fires burn themselves out. The huge walls still stood, as did the more robust buildings, including the palaces of the High Pontiff, the cathedral and other public buildings. But the poor brick of much of the city had collapsed in the intense heat of the burning and vast expanses of the space within the walls were levelled plains of dust, rubble and ash.

The rubble and the ash had cost his army almost fifty thousand men to win.

Three leagues to the east of the city, the female prisoners covered almost nine acres. A good proportion of those would remain with the army. His men had earned them. And trundling back to Orkhan was a train of waggons two leagues long; the spoils of Aekir sent back to the Sultan Aurungzeb. The richest city in the world should have yielded more in the way of plunder, but most of it had gone up in smoke ere his troops were able to come to it. The men were restless as a result. Well, that restlessness would be put to good use.

Aekir was a shell. It would require the labour of several lifetimes to rebuild it, but Shahr Baraz did not doubt that it would be done. Aurungzeb wanted Aekir to be his capital some day. Aurungabar he had said he would rename it, but he had been drunk at the time.

A cat darted out of a cleft between the stones and sped across the street, startling the lead horses. The staff officers fought the excited animals into submission. Shahr Baraz's own mount laid back his ears, but the old general talked to him softly and he remained quiet. The young men were too impatient with horses these days. They treated them like tools instead of companions. He would have a word with the cavalry-quartermaster when they returned to camp.

Jaffan had regained his composure. He was pointing out something else . . . ah, yes. The spires of Carcasson. They loomed through the smoke haze like the horns of some huge, crouching beast. What would they do with that place? Baraz wondered. It was his own ambition to found a university in

Aekir before he died, and Carcasson—what a library it would
make! And in the centre, where the Ramusians had worshipped
their idols, would be the prayer mats of Ahrimuz.

Baraz's thoughts darkened. The retreating Torunnans had
fired the library of Gadorian Hagus as they retreated. Two
hundred thousand books and scrolls, some of them dating back
into the dim history before the days of the Fimbrian Hegemony. All of them had been lost. Horb, Shahr Baraz's secretary,
had been in tears at the news.

John Mogen would not have done that. He would have
known that the Merduks would have preserved the library and
would have left it intact behind him. But this Lejer fellow, he
was a barbarian. He deserved the fate which awaited him.

They were riding to view his crucifixion.

The cavalcade turned left, into the afternoon sun. The buildings, or their remnants, receded on either side and all of a
sudden there was a space before them, a square fully a sixth
of a league wide. This was the Square of Victories, built by
the Fimbrian Elector Myrnius Kuln himself. It was the largest
square in the world, and drawn up in it to meet their general
were a hundred and twenty thousand Merduk troops in full
battle array.

The cavalcade halted before that sea of faces. Rank on rank
of soldiers with their pikes held upright in salute, the slow-
match of the *Hraibadar* arquebusiers drifting in blue streamers
down the breeze, the drawn tulwars of the Subadars and Je-
fadars and Imrahins catching the faint sunlight in serried glitters. The cavalry was there, regiment by regiment, the tall
headdresses of the horses nodding and waving, their riders
stock-still. Beyond them the elephants stood in long lines, so
fantastically caparisoned so as to seem like animals out of
some fabled bestiary. In the towers that perched on their broad
backs their crews swayed as the beasts shifted from foot to
foot; they did not like the feel of the grit underfoot. Notoriously footsore creatures, elephants. Dozens had been crippled
by caltrops in the last assault.

Shahr Baraz's staff took up their places behind him in a
momentary stillness. The old Khedive was helmetless and the
wind swayed the long white hair of his topknot, the two ends
of his drooping moustache. His face seemed hardly lined despite his age, and his eyes were almost invisible within their

slits. He sat his steed as easily as a young man, in black and gold lacquered armour, his scimitar sheathed at one thigh. His horse, a tall grey gelding, bore a black chamfron and a tall yellow crest, and its tail was bound up with white ribbons.

Shahr Baraz tightened his knees, and his mount started forward into the square at an easy canter.

There was a murmur of sound from the assembled army. As the old Khedive approached the centre of the square it swelled into a roar. The army was cheering him, three sides of the gargantuan space erupting as the thousands upon thousands of throats joined in an air-shaking storm of noise. Then it began to form words, a phrase repeated over and over again:

"Hor-la Kadhar, Hor-la Khadar!"

Glory to God they were chanting, thanking their creator for this moment of triumph, this spectacle of their greatness. And their cheers were directed at Shahr Baraz on his horse near the heart of their formations. Glory to God for this evidence of His love for them, this victory of victories.

"Hor-la Kadhar," Shahr Baraz whispered, his eyes stinging with tears that he would not let fall. He whipped out his scimitar so that it was a white flash in the sunlight, and the cheering redoubled. They would hear it for leagues, he thought. They would hear the Merduk army giving praise to the One True God, and they would tremble, those unbelievers, knowing at last that the time of the Saint had ended and the time of the Prophet was beginning.

Shahr Baraz sheathed his scimitar. The blood was racing through him like a spring tide, making him young again. The gelding caught his mood and began to dance beneath him. The pair continued on their way to the scaffold that had been set up in the square where the statue of Myrnius Kuln stood looking on with granite eyes, as he had looked on for six centuries in this city he had founded. The Khedive's staff caught up with him, their silk surcoats flapping like banners, the battle fanions streaming like brightly coloured serpents above their heads.

The cheering abated like a retreating gale, became a murmur again and then a silence, so that the hooves of the Khedive's entourage were loud on the flagged surface of the square.

When Shahr Baraz reached the scaffold he halted and donned his war-helm. It was black with a long neck guard and full cheekpieces that made the wearer's face into a mask. Set atop it was a representation of a crescent moon, a curving horn two feet across encased in silver. It was the badge of the Baraz clan.

At the foot of the scaffold Sibastion Lejer stood in tattered rags, a hooded Merduk soldier on either side of him. His dark eyes glowed with hatred.

The last stand of the Torunnans had ended a few leagues outside the city, on a low hillock beside the Searil road. There the remnants of John Mogen's once great army had turned at bay, to be annihilated by the massed Merduk forces. Only a handful had survived the last savage hand-to-hand struggle, and these, having refused service in the Merduk army, were already on their way eastwards in chains so that the people of Ostrabar might have a look at the soldiers who had defied them for sixty years, since the crossing of the Jafrar Mountains and the first battles between Merduk and Ramusian.

But Lejer—for him a different fate was reserved.

It would be good for the army to watch his death. He had baulked them of a fortune in loot, and left them masters of a dead city. Now they would see their general make him pay for it, and know that he shared their anger.

Shahr Baraz spoke, his voice hollowed by the tall-crested helm.

"I had thought to have you killed by the elephants, like the criminal you are," he told Lejer matter-of-factly. "You destroyed the jewel of the world out of sheer malice. My people would have made the Aekir you knew into an even more wondrous place, a fit capital for the greatest of the Seven Sultans.

"And yet this I could have forgiven, it being the act of a desperate mind in its greatest extremity. It may be that had your men been knocking on the gates of Orkhan, my own city, I would have burned it rather than see unbelievers trample the prayer mats in the Temple of Ahrimuz.

"And your conduct in the last fight was admirable. You Torunnans will be long remembered by us as the noblest enemy we ever had, and in John Mogen I had a worthy adversary. I would that he had survived, so that we might speak of the future together. The Prophet tells us that all men take different roads to the same place. For men such as us the roads lead to a soldier's death. We have that in common.

"But you destroyed one thing that cannot be replaced. You took the wisdom of the past ages, the voices of great men, the accumulated knowledge of centuries, and you wantonly burned it, removing it for ever from the earth and ensuring that your people and mine could never enjoy it again. For that you have earned death, and you will die like the traitor to later generations that you are. You will be crucified. Have you anything to say, Sibastion Lejer?"

The man in rags straightened to his full height.

"Only this, Merduk. You will never conquer the west. There are too many men there who love their freedom and their faith. Your God is but a shadow cast by ours, and in the end the Blessed Saint will prevail. Kill me and have done with it. I weary of your philosophizing."

Shahr Baraz nodded, and gestured to the hooded soldiers. Lejer was forced on to his back and his rags torn away. Other Merduks came, also hooded, bearing mallets and iron spikes. The Torunnan's arms were stretched out across a stout beam of wood and the spikes poised over his wrists.

The kettledrums of the elephants began a low, thunderous roll.

The spikes were hammered in, blood jetting bright in the sunshine. Then Lejer was hauled to his feet, attached to the heavy beam.

A pair of ropes snaked down and were swiftly tied to the two ends of the beam. Men behind the scaffold began to haul, and Lejer was hoisted up on to it. For the first time his mouth opened in a scream, but it was drowned out by the roar of the kettledrums.

They fastened him to the scaffold, the hooded men clambering up after him. Finally they hammered a last spike through both his ankles before climbing down.

The drums stopped. Lejer's eyes were wide and white in his filthy face. A ribbon of blood trickled down over his chin where he was biting through his lower lip, but he made no sound. Shahr Baraz nodded approvingly, then twitched his reins and began his stately progress back across the square. His aides and staff officers streamed after him.

"What now, Khedive?" Jaffan, his adjutant, asked.

"I want the men redeployed, Jaffan, as soon as is practicable. We must start planning our next move. You will send the

quartermaster-general to me after lunch and we will discuss a
new supply route."

"We are advancing on the Searil, then?" Jaffan asked, his
eyes shining.

"Yes. It will take time, of course; time to reorganize and to
consolidate, but we are advancing on the Searil. May Ahrimuz
continue to bless our arms as he has done in this place. I will
call an indaba of general officers this evening to discuss things
in detail."

"Yes, Khedive!"

"Oh, and Jaffan—"

"Khedive?"

"Make sure that Lejer is dead within the hour. With all his
faults, he is a brave man. I do not like to see brave men hanging on gibbets."

SEVEN

FURTHER west, along the Searil road.

The rain was falling steadily, mourning perhaps the fall of the City of God. The Thurians were hidden behind its diffuse, livid veil; the moisture beaded the air in a mother-of-pearl dimness so all Corfe could see were shapes moving off on every side, occasionally becoming darker and clearer as they staggered nearer then, wraithlike, fading again.

His boots sank calf-deep in the clutching mud, and water rolled down his face as though it were the sweat of his toil. He was tired, chilled to the marrow, numb as a stone.

The fleeing hordes had been passing this way for days. They had scoured a scar across the very face of the earth, a long snake of churned mud almost a third of a league wide obscuring the original slim track that had been the route west. The rain was filling up the broken soil, turning it into something near liquid glue. Along it bodies lay partly submerged every few yards: the ranks were beginning to thin. Folk who had fled Aekir with nothing more than the tunics on their backs were shivering and shuddering as they trudged towards the dubious sanctuary of the Torunnan lines. The very old and the very young were the first to falter; most of the bodies Corfe had passed were those of children and the elderly.

Here and there was the angular shape of a cart askew, sinking in the mud, the carcass of a mule or a pair of oxen sprawled between its shafts. People had already been at the flesh, stripping the bodies clean so that bones glinted palely in the unending rain.

There was shouting away in the rain mist. A fight up ahead by the sound of it. Corfe heard an old man's voice cry out in pain, the sound of blows. He did not quicken his pace, but slogged wearily along. He had seen a score of such encounters since Aekir; they were as unremarkable as the falling rain.

But suddenly he was in the midst of it. An elderly man, his clothes black with mud and his face hideously scarred, came blundering out of the mist with one hand stretched before him as though feeling his way through the damp air. His other hand clutched something at his breast. There were half a dozen shapes in pursuit, snarling and shouting to one another.

The old man tripped and fell full length in the mud. For a second he lay as if struck down; then he began moving feebly. As he lifted his head Corfe saw that his eyes had been gouged out. They were dark, scabbed pits filled with mud and rain.

The pursuers became more visible, a rag-tag crowd of wild-eyed men. They carried cudgels and poniards. One bore a pike with a broken shaft. He poked the old man with the splintered end.

"Come on, grandfather, let us have the pretty bauble and perhaps we will let you live. It's little good to you anyway. You'll never see it glitter no more."

The old man tried to struggle to his knees, but the mud held him fast. His breath was coming in hoarse whines.

"I beg you, my sons," he bleated, "in the name of the Blessed Saint, let me be." Corfe could see now that dangling from a chain around his wizened neck was the A-shaped symbol of the praying hands, the badge of a Ramusian cleric. It was smeared with mud, but the yellow gleam of gold and precious stones could be made out through the filth.

"Have it your own way then, you God-damned Raven."

The men closed in on the prone figure like vultures moving in on a carcass. The old man's body began jerking up and down as they tried to wrest the chain off his neck.

Corfe was level with the scuffle. He could either step off to one side and continue on his way or walk right through the middle of them. He stopped, hesitating, furious with himself for even caring.

There was a squawk of anguish from the old man as the chain broke free. The men laughed, one holding it aloft like a trophy.

"You accursed priests," he said, and kicked the old man in the ribs. "Your sort always have gold about you, even if all around is ruin and wreckage."

"Cut his saintly throat, Pardal," one of the men said. "He should have stayed to burn in his precious holy city."

The man named Pardal bent with a steel glitter in his fist. The old man groaned helplessly.

"That's enough, lads," Corfe heard himself say, for all the world as though he were back in barracks breaking up a brawl.

The men paused. Their victim blinked withered eyelids on bleeding holes. One side of his face was as black as a Merduk's with the mud.

"Who's that?"

"Just a traveller, like yourselves. Has not there been enough murder done these past days, without you adding to it? Leave the old crow alone. You have what you want."

The men peered at him, curious and wary.

"What are you, a Knight Militant?" one asked.

"Nay," another said. "See his sabre? That's the weapon of Mogen's men. He's a Torunnan."

The man called Pardal straightened. "The Torunnans died with Mogen or with Lejer. He's got that pig-sticker off a corpse."

"What else do you think he's got?" another asked greedily. The men growled and moved into a line confronting Corfe. Six of them.

Corfe drew out the heavy sabre in one fluid movement.

"Who'll be first to test whether I be one of Mogen's men or no?" he asked. The sabre danced in his hand. He loosened his feet in the gripping muck.

The men stared at him doubtfully, then one said: "What's that in your pouch, fellow?"

Corfe tapped his bulging belt pouch, smiling, and said truthfully: "Half a turnip."

"Throw it over here, and maybe we won't cut off your prick."

"Come and get it, you long streak of yellow shit."

The six paused, greed and fear fighting a curious battle on their countenances.

Then: "Take him!" one of them bellowed, and they were lurching towards Corfe with their weapons upraised.

He moved aside. They bunched on him, which was what he had hoped for. A jab of the sabre point made one throw himself backwards, to slip and tumble in the slithery mud. As he brought the blade back Corfe smashed the heavy basket hilt into another of their faces. The short spike on the hilt ripped up the man's nostril with a spray of dark blood, and he turned aside with a cry.

Corfe whirled—too slowly. A cudgel caught him just above the ear, grazing his skull and tearing the skin and hair. He hardly felt the blow, but ducked low and swung at the man's knee, feeling the crunch of bone and cartilage up his forearm as the keen blade destroyed the joint.

He tore the sabre free and the man fell, tripping up another. Corfe swung at the nape of the tripped man's neck, saw the flesh slice apart and again felt the familiar jar as the sabre broke through the bone.

No more of them came at him. He stood with the sword held at the ready position, hardly panting. His head was ringing and he could feel the burning swell of the blow that had landed there, but he felt as light as thistledown. There was laughter fluttering in his throat like some manic, trapped bird.

One man lay dead, his head attached to his body only by the clammy gleam of the windpipe. Another was sitting holding his mangled knee, groaning. A third had both hands clutched to the hole in his face. The other three looked at Corfe darkly.

"The bastard is a Torunnan after all," one said with disgust. "Aren't you?" he asked Corfe.

Corfe nodded.

"We'll leave you to your Raven then, Torunnan. May you have joy of each other."

They helped up the crippled man and stumbled off into the curtain of the rain, joining the other anonymous shapes who were staggering westwards. The dead man's blood darkened the mud, rain-stippled. Corfe felt strangely let down. With a flash of insight he realized he had been hoping to die and leave his own corpse on the churned ground. The knowledge sapped his strength. His shoulders sagged, and he sheathed the sabre without cleaning it. There was only himself again, and the rain and the mud and the shadows passing by.

Someone else was stumbling towards him: a robed shape bent over as if burdened with pain. It was a young monk, his tonsure a white circle in the gloom. He splashed to his knees beside the old, eyeless man who lay forgotten on the ground.

"Master," he sobbed. "Master, they have killed you." There was a black bar of blood striping the young monk's face. Corfe joined him, kneeling in the mud like a penitent.

The terrible face on the ground twitched. The mouth moved, and Corfe heard the old man say in a whisper of escaping breath:

"God has forsaken us. We are alone in a darkening land. Sweet Saint, forgive us."

The monk cradled his master's head in his lap, weeping. Corfe stared at the pair dull-eyed, still somewhat blasted at finding himself yet living. But there was something here at least—something for him to do.

"Come," he said, tugging at the monk's arm. "We'll find us some shelter, a space out of the rain. I have food I'm willing to share."

The young man stared at him. His face was swollen grotesquely on one side and Corfe thought there were bones broken there.

"Who are you, that has saved my master's life?" he asked. "What blessed angel sent you to watch over us?"

"I'm just a soldier," Corfe told him irritably. "A deserter fleeing west like the rest of the world. No angel sent me." The young man's piety soured his humour further. He had seen too many horrors lately to give it credence.

"Well, soldier," the monk said with absurd formality, "we are in your debt. I am Ribeiro, a novice of the Antillian Order." He paused, almost as if he were weighing something up in his mind. Then he looked down at the wreck of a man whose savaged head was pillowed on his knees. "And this is His Holiness the High Pontiff of the Five Monarchies, Macrobius the Third."

•   •   •

THE rain had stopped with the rising of the moon, and it looked as though the night sky would clear. Already Corfe could see the long curve of Coranada's scythe twinkling around the North Star.

He threw another piece of wood on the fire, relishing the heat. His back was sodden and cold, but his face was aglow. The saturated leather of his boots was steaming and beginning to split, what with the heat and the rough usage. Mud was dropping in hard scales from his drying garments.

He shook his head testily. The blood pooled in his ear had dried to a black crust, affecting his hearing. He would see about that when dawn came.

He was huddled under an ox-waggon, burning the spokes of its shattered wheels for fuel. Ribeiro was asleep but the old man—Macrobius—was awake. It was somehow awful to see him blink like that, the eyelids sunken and wrinkled over the pits which had once housed his sight. Corfe could see now that he wore the black habit of the Inceptines, and that once the garment had been rich and full. It was a mosaic of mud and blood and broken threads now, and the old man shivered within it despite the warmth of the flames.

"You do not believe us," the old priest said. "You do not believe that I am who I say I am."

Corfe stabbed a stick into the fire's glowing heart and said nothing.

"It is true, though. I am—or was—Macrobius, head of the Ramusian Faith, guardian of the Holy City of Aekir."

"John Mogen was its guardian, and the men who died there with him," Corfe said roughly.

"And were you, my son, one of Mogen's men?"

It was eerie, having a conversation with an eyeless man. Corfe's glare went unheeded.

"I heard those brigands talk. They called you a Torunnan. Were you one of the garrison?"

"You talk too much, old man."

For a second the man's face changed; the saintly look fled and something like a snarl passed over it. That too faded, though, and the old man laughed ruefully.

"I ask your pardon, soldier. I am not much used to blunt speech, even yet. It must be that God is chastising me for my pride. 'The Proud shall be humbled, and the Meek shall be raised above them.' "

"There aren't many meek folk abroad tonight," Corfe retorted. "It surprises me that the pair of you got so far without getting your holy throats slit." As he spoke, he saw again the place where the old man's eyes had been and cursed himself for his clumsiness.

"I'm sorry," he grated. "We have all suffered."

Macrobius' fingers touched the ragged pits in his face gingerly. " 'And those who do not see me, though they have eyes, yet they will be blind,' " he whispered. He bent his head, and Corfe thought he would have wept had he been able.

"The Merduks found me cowering in a storeroom in the palace. They gouged out my sight with glass from the windows. They would have slain me, but the building was in flames and they were in haste. They thought me just another priest, and left me for dead as they had left a thousand others. It was Ribeiro who found me." Macrobius laughed again, the sound more like the croak of a crow. "Even he did not know at first who I was. Perhaps that is my fate now, to become someone else. To atone for what I did and did not do."

Corfe stared closely at him. He had seen the High Pontiff before, conducting the ritual blessings of the troops and sometimes at High Table when he had been commanding the guard for the night, but it had been at a distance. There was only the vague impression of a grey-haired head, a thin face. How much we need the eyes, he thought, to truly know someone, to give them an identity.

It was true that Mogen had purportedly made the High Pontiff a prisoner in his own palace to keep him from fleeing the city—the Knights Militant in the garrison had almost created an internal war when they had heard—but surely it was impossible that this wreck, this decrepit flotsam of war, was the religious leader of the entire western world?

No. Impossible.

Corfe poked the blackened turnip out of the fire and nudged the old man beside him, who seemed lost in some interior wilderness.

"Here. Eat."

"Thank you, my son, but I cannot. My stomach is closed. Another penance, perhaps." He bent over the young monk who was sleeping to one side and shook his shoulder gently.

Ribeiro woke with a start, his eyes brimming with night-mares. His mouth opened and for an instant Corfe thought he would scream, but then he seemed to shiver and, scrubbing at one eye with a grubby knuckle, he sat up. His face was a dark purple bruise, and the cheekbone on one side had swollen out to close the eye and stretch the skin to a shiny drum tightness.

"The soldier has food here, Ribeiro. Eat and keep up your strength," Macrobius said.

The young monk smiled. "I cannot, Master. I cannot chew. There is nothing left of my teeth but shards. But I am not so hungry anyway. You must have sustenance—you are the important one."

Corfe stared towards the starlit heaven, stifling his exasperation. The smell of the charred turnip brought the water running round his tongue. He wondered what ridiculous impulse had made him risk his life to save these two pious fools.

But he knew the answer to that. It was the darkest impulse of all.

He almost laughed. A soldier, a monk and a blind lunatic who believed himself Pontiff sitting under an ox-cart arguing over who should eat a burnt turnip, whilst behind them burned the greatest city in the world. It might have been a comedy written by one of the playwrights of Aekir, a sketch to keep the mob happy when bread was scarce.

But then he thought of his wife, his sweet Heria, and the thin, bitter humour ran cold. He sat and stared into the flames of the fire as though they were the conflagration that blazed at the heart of his very soul.

IT took an hour of soaking in the big copper bath for Hawk-wood to lose the stink and filth of the catacombs, even with the perfumes he had poured into the water.

He could see them in his mind's eye: the low arched ceilings of rounded brick, the torches in the hands of the jailers guttering blue with the stench and the lack of air. And the countless figures lying as still as corpses in row on row with heavy irons at their wrists and ankles. A white face would flash as one looked up, but the rest remained prone, or sitting with their backs to the streaming damp of the walls. Hundreds of men and women and even children sprawled together. There was blood here and there where they had fought amongst themselves, and a woman keened softly because of some violation. Hawkwood had been in sties where the pigs were fifty times better looked after. But these, of course, were dead meat already. They were destined for the pyre.

"Radisson!" he had called out. "Radisson of Ibnir! It is the Captain, Hawkwood, come to free you!"

Someone reared up, snarling, and one of the turnkeys beat him down savagely, his arm with its club descending again and again until the man lay still, a broken place shining in his skull. The other prisoners stirred restlessly. There were more faces turned to Hawkwood, ovals of white flesh in the gloom with holes for eyes.

"Lasso! Lasso of Calidar! Stand up, damn you!" An unwise order. Though Hawkwood was short himself, he had to crouch under the low vaulted ceiling. The turnkeys seemed permanently bent, as though warped by their ghastly labour.

"I am here for the crew of the *Grace of God*. Where are you, shipmates? I am to take you out of here!"

"Take me, take me!" a woman screamed. "Take my child, sir, for pity's sake!"

"Take me!" another shouted. And suddenly there was a cacophony of shouting and screaming that seemed to echo and re-echo off the walls, pounding Hawkwood's brain.

"Take me, Captain! Take me! Save me from the flames in the name of God!"

H E poured more water over himself and relaxed in the rose-scented steam. He did not like the perfumes Estrella used. They were too sickly for his tastes, but today he had poured vial after vial of them into the water to wash away the stink.

He had his men—most of them, at any rate. One had died, beaten to death by his fellow prisoners for the blackness of his face, but the rest were back on board ship, no doubt being scrubbed down in seawater by Billerand, the new first mate, if Billerand had time for such niceties in the chaos of outfitting for the voyage.

The voyage. He had not yet told his wife that he was leaving again within two sennights. He knew only too well the scene that would provoke.

The door to the bathing chamber swung open and his wife

walked in, averting her eyes from Hawkwood's nakedness. She carried clean clothes and woollen towels in her arms, and bent to set them down on the bench that lined one wall.

She was wearing brocade, even in the heat. Her tiny fingers were covered with rings, like so many gilded knuckles, and the steam in the air made the tong-curled frizz of her hair wilt.

"I burned the other things, Ricardo," she said. "They were fit for nothing, not even the street beggars . . . There is cold ale waiting in the dining chamber, and some sweetmeats."

Hawkwood stood up, wiping the water out of his eyes. The air in the room seemed scarcely cooler than the liquid in the tub. Estrella's eyes rested on his nakedness for a second and then darted away. She coloured and reached for a towel for him, her eyes still averted. He smiled sourly as he took it from her. His wife and he only saw each other nude when in the bed chamber, and even then she insisted on there being no light. He knew her body only by moonlight and starlight, and by the touch of his hard-palmed hands. It was thin and spare, like a boy's, with tiny, dark-nippled breasts and a thick fleece of hair down in her secret part. Absurdly, she reminded Hawkwood of Mateo, the ship's boy who had shared his bunk a few times on that last long voyage to the Kardian Sea. He wondered what his wife would make of that comparison, and his smile soured further.

He stepped out of the bath, wrapping the towel about himself. Ricardo. Like Galliardo, she had always used the Hebrionese rendering of his name instead of his native version. It irked him to hear it, though he had heard it ten thousand times before.

Estrella had been a good marriage. She was a scion of one of the lesser noble houses of Hebrion, the Calochins. His father had arranged the match, terrible old Johann Hawkwood who had wanted a toe in the door in Abrusio, even in his day the fastest-growing port in the west. Johann had convinced the Calochins that the Hawkwood family was a noble Gabrionese house when in fact it was nothing of the sort. Johann had been given a set of arms by Duke Simeon of Gabrion for his services at the battle of Azbakir. Before that he had been merely a first mate on board a Gabrionese dispatch-runner with no pedigree, no lineage, no money, but a vast store of ambition.

He would be pleased if he could see me, Hawkwood thought

wryly, consorting with the emissaries of kings and with a Royal victualling warrant in my pouch.

Hawkwood dressed, his wife leaving the room before the towel fell from his waist. His hair and beard dripped water but the arid air would soon put paid to that. He padded barefoot into the high-ceilinged room that was at the centre of his house. Louvred windows far above his head let in slats of light that blazed on the flagged floor. When his bare foot rested on one of the sun-warmed stones he felt the pain and the heat of it. Abrusio without the trade wind was like a desert without an oasis.

High-backed chairs, as stiffly upright as his wife's slender backbone, a long table of dark wood, various hangings as limp as dead flowers against the whitewashed plaster of the walls—they seemed unfamiliar to him because he had had no part in choosing them—and the balcony with its wooden screens, closed now, dimming the light in the room. The place is like a church, Hawkwood thought, or a nunnery.

He stepped to the balcony screens and wrenched them aside, letting in the golden glare and heat and dust and noise of the city. The balcony faced west, so he could see the bay and the Inner and the Outer Roads, as the two approaches to the harbour were called; the quays, the wharves, the seaward defence towers and the watch beacons on the massive mole of the harbour wall. He noted half a dozen vessels standing out to sea, their sails flaccid as empty sacks, their crews hauling them in with longboats. He listened to the clatter of wheels on cobbles, the shouts of hawkers and laughter from a nearby tavern.

Not for him the isolation of a nobleman's villa on the higher slopes of Abrusio Hill. He was looking out from one of the lower quarters, where the houses of the merchants clung to the slopes like tiers of sand martins' nests and it was possible to sniff bad fish and tar and salt air, a reek more welcome to him than any perfume.

"The ale will get warm," Estrella said hesitantly.

He did not reply, but stood drinking in the life of Abrusio, the sight of the flawless sea, as calm as milk. When would the trade start up again? He did not want to begin the voyage with his ships being towed out of the bay, searching for a puff of air on the open ocean.

That thought made him feel guilty, and he turned back into

the room. It was full of light now, the early afternoon sun pouring down to flood the stone and touch off the gilt thread in the tapestries, bring out a warmer glow from the dark wood of the furniture.

He sat and ate and drank, whilst Estrella hovered like a humming-bird unable to settle upon a flower. There was a sheen of sweat on her collar-bone, gathering like a jewel in the hollow of her throat before sliding gently below the ruff and down into her bodice.

"How long have you been back, Ricardo? Domna Ponera says her husband spoke to you days ago, when there was that shooting in the harbour . . . I have been waiting, Ricardo."

"I had business to attend to, lady, a new venture that involves the nobility. You know what the nobility are like."

"Yes, I know what they are like," she said bitterly, and he wondered if court gossip about Jemilla had come this far down from the Noble Quarter. Or perhaps she was just reminding him of her own origins. It mattered not, he told himself, though again the remorse edged into his mind, making him defensive.

"Half my crew were taken away by the Ravens when we docked. That is why I stank like a privy when I arrived. I have been in the catacombs trying to get them released."

"Oh." Her face slumped, some of the energy going out of her. He noted with satisfaction that not even she could find fault with such a virtuous cause. She loved virtuous causes.

She sat down on one of the high-backed chairs and clapped her small hands together with a snap. A servant appeared at once and bowed low.

"Bring me wine, and see it is cold," she said.

"At once, my lady." The servant hurried away.

She could order the common folk like a true noble at any rate, Hawkwood reflected. Let her try that tone of voice once with me and we'll see how that narrow rump of hers likes a seaman's belt across it.

"Berio, was that?" he asked, slugging thirstily at his ale.

"Berio is gone. He was slovenly. This new one is named Haziz."

"Haziz? That's a Merduk name!"

Her eyes widened a little. He could see the pulse beat in her neck. "He is from the Malacars. His father was Hebrionese. He was afraid of the burnings, so I gave him a position."

"I see." Another stray dog. Estrella was a strange mixture of the petulant and the soft-hearted. She might take in a man off the street out of pity and throw him out again a week later because he was slow in serving dinner. Jemilla at least was unrelentingly hard on her attendants.

And her lovers, Hawkwood added to himself.

The wine came, borne by the ill-favoured Haziz who had the look of a seaman about him despite the fine doublet Estrella had procured for him. He looked at Hawkwood as though Richard were about to strike him.

They sat in silence, the husband and wife, drinking their tepid drinks slowly. As he sat there, Hawkwood had an overwhelming longing to be at sea again, away from the torrid heat, the crowds, the reek of the pyres. Away from Estrella and the silences in his home. He called it his home, though he had spent more time in either of his two ships and felt more at ease in them.

Estrella cleared her throat. "Domna Ponera was also saying today that your ships are being outfitted for a new voyage in great haste, and that all the port is buzzing with talk of the issue of a Royal warrant."

Hawkwood silently cursed Domna Ponera. Galliardo's wife was a huge woman with a moist moustache and the appetite of a goat for both food and information. As wife to the port captain she was in a fine position to acquire the latter, and her mine of information obtained her invitations to households where ordinarily she would not have been countenanced. Hawkwood knew that Galliardo had upbraided her many times for being too free with her tongue, but he was as much to blame. He could not, he had once told Hawkwood with a sigh, keep his tongue from wagging in the marriage bed, and he so loved the marriage bed. Hawkwood preferred not to dwell on that. His friend was an admirable fellow in many respects, but his unbridled lust for his enormous wife was inexplicable.

It was Domna Ponera who took the bribes, and then bullied her husband into carrying out her promises. A convenient berth, a vacant warehouse, an extra gang of longshoremen, or an eye turned aside for a special cargo. There were many ways a port captain might be of service to the high and the low of Abrusio; but though it made Galliardo rich, it did not make him happy, even if it did make his wife gratifyingly agile in the afore-mentioned bed. Sometimes though, Hawkwood thought that Galliardo would give it all up to be master of a swift caravel again, plying the trade-routes of the Five Seas and raising a riot in every port he put into to wet his throat.

As for Domna Ponera's Royal warrant, Hawkwood had already seen it. The scarred nobleman, Murad of Galiapeno, was in possession of it, and had sent the victualling documents to Hawkwood as soon as he had received Richard's agreement on the proposed voyage. Hence his visits to the catacombs this morning. Some other poor devils had gone to the pyre today, but not Hawkwood's crew. There was that to be thankful for.

"Do you know anything about this warrant?" Estrella asked him. She was trembling. She probably hated the silences even more than he did.

"Yes," he said heavily at last. "I know about it."

"Perhaps you would be so good as to tell your wife then, before she hears about it from someone else."

"Estrella, I would have told you today in any case. The commission is for my ships. I have been hired to undertake a voyage by the nobility, and ultimately by the King himself."

"Where to? What is the cargo?"

"There is no cargo as such. I am carrying . . . passengers. I cannot tell you where, because I am not yet entirely sure myself." He hoped she would recognize the element of truth in that statement.

"You do not know how long it is to be for, then?"

"No, lady, I do not." Then he added, out of some belated sense of decency, "But it is likely to be a long time."

"I see."

She was trembling again and he could see the tears coming. Why did she cry? He had never worked it out. They took little pleasure in each other's company, in bed or at board, and yet she always hated to see him go. He could not decipher it.

"You would not have told me—not until you had to," she said, her voice breaking.

He stood up and padded barefoot out to the balcony. "I knew you would not like it."

"Does it matter greatly to you what I like and do not like?"

He did not reply, but stared out at the crescent of the teeming harbour and its forest of masts and, further out, the blue of the horizon where it met the sky in the uttermost west. What lay out there? A new land ready for the taking, or nothing but the rim of the earth as the old sailors had believed, where the Western Ocean tipped away eternally into the gulf wherein circled the very stars?

He heard the swish of her heavy robe as she left the room behind him, the gulp of breath as she swallowed a sob. For a second he hated himself. It might have been different had she borne him a son—but then he could imagine the scenes when first the father took the son to sea with him. No, they were too far apart from each other ever to find some middle ground.

And did it matter? It had been a political marriage, though the Hawkwoods had done better out of it than the Calochins. Estrella's dowry had bought the *Osprey*. He forgot that sometimes.

I'd as lief have the ship, he thought, without the wife.

He was the last of his line; after Richard Hawkwood the name would disappear. The last chance to perpetuate it had died with the abortion he had procured for Jemilla, unless by chance there was a whore in some port who had borne his progeny in a moment of carelessness.

He wiped his eyes. The dry heat had baked the bathwater out of his hair and now he stank of roses. He would go down to the yards and see how the outfitting was coming along. He would regain the smell of cordage and salt and sweat that was his proper scent, and he would ready his ships for the voyage ahead.

EIGHT

D OWN near the Guilds' Quarter of the city the streets were
quieter than at the rowdy waterfront. Here the merchants
rented or owned the stoutest warehouses for the most expensive of their commodities. It was a district of clean alleyways
and bland shopfronts, with privately hired guards at most corners and the odd, cramped little tavern where men of business
might meet in peace without being disturbed by the drunken
antics of paid-off sailors or off-duty marines.

Most of the guilds of Abrusio owned property here, from
the humble Potters' Guild to the mighty Guild of Shipmasters.
The Thaumaturgists' Guild owned towers and mansions further up the hillside, near the courts as befitted their role. But
those towers were closed now, by order of the Prelate of Abrusio, and Golophin the Mage, Adviser to King Abeleyn of Hebrion, was waiting patiently in a tiny tavern tucked behind one
of the warehouses built of stone that was for the storage of
ship timber. His wide-brimmed hat was pulled down to shade
his eyes, though the lights were low in the place, as if to
encourage conspiracy. He smoked a long pipe of pale clay
whilst a flagon of barley beer grew ever warmer on the table
in front of him.

The door of the inn opened and three men entered, all

cloaked despite the closeness of the night. They ordered ale, and two took theirs to a table on the other side of the inn while the third sat down opposite Golophin. He threw back his hood and raised his flagon to the old wizard, grinning.

"Well met, my friend."

Golophin's narrow, lined face cracked into a smile. "You might order me another beer, lad. This one is as flat as an old crone's tit."

A fresh flagon came, and Golophin drank from its moisture-beaded pewter gratefully.

"The landlord seems singularly incurious about the nature of his customers," King Abeleyn of Hebrion said.

"It is his business. This will not be the first whispered discussion he will have seen in his tavern. In places such as this the commerce of Abrusio is directed and misdirected."

Abeleyn raised one dark eyebrow. "So? And not in the court or the throne room then?"

"There as well, of course, sire," said Golophin with mock sincerity.

"I do not see why you could not have made your way into the palace invisibly or suchlike. This trysting in corners smacks of fear, Golophin. I don't like it."

"It is for the best, sire. It may seem to complicate things, but in fact it keeps life a lot simpler. Our friend the Prelate may be out of the city, but he has spies aplenty to do his watching for him. It were best you were not seen in my company while this current purge lasts."

"It is you he aims at, Golophin."

"Oh, I know. He wants my hide nailed to a tree, to halt what he sees as the Guild's meddling in the affairs of state. He would rather the clergy did the meddling. The Prelate has a whole host of issues he means to address, sire, and this edict he badgered you into signing is one way of getting to the heart of several of them."

"I know it only too well, but I cannot risk excommunication. With Macrobius gone there is no voice of reason left among the senior Church leaders, except possibly Merion of Astarac. By the way, how is the Synod coming together? What have you seen in your sorcerous travels?"

"They are still gathering. Our worthy Prelate had a good passage once he was out of the calms around these coasts. His vessel is currently crossing the Gulf of Almark, south of Alsten Island. He will be in Charibon in ten days, if the weather holds."

"Who is there already?"

"The Prelates of Almark, Perigraine and Torunna have preceded him. Their colleague, Merion of Astarac, had a longer journey to make than any of the others, and the Malvennor Mountains to cross. It will be two weeks, I fear, before the Synod is convened, sire."

"The longer the better, if it keeps that tonsured wolf from my door. I will soon be setting off myself for the Conclave of Kings at Vol Ephrir. Can you keep me informed about the doings here while I am away, Golophin?"

The old mage sucked deeply on his pipe, and then shrugged with a twitch of his bony shoulders.

"It will not be easy. I will have to cast through my familiar, something no mage likes to do at any time, but I will do my best, sire. It will mean losing our eye on the east, though."

"Why? I thought all you wizards had to do was gaze into a crystal and see what you wanted to see."

"If only it were that simple. No, if my gyrfalcon accompanies you I will be able to send you news from here through it, but do not expect regular bulletins. The process is exhausting and dangerous."

Abeleyn looked troubled. "I would not ask, except—"

"No, you have a right to ask, and it is a thing which must be done. Let us speak no more of it."

No one else could have spoken thus to the King of Hebrion, but Golophin had been one of Abeleyn's tutors when he had been a runny-nosed little miscreant, and the young prince had felt the back of the wizard's hand many times. Abeleyn's father, Bleyn the Pious, had believed in a stern upbringing laden with religious instruction, but Abeleyn had always hated the Inceptine tutors, dry men whose imagination was a thing of dust, a storehouse of past aphorisms and never-to-be-questioned rules. It was Golophin who had saved him, who had defused the incipient rebellion in the youngster and coaxed him into an appearance at least of dutiful submission. The wizard's closeness to the King's son had been one of the things which had protected him from the malice of the Inceptines when they had tried to rid the court of all vestiges of unorthodoxy and sorcery. The irony was that with the wizard's pupil at last on the throne, they had finally succeeded. Aekir's fall, Golophin thought with real bitterness, had been a Godsend to them.

"Speaking of the east," Abeleyn said conversationally, "how are the Torunnans holding out?"

Golophin tapped his long pipe out delicately on the table. He preferred leaf imported from Ridawan flavoured with cinnamon. The smoking pile of ashes smelled like an essence of the east itself. Abeleyn wondered if there were a tinct of *kobhang* in the leaf, the mild euphoric that easterners chewed or smoked to fight tiredness and clear their thinking. Golophin made patterns in the ashes with one long, white finger.

"I have been working the bird hard lately. He is tired, and when he is tired he begins to slip away from me, and I receive pictures of the stoop, the kill, blood and feathers drifting in the air. It is said that a tired or a despairing mage will sometimes let his self slip wholly into his familiar and become one with it, leaving his body an empty husk behind him. He glories thereafter in the animal emotions of the creature, and eventually forgets what he once was."

Golophin smiled thinly.

"My familiar sleeps on a withered tree not far from Ormann Dyke. Today he has seen a hundred thousand people go by, dragging their feet through the mud towards the last Torunnan fortress before the mountains. They have left thousands on the road behind them, and on their flanks the Merduk light cavalry prowl like ghouls. Ormann Dyke itself is in chaos. Half its defenders are taken up with dealing with the refugees, and the land to the west of the dyke resembles an enormous shanty town. The poor folk of Aekir can walk no more. Perhaps they will squat in the rain and await the outcome of another battle before they will have the strength to trek further west. But after Ormann Dyke, where can they go?"

"You believe the dyke will fall," Abeleyn said.

"I believe the dyke will fall, but more importantly so do its defenders. They feel forsaken by God, and King Lofantyr of Torunna they believe has abandoned them. He has drawn off men of the garrison to defend the capital."

Abeleyn thumped a fist down on the table, making the beer

jump in the flagons. "The damned fool! He should be concentrating all he has at the dyke."

"He is afraid he will lose all he has," Golophin said calmly. "There are less than eighteen thousand men left in the garrison, and the Knights Militant have been riding away to the west in large bodies for days. If Shahr Baraz finds more than twelve thousand manning the defences when he arrives I will be surprised. And even leaving troops to garrison Aekir and their supply lines, the Merduk can still put a hundred thousand men before the dyke, probably more."

"How long do we have before the assault?" Abeleyn asked.

"More time than you might imagine. Sibastion Lejer's fighting rearguard badly mangled the *Hraibadar*, the shock-troops of Shahr Baraz's forces. He will wait for them to come up before launching a serious assault, and with the Western Road in a shambles and the weather showing no sign of changing, his transport will have difficulties moving with the troops. The River Searil is swollen. Once the Torunnans cut the bridges, the Merduks will have to force a river crossing under fire; but the Torunnans will not cut the bridges whilst there are refugees on the eastern bank. If I were the Khedive, I'd wait until the roads improved before I advanced. The refugees are still pouring west, so for the moment time is on his side. That is not to say that his cavalry will not attack the dyke first, before the main body comes up, but the dyke will hold them for a little while. Its defenders are Torunnans, after all."

Abeleyn nodded absently. "I begin to see that Ormann Dyke is not solely a Torunnan affair. Lofantyr needs troops, needs them desperately. But what do I have to give him, and how could they get there in time? An army would take five or six months to march to the dyke."

"By sea it might take five weeks, with fair winds or the aid of a weather-worker," Golophin said.

"By sea?" Abeleyn shook his head. "The navy has its hands full patrolling the Malacar Straits against the corsairs; and then there is Calmar to consider. A western armament sailing into the Levangore would have to contend with the Calmaric Sea-Merduks. They have been quiet since Azbakir, but they would not tolerate an incursion of that size. It would be Azbakir all over again, save we'd be fighting it with transports instead of war-carracks. No, Golophin, unless you can magically spirit a few thousand men halfway across the world there is nothing we can do about the dyke. Lofantyr will love hearing that when I meet him at the conclave. Already he thinks the other monarchies have abandoned Torunna."

"Perhaps he is right," the mage said sharply. "There were seven great Kingdoms after the Fimbrian Hegemony ended; now the Merduks have reduced it to five. Will you sit in Abrusio until their elephants come tramping over the Hebros?"

"What would you have me do, teacher?"

Golophin paused, looking suddenly weary. "Teachers do not always know the answers."

"Nor do kings." Abeleyn set his brown fingers atop the old mage's lean wrist and smiled.

Golophin laughed. "What a jest it is to sit and try to put the world to rights. The earth was a flawed place ere man arrived to skew it further; we shall never set it straight upon its foundations. Only God can do that, or the 'Lord of Victories'," as the Merduks call Him."

"We will do our best, nonetheless," Abeleyn said.

"Now, my King, you are beginning to sound like your father."

"God forbid that I should ever sound like that sanctimonious, cold-eyed old warhorse."

"Do not be so hard on his memory. He loved you in his own way, and everything he did was for the good of his people. I do not believe he ever committed one act which could be attributed to personal motives."

"That much is certainly true," Abeleyn said tartly.

"Were he Torunna's king, sire, I'll guarantee you that Aekir would be standing and the Merduks would be breaking their heads against its walls as they have done for the past sixty years. And the Knights Militant would be there in number also, instead of carrying out purges up and down the continent. It is hard to argue with a man of perfect convictions."

"That I know."

"John Mogen was such a man, but he was too abrasive. He inspired either love or hate, and alienated those who should have been his allies in Aekir's defence. A king must appear to be as solid as a stone in his beliefs, lad, but he must bend like a willow when the gale blows."

"And bend invisibly," Abeleyn pointed out.

"Even so. There is a vast difference between blinkered intolerance and the ability to compromise without being seen to compromise."

"Ironic, Golophin, isn't it, that the best soldiers in the world, the Torunnans, are ruled by a king who has never seen battle, a young man who knows nothing of war?"

"The old monarchs are gone or going, sire. There is you, Lofantyr, King Mark of Astarac and Skarpathin of Finnmark—young men only a few years on the throne. The older kings who remember the earlier struggles with the Merduk are on their way out. The fate of Normannia rests on the shoulders of a new generation. I pray they will prove equal to the burden."

"Thank you for your confidence, Golophin," the King said dryly.

"You have it, sire, insofar as any man can have it. But I worry. The Ramusians have stood off the Merduk threat so long because they were united, strong, and of one faith. Now the holy men of the west seem intent on splitting each kingdom apart in the search for—what? Piety or earthly authority? I cannot yet say, but it worries me. Perhaps it is time there was a change. Perhaps Macrobius' downfall and the loss of Aekir is a new beginning—or the beginning of the end. I am no seer; I do not know."

Abeleyn stared into the cloudy heart of his beer. The tavern around them was quiet. There were a few murmuring knots of men in the corners, and the landlord stood at the bar smoking a short, foul-smelling pipe and whittling a piece of wood. Only Abeleyn's bodyguards, across the dim room, were looking about them, ever alert for the safety of their king.

"I need something, Golophin," Abeleyn said in a low voice. "Some morsel to take with me to the Conclave of Kings, some means of raising hope."

"And of staving off requests for troops," Golophin told him.

"That too. But I cannot think of anything."

"You just spoke of the Torunnans, sire, and how they were the best soldiers in the world. That was not always true."

"I don't follow you."

"Think, lad. Who once held all of Normannia in their fist? Whose tercios marched from the shores of the Western Ocean to the black heights of the Jafrar in the east? The Fimbrians, whose hegemony lasted two hundred years before they tore themselves apart in their endless civil wars. The Fimbrians, whose hands built Aekir and laid the foundations of Ormann Dyke, who broke the power of the Cimbric tribes and founded the Kingdom of Torunna itself."

"What about them?"

"They are still there, aren't they? They have not disappeared."

"They have shut themselves off in their electorates for this past century and more, endlessly quarrelling amongst themselves. They are no longer interested in empire, or in any events east of the Malvennor Mountains."

"They have fine armies, though. *There* is something you can take to your meeting of kings, Abeleyn. The west needs troops? There are untold tens of thousands of them in Fimbria contributing nothing to the defence of the continent."

"The Five Kingdoms distrust Fimbria; men have long memories. I am not sure even Torunna would welcome Fimbrian troops on its soil, despite the urgency of its needs—and even if we could persuade the Fimbrians to send them. They are an isolationist power, Golophin. They are not even sending a representative to the conclave."

Golophin leaned back from the table and flapped a hand in exasperation. "So be it then. Let the men of the west keep their fears and prejudices. They will no doubt still possess them when the hordes of Ahrimuz have cast the shadow of their scimitars over all the Ramusian kingdoms."

Abeleyn scowled, feeling as though he were the pupil again and Golophin the teacher who had just received the wrong answer.

"All right then, blast you! I'll see what can be done. It can do no harm, after all. I'll send envoys to the four Fimbrian Electorates, and I'll bring the whole thing up at the conclave. Much good it will do me."

"That's my boy," Golophin said, knowing how much that phrase irritated the King. "But there is one thing you might remember when dealing with the Fimbrians, sire."

"Yes?"

"Do not be proud. They hoard memories of empire, even if they say they no longer hanker after it. You must make yourself into a supplicant, no matter if it galls your pride."

"I must be a willow, eh, bending in the wind?"

Golophin grinned. "Exactly—but not, of course, *seen* to be bending. You are a king, after all."

They clinked flagons like men sealing a bargain or toasting a birth. The King drank deeply, and then pinched foam from his upper lip.

"There is one last thing tonight, something near to your heart, perhaps."

Golophin cocked an eyebrow.

"The list. The list we drew up of those of your own kind who might be saved from the pyre." The King did not meet the old wizard's eyes as he spoke. He seemed oddly abashed. "Murad tells me he will be ready to sail within two sennights. He takes a demi-tercio with him, fifty Hebrian arquebusiers and sword-and-buckler men. Counting the crews, that leaves space for some hundred and forty passengers."

"Less than we had hoped," Golophin said tersely.

"I know, but he is convinced he will need the soldiers once landfall is made."

"To deal with the wild natives he may meet, or with the passengers he must travel with?"

Abeleyn shrugged helplessly. "I have hamstrung his scheme enough as it is, Golophin. If I prune away at it any further he may throw it all up, and then we are back where we started. A man like Murad needs some kind of incentive."

"The viceroyship of a new colony."

"Yes. He has few superstitious prejudices against the Dweomer-folk. He should treat them fairly. They could be said to be the backbone of his ambitions."

"And your ambitions, sire. How do the Dweomer-folk fit into those?"

The King coloured. "Let us say that Murad's expedition eases my conscience and—"

"So many fewer innocents consigned to the flames."

"I do not relish being interrupted, Golophin, not even by you."

The old mage bowed in his seat.

"As you have said, it is a means of putting these folk beyond the reach of the Church, but you know also that there are other motives involved."

"As always."

"If there is a Western Continent, it must be claimed by Hebrion—must be. We are the westernmost seafaring power in
the world. It is our right to expand in that direction whilst
Gabrion and Astarac look to the Levangore for trade and influence. Think of it, Golophin. A new world, an empty world
free of monopolies or corsairs. A virgin continent waiting for
us."

"And if the continent is not virgin?"

"What do you mean?"

"What if this fabled western land is inhabited?"

"I cannot imagine that it is, or at least that they have a
civilization comparable to ours. And I am certain that they will
not possess gunpowder. That is something we ourselves have
had for only a century and a half."

"So Murad will slaughter his way to a Hebrian hegemony
on the shores of this primitive land, and the sorcerers who are
his cargo will be the living artillery which backs him up?"

"Yes. It was the only way, Golophin. The colonists must be
hardy, talented, able to defend themselves. What better way to
ensure that they survive than to make every one a sorcerer, a
herbalist, a weather-worker, or even a true thaumaturgist?"

Or a shifter, Golophin thought to himself, remembering Bardolin's new ward. But he said nothing of that.

"A king's motives are never simple," he intoned at last. "I
should have remembered that."

"I do my best with what God sees fit to give me."

"God, and Murad of Galiapeno. I would you had found
another man to lead this expedition. He has a face I do not
like. There is murder written in it and as for the ambition of
which you spoke I do not think even he has yet plumbed the
depths of it."

"It was his discovery, his idea. I could not take it away from
him without making an enemy."

"Then tie him to you. Make sure he knows how long the
arm of the Hebrian crown can be."

"You are beginning to sound like an old woman, Golophin."

"Maybe I am, but there is wisdom in the words of old
women too, you know."

Abeleyn grinned, looking boyish in the dim tavern light.

"Come, will you not return to the court and assume your
rightful place?"

"What, crouching behind your throne and whispering in your ear?"

It was the popular Inceptine image of the King's wizardly advisor.

"No, sire," Golophin went on. "It is too early yet. Let us see how the Synod goes, and this conclave of yours. I have a feeling, like the ache in an old wound before a storm. I think the worst is yet to come; and not all of it is drawing in from the east."

"You were ever free with prophecies of doom, despite the fact that you are no seer," Abeleyn said. His good humour had thinned. The boy had disappeared. It was a man who stood up and held out a strong hand to the old mage. "I must go. Tongues wag in the court. They think I have a woman down near the waterfront."

"An old woman?" Golophin asked, with one eye closed.

"A friend, Golophin. Even kings need those."

"Kings most of all, my lord."

THE night was as close as ever. Abeleyn and his bodyguards strolled up the street as nonchalantly as if they were three night-watchmen. The closed carriage was in a courtyard at the top, the horses standing stock-still, patient as graven images. The bodyguards clambered up behind whilst Abeleyn let himself inside.

There was a scratch of steel, a shower of sparks, then a glow. As the candle lantern took the flame, the interior of the curtained coach flickered with glowing gold. The carriage lurched into motion, the hooves of the horses clicking on the cobbles.

"Well met, my lord," the lady Jemilla said, her white face olive-coloured in the swaying candlelight.

"Indeed, my lady. I am sorry to have kept you waiting for so long."

"The wait was no trouble. It sharpens the anticipation."

"Indeed? Then I must make sure to keep you waiting more often." The King's tone seemed casual, but there was a tenseness about him that he had not evidenced whilst in the tavern with Golophin.

Jemilla threw off her dark, hooded cloak. Underneath she wore one of the tight-fitting dresses of the court. It emphasized the perfect lines of her collar-bones, the smoothness of the skin on her breastbone.

"I hope, my lord, that you have not been squandering yourself on one of the lower-city doxies. That would grieve me extremely."

She was ten years older than the King. Abeleyn felt the difference now as he met the dancing darkness of her eyes. He was no longer the ruler of a kingdom, the commander of armies. He was a young man on the brink of some glorious dispensation. It had always been this way with her. He half resented it. And yet it was the reason he was here.

The lady Jemilla unfastened the laces of her bodice whilst Abeleyn watched, fascinated. He saw the high, dark-nippled breasts spring out, red-marked where the tight clothing had imprisoned them.

Their quiet noises were hidden by the creak of leather and wood, the rattle of the iron-bound wheels, the clatter of the horses' progress. The carriage wound its leisurely way up Abrusio Hill towards the Noble quarter, whilst down on the waterfront the gaudy riot of the pothouses and brothels continued to paint the hot night in hues of flesh and scarlet, and in the harbour the quiet ships floated stark and silent at their moorings.

The high clouds shifted; the stars wheeled overhead in the nightly dance of heaven. Men sitting on the sea walls in the reek of fish and weed with bottles at their feet paused in their low talk to sniff the air and feel its sudden caress as it moved against their faces. Canvas flapped idly once, twice; then it bellied out as the moving air took it. The glassy sea, a mirror for the shining stars, broke up in swell on swell as the clouds rose higher out on the Western Ocean. Finally the men on the sea wall could feel it in their hair, and they looked at one another as if they had experienced some common revelation.

The breeze grew, freshening and veering until it was blowing steadily from the north-west, in off the sea. It swayed the countless ships at their moorings until the mooring ropes creaked, raised smokes of dust off the parched streets of the city and stirred the branches of the King's cypresses, moving inland to refresh sweat-soaked sleepers. The Hebrian trade wind had started up again at last.

NINE

BARDOLIN stared impassively at the wreckage of his home. The tower's massive walls had shrugged off the fury of the mob but the interior had been gutted. The walls were black with soot, the floor inches deep in it. Someone had smashed the jar of Ur-blood and it had gelled into a slithering, gelatinous, slug-like creature, incorporating the ashes and the fragments of scale and bone that were all that was left of his specimen collection. It was the Ur-creature that had finally frightened them off, he guessed. He stared at it as its pseudopodia blindly touched the air, trying to make sense out of this new world it had been so violently born into.

For a second Bardolin felt like reshaping it, adding the crocodile skull that lay mouldering in a corner, giving it the sabre-cat claws he had picked up on a trip to Macassar, and then launching the finished, unholy beast into the streets to wreak his revenge. But he settled for unbinding the Ur-blood from its gathered organic fragments and letting it sink, mere liquid again, into the scorched floor.

All gone—everything. His books, some of which dated back to before the Fimbrian Hegemony, his spell grimoires, his references, his collections of birdskins and insects, even his clothes.

The imp tiptoed across the ravaged chamber with wide, bewildered eyes. It clambered up Bardolin's shoulder and nestled in the hollow of his neck, seeking reassurance. He could feel the fear and confusion in its mind. Thank God he had removed it from the rejuvenating jar before he had left and had taken it with him, hidden in the bosom of his robe. Otherwise it would be one more rotting mess amid the littered debris.

There were things here which disturbed him, unanswered questions amid the ruin of his home which hinted at larger answers; but he was too blasted and bewildered to tackle them now. How had they forced the mage bolt on the door? How had they known he was not at home, but was away watching poor Orquil burn?

Orquil. He shut his eyes. Despite the cool sea breeze that washed over the city like a blessing, he could still smell burnt flesh. Not in the air, but off his own clothes. He had stood at the foot of the boy's pyre looking up into his apprentice's pitifully young face, as pale as chalk, but smiling somehow; and he had smote him with a bullet of pure thaumaturgy as potent as his grief and rage could make. The boy had been dead before the first flames began to lick round his shins. The first life Bardolin had ever taken with magic, though he had taken many more with blade and arquebus ball.

There will be more taken by magic before I am done, he promised himself, the bitter anger rising in him. He wondered if Griella felt like this when the black change was upon her. That unfocused hatred, the mounting fury craving outlet in some act of extreme violence.

But that was not the mage way. Anger did no one any good. And besides, if Bardolin were truly honest with himself, he would have to admit that it was guilt that fuelled his rage as much as grief. The fact that he himself had not burned.

Griella entered the blasted room. She had a sack slung over one slim shoulder and her hands were black with ash.

"I tried to salvage some things, but there's not much left." She smiled as the imp chirruped at her, but then her face went flat again. "If you had let me stay, I would have stopped it," she said.

Bardolin did not look at her.

"How? By slaughtering them like cattle? And then the city

guard would have been swarming over this place like flies around summer dung."

"I don't think so. I think they would not have come here whatever happened. I think they were told to stay away."

Bardolin did look at her now, startled by the depth of her reasoning.

"Something does not smell right, it is true," he admitted. "Golophin has ensured our safety, by order of the King himself; but someone else is determined to hurt us ere we take ship for the West."

"Well, we've less to pack at any rate," Griella said brightly.

Her smile eventually drew an answering one from him. The heavy sun pouring through the splintered windows gave her hair the aspect of beaten bronze. Her very skin seemed golden.

"You are still sure you want to take ship with me, then?" Bardolin asked.

"Of course! I shall become your new apprentice, to replace the one they burned today. And I shall keep you safe. Not even when the change is upon me would I hurt you, I think."

Bardolin said nothing. When she had come round from the spell of unconsciousness she had been both furious and fascinated. She had never dreamed there could be a power to knock out a full-blooded shifter in the midst of the change. She had been a little in awe of him afterwards. But she was young, and she was not apt for an apprenticeship in the Seven Disciplines; shifters never were. And there was an aspect of her he had glimpsed whilst wrestling the beast down into oblivion, a hunger that was not part of the werewolf she became, but that was buried in her human soul. He had seen it only briefly, flickering as if in the depths of a long abyss, but it gave him doubts as to the wisdom of letting her accompany him on the voyage.

But what alternative was there for her here in Abrusio? She had been abused before; it would happen again, and then she would become the beast once more, and she would be hunted down. They would cut off the beast's head with a silver knife and stick it on a spear in the market place. In a few hours the head would change, and it would be her brown eyes staring down, that bronze helmet of shining hair atop the ragged stump of the neck. He had seen it before. He could not allow it to happen to her, and he would not yet allow himself to ask why.

He rose to his feet. He had only a leather satchel to carry; they had saved pitifully little. His magicks would be crude for a while, and reduced in power, for his memory was not up to the task of remembering all the subtleties and nuances of casting that were necessary to make a piece of thaumaturgy perfect. He hoped that some of his fellow passengers on the voyage would be able to help him regain his lost knowledge.

The imp crawled into the bosom of his robe, not minding the smell of the pyre. New clothes; he must have new clothes, and get rid of this reek.

"Let us leave this place," he said. "We have things to do. I would like to see these ships that are to bear us, and perhaps buy a few things to make the voyage more tolerable."

"Salt beef and wormy bread are what sailors eat," Griella informed him. "And unwatered wine. They wash in seawater, when they wash at all, and they use each other in the way a man uses a woman."

"Enough," Bardolin said, uncomfortable with hearing such things from such a young mouth. "To the harbour, then. Let's take a look at these terrible seafarers."

There was one thing he could still do, though. As they left through the shattered doorway of his burned-out tower, Bardolin traced in the stone lintel a glyph of warding. It flamed briefly as his fingers brushed the stone, then died into invisibility. If anyone came after, picking around the bones of his home, the glyph would burst into an inferno and mayhap burn the bastards while they rummaged.

TO a landsman, the Great Harbour of Abrusio was a vast and labyrinthine place. Now that the Hebrian trade had started up again, ships that had lain becalmed beyond the curve of the horizon were working in under all the canvas they could bear. The place was a stinking chaos of shouting men, squealing trucks and pulleys, creaking rope and thundering noise as a convoy of caravels out of Cartigella disgorged their cargoes of wine tuns on the quays and the enormous barrels were rolled up into waiting waggons which in turn would transport them to the public cellars.

On another wharf a beast transport had her square hull doors open wide, letting out a stench of animal excrement as the frightened cattle within were prodded and cursed down the ramps, scattering dung and straw as they went.

Bardolin and Griella paused to watch a Royal dispatch-runner, a lateen-rigged galleass, come sweeping into the harbour like some precisely rhythmed sea insect, the oars soaring up and out of the water at the same moment and the crew backing the mizzen to heave her to within yards of a free berth. These were the famous deep-water berths of Abrusio, hollowed out by the Fimbrians in past centuries using forced Hebrian labour. Abrusio could accommodate a thousand fully rigged ships at her wharves, it was said, and still have space for more.

Here were boxes of fish and sea squid shining in the hard sunlight, sacks of pepper from Punt or Ridawan, gleaming piles of marmorill tusks from the jungles of Macassar and, stumbling, chained lines of slaves bought from the Rovenan corsairs to work the estates of the Hebrian nobility.

Sailors, fishermen, marines, merchants, vintners and longshoremen. They worked without pause in the unrelenting heat with the sweat shining on their faces and limbs unable, it seemed, to communicate in anything less than a bellow. Bardolin and Griella found themselves holding hands in the crush to avoid being separated, for all the world like father and daughter. The heat glued their palms together with slick perspiration, and inside Bardolin's robe the imp whimpered with the noise and the smells and the jostling press of it.

They stopped half a dozen times to ask for the Hawkwood vessels, but each time were regarded pityingly, like imbeciles abroad by mistake, and then the throng pushed them along again. Finally they found themselves inside the tall, stone-built harbour offices, and there were told by a harried clerk to go to the twenty-sixth outfitting berth and ask for the *Grace of God* or the *Gabrian Osprey*, Ricardo Hawkwood, Master. They would find them easily, they were told. A ship-rigged caravel of one hundred tons, and a low-fo'c'sled carrack twice that tonnage with a mouldy looking bird for a figurehead.

They left the place only slightly less bewildered than when they had entered. This was a different world, down here by the water's edge. This was the world of the sea, with its own rules, laws, and even language. They felt like travellers in a foreign country as they pushed past ship after ship, wharf after wharf, and passed men of every land and faith and colour as they went. Since the easing of the edict in the wake of the Prelate of Abrusio's departure for the Charibon Synod, foreign ships had been putting into Abrusio without let-up. It was as though they were trying to make up for the time they had lost—or would lose again once the Prelate returned and for- eigners were once more hauled off their ships and into the catacombs by the hundred.

"There," Bardolin said at last. "I think that's them. See the bird figurehead? It's a sea osprey from the Levangore. One knows from the speckles on its breast."

They stood before a wide stone dock dotted with mooring bollards and littered with guano. Snug in the berth behind the dock were two ships, their bowsprits projecting out over Bardolin's head and their masts tall, rope-tangled edifices tower- ing up into the blue sky.

There were men everywhere it seemed, clinging to every piece of rigging and every rail. Some were out on the hulls on stages, painting the sea-battered wood with what looked like white lead. Others were knotting and splicing furiously in the shrouds. A gang of them were heaving on the windlass, and Bardolin saw that they were replacing a topmast. He knew little of ships, but he knew it was unusual, not to say revolu- tionary, to have masts in several pieces instead of one long, massive yard. This Hawkwood seemed to take his calling se- riously.

Yet more men were on the dock, hauling on tackles attached to the mainyard, lifting net-wrapped bundles of casks and crates up over the ships' sides and on to the decks. On the decks themselves the hatches were wide open and gaping to receive the dangling goods, and Bardolin was astonished to see sheep, goats and cages of chickens go up in the air along with the wine barrels and boxes of salt meat and ship's biscuit. He noted with approval a huge sack of lemons being loaded also. It was thought by many that they combated the killer disease of scurvy, though many others believed the condition was caused by the unsanitary conditions aboard any ship.

"Who are we to talk to?" Griella asked wide-eyed. Her grip on the wizard's hand had not relaxed one whit.

Bardolin pointed to a burly, ornately mustachioed figure on the larger of the two ships. He was standing at the back—the quarterdeck?—and shouting furiously at a group of men down in the waist of the ship. He had a long, eastern water-pipe in one hand and he shook it at the men as though it were a weapon. His hair was cut so short that the sunlight made his scalp gleam through the bristle.

"I would say he is in charge," Bardolin decided.

"Is he this Hawkwood man?"

"I don't know, child. We'll have to ask."

He and Griella made their tortuous way through the piled provisions and cordage and timber on the wharf to where a gangway with raised planks for steps had been thrown down from the waist of the larger ship. Some of the sailors stopped to stare at the hard-faced, soldierly looking man and the shining-haired girl on his arm. There was an appreciative whistle and ribald chatter in a language even Bardolin did not recognize; but the meaning and the gesture that accompanied it were obvious.

Griella spun round on the obscenely capering seamen. With the sunlight in her eyes it seemed they had a yellow glow, and the lips drew back from her white teeth in a snarl.

Bardolin tugged her on, leaving the sailors staring after the pair. One man hurriedly made the Sign of the Saint.

They laboured up the precarious gangplank, which seemed designed for the agility of apes rather than that of men. Once on deck, Bardolin raised a hand to the furious mustachioed man and shouted in his best sergeant of arquebusiers voice:

"Ho there, Captain! Might we have a word with you?"

The man yanked his water-pipe out of his mouth as though it had bitten him and glared at the pair.

"Who in the name of the Prophet's Arse are *you*?"

"Someone who is to take ship with you in a short while. May we speak to you?"

The man's eyes rolled in his head. "A warlock I shouldn't wonder, and his doxy with him too. Sweet Saints, what a trip this is promising to be!"

He turned away from the quarterdeck rail, muttering to himself. Bardolin and Griella looked at one another, and then clambered up towards him, feeling two dozen baleful stares on their backs as they went. It was like intruding on the territory of some alien, primitive tribe.

The quarterdeck was littered with coiled ropes and light spars of timber. Everywhere lines of the running rigging came down to be hitched about fiferails. A brass bell glittered, painfully bright in the sun, and the huge tiller that steered the ship from the half-deck below had been unshipped and lay to one side. The man was leaning on the taffrail and puffing on his gurgling pipe. His eyes were slits of suspicion.

"Well, what do you want? We're outfitting for a blue-water voyage and we're short of men. I have things to do, and passing the time of day with landsmen is not one of them."

"I am Bardolin of Carreirida and this is my ward, Griella Tabard. We have been told we are to be passengers on one of the vessels of Ricardo Hawkwood, and we wanted to see them and ask for advice on preparing for the coming voyage."

The man looked as though he were about to give a sneering answer, but something in Bardolin's eye stopped him.

"You've been a soldier," he said instead. "I can see the helm scar. You don't look like a wizard." He paused, staring into the glass-sided bubble of his pipe for a second, then grudgingly said: "I am Billerand, first mate of the *Osprey*, so don't call me captain, not yet at least. Richard is up in the city wrestling with the provisioners and moneylenders. I don't know when he'll be back."

The imp squirmed in Bardolin's bosom, making Billerand gape.

"Might we talk below?" Bardolin asked. "There are many sets of ears up here."

"All right."

The mate led them down a companionway in the deck and they blinked in the gloom, startling after the harsh brightness of the day. It was close down here; the heat seemed to hang like a tangible thing in their throats. They could smell the wood of the ship, the pitch that caulked the seams, soft and bitter-smelling, and the faint stink of the bilge, like filth and water left to lie stagnant in a warm place. They could hear, too, the thumps and shouts of men off in the ship's hold. It sounded like a fight going on in the adjacent room of a large house, muffled but somehow very near.

They went through a door, stepping over a high storm sill, and found themselves in the Master's cabin. One side of it was taken up by the long stern windows. They could look out and see the harbour sunlit and framed by the curving lines of the interior bulkheads, like a backlit painting of sharp brilliance.

There were two small culverins on either side of the cabin, lashed up tight against their closed gunports. Billerand sat down behind the table that ran athwartships, the scene of the harbour behind him.

"Is that a familiar you have there?" he asked, pointing to the wriggling movement in the breast of Bardolin's robe.

"Aye, an imp."

The mate's face seemed to lighten somewhat. "They're lucky things to have on a ship, imps. They keep the rats down. The men will be pleased with that at least. Let him out, if you please."

Bardolin let the imp crawl out of the neck of his robe. The tiny creature blinked its eyes, its ears moving and quivering on either side of its head. Bardolin could feel its fear and fascination.

Billerand's fierce face relaxed into a smile. "Here, little one. See what I have for you?" He produced a small quid of tobacco from a neck pouch and held it out. The imp looked at Bardolin, and then leapt on to the table and sniffed at the tobacco. It took it delicately in one minute, clawed hand and then began to gnaw on it like a squirrel working at a nut. Billerand scratched it gently behind the ear and his smile widened into a grin.

"As I said, the hands will be pleased." He leaned back again. "What would you have me tell you then, Bardolin of Carreirida?"

"What do you know of this voyage we are to undertake?"

"Very little. Only that it is to the west. The Brenn Isles, maybe. And we are not taking cargo, only passengers and some Hebrian soldiery. We'll be packed in these two ships tighter than a couple on their honeymoon night."

"And the nature of the other passengers, besides the soldiers?"

"Dweomer-folk, like yourself. The hands do not know it yet, and I'd as soon leave it that way for the moment."

"Do you know who is sponsoring the voyage?"

"There is talk of a nobleman, and even of a Royal warrant. Richard has yet to brief his officers."

"What kind of a man is this Hawkwood?"

"A good seaman, even a great one. He has redesigned his ships according to his own lights, despite the grumbling of the older hands. They'll make less leeway than any vessel in this port, I'll promise you. And they're drier than any other ships of their class. I've been in this carrack in a tearing gale off the Malacar Straits with a lee shore a scant league away and a south-easter roaring in off the starboard quarter, but she weathered it. Many another ship, under many another captain, would have been driven on to the shoals and broken."

"Is he a Hebrian native?"

"No, and neither are most of his crews. Nay, our Richard is Gabrionese, one of the mariner race, though he has made his home in Abrusio these twenty years, ever since his marriage to one of the Calochins."

"Is he a . . . pious man?"

Billerand roared with laughter, and a spit of fluid sparked out of the brim of his pipe. The imp jumped, afraid, but he soothed it with the caress of one callused hand.

"Easy, little fellow, it's all right. No, wizard, he is not particularly pious. Do you think he'd take your sort as supercargo if he was? Why, I've seen him make a sacrifice to Ran the god of storms to placate the tribesmen among the crew. If the Inceptines had heard of that he'd have been burnt flesh a long time ago. You need not fear; he loves the Ravens even less than the next man. They had Julius Albak, the first mate before me and a damned good shipmate, shot in front of our eyes and then they hauled half the crew of the *Grace* off to the catacombs to await the pyre—but our Richard got them back, God knows how."

"Which lands do your seamen come from?" Bardolin asked with interest, perching on a seachest that rested against the forward bulkhead.

Billerand sucked a moment on his gurgling pipe.

"What are these questions in aid of, wizard? You wouldn't be a spy of the Inceptines yourself, would you?"

"Far from it." Bardolin's face changed, going as white as marble, but his eyes flashed. "A friend of mine they burned today, sailor, a boy who was like a son to me. They have wrecked my home and the researches of thirty years. I am about to be exiled because of them. I have no love for the Ravens."

Billerand nodded. "I believe you. And I'll tell you that our crews are from every kingdom and sultanate in Normannia.

We've men from Nalbeni and Ridawan, Kashdan and Ibnir. Men of Gabrion who sailed under Richard's father; Northmen from far Hardalen, and even one from the jungles of Punt, though he don't speak much on account of the Merduks cutting out his tongue. We have tribesmen from the Cimbrics captured by the Torunnans and sold as slaves. They were oarsmen in a Macassian galley which we took last year. Richard is their headman now. They have blue faces, with the tattooing.

"Myself, I'm from Narbosk, the Fimbrian electorate that broke off from the empire and went its own way back in my great-grandfather's time. I've served my stint in the Fimbrian tercios, but it's a boring life fighting the same battles on the Gaderian river every year. I tired of it, and took to the sea. Which army did you serve with?"

"The Hebrian. I was a sword-and-buckler man, and later an arquebusier. We fought the Fimbrians at Himerio, and they trounced us up and down. They pulled out of Imerdon, though, and thus it now belongs to the Hebrian crown."

"Ah, the Fimbrians," Billerand said, his eyes shining. Abruptly he reached under the table and produced a wide-bottomed bottle of dark glass. "Have a taste of *Nabuksina* with me, in memory of battling Fimbrians," he said, his smile baring teeth as square and yellow as those of a horse.

They shared the fiery Fimbrian root spirit, slugging in turn from the bottle. The imp watched, grinning from ear to long, pointed ear, the tobacco a bulge in one cheek. Griella stirred restlessly. She was bored with this talk of battles and armies. When Bardolin noticed he wiped his mouth on his sleeve, as he had not done in years, and held up a hand when the bottle was proffered to him again.

"Some other time, perhaps, my friend. I have other questions for you."

"Question away," Billerand said expansively, curling one end of his luxurious moustache on a finger.

"Why are the soldiers taking ship with us? Is that usual?"

Billerand belched. "If a king's warrant is involved, why then yes."

"How many are coming?"

"We've been told to provision for fifty—a demi-tercio."

"That's a lot of fighting men for two vessels such as these."

"Indeed. Perhaps they're to keep the Dweomer-folk from

magicking us when we've put to sea. We've to provide berths for half a dozen nags, too, both mares and stallions, so the nobles don't wear out their boots when we make landfall."

"And you're sure you don't know where that landfall will be?"

"Upon mine honour as a soldier, no. Richard is keeping that nugget to himself. He does that sometimes if we're putting to sea in search of a prize, so that word will not get out over the harbour. Sailors can be like a bunch of gossiping old women when they choose, and they dearly love a prize."

"This ship is a privateer also, then?"

"It is anything it has to be to make a little money; but we don't like that too widely known in Hebrion. Our good captain has contacts with the sea-rovers, the corsairs of Rovenan, or Macassar as they call it now. Our culverins and falconets are not for decoration alone."

"I'm sure," Bardolin said, standing up. "Can you tell me when you expect to sail?"

Billerand shook his head mournfully. The drink was beginning to trickle into place behind his eyes, making them as glassy as wet marbles. "We weigh anchor some time in the next fortnight, that's all I know. I doubt if even Richard himself knows the exact date yet. A lot depends on these nobles."

"Then we'll see you again, Billerand. Let us hope the voyage will be a prosperous one."

Billerand winked one eye slowly, showing them his square-toothed grin again.

BACK out on the dock Bardolin strolled along lost in thought, the imp fast asleep in his bosom. Griella had to jog beside him to keep up.

"Well?" she demanded.

"Well what?"

"What have you learned?"

"You were there—you heard what was said."

"But you've guessed something. You're not telling me everything."

Bardolin stopped and gazed down at her. Her lower lip was caught up between her teeth. She looked absurdly fetching, and incredibly young.

"It is the presence of so many soldiers, and the nobles who command them. And the horses."

"What about them?"

"We cannot be sailing to any port in any of the civilized kingdoms or principalities; their authorities would not readily permit so many foreign soldiery to put ashore. And the horses. Billerand said they were mares and stallions. Warhorses are geldings. Those horses are for breeding. And did you see the sheep being taken on board? I'll wager they are for the same purpose."

"What does it all mean?"

"That we are going somewhere where there are no sheep and no horses; where there is no recognized authority. We truly are sailing into the unknown."

"But where?" Griella insisted, growing petulant.

Bardolin stared out across the maze of docks and ships and labouring men, out to where the flawless sky came down and merged with the brim of the horizon.

"West, we were told; maybe the Brenn Isles. But I reckon our worthy first mate was not telling us everything he knows. I think our course is set beyond them. I believe we are to sail further than any ship ever has before."

"And what are we supposed to find?" Griella asked him irritably.

Bardolin smiled and put an arm about her slim shoulders.

"Who knows? A new beginning, perhaps."

TEN

OUTSIDE, the tramp of cadenced feet and the bark of orders were filling up the afternoon. Little zephyrs of dust swirled in the doorway to curl up on the floor. A lizard clung motionless to the whitewashed wall.

Lord Murad of Galiapeno sipped wine, his eyes running down the muster lists. Unlike many nobles of the old breed, he could read and write perfectly and did not consider it beneath him. The older generation had cooks to feed them, grooms to care for their horses and scribes to read or write their books and letters. Murad, like King Abeleyn, had never thought that a prudent state of affairs. He liked to decipher evidence with his own wits without having to rely on a commoner. And there were some things which he liked to reserve for his eyes alone.

Fifty-two men, including two sergeants and two ensigns. They were the best in the Abrusio garrison, and Murad had commanded the bulk of them himself for more than two years. No cavalry, alas. The only horses they were taking were breeding stock. There were arquebuses for every man, though not all of them were yet trained in their use; and Hawkwood's crews—they were familiar with firearms. Many of them were no better than pirates.

Murad dipped his quill in the inkwell and did some calculations. Then he leaned back, gnawing the end of the goose-feather with his teeth. Two hundred and sixty-two souls all told, in two ships. Of that total perhaps a hundred and twenty were able to bear arms, plus an unknown quantity of these God-cursed sorcerers. They might well be more useful than field guns if their powers were as great as rumour made them, but it was best not to expect too much. They would know nothing of discipline, and would have to be herded like the cattle they were.

His eye fell on another list, and he examined it carefully. Of the passengers on the ships, some sixty were women. That was good. His men would need recreation, to say nothing of himself. He would look them over ere they sailed and pick out a couple of the comeliest for his servants.

Murad put down his pen and stretched, the new leather of his doublet creaking. There was a shadow in the doorway, backlit by the glaring sunlight.

"Come."

Ensign Valdan di Souza entered, ducking his head a little. He snapped to attention before his superior officer, his armour clinking. He seemed half broiled, his face a mask of dust save where the sweat had cut long runnels down it. There was sweat dripping off his nose also, Murad noted with distaste. The man smelled like a Calmaric bathing room.

"Well, Valdan?"

"My men have drawn all weapons and equipment, sir, and I have quartered them apart from the others as you ordered. Sergeant Mensurado is inspecting them now, prior to your own inspection."

"Good." Mensurado was the best sergeant in the city, a filthy beast of a man and an inveterate whoremonger, but a born soldier.

"Sit down, Valdan. Loosen your harness for the sake of the Saint. Have some wine."

Valdan sat gratefully and plucked at his armour straps. He was a big, lanky youth with straw-yellow hair, unusual in Hebrion. His father was a prosperous merchant who had paid for his son to be adopted by one of the lesser noble houses, the Souzas. That was the way noble blood was watered down these days. Nobles without money sold their names to commoners with it. A century previously it would have been much different, but times were changing.

Still, di Souza was a good officer and the men liked him—perhaps, Murad thought wryly, because he was on their level. He was one of the two junior officers who would be accompanying him on the voyage. The other was Ensign Hernan Sequero, a member of the noblest family in the kingdom save for the Royal line of the Hibrusios. He might even be a closer relation to the King than Murad himself. But however blue his blood, he was late.

Sequero eventually arrived as Ensign di Souza was gulping down his second glass of the chilled wine. Murad looked him up and down coolly as he stood at attention. He smelled of Perigrainian perfume. His forehead shone with the heat, yet he somehow contrived to appear completely at ease despite his heavy half-armour.

"Sit." Sequero did so, flashing a glance of contempt at the gasping di Souza.

"The horses, Hernan. Have you seen to them?" Murad drawled.

"Yes, sir. They are to be loaded on to the ships the day before we sail. Two stallions and six mares."

"That's two more than this fellow Hawkwood bargained for, but no doubt he will find room for them somewhere. We need the wider range of brood mares for a healthy line."

"Indeed, sir," Sequero said. Horsebreeding was a passion of his. He had selected the stock himself from his father's studs.

"What about their feed?"

"Being loaded tomorrow: hay and best barley grain. I hope, sir, that there will be good pasture at our landfall. The horses will need fresh grass to get back into condition."

"There will be," Murad said confidently, although he did not know for sure himself.

There was a silence. They could hear cicadas singing in the trees that bordered the parched parade ground. Here, on the eastern side of Abrusio hill, the landward breeze was blocked and the country was as dry as a desert. Still, it was moving into autumn and rain could not be far away.

Where will autumn find us? Murad thought momentarily. Somewhere on the face of an unexplored ocean, or maybe a league below it.

He stood up and began pacing back and forth in the small room. It was stone-floored and thick-walled to keep out the worst of the heat. There was a bunk in one corner, a tall wall cupboard and a table covered in papers with his rapier lying across it. The two ensigns sat uncomfortably by the small desk. The window had been shuttered, and the place was dim save where the afternoon light flooded in through the open door. Murad's quarters were monk-like in their austerity, but he made up for it when he had time to spend in the city. His conquests were almost as legendary as the duels they engendered.

"You know, gentlemen," he said, continuing to pace, "that we are to undertake a voyage in a few days' time. That we are taking the best of the garrison and enough stock to breed us a new line of warhorses. Thus far, that is all you have known."

The two ensigns leaned forward in their chairs. Murad's black eyes swept over them both balefully.

"What I am about to tell you will not leave this room, not until the day and very hour we sail. You will not repeat it to the sergeants, to the men, to your sweethearts or your families. Is that understood?"

The two younger men nodded readily.

"Very good. The fact is, gentlemen, that we are taking ship with a Gabrian sea captain and a crew of black-faced easterners, so I want you to watch the men once we are aboard. Any fighting when we are at sea will not be tolerated. No man of any piety likes having veritable Sea-Merduks as travelling companions, but we make do the best we can with what God sees fit to give us. On that note, you had best be aware that we are not the only passengers on these ships. Some one hundred and forty other folk will be sailing with us, as . . . colonists. These people are, to put it bluntly, sorcerers who are fleeing the purges in Abrusio. Our king has seen fit to allow them to take ship for a place of sanctuary, and they will be the citizens of the state we intend to found in the west."

Hernan Sequero's face had darkened at the mention of sorcerers, but now it took on a narrow-eyed intensity at Murad's last word.

"West, sir? Where in the west?"

"On the as yet undiscovered Western Continent, Hernan."

"Is there such a place?" di Souza asked, shocked out of his respectful silence.

"Yes, Valdan, there is. I have proof of it, and I am to be the viceroy of a new Hebrian province we will establish there."

Murad could see that his officers' minds were working furiously, and he had to smile. They were the only other Hebrians of any rank who would be on the voyage; they were busy calculating what that meant in terms of personal position and prestige.

"As viceroy," Sequero said at last. "You are not expected to command troops, but to be the administrative head of the province. Is that not true, sir?"

Trust Sequero to work it out first.

"Yes, Hernan."

"Then someone will have to be appointed overall commander of the military part of the expedition once it reaches this Western Continent."

"Eventually, yes."

Di Souza and Sequero were looking at one another sidelong and Murad had to make an effort not to laugh. He had planned it well. Now they would be striving like titans to gain his favour in the hopes of promotion. And there would be no conspiring behind his back, either. They would trust each other too little for that.

"But that is in the future," he said smoothly. "For the moment, I want you both to begin drawing up guard rosters and training routines with the assistance of your sergeants. I want the men well drilled while we are at sea, and they must be proficient with arquebuses by the time we make landfall. That includes the officers."

He saw Sequero wrinkle up his nose at the thought. Nobles disliked firearms, considering them the weapons of commoners. Swords and lances were the only arms a man of any quality should have to know how to use. Murad had had to overcome that prejudice himself. Di Souza, who was closer to his troops, already knew how to use an arquebus and how to read and write, whereas Sequero, though quicker witted, was of the old school. He was illiterate and fought with sword alone. It would be interesting to see how they both developed in the voyage west. Murad was pleased with his choice of subordinates. They complemented each other.

"Sir," Sequero asked, "do you expect any kind of resistance in the west? Is the continent inhabited?"

"I am not entirely sure," Murad said. "But it is always best to be prepared. I am positive, though, that we will meet nothing which can overcome a demi-tercio of Hebrian soldiers."

"These sorcerers we are sailing with," di Souza said. "Are they convicts being deported, sir, or are they passengers embarking of their own free will? The Prelate of Abrusio—"

"Let me worry about the Prelate of Abrusio," Murad snapped. "It is true that we could choose better stuff to form the seed of a new province, but I do as the King wills. And besides, their abilities could prove useful."

"I take it, then, that we will not be embarking a priest, sir?" Sequero asked.

Murad glared blackly at him. Sequero sometimes liked to walk a narrower line than most.

"Probably not, Hernan."

"But sir—" di Souza began to protest.

"Enough. As I said, we are all subject to the will of higher authorities. There is no cleric in our complement, nor to be honest would I expect one to take ship with such fellow travellers. The new province will have to do without spiritual guidance until the first ships make the return voyage."

Di Souza was obviously troubled and Murad cursed himself. He had forgotten how God-damned pious some of the lower classes could be. They needed religion like the nobility needed wine.

"The men will not be happy, sir," di Souza said, almost sullenly. "You know how they like to have a priest on hand ere they go into battle."

"The men will follow orders, as they always do. It is too late now to do any differently. We sail, gentlemen, in eight days. You may inform your sergeants of the timing two days before departure—no sooner. Are there any other questions?"

Both ensigns were silent. Both looked thoughtful, but that was as it should be. Murad had given them a lot to think about.

"Good. Then, gentlemen, you are dismissed to your duties."

The two rose, saluted, and then left. There was a charming pause at the doorway as they silently wrangled over who should precede whom. In the end di Souza exited first, and Sequero followed him smiling unpleasantly.

Murad sat at his desk once more and steepled his fingers together. He did not like di Souza's emphasis on the priest. That was the last thing the King wanted—a cleric accompanying the ships westward to send back reports to the Prelate of Hebrion. It would seem odd, though, to the men not to have one.

He shook his head angrily. He felt like a warhorse beset by horseflies. It would be better once they were at sea and he had his own little kingdom to rule. And the Saints protect anyone who tried to gainsay him.

He opened the locked drawer of the desk and heaved out an ancient-looking book, much battered and stained. Hawkwood had sent him a letter, in his insolence, asking for a perusal of it. It was the rutter of the *Cartigellan Faulcon*'s master, the ship which had returned an empty and leaking hulk to the shores of Hebrion over a century before, with no thing living on board save a werewolf.

He flipped through the worn tome, squinting sometimes at the spidery scrawl of the entries. Finally he lit a candle, shut the door and sat peering at page after page in the yellow light as though it were the middle of the night. The parade-ground noises faded. In the sour salt and water snell of the rutter it seemed he was transported to another age, and heard instead the slap and rush of waves against a wooden hull, the creak of timbers working, the flap of canvas.

> *On leaving Abrusio, steer west-south-west with the wind on the starboard bow. With the Hebrian trade, it is 240 turns of the glass or five kennings to North Cape in the Hebrionese. Half a kenning from the shore the lead will find white sand at 40 fathoms. Change course to due west and keep on the latitude of North Cape for 42 days more of good sailing. Thereafter the trade veers to north-north-west. With the wind on the starboard bow it is 36 days more on that latitude before sounding will find a shelving shore from 100 fathoms and shallowing. At 80 fathoms there will be shells and white clay, and land will be a kenning and a half away. Keep a good lookout and at 30 fathoms there will be sighted green hills and a white strand. There is a bay there one league north of the latitude of North Cape. Behind it stands a*

mountain with two summits, clothed in trees. Stand off and let go anchor in fifteen fathoms. Low surf, high water when moon is north-north-west and south-south-east. A sixth of a league inland there is a sweet spring. Greenstuff is to be found all along the shore, and fruit. Winds freshen coming on to late autumn. Use the best bow and a stern anchor or else she is liable to drag in the soft ground.

These instructions had I from the rutter of the God-speed's master, gone to his rest these three hundred years and eleven, the Lord God rest his soul. I am—

Tyrenius Cobrian
Master, Cartigellan Faulcon
St. Mateo's Eve
Year of the Blessed Saint, 421

Murad knuckled his eyes irritably. So much of what was written in the rutter seemed to him utterly incomprehensible, though no doubt to a sailor it would make perfect sense. He was not going to let Hawkwood see this, though. No, he would give the good captain as much information as it suited him to give.

Conjoined to the rutter was the log of the *Faulcon*, and it made better reading though there were still long lines of boring entries.

16th day of Enmian 421. Wind NNW, fresh. Course due west. 206 leagues out of Abrusio by dead-reckoning. Four knots with courses and topsails. Killed the last pig, weight 123lbs. Body of Jann Toft of Hebriero, seaman, this day committed to the deep. May the Lord God have mercy on his soul. Hands employed about the ship. Re-caulked the cutter.

It was the record of an uneventful voyage westwards. The health of the crew seemed good apart from a few minor accidents, and there was only one major storm.

14th day of Forlion 421. Wind NNW backing to NW. Running before the wind under bare poles. Three foot of water in the hold. Preventer-stays aloft and eight men on the tiller. Estimate we are making over eight knots, and have been blown some fifteen leagues to SE.

15th day of Forlion 421. Wind NW, slacking. Course due west under unbonneted topsails. Speed three knots. Hands employed pumping ship and knotting and splicing rigging. Small cutter carried away. Seaman Gabriel Timian unaccounted for when all hands called in the forenoon watch. Ship searched from tops to bilge, but no sign. Presumed lost overboard, may God have mercy on him.

From here the log began to grow more interesting.

22nd day of Forlion 421. Wind NNW, moderate breeze. Course WNW, wind on starboard bow. Four knots, under topsails and mizzen course. Estimate we are three leagues south of North Cape latitude. 37 days out of Abrusio.

The first mate has reported to me that three casks of salt meat have been broken in the hold and their contents half gone. Hands restless at being so long out of sight of land. Gave speech in first dog-watch to encourage hands. Isreel Hobin, bosun's mate, stated our voyage was cursed. Had him put in irons in the bilge.

23rd day of Forlion 421. Wind NNW. Course due west. Four knots under unbonneted courses and topsails. By cross-staff reckoning we are back on North Cape latitude.

Isreel Hobin found dead in irons this day. Hands frightened. First mate, John Maze of Gabrir, reported privately to me that Hobin's throat had been torn out. Doubled the men on the night watches at their own request. The hands believe something haunts the ship.

24th day of Forlion 421. Wind NNW. Course due west. Six knots under courses and topsails. 215 leagues due west of Abrusio by dead-reckoning.

This day committed the body of Isreel Hobin, bosun's mate, to the deep. May the Lord have mercy on his soul.

*All hands engaged in carrying out search of the ship,
but nothing found. Passengers worried and hands uneasy. May the Blessed Saint watch over us all, and give
me the strength to take us across this accursed ocean.*

The Blessed Saint must indeed have been watching over
Tyrenius, for the *Faulcon* made landfall five and a half weeks
later, dropping anchor in a sheltered bay on the Western Continent. By that time three more crewmen had disappeared without trace, presumed lost overboard, and the crew were refusing
to venture down into the deeper, darker parts of the ship below
the hold.

Murad poured himself more wine. There was no sound from
the parade ground outside; it must have been near time for the
men's evening meal. He sat and stared at page after page of
the century-old log, his puckered scar twitching as he went
over the entries one by one.

Something had been aboard the ship with them, that much
was clear. But had it been the shifter which was the *Faulcon's*
sole occupant on its arrival back off the shore of Hebrion, or
was there something else? In any case, the men had been glad
to leave the ship on making landfall. Tyrenius could not even
prevail upon them to mount an anchor watch. They had all
slept ashore, save one.

The master had stayed with his vessel, had slept alone on
board whilst the crew threw up shelters on the shore. A brave
man, this Tyrenius, to face down his own fear and stick by his
duty. Murad drank a silent toast to him.

*8th day of Endorion 421. Wind NNW, veering to north,
light breeze. One foot swell. At anchor.
    This day I named the bay in which we rest Essequibo
Bay after our good king of Astarac, whose humble subject I am. Crew on shore gathering provisions and preparing with certain of the passengers to mount an
expedition into the interior. I remain aboard alone, for
no man will stand with me in this hour.*

Here the clipped, precise nature of the entry slipped and the
jagged uprightness of Tyrenius' handwriting became more ragged. The pen-strokes began flying both higher and lower along

the line, and tiny spatters of ink here and there spoke of the force he was exerting on his quill. He had been drinking, Murad guessed, trying to swallow his fear.

It is the last glass of the middle watch, and only I remain on the ship to turn the glass and keep the time which we have kept faithfully since leaving Abrusio. I hear the ship moving on the swell, and I think of the faces of the men whose lives this voyage has claimed. In the last First Watch one of the men swore he saw a pair of eyes staring up out of the open hatchway at him. Bright eyes, glowing in the night. After that no one would remain on board save me. But Sweet Blessed Saints forgive me, I do not remain on this ship out of duty alone. Fear also keeps me at my post.

Half a glass ago I was on deck, watching the fires of the men on the shore burning in the night, and something came up out of the main hatch, something monstrous. It padded across the deck whilst I remained on the quarterdeck above, and then it slipped over the rail and into the sea with never a splash to mark its passing. I saw it once, the dark head of it breasting the swell as it struck out for shore, and then it was gone. I sit here now and know that whatever unholy thing it was that took ship with us is gone. It is ashore, among the men on the beaches—whilst they sleep on under the trees, believing themselves safe. May God forgive me, I cannot leave the ship. I must sit and wait, and watch for the return of my men and whatever stories of horror they may bring with them. I would to God that we had a priest with us in this God-forsaken land, if only to give the last blessing which our frail souls crave before the final closing of death's curtain.

There were pages missing from the log, ripped out. Some of them Murad had removed himself, lest the King see them in his brief perusal of the volume; but others had been removed long before. Murad found himself staring at one page which seemed to have been spattered with thick, black ink. It was blood, old blood, and it had soaked through several pages, gluing them irrevocably together.

He sat back, trying to clear his head of the mouldy parchment smell, breathing in instead the dry heat of Hebrion in late summer.

Tyrenius' passengers—who had they been? And had they remained there in the west, or had they taken ship back with him to the Kingdoms of God? Whatever they had done, not one had survived to tell his story; all that was left of it was housed in the fragments of the document that was now before Murad.

It had to be a shifter, the same that had jumped from the ship on its return to Hebrion; but its behaviour tallied with nothing that Murad knew about the beasts. And why had it taken ship with the *Faulcon* in the first place? Had it signed on as a crew member in human form, or had it stowed away as a beast? The former was far more likely.

Murad flipped back to the rutter, turning page after page with a frown until he found what he was looking for. There.

> *Sailing directions for the western route as per the rutter of the* Godspeed, *bound out of Abrusio in the year of the Saint 109, Pinarro Albayero Master. Given to me by Tobias of Garmidalan, Duke of East Astarac, this 14th day of Miderialon 421 on the understanding that the rutter be destroyed after the relevant parts are copied. Witnessed by Ahern Abbas, Mage to the Court of King Essequibos of Astarac.*

That reference to an earlier voyage was not unique; there were others throughout the rutter. It seemed that high-ranking men from both Hebrion and Astarac had sailed into the west three centuries before the *Faulcon*'s ill-fated voyage. Tyrenius had been able to draw from their experience in his own journey, which meant they must have sent a ship back at some point. If so, what had happened to them, out in the west? There was no reference to finding them or their descendants in the *Faulcon*'s log. If they had not come back in the returning ship then they must have died there and left nothing but their bones for posterity.

It was hard to be sure, though. So much of Tyrenius' log had been removed. There were cryptic references to the earlier expedition, talk of sorcery and madness; a fever that struck down men and destroyed their reason. Darker still were veiled references to theurgical experiments carried out by the members of the first expedition—experiments that had gone badly awry.

What it added up to, Murad thought, was that there had been two previous expeditions to the west, the first sponsored by what seemed to be a group of high-born mages, the second by the government—or at least some of the nobility—of Astarac. Both had ended in disaster; but had the first disaster somehow contributed to the second?

Murad stared moodily into the candlelit depths of his wine. Here he was, again sailing into the west, again with a crowd of sorcerers on board. But the earlier voyages had not had Hebrian soldiery as part of their complement. Or Murad of Galiapeno, he added to himself.

He looked again over the part of Tyrenius' log that detailed the anchorage he called Essequibo Bay. From the description, the Western Continent seemed rich, heavily vegetated, and uninhabited.

He flipped the pages. More of the crew had died in Essequibo Bay, and the expedition into the interior had been abandoned. They had reprovisioned and sailed away leaving nothing behind.

Nothing at all, for the beast had been back on board ship by the time they had weighed anchor. Two weeks out to sea, and the first disappearances had begun. The return voyage had been a nightmare. A dwindling ship's company, contrary winds, and terror down in the hold.

The last pages of the log were missing. There was no word of how Tyrenius had met his end, or how he had managed to pilot his ship to the very coasts he had left six months before. The writing was hard to decipher. It shook and scratched as though written in haste or terrible apprehension. Murad was surprised to find that he pitied long-dead Tyrenius and his haunted crew. They had found hell within the wooden walls of a ship, and had carried it with them across half the world and back again.

There was a knock on the door and he started, spilling his wine. He cursed and snapped: "Who is it?"

"Renaldo, my lord, come with your supper."

"Enter."

His servant eased the door open and entered bearing a wooden tray. He cleared a space on the large table and began to set out a place. Murad put away the log and rutter and sat down before a plate of sliced roast boar and wild mushrooms, fresh-baked bread and olives, and a chunk of gleaming goat's cheese.

"Will that be all, sir?" Renaldo asked.

Murad was still screwing up his eyes against the flood of light that the open door admitted. He was surprised to see it, for he had thought it later in the day. But he liked to eat early; it gave him a chance to ride up to the city afterwards if he felt in need of amusement.

"Yes. You are dismissed."

The servant left, and Murad paused a moment in his tearing of the fragrant bread. They were sailing in eight days. There was time enough to call off the voyage.

He shook his head incredulously, wondering what had prompted that thought. This was the chance he had been waiting for all his life, the chance to carve out a principality for himself. He could not throw it away.

As he ate, though, not tasting the food, he could see in his mind's eyes the picture of a deserted ship sailing across an endless ocean with a dead man's hand on the tiller. And the eyes of a beast burning as bright as candles in the depths of its hold.

ELEVEN

IT had been a busy time, but now the worst was over. Hawk-wood's two ships had been towed out of their berths by sweating harbourmen and were anchored in the Inner Roads, yards crossed and the last of the water completed. They were ready for sea, and rose and fell slowly on the swell that the trade wind had brushed up in the bay. Even this small distance from the land, it was cooler. There was no dust hanging in the throat out here, only the tang of the ocean and the shipboard smells that to Richard Hawkwood had always been the aroma of home.

The deck of the *Gabrian Osprey,* Hawkwood's flagship, was a scene of utter chaos. Billerand could be seen down in the waist of the ship bellowing and shoving along with a pair of bosun's mates. The goats were bleating madly in their pen aft of the main hatch and at least threescore of the passengers and soldiers who were aboard were lining the lee bulwark and peering up at Abrusio hill as it towered over the shining expanse of the bay.

The ship was dangerously overcrowded, and when sailing as close to the wind as they would need to in order to clear the bay itself, Hawkwood would have to make sure that the passengers manned the weather side of the ship to stiffen her

against the breeze. A beam wind—not the *Osprey*'s best point
of sailing, not by a long chalk. Richard had lost count of the
times he had beaten out of this port with the north-west trade
in his right eye. It was an ordeal every sailor leaving Hebrion
had to undergo, except in the hottest of the summer months
when the trade might fail altogether, or veer a point and make
it necessary to tack out of the bay, for there was not enough
sea room here for wearing. Old salts had a saying that Abrusio
loved to welcome ships, but hated to let them go.

"Take your hands off me!" a shrill voice cried. A girl down
in the waist, her hair a dark golden bob. One of the crew was
lifting her bodily from the ship's side to get at the fiferail. But
then, unaccountably, the sailor was lying clear across the other
side of the ship, looking dazed, and the girl was standing with
her hands on her slim hips, eyes aflame. The rest of the crew
roared with laughter, loving it. Eventually an older man, who
looked like a soldier or a prize fighter, calmed her down and
led her away. The dazed seaman had to endure the derision of
his comrades, but he went back to his work readily enough.

Hawkwood frowned. Women on board ship, and in such
numbers. And soldiers, too. That was a potentially explosive
mixture. He must have a formal meeting with Murad and his
officers as soon as possible and lay down a few ground rules.

Billerand was restoring some sort of order to the deck in
his rough way. The passengers were being hustled below, the
last of the goats lowered down through the main hatch by a
gang of men with tackles, and the soldiers were being patiently
ushered up to the forecastle, their armour clinking and glittering in the bright air.

The breeze was freshening. Over an hour still to the evening
tide. But it was a long pull to the Inner Roads with the trade
blowing, half a league at least. Hawkwood hoped Murad
would not cut it too fine.

The scar-faced nobleman was in Abrusio tying up some last
matters of his own, and the *Osprey*'s longboat, along with
eight good oarsmen, was waiting for him at the harbour wall.

The past week had been a nightmare in every way possible. Hawkwood swore to himself that he would never allow
himself to be threatened or cajoled into a joint expedition
again. It was the old story of soldier versus sailor, noble versus
commoner. At times he had almost believed that Murad was

throwing obstacles in his path and disregarding his arrangements for the sheer satisfaction of seeing him rant.

Billerand joined him on the quarterdeck, sweating and red-faced. His fantastic moustache seemed to bristle with suppressed fury.

"God-damned landsmen!" was all he could utter for several moments. Hawkwood grinned. He was glad he had kept Billerand here with him on the *Osprey* instead of giving him command of the *Grace*. He looked across at the smaller vessel. The rigging of the caravel was black with men. They were just finishing the job of rerigging her with the long lateen yards; she carried them on all three masts now. They would serve her well in the beam wind they would be sailing on. Haukal of Hardalen, the master of the *Grace*, had been brought up on the square-rigged, snakelike ships of the far north, but he had soon picked up the nuances of sailing with lateen yards. Hawkwood could see him, a tall, immensely bearded man who habitually carried a hand axe slung at his waist. He was standing on the *Grace*'s tiny quarterdeck waving his arms about. He and Billerand were close friends; their exploits in the brothels and taverns of half a hundred ports had become the stuff of legend.

The *Grace*'s decks were also crowded with soldiers and passengers, hampering the work of the sailors. It was to be expected; this would be the iast real sight of land they would have for many days. For most of them, Hawkwood supposed, it was probably their last ever sight of Hebrion and gaudy old Abrusio. Their fates were set in the west, now.

"How is the supercargo settling in?" he asked the fuming Billerand.

"We've hammocks slung fore and aft the length of the gundeck, but God help us if we're brought to action, Captain. We'll have to cram the whole miserable crowd of them down with the cargo or in the bilge." That thought made his face brighten a little. "Still, the soldiers will be useful."

Billerand had time for soldiers; he had been one himself. For Hawkwood, they were just another nuisance. He had thirty-five of them here on the *Osprey,* the rest on the caravel. Two-thirds of the expedition travelled in the carrack, including Murad and both his junior officers. Hawkwood had had to partition the great cabin with an extra bulkhead so the nobility

might sail in the style it was accustomed to. The sailors were
berthed in the forecastle, the soldiers in the forward part of
the gundeck. They would be living cheek by jowl for the next
few months. And they had so many stores on board for the
setting up of the colony, to say nothing of provisions for the
voyage, that both ships sat low in the water and were sluggish
answering the tiller. It would take very little to put the tall-
sterned *Osprey* in irons or make her miss stays. Hawkwood
was not happy about it. It was like mounting a normally fiery
horse and finding it lame.

"Longboat on the larboard beam!" the lookout called from
the foretop.

"Our tardy nobleman, at last," Billerand muttered. "At least
he will not make us miss our tide."

"What have you heard of this Murad fellow?" Hawkwood
asked him.

"Only what you already know, Captain. That he has an eye
for the ladies, and is as swift as a viper with that rapier of his.
A good soldier, according to his sergeants, though he's over-
fond of flogging."

"What nobleman is not?"

"I've been meaning to tell you, Captain. This Murad is to
bring no valet on board with him. Instead he has selected a
pair of girls from among the passengers as his cabin servants."

"So?"

"I've heard the soldiers talking. He'll have them as bed-
mates and the soldiers intend to try and follow his example.
We have forty women on the carrack alone, married most of
them, or someone's daughter."

"I hear you, Billerand. I'll talk to him about it."

"Good. We don't want the mariners feeling left out. There's
enough friction as it is, and raping a sorcerer's wife or daughter is no light matter. Why, I saw a man once—"

"I said I'd talk to him."

"Aye, sir. Well, I'd best see to the windlass. We'll weigh
as soon as the tide is on the ebb?"

"Aye, Billerand." Hawkwood slapped his first mate on the
shoulder, and the man left the quarterdeck, sensing his captain
wanted to be alone.

Or as alone as it is possible to be in a ship thirty yards long
with ninescore souls on board, Hawkwood thought. He peered

out towards the land and saw the longboat skimming along like a sea-snake half a mile away. Murad was standing in the stern, straight as a flagstaff. His long hair was flying free in the wind. He looked as though he were coming to lay claim to the ships and all in them.

Hawkwood moved over to the weather side of the deck, pausing to shout down through the connecting hatch to the tillerdeck below.

"Relieving tackles all shipped there?"

"Aye, sir," a muffled voice answered. "Course west-sou'-west by north as soon as we weigh."

The men knew their job. Hawkwood was fidgeting, anxious to get started, but they needed the ebb of the tide to help pull them out of the bay. There was a while to wait yet.

He had said his farewells, for what they were worth. He and Galliardo had drunk a bottle of good Gaderian and chewed half a dozen pellets of *Kobhang* so they might talk the night through. The port captain would look after his affairs while he was gone, and call in on Estrella occasionally.

Estrella. Saying farewell to her had been like ridding one's hands of fresh pitch. She knew this was no common voyage— no coasting trip, or ordinary cruise after a prize. He could still feel her thin arms about his waist as she knelt before him, sobbing, the tears streaking kohl down her cheeks.

And then Jemilla. What was it she had said?

"I'll look for you in the spring, Richard. I'll look out over the harbour. I'd know that absurd carrack of yours anywhere."

She had been naked, lying on the wide bed with her head resting on one hand, watching him with those feline eyes of hers. Her thighs had been slick with the aftermath of their loving and his back was smarting from where she had clawed him.

"Will you still be the King's favourite when I return?" he had asked, lightly enough.

That smile of hers, infuriating him.

"Who knows? Favourites come and go. I live in the present, Richard. This time next year we could all be under the Mer-duks."

"In which case you would no doubt be chief concubine in the Sultan's harem. Still spinning your webs."

"Oh, Richard," she said, feigning hurt, "you wrong me." But

then her face had changed at seeing the anger on his. The dark eyes had sparked in the way that never failed to raise the hair on his nape. She opened her legs so he could see the pink flesh amid the dark fur at her crotch, and then she spread herself wide there with shining fingers so that it seemed he was looking at some carnivorous flower from the southern sultanates.

"You have your ships, your culverins, your crews. I only have this, the one weapon all women have possessed since time began. You would prate to me of love, fidelity—I can see it in your great sad eyes. You who have a wife weeping the night away at home. The sea is your real mistress, Richard Hawkwood. I am only your whore, so let me pursue the same aims in life as you, in my own way. If that means bedding every noble in the kingdom, I will do it. Soon enough my charms will be taken from me. My skin will wither and my hair will grey, while your God-cursed sea will always be there, always the same. So let me play what games I can while I can."

He had felt like a child groping for an adult's comprehension. It was true that he had been about to tell her that he loved her. In her own way, he thought she returned his love— if it was in her to love any man at all. And he realized that, in her own way, she hated his leaving as much as Estrella did, and resented it similarly.

They had loved again, after that. But this time there was no hectic passion; they had coupled like two people grown old together, savouring every moment. And Hawkwood had known somehow that it was the last time. Like a ship, she had slipped her cables and was drifting away, letting the wind take her further on her voyage. He had been discarded.

"Longboat alongside!" someone shouted, and there was a commotion on deck, a glittering clatter as a file of soldiers shouldered arms and Murad of Galiapeno hauled himself up the carrack's sloping side.

Murad sketched a salute to his officers and went below without further ceremony. He had a small chest under one arm. Hawkwood saw his face as a pale, sneering flash before the lean nobleman had stepped into the companionway and disappeared.

"Sir, shall we stow the longboat on the booms?" Billerand shouted.

"No, we'll tow her. The waist is crowded enough as it is."

Hawkwood had a momentary, silent argument with himself, and then left the quarterdeck. He went below, following in Murad's footsteps, and knocked on the new door the ship's carpenter had wrought in the bulkhead next to his own.

"Come."

He went in. At the back of his mind he was counting off the minutes before they weighed anchor, but it was best to do this now, to get it over with. Billerand would manage if he were detained.

Murad had his back to him when he entered. He was studying something on the long table that spanned the cabin. He locked it away, whatever it was, in the chest he had brought aboard before turning round with a smile.

"Well, Captain. To what do I owe the pleasure?"

"I would have a word with you, if I may."

"I am entirely at your disposal. Speak freely." Murad leaned back against the table and folded his arms. Hawkwood stood awkwardly before him as though he had been summoned to the cabin. He noted with some satisfaction, however, that the nobleman was finding the slight roll and pitch of the ship awkward. He swung like a reed in a thin breeze, whereas to Richard the deck was solid and steady under his feet.

Wait until the bastard gets his first taste of seasickness, he thought malevolently.

"It is about your men. It has been brought to my attention that they seem to think they can have the pick of the women on board."

Murad frowned. "So?"

"They cannot."

Murad straightened, his arms coming down by his sides. *"Cannot?"*

"No. There will be no women molested on my ships, not by my men and not by yours. These are not strumpets from the back alleys of Abrusio we have embarked. They are decent women, with families."

"They are Dweomer-folk—"

"They are passengers, and thus my responsibility. I have no wish to challenge your authority with your own men, especially in public; but if I hear of a rape, I'll give the man involved the strappado, be he seaman or soldier. I'd as lief have

you order it, though. It would help relations between the services."

Murad stared silently at Hawkwood as though he were seeing him for the first time. Then, very softly, he said:

"And I? If I choose to take a woman, Captain, will you give
me the strappado?"

"Rules are different for the nobility—you know that. I cannot touch you. But I beg you to consider what such an example
would do for the men. There is also the fact that the passengers
are, as you have said, Dweomer-folk. They are not defenceless.
I've no wish to have my vessel blown out of the water."

Murad nodded curtly, as if finally accepting the justice of
this. "We must get along as best we may, then," he said pleasantly. "Perhaps your crews can persuade my men to follow
their example and fuck each other's arses as sailors are wont
to do, I am told."

Hawkwood felt the blood rising into his face and his sight
darkened with fury. He bit back the words that were forming
in his mouth, however, and when he spoke again his tone was
as civil as Murad's.

"There is another thing."

"Of course. What is it?"

"The rutter. I need it if I am to plot a proper course. So far
you have told me to set sail for North Cape in the Hebrionese,
but after that I am wholly in the dark. That is no way for the
master of a ship to be. I need the rutter."

"Don't you mariners ever use the proper form of address,
Hawkwood?"

"I am Captain Hawkwood to you, Lord Murad. What about
the rutter?"

"I cannot give it to you." Murad held up a hand as Hawkwood was about to speak again. "But I can give you a set of
sailing instructions copied out of it word for word." He
snatched up a sheaf of papers from the table behind him. "Will
that suffice?"

Hawkwood hesitated. The rutter of a true seaman, an open-
ocean navigator, was a rare and wonderful thing. Shipmasters
guarded their rutters with their lives, and the knowledge that
this ignorant landsman had in his possession such a document—and containing the details of such a voyage—was mad-
dening. Perhaps he even had a log as well. So much

information would be there, information any captain in Hebrion would give an arm for, and this ignorant swine kept it to himself where it was useless. What was he afraid that Hawkwood might see? What was out there in the west that had to be kept so secret?

He snatched the papers greedily out of Murad's hand but forced himself not to look at them. There would be a better time. He would lay his hands on the rutter yet. He had to, if he was to be responsible for his ships.

"Thank you," he said stiffly, stuffing the papers in his bosom as though they were of little account.

Murad nodded. "There! You see, Captain, we can work together if we've a mind to. Now will you sit with me and have some wine?"

They would be weighing anchor soon, but Hawkwood took a chair, feeling that the scarred nobleman had somehow outfoxed him. Murad rang a little handbell that sat on the table.

The cabin door opened and a girl's voice said, "Yes?"

Hawkwood turned in his chair, and found himself staring at a young woman with olive-coloured skin, green eyes and a mane of tawny, shining hair that was cropped short just below her ears. She wore the breeches of a boy, and could almost have passed for one were it not for the subtle delicacy of her features and the undeniable curves of her slim figure. He saw her hand on the door handle: brown fingers with close-bitten nails. A peasant girl, then. And he remembered—she was the one the sailor had tussled with up on deck.

"Wine, Griella, if you please," Murad drawled, his eyes drinking in the girl as he spoke. She nodded and left without another word, eyes blazing.

"Marvellous, eh, Captain? Such spirit! She hates me already, but that is only to be expected. She will grow used to me, and her comrade also. It promises to be a pleasant tussle of wills."

The girl came in with a tray, a decanter and two glasses. She set them on the table and exited again. She met Hawkwood's stare as she went, and her eyes made him sit very still. He was silent as Murad poured the wine. Something in the eyes was not right; it reminded Hawkwood of the mad eyes of a rabid dog, windows into some unfathomable viciousness. He thought of saying something, but then shrugged to himself.

Perhaps Murad liked them that way, but he had best be wary when bedding such a one.

"Drink, Captain." The nobleman's normally sinister face was creased with a smile: the sight of a girl seemed to have quickened his humour. Hawkwood knew that he had called her in for a reason, to make a point. He sipped at his glass, face flat.

A good wine, perhaps the best he had ever tasted. He savoured it a moment.

"Candelarian," Murad told him. "Laid down by my grandfather. They call it the wine of ships, for it is said that it takes a sea voyage to age it properly, a little rolling in the cask. I have half a dozen barrels below, thank the Saints."

Hawkwood knew that. It had meant carrying six fewer casks of water. But he said nothing. He had come to realize that he could do little about the whims of the nobleman whilst Hebrion was in sight. Once they were on the open ocean, though— then it would be different.

"So tell me, Captain," Murad went on, "why the delay? We are all aboard, everything is ready, so why do we sit at anchor? Aren't we wasting time?"

"We are waiting for the tide to turn," Hawkwood said patiently. "Once it reverses its flow and begins pulling out of the bay, then we'll up anchor and have the current to aid us when we're trying to get past the headland. A beam wind—one that hits the ship on the side—is not the best for speed. With the *Osprey* I'd sooner have one from the quarter, that is coming up at an angle from aft of amidships."

Murad laughed. "What a language you sailors have among yourselves!"

"Once we clear Abrusio Head we'll be steering a more southerly course and we'll have that quartering wind; but it'll be pushing us towards a lee shore so I'll be taking the ships further out to gain sea room."

"Surely it would be quicker to remain inshore."

"Yes, but if the wind picks up, and with the leeway the ships make, we could find ourselves being pushed on the shore itself, embayed or run aground. A good mariner likes to have deep water under him and a few leagues of sea room to his lee."

Murad waved a hand, growing bored. "Whatever. You are the expert in this matter."

"When we hit the latitude of North Cape," Hawkwood went on relentlessly, "if we sail due west we'll have that beam wind again. Only the rutter of the *Cartigellan Faulcon's* master can tell me if we can expect to have the Hebrian trade with us out into the Western Ocean, or if we pick up a different set of winds at some point. It is important; it will dictate the length of the voyage."

"It is there in the sheets I copied for you," Murad said sharply. His scar rippled on his face like a pale leech.

"You may not know what should be copied and what should not. You may not have given me everything I need to navigate this enterprise with any safety."

"Then you will have to come back to me, Captain. There will be no more discussion of the matter."

Hawkwood was about to retort when he heard a cry beyond the cabin.

"*Osprey* ahoy! Ahoy the carrack there! We've a passenger for you. You left him behind, it seems."

Hawkwood glanced at Murad, but the nobleman seemed as puzzled as himself. They rose as one and left the cabin, stepping along the passage to the waist of the ship. Billerand and a crowd of others were leaning over the side.

"What is it? Who is this?" Murad demanded, but Billerand ignored him.

"Seems we left someone behind, Captain. They've an extra passenger for us, brought out in the harbour scow."

Hawkwood looked down the sloping ship's side. The scow crew had hooked on to the carrack's main chains and a figure was clambering up the side of the ship, his robe billowing in the sea breeze. He laboured over the ship's rail and stood on deck, his tonsured head shining with effort.

"The peace of God on this ship and all in her," he said, panting.

He was an Inceptine cleric.

"What foolishness is this?" Murad shouted. "By whose orders are you come aboard? You there, in the boat—take this man off again!" But the scow had already unhooked and her crew were pulling away from the carrack, one waving as they went.

"Damnation! Who are you, sir? On whose authority do you take ship with this company?" Murad was livid, furious, but the Inceptine was calm and collected. He was an oldish man, white-haired, but ruddy and spare of feature. His shoulders were rounded under the habit and he had the stocky build of a longshoreman. The Saint symbol glinted at his breast.

"Please, my son, no blasphemy on the eve of so great an undertaking as this."

For a moment Hawkwood thought that Murad was going to draw his sword and run the priest through. Then he spun on his heel and left the deck, disappearing down the companion-way.

"Are you the master of this vessel?" the Inceptine asked Hawkwood.

"I am Richard Hawkwood, yes."

"Ah, the Gabrian. Then, sir, might I ask you to find me some quarters? I have little in the way of belongings with me. All I need is a space to lay my head."

Men were gathering in the waist, soldiers and sailors both. The sailors looked uneasy, even hostile, but the soldiers seemed pleased.

"Give us a blessing, Father!" one of them cried. "Call God and the Saints to watch over us!"

His cry was taken up by a score of his comrades. The Inceptine beamed and held up an open hand. "Very well, my sons. Kneel and receive the blessing of the Holy Church upon your enterprise."

There was a mass movement as the soldiers knelt on the deck. A pause, and then most of the sailors joined them. The ship creaked and rolled on the swell, and there was almost a silence. The Inceptine opened his mouth to speak.

In the quiet came the four, distinct, lovely notes of the ship's bell marking the end of the second dog-watch, and the turn of the tide.

"All hands!" Hawkwood roared instantly. "All hands to weigh anchor!"

The sailors leapt up, and the waist became a massive confusion of figures. Billerand began shouting; some of the kneeling soldiers were knocked sprawling.

A series of orders were bandied back and forth as the seamen hurried to their duties. There were casks, crates, boxes and chests everywhere on the deck and they along with the bewildered soldiers impeded the working of the ship, but there was no help for it; the hold was filled to capacity already. Hawkwood and Billerand shouted and shoved the crew to their well-known stations, whilst the cleric was left with his hand hanging impotently in the air, his face filling with blood.

In a twinkling, the crew were in position. Some were standing by at the windlass and the hawse-holes ready to begin winding in the thick cables that connected the ship to the anchors. More were busy on the yards, preparing to flash out the courses and topsails as soon as the anchor was weighed. The sailmaker and his mates were bringing up sail bonnets from below-decks so they would be handy when the time came for lashing them to the courses for a greater area of sail.

"Brace them round!" Hawkwood shouted. "Brace them right round, lads. We've a beam wind to work with. I don't want to spill any of it!"

He felt the ship tilt under his feet, like a horse gathering its legs under it for a spring. The ebb was flowing out of the bay.

"Weigh anchor! Start her there, at the windlass. Stand by at the tiller!"

The anchor ropes began to come aboard, mud-slimed and foul-smelling. They were like thick-bodied serpents that slithered down the hatches to be coiled in the top tiers by men below.

"Up and down!" a sweating master's mate cried.

"Tie her off," Hawkwood told him. "On the yards there— courses and topsails. Bonnet on the main course!"

The crackling and booming expanses of creamy canvas were let loose, billowing and filling against the blue sky. The carrack staggered as the breeze hit her. Hawkwood ran up to the quarterdeck. The ship had canted to larboard as the sails took the wind.

"Brace her, brace her there, damn you!"

The men hauled on the braces—ropes which angled the yards at the best attitude to the wind. The carrack began to move. Her bow dipped and cut through the rising swell, coming up again with the grace of a swan. Spray flew round her bows, and Hawkwood could feel the tremor of her keel as it gathered way. He looked across at the *Grace* and saw that she was pulling ahead, her great lateen sails like the wings of some monstrous, beautiful bird. Haukal was on her quarterdeck, waving and grinning through his beard like a maniac. Hawkwood waved back.

"Let loose the pennants!"

Men on the topmasts shimmied up the shrouds and pulled loose the long, tapering flags so that they sprang free at the mastheads, snapping and writhing in the wind. They were of shimmering Nalbeni silk, the dark blue device of the Hawkwoods at the main and the scarlet of Hebrion on the mizzen.

"Light along the log to the forechains there! Let's see what she's doing."

Men ran along the decks with the log and rope that would let them know the speed of the carrack once she had fully taken the wind. Hawkwood bent down to the tiller hatch.

"Helm there, west-sou'-west by north."

"Aye, sir. West-sou'-west by north it is."

The larboard heel of the carrack became more pronounced. Hawkwood hooked an arm about the mizzen backstay as the ship rose and dipped, cleaving the waves like a spearhead, her timbers groaning and the rigging creaking as the strain rose on it. She would make a deal of water until the timber of her upper hull became wet and swollen again, but she was moving more easily than he had dared hope, even with the heavy load. It must be the ebb tide, pushing her out to sea along with the blessed wind.

The soldiers had mostly been cleared from the decks, and the Inceptine had vanished below, his blessing unsaid. Some of the passengers were in sight, though, being shunted about by sailors intent on their work. Hawkwood saw Murad's cabin servant, the girl Griella. She was on the forecastle, her hair flying and the spray exploding about her. She looked beautiful and happy and alive, her eyes alight. He was glad for her.

He stared back over the taffrail. Hebrion and Abrusio were sliding swiftly astern. He guessed they must be doing six knots. He wondered if Jemilla were on her balcony, watching the carrack and the caravel grow smaller and smaller as they forged further out to sea.

The *Osprey* rose and fell, rose and fell, breasting the waves with an easy rhythm. The sails were drum-taut; Hawkwood could feel the strain on the mast through the twanging-tight backstay. If he looked up all he could see were towering expanses of canvas criss-crossed with the running rigging, and beyond the hard unclouded blue of heaven. He grinned fiercely as the ship came to life under his feet. He knew her as well as he knew the curves of his wife's body; he knew how the masts were creaking and the timbers stretching as his ship answered his demands, like a willing horse catching fire from his own spirit. No landsman could ever feel this, and those who spent their time politicking on land would never know the exhilaration, the freedom of a fine ship answering the wind.

This, he thought, is life; this is living. Maybe it is even prayer.

The two ships sailed steadily on as the afternoon waned, leaving the land in their wake until Abrusio hill was a mere dark smudge on the rim of the world behind them. They crested the rising swell of the coastal sea and touched upon the darker, purer colour of the open ocean. They left the fishing boats and the screaming gulls behind, carving their own solitary course to the horizon and setting their bows toward a gathering wrack and fire of cloud in the west, a flame-tinted arch which housed the gleam of the sinking sun.

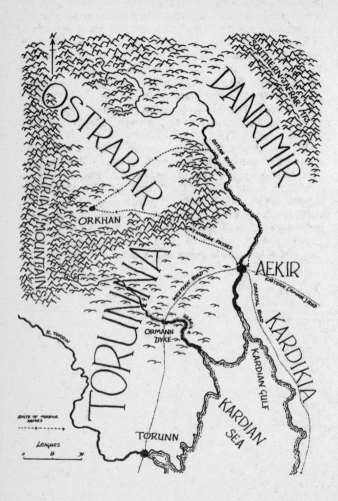

PART TWO

THE DEFENCE OF THE WEST

TWELVE

THEY had been three weeks on the road, this giant convoy, this rolling city. They had fought against slime and snow and marauding wolves to force the waggons over the narrow passes of the Thurian Mountains before beginning the long, downward haul to the green plains of Ostrabar beyond.

The Sultanate of Ostrabar, now first in the ranks of the Seven Sultanates, its head, Aurungzeb the Golden, one of the richest men in the world—or he would be when this caravan reached him.

This had been a Ramusian country once, a settled land of tilled fields and coppiced woods with a church in every village and a castle on every hill. Ostiber had been its name, and its king had been one of the Seven Monarchs of Normannia.

That had changed with the advent of the Merduks sixty years ago. They had poured over the inadequately defended passes of the terrible Jafrar Mountains to the east, crossed the headwaters of the Ostian river and had overrun Ostiber in less than a year, exposing the city of Aekir's northern flank and coming to a halt only when faced with the defended heights of the Thurians manned by grim Torunnans who included in their ranks a youthful John Mogen. Ostiber had become Ostrabar, and the wild steppe chieftain who had conquered this

country took that as his family name. The captain of his guard
had been Shahr Baraz, who would in time rise to command
all his armies. And his sons, when they had finished poisoning
one another, became sultan after him. Thus was the Kingdom
of Ostiber lost to the west, its Royal line extinguished, its
people enslaved, tortured, ravished and pillaged and, worst of
all, forced to change their faith so their eternal souls were lost
to the Company of the Saints for ever.

Thus were the children of the Western Kingdoms taught. To
them the Merduk were a teeming tribe of savages, held at bay
only by the valour of the Ramusian armies and the swift terror
of horse and sword and arquebus.

For the folk living in Ostrabar now it was different. True,
they must needs pray to Ahrimuz every day in one of the
domed temples that had been erected throughout the land, and
they yielded yearly tribute to the Sirdars and Beys who now
inhabited the hilltop castles; but there had always been nobles
in the castles exacting tribute, and they had always prayed.
The terror of the first invasion was long past, and many descendants of those who had fought in Ramusian armies six
decades before wielded tulwar and scimitar in the ranks of
Aurungzeb's regiments.

For some, indeed, life had improved under the Merduk
yoke. Wizards and thaumaturgists and alchemists were tolerated under the new regime, not persecuted as they occasionally
had been when the Knights Militant roved the land. Many, in
fact, had wealthy patrons, for the Merduk nobility treasured
learning above all things save, perhaps, the profession of arms
and the breeding of horses.

So for those among the long train of waggons who had
expected to see a nightmarish, unholy land upon their descent
from the heights of the Thurians, there was a shock. They saw
the same countryside, the same houses, and in the main the
same people whom they had encountered every day in Aekir
before its fall. The only differences were the domes of the
temples glittering across the peaceful landscape, and the fan-
tastical shapes of elephants working in the woods and along
the well-kept roads. Those and the flashing silk finery of the
Merduk nobility who gathered to see the train that held the
spoils of Aekir.

Six miles long, it straggled out of the high land to the south.

Over nine hundred waggons hauled by patient oxen, their tarred covers ragged and flapping in the wind. Trudging beside them in long lines were thousands upon thousands of captives who had been brought back as trophies for Aurungzeb to view. Most were women destined for harems and brothels, or the kitchen. Others were Torunnan soldiers, bitter-faced and savage. For them crucifixion awaited; they were to be made an example of, and were too dangerous to be allowed to live. And there were the children: young boys who would be made into eunuchs for the courts or the more specialized of the pleasure houses, young girls who would serve the same ends as the women, despite their age. There were all tastes and persuasions among the nobles of Ostrabar.

Along the flanks of the train rode bodies of Merduk light cavalry. During the crossing of the mountains they had been muffled in furs and cloaks, spattered with mud and haggard with exhaustion, but before nearing the country of their homes they had spruced themselves up, grooming their mounts and donning coloured silk surcoats over their chainmail. Pennons snapped and danced in the wind, and decorations glittered on the breasts of the horses. They made a fine sight as they stepped out, regiment by regiment, the very picture of a victorious army escorting a beaten foe.

In the better covered of the waggons the occupants shuddered as they listened to the thunder of hooves and the voices shouting gaily in the harsh Merduk tongue. Not for these select ones the killing labour of marching and scrambling in the rutted path of the train; they were to be kept apart, and spared the ordeal of the journey. They knelt in chains and rags, hardly looking at one another, whilst the waggons bounced and jolted under them, carrying them closer to their fate by the hour.

They were the pick of the spoils, the choicest treasures that Aekir had to offer. Two hundred of the most beautiful women in the city, rounded up like cattle to await the appraising eye of the Grand Vizier and in turn the perusal of Aurungzeb himself. The lucky ones would be taken into the harem to join the numerous ranks of the Sultan's concubines. The rest would be shared out amongst court officials and senior officers—rewards for men of ability and loyalty in this happy time.

The woman named Heria pulled her rags closer about her, the chains on her wrists clinking as she moved. Her bruises

were fading. As they had begun to near their destination the
soldiers had left the women in the waggons alone; they had to
reach the capital looking relatively unabused. At night she and
her sister slaves had huddled under the canopy and listened to
the screams of the less fortunate outside, and the laughter of
the soldiers.

Corfe, she thought yet again. Do you live? Did you get
away, or did they kill you like the others?

There was a red memory in her mind, the picture of the
city's fall and the fury that had followed. Merduks everywhere,
looting, killing, running. And the flames of Aekir's burning
rising as high as hills into the smoke-black night beyond.

She had been caught whilst trying to flee towards the western gate. A grinning devil with a face as black as leather had
seized her and dragged her into the ruin of a burning building.
There she had been raped.

As he had worked busily upon her the blade of his sword
had rested against her throat, already bloody, and sparks had
come sailing down out of the air to land on his back and gleam
like little leering eyes on his armour. She remembered staring
at them and watching them go dark one by one to be replaced
by others. Not feeling anything much.

His breastplate had bruised her and her back had been cut
by the glass and broken stones on the floor. Then the officer
had come, his horsehair plume nodding above his helm and
his eyes as greedy as a child's. He had taken her, despite the
first soldier's protests, and hauled her to the city wall where
she had been raped again. Finally she had joined the thousands
of others herded into the pens on the hillsides beyond the city,
all weeping, all bloody and terrified and ashamed like herself.
That had been the first stage in her journey.

For days the terrified masses had shivered on the hills and
watched the ruin of the City of God. They had seen the Merduks withdraw in the face of the flames and then had been
witness to the final conflagration, a holocaust that seemed
caused by the hand of God, so immense was the scale of it.
In the morning the ashes had covered the ground like a grey
snow, and the sun had been shrouded so that the land about
was in twilight. It had seemed like the end of the world.

And, in a way, it was.

They had started north on the eighth day after her capture,

herded by hordes of Merduk soldiers. The entire country had seemed covered with moving people, soldiers, horses and elephants, and untold hundreds of waggons bumping and lurching in the mud. And all the while the rain had poured down, numbing their very souls.

But the worst thing had been the sight of hundreds of Ramusian soldiers, the much-vaunted Torunnans of John Mogen, trudging north with their arms in capture yokes. From stolen conversations and whispered words the women learned that Sibastion Lejer was dead, his command annihilated; Lejer himself had been crucified in the square of Myrnius Kuln. The garrison of Aekir no longer existed, and the inhabitants of the city were fleeing westwards to Ormann Dyke, blackening the very face of the earth with the vastness of their exodus.

The train had laboured north at a snail's pace, the bodies of the weak and injured littering the land in its wake. They had passed the enormous camps of the Merduk army, cities of canvas and silk flags sprawled out across the blasted countryside. They had seen the wrecked churches, the gutted castles and burned villages of the north of the country. And the Thurians had loomed closer and closer on the horizon, and ice had begun to collect on the muzzles of the oxen.

A hard, timeless nightmare of mud and snow and savage faces. The wind had come down from the north like an avenging angel, ripping the covers from the waggons and making the horses scream. There had been brief snowstorms, snap freezes that had given the mud the consistency of wood. The Merduks had dined on horseflesh, their captives occasionally on each other.

A few of the Torunnans had tried to escape, and the Merduks had shot them full of arrows, perhaps wary even now of coming to grips with them.

They had lost waggons by the score. Heria had seen ancient tapestries trampled into the mud, incense sticks scattered across the snow, little children wide-eyed and dead, their faces grey with frost. The Merduks had been brutal in their haste, striving to get the train over the high passes before the first heavy snows of autumn. And somehow they had done it, though fully two thousand of the prisoners were left dead in the drifts of the mountains.

Heria had been one of the lucky ones. A Merduk officer

had taken her out of the long line of chained women on seeing
her face, and put her in one of the waggons and given her a
blanket. That night he had taken her against a waggon wheel
watched by a laughing score of his fellows, but had stopped
the rest from following suit. From then on he had visited the
waggon from time to time, to bring her morsels of food—even
wine once—and to take her again. But he had stopped coming
once the Thurians were behind them. Perhaps he too lay dead
in the snows.

So she had remained alive, for what it was worth. The rutted
quagmires of the mountain roads had given way to good paved
highways, and the air had become warmer. There was food
again, though never enough to banish hunger entirely. And she
had been left in peace at night.

Ceasing to think, to wonder or to hope, she had crouched
in the waggon, feeling the lice move in her hair, and had stared
at the blank canvas, rocking with the movement of the vehicle
as though she were in a ship at sea. A thousand fantasies had
glimmered in her mind, dreams of rescue, images of scarlet
carnage. But they had burned down to black ash now. Corfe
was dead and she was glad, for she was no longer fit to be his
wife. The body she had kept for him alone was an item of
property to be bartered for a crust of bread, and the looks she
had been so secretly proud of had gone. Her eyes were as dull
as slate, her heavy mane of raven hair matted and infested, her
body covered with bites and sores, and her ribs saw-toothed
ridges down her sides.

I am carrion, she thought.

Thirty-six days out of Aekir, though, something pricked her
apathy. There was a shout at the head of the train, men cheering and horses neighing. The women in the waggon shifted
and looked at one another fearfully. What was it now? What
devilish torment had the Merduks contrived for them?

Suddenly there was a ripping sound, and the entire canopy
of the waggon was peeled off and torn away. A pair of
horsemen rode off with it flapping between them, grinning like
apes.

Sunlight, blinding and searingly painful to their shadow-
accustomed eyes. The women covered their faces and tried to
pull their rags about them. There were hoots of laughter, and
the world was a chaos of galloping shapes, half-glimpsed dark

faces, capering horses. Then they cleared away, leaving the women staring.

The land before them dipped in a great shallow bowl leagues across. At its bottom was the sword-blade glitter of a large river, lightning-bright in the sun. All around were broken and rolling hills, green or gold with crops or dotted with grazing herds. They stretched to every horizon, gilded by the sunshine and ruffled to glimmering waves by the northern breeze.

As the expanse rose up to meet the blue shadows of the mountains in the north, so the watchers saw a wider hill there. It was a city, white-walled and towered, the smoke of its hearths rising to haze the cerulean arch of the cloudless sky. Everywhere amid the clotted disorder of its streets minarets and cupolas caught the sun, and at the height of the hill gleamed the massive dome of the Temple of Ahrimuz, the biggest in the world after its older rival in Nalbeni.

There were palaces there, in the shadow of the temple. The women could see parks amid the city, the ripple of water in tended gardens. And even at this distance they could hear the chanters in the towers calling the faithful to prayer. Their oddly harmonious wails drifted down the wind, and the Merduk escort bowed their heads for a moment in acknowledgement.

"Where are we? What is this place?" one of the women demanded in a panic-shrill whisper.

But one of the escort had heard her. He bent from his horse into the waggon and gripped the woman's jaw with one brown hand.

"We are home," he said distinctly. This is *Orkhan*, home for me and you. This is the city of Ostrabar. *Hor-la Kadhar, Ahrimuzim-al kohla ab imuzir . . .*" He trailed off into his own language as if he were reciting something, then turned to the women in the waggon again.

"You go to Sultan's bed!" And he laughed uproariously before touching spurs to his horse's belly and cantering off.

"Lord God in heaven!" someone murmured. Others began sobbing quietly. Heria bent her head until her filthy hair covered her face.

Can you remember him? How he was when he had that devil-may-care grin on his face, his eyes alight? Can you remember?

• • •

A long summer's day, the sun hanging in a cobalt sky and the Thurians mere guesses of shadow at the edge of the world. They were in the hills above the city, watching the huge length of Aekir sprawl out along the shining length of the Ostian river. Far enough to view the whole of the city walls but near enough to hear the bells of Carcasson tolling the hour, the sound drifting up into the hills along with a faint rush of noise; the echo of a distant throng.

Wine they had had, and white bread from the city bakeries. Apples from last year's crop, wrinkled but still sweet and moist. If they looked out to the south, beyond the city, they could see where the Ostian river widened in its estuary before opening out into the Kardian Sea. Sometimes when the wind was from the south, the gulls wheeled and cried in the very streets of the city itself and the salt tang was in the air so that Aekir might have been a harbour city on the rim of an ocean. Heria had always loved to come into the hills and see the Kardian glittering on the horizon. It was like seeing the promise of tomorrow, a doorway into a wider world. She had often wondered what it would be like to have a ship, to ply the sea routes of the wide world, sleep beneath a wooden deck and hear the waves lapping at her ear.

Corfe had laughed at her fantasies, but never tired of hearing them. He had been wearing his ensign's uniform that day— Torunnan black edged with scarlet. Blood and bruises, they called it. His sabre had lain scabbarded at his side.

She could not remember what they had said, only that they had been content. It seemed to her now that they had never thought how lucky they might be to have each other, the sun flooding down on the grass-covered hillside, Aekir spread out on the earth below them like a brilliantly coloured cloak let slip upon the world and the sea glimmering at the limit of vision, full of possibilities. Everything had been possible; though even then, in that last, glorious summer, the Merduk host had already been on the move. Their fates had been fixed, and their snatched seconds were trickling away like sand in an hourglass.

The train of booty and prizes lurched and trundled downhill towards Orkhan, capital of the Northern Merduks, whilst in the waggons the women sat stark and silent and the Merduk horsemen sang their songs of victory all around.

THE rain had held off and a weak sun was pouring down over the blasted expanse of the land. Corfe helped the old man up the muddy slope, using his sabre as a staff. Ribeiro came behind them, his face swathed in filthy rags, one eye invisible with the awful swelling.

They reached the top of the hill and stood panting. Macrobius leaned on Corfe with his head bent, his bony chest sucking in and out. Corfe looked down the western slope and suddenly went very still. Macrobius tensed at once, his liver-spotted fingers gripping Corfe's arm.

"What is it? What do you see?"

"We're there, old man, there at last. Ormann Dyke."

The land levelled out west of where they stood. It dipped down into a broad valley in which the wide expanse of the Searil river foamed and churned, full after the recent rains. There was a bridge there, spanning the current. On the western bank it was constructed of weatherbeaten stone, but here on the eastern side the supports were of fresh timber.

On the eastern side of the Searil great works of earth and stone had been thrown up, revetments and trenches and stockades. The smoke of burning slow-match drifted down the breeze along with the cooking fires, and above the fortifications the black and scarlet Torunnan flag flapped. Corfe felt a strange ache in his breast at the sight of it.

The eastern fortifications extended maybe half a mile on either side of the bridge. Corfe could see culverins gleaming with brass behind gabion-strengthened emplacements, soldiers walking up and down, a knot of cavalry here and there. But the entire rear of the position seemed choked with people. There were thousands there in the spaces behind the battlements, some obviously cooking, others sleeping in the mud and more trudging purposefully towards the river.

The bridge was clogged with them. All along its length it was jammed with handcarts, animals, people on foot and in waggons. Torunnan troopers were trying to direct the traffic. There was nothing panicked about it. It was more like a sullen retreat, as though the crowds of refugees were too exhausted to feel fear.

Corfe peered further west, across the river. The land rose there in two ridges running parallel to the Searil. The ridges themselves were steep and rocky, and their summits were dotted with watchtowers and signal stations. But there was a gap close to where the bridge arched out from the western bank, and in this gap, maybe a league wide, the fortress of Ormann Dyke proper stood.

The walls were sixty feet high and wide enough for a waggon to drive along. Every cable or so their length was interrupted by a tower which jutted up to a hundred feet, guns glinting in the embrasures. There were odd kinks in the layout of the walls, and the sides of the towers met at strange angles. These were recent innovations, designed to concentrate the gunfire of the defenders so that anyone approaching the dyke would be caught in a deadly crossfire.

At the southern end of the Long Walls was the citadel. It was built on a steep-sided spur that jutted out from the main line of the ridges. Its guns would dominate the whole frontage of the dyke itself.

In front of the walls, and constructed at least six centuries before them, was a vast ditch, carved out of the very bones of the land. It was forty feet deep and at least two hundred wide, a work of unimaginable labour built by the Fimbrians when Ormann Dyke had marked the limits of their empire, before the first ships sailed up the Ostian river to found the trading post that would eventually become Aekir. This ditch extended for fully three miles in front of the walls, like a second river to mirror the brown flow of the Searil. It, too, was full of muddy water, and its sides were constructed of slick, close-joined brick. Corfe knew that under the water were entanglements, impaling caltrops, and all manner of devilry designed to rip out the bottoms of any boats foolish enough to try and cross. He knew also that once there had been charges of gunpowder placed in waterproof caches along the ditch, with underground fuse tunnels connecting them to the main fortress. These had fallen into disrepair within the past few years, but he did not doubt that the dyke's defenders had remedied that by now.

The garrison of Ormann Dyke usually numbered some twenty thousand men. It was one of the three great Torunnan armies. The others were stationed at Aekir and Torunn itself.

The Aekir army no longer existed, and the Torunn force was some thirty thousand strong. Corfe was sure that most of the capital's garrison were here at the dyke now. The Torunnan king would concentrate his forces here, at the Gateway to the West.

"It still stands then, the dyke?" Macrobius asked querulously.

"It stands," Corfe told him, "though it looks as though half the world is trekking westwards through it."

Ribeiro joined them at the hilltop and stared down at the teeming fortress, the river, the bristling ridges beyond.

"God be praised!" he said thickly. He knelt and kissed Macrobius' knuckle. "We will find someone who will recognize you for who you really are, Your Holiness. Your sojourn in the wilderness is ended. You are come back into your kingdom."

Macrobius shook his head, smiling slightly.

"I have no kingdom. I never had, unless it be in the souls of men. Always I was a mere cipher, a figurehead. Perhaps my hand helped guide the tiller a little, but that is all. I know that now, and I do not know if I would greatly care to be such a figure again."

"But you must! Holiness—"

"Patrol coming," Corfe said brusquely, wearying of this pious raving. "Torunnan heavy horse—cuirassiers by the look of them."

The cavalry troop was forcing a way out of the clogged gate of the eastern defences. They parted the flow of refugees like a rock splitting a wave, and then their mounts were stepping through the broken mud of the hillside below Corfe and his companions. Corfe did not move. He doubted that, what with the filth and wear of the past days, his clothing was recognizable as a Torunnan uniform. There was no reason for the horsemen to note three more ragged refugees.

But Ribeiro was sliding and tumbling down the sodden hillside, waving his arms and shouting. His habit billowed out above his thin limbs like the wings of an ungainly bird. The lead horsemen reined in. Corfe swore rabidly.

"What is he doing?" Macrobius asked. There was real fear in his voice.

"The damn fool is . . . ach, they'll think he's merely mad."

Ribeiro was talking to the halted cavalry. Corfe could not make out what he was saying, but he could guess.

"He's probably trying to convince them that you're the Pontiff."

Macrobius shook his head as if in pain. "But I am not—not any more. That man died in Aekir. There is no Macrobius any more."

Corfe looked at him quickly. Something in the tone of the old man's voice, some note of loss and resignation, struck a painful chord in his own breast. For the first time he wondered if this Macrobius might indeed be whom he said he was.

"Easy, Father. They'll put his claims down to the ravings of a demented cleric, no more."

Macrobius sank to his knees in the mud. "Let them leave me alone. I am in darkness, and always will be. I am no longer even sure of the faith which once sustained me. I am a coward, soldier of Mogen. You fought to save the City of God whilst I cowered in a storeroom, imprisoned in my own palace lest I flee and take the heart of the city with me."

"We are all cowards, in one way or another," Corfe said with rough gentleness. "Were I a braver man, I'd be lying dead before Aekir myself, along with my wife."

The old man raised his head at that. "You left your wife in Aekir? I am sorry, my friend, very sorry."

The horsemen rode on, leaving Ribeiro behind them. The young monk shook his fist at them, and then his whole frame seemed to sag. Corfe helped Macrobius to his feet.

"Come on, Father. We'll see if we can't get you a roof over your head tonight, and something warm in your belly. Let the great ones argue over the fate of the west. It is our concern no more."

"Oh, but it is, my son, it is. If it is not the concern of us all, then we may as well lie down here on the ground and wait for death to take us."

"We'll think about that another time. Come. Ho! Ribeiro! Give me a hand with the old man!"

But Ribeiro seemed not to have heard. He was standing with one hand over the eye he could still see out of, and his lips were moving silently.

They joined the straggling crowds of ragged and wild-eyed people who were disappearing into the eastern gate of the dyke. They sank calf-deep in mud—what was left of the Western Road—and were shoved and jostled as they went. Eventually, though, the darkness of the barbican was around them, and then they were within the walls of the last Ramusian outpost east of the Searil river.

There was chaos within the defences.

People everywhere, in all states of filth and desperation. They stood in huddles around fires on the very drill ground and the interior walls of the fortifications were lined with primitive shelters and lean-tos that had been thrown up to combat the rain. Some enterprising souls had set up market stalls of sorts, selling whatever they had brought with them out of the wreck of Aekir. Corfe saw a mule being butchered, people hanging round the carcass like gore-crows. There were women, pathetically haggard, who were offering themselves to passers-by for food or money, and here and there some callous souls were playing dice on a cloak thrown over the mud.

Corfe glimpsed violence, also. There were groups of men with long knives extorting anything of value from fellow refugees, once the Torunnans had passed by. He wondered if Pardal's comrades had made it this far.

What he saw disturbed him. There seemed to be little order within the fortress, no organization or authority. True, men in Torunnan black were on the battlements, their armour gleaming darkly, but they appeared thin on the ground, as though the garrison were not up to strength. And no effort had been made, it seemed, to bring the mob of fleeing civilians under control. If Corfe were in command here, he'd have them herded west, well clear of the dyke, and then perhaps try and rig up provisions for them and police the camps with what men he could spare. But this—this was mere anarchy. Was Martellus still in command, or had there been some reshuffle which had engendered this chaos?

He found a spot to stop in the shadow of one of the eastern revetments, kicking a couple of sullen young men from the space. They left after a hard stare at the sabre and the ragged remnants of the uniform, but Corfe was too weary and troubled to care. He collected pieces of wood—there were plenty lying about, and he guessed that the refugees had demolished some of the inner stockades and catwalks—and got a fire going with

the greatest difficulty. By that time the light was beginning to
fail, and across the open ground within the fortress campfires
were flickering into life like lambent stars, whilst if he stood
up he could see across the Searil river to where the lights of
the dyke burned by the thousand. People were crossing the
bridge by torchlight in an unending procession and the eastern
gates remained open despite the dimming light, which seemed
to Corfe to be the merest madness: in the dark, Merduks might
mingle with the swarm of civilians entering the fortress and
gain access to the interior. Who was in command here? What
kind of fool?

Ribeiro was uncommunicative and seemed shaken by the
fact that Macrobius had not immediately been recognized. He
sat with his swollen head in his hands and stared into the
flames of Corfe's fire as though he were looking for some
revelation.

Macrobius, however, was almost serene. He sat on the wet
ground, the firelight making a hideous mask out of his savaged
face, and nodded to himself. Corfe had seen that look before,
on men about to go into battle. It meant they no longer feared
death.

Could this crazy old man really be the High Pontiff?

His stomach rumbled. They had eaten nothing in the past
day and a half, and precious little in the days before that. In
fact, the last time he had eaten a solid meal . . .

The last time, it had been Heria who had prepared it, and
brought it to him at his post on the wall of Aekir. It had been
dark then, as it was now. They had stood together on the catwalk looking out at the campfires of the Merduk thousands,
smelling the tar and smoke of the siege engines, the stench of
death that hung over the city continually. He had begged her
to go once more, but she would not leave him. That had been
the last time he had ever seen his wife; that heartbreaking
smile, one corner of her mouth quirking upwards, one eyebrow
lifting. He remembered her going down the steps from the
wall, the torchlight shining on her hair.

Two hours later the final assault had begun, and then his
world had been utterly destroyed.

He felt a hand on his arm and started. It was wholly dark
but for the fire. The open ground within the fortress was a
flame-stitched blueness in which shadows moved aimlessly.

"She is gone to God's rest, my son. You no longer have to fear for her," Macrobius said softly.

"How did you—?"

"You had relaxed, as though in a dream, and then I felt your muscles go as rigid as wood. I am good, I find, at recognizing suffering in others these days. She is with Ramusio in the company of the Saints of heaven. Nothing more can touch her."

"I hope so, old man. I hope so."

He could not voice, even to himself, the fear that Heria might yet be alive and suffering torment at the hands of those eastern animals. And so he prayed that his wife was dead.

He stood up abruptly, shaking off the priest's hand.

"Food. We have to eat if we're to be good for anything. Ribeiro, look after the old man."

The young monk nodded. His face was shiny and discoloured, like a bruised fruit, and he kept spitting out bits of teeth. Privately Corfe did not give much for his chances.

He strode off between the fires, stepping over exhausted bodies lying unconscious on the sodden ground, brushing aside two women who tried to solicit him. It was only in extremity that the true depths and heights of human nature were visible. Folk who had been civilized, upright, even downright saintly in Aekir before its fall were now whores and thieves and murderers.

And cowards, he added to himself. Let us not forget cowards.

No man could truly say what he was until he had been pushed to the edge of things with the precipice of his own ruin staring up at him. Things changed that close to the brink, and people changed too. Rarely, Corfe believed, for the better.

He turned aside at the approach of two Torunnan troopers, twitching his sabre behind his body so it would not be seen. He was not sure what his position might be with the army, whether he was a deserter or a mere straggler, but he felt guilty enough in his own mind not to want to find out.

He had not been afraid on abandoning Aekir. He had seen most of the men he commanded slaughtered on the walls, and had been caught up in the headlong retreat that followed. After that, knowing Heria was lost to him, one way or another, he had merely wanted to leave the blood and the smoke behind.

It had been a bitter thing, but he could not remember being afraid. He could not remember feeling anything much. The events in which he had been caught up had seemed too vast for human emotion.

But away from the roaring chaos of that day, he was not so sure. *Had* it been fear? At any rate, his duty would have been to stay with Lejer's rearguard and fight on. He would be dead by now in that case, or marching east under a Merduk capture yoke.

"You there!" a voice barked. "Halt where you are. What's that you're carrying?"

Two fellow Torunnans. They had noticed the sabre after all. Corfe contemplated running for a second, but then smiled at the absurdity of the idea. He had nowhere else to go.

The Torunnans were in black and scarlet, their half-armour lacquered so that it was like shining ebony. Sabres that were the twin of Corfe's hung by their sides and they wore the light helms with beak-like nose guards that were typical of their race. One also carried an arquebus over his shoulder, but the slow-match was not lit.

"Where did you get that weapon?" the one without the arquebus demanded.

"From a dead Torunnan," Corfe said carelessly.

The man's breath hissed through his teeth. "You God-damned vulture, I'll stick you like a pig—" But then his companion stopped him.

"Wait, Han. What's that he's wearing?"

They both stared, and Corfe could almost have laughed at the dawning comprehension on their faces.

"Yes, I am Torunnan also. John Mogen was my general, and I saw him die on the eastern wall of Aekir. Any other questions?"

IT puzzled Corfe that he was being taken so seriously. He paced the stone floor of the anteroom, listening to the voices rising and falling on the other side of the door. The two troopers had brought him here at once, across the crowded Searil bridge to the dyke and into the very heart of the fortress on the western bank.

Here the chaos had been even greater than it was across the river. The refugees had set up a kind of shanty town of sticks and canvas and whatever else they could find within the fortress, and it spilled beyond the towering walls out into the surrounding countryside. Everywhere fires glittered in the night, stretching far across the land and roughly following the line of the Western Road. Everywhere there was the hubbub and stink of an enormous camp.

It troubled Corfe to see Ormann Dyke in this state. He had always thought of it as impregnable, but then he had thought the same about Aekir in the months before its fall. He had a hollow feeling in the pit of his stomach as he waited to be called in by General Pieter Martellus, the commanding officer. He had seen the long lines of waggons waiting in the drill yards piled high with supplies, and he had seen the activity along the horse lines, the blacksmiths working through the night, their forges like little hell-lit caverns. He had a feeling the dyke was being abandoned without a battle, and despite the detachment he affected the knowledge shook him to the core. If the dyke fell, what hope was there for Torunn itself?

He was called in at last, and found himself in a high-ceilinged room built entirely of stone but for black beams as thick as his waist criss-crossing near the roof. A fire burned in a deep brazier and there was a long table covered with maps and papers, and so many quills that it seemed a flock of birds had just been startled into flight from there. A group of men stood or sat around the table, some smoking pipes. They stared at him as he entered.

He saluted, acutely conscious of his wretched appearance and the mud that was falling from his boots to clod the floor.

One man, whom Corfe recognized as Martellus, stood up, throwing aside a quill as though it were a dart.

The troops called him "the Lion," not without reason. He had a mane and beard of shaggy black hair shot through with grey and russet tints, and his eyebrows shadowed his cavernous sockets. He was a huge man, but surprisingly slim-waisted—quite unlike the barrel-chested firebrand that had been John Mogen. He had been Mogen's lieutenant for ten years and had a reputation for cold-blooded severity. There were also barrack rumours that he was a wizard of sorts. His pale eyes regarded Corfe unblinkingly.

"We are told you were at Aekir," he said, and his voice was as deep as the splash of a coin at a well's bottom. "Is this so?"

"Yes, sir."

"You were one of Mogen's command?"

"I was."

"Why did you not join Lejer in his rearguard?"

Corfe's heart hammered as the officers watched him intently, some with their pipes halfway to their mouths. They were Torunnans like himself, the much-vaunted warrior race. It had been the Torunnans who had first thrown off the Fimbrian yoke, Torunnans who had beaten back the first of the Merduk invasions. That tradition seemed to hang heavy in the room now, along with the unfamiliar taste of defeat. Mogen had been their best, and they knew it. The garrison of Aekir had been widely recognized as the finest army in the world. No one had ever contemplated its defeat—especially these men, the generals of the last fortress of the west. But none of them had been at Aekir: how could they know?

"There was no time. After the eastern bastion fell—after Mogen died—there was a rout. My men were all dead. I got cut off . . ." His voice trailed away. He remembered the flames, the panic of the mobs, the falling buildings. He remembered his wife's face.

Martellus continued to stare at him.

"I'd had enough of the killing," he said, his words grating out unwillingly. "I wanted to look for my wife. When I failed to find her it was too late to join Lejer. I got caught up in the crowd. I—" He hesitated, then went on, his gaze never leaving Martellus's cold eyes: "I fled with the rest into the countryside."

"You deserted," someone said, and there was a murmur round the table.

"Maybe I did," Corfe said, surprising himself with his calmness. "Aekir was burning. There was nothing left in the city to fight for. Nothing I cared about. Yes, I deserted. I ran away. Do with me what you will. I am tired, and have come a long way."

One man thumped the table angrily at this, but Martellus held up a hand then stood with his hands behind his back, the red light from the brazier making his face seem more than ever like that of a feline predator.

"Easy, gentlemen. We did not bring this man here to judge him, but to gain information. What is your name, Ensign?"

"Corfe. Corfe Cear-Inaf. My father served under Mogen also."

"Inaf, yes. I know the name. Well, Corfe, I have to tell you that you are the first Torunnan soldier we have seen who came out of Aekir alive. The best field army of the Five Monarchies is no more. You may be its last survivor."

Corfe gaped, unable to believe it. "There have been no more? None?"

"Not one. The Merduks took many hundreds prisoner after Lejer's last battle, that much we know. They are destined for crucifixion in the east. No others have got this far."

Corfe bowed his head. He was alive, then, when every other Torunnan who had fought under Mogen was dead or captured. The shame of it made his face burn. Small wonder the men around the table seemed so hostile. In all the thousands of men who had been part of that army, only Corfe had fled and saved his own skin. The knowledge staggered him.

"Take a seat," Martellus said, not unkindly. "You look as though you need it."

He fumbled for a chair and sat down, his head in his hands. "What do you want of me?" he whispered.

"As I said, information. I want to know the composition of the Merduk army. I want to know how badly Mogen's men damaged it before the end. And I want to know why Aekir fell."

Corfe looked up. "Are you going to stay here, to fight the Merduk again?"

"Yes."

"It doesn't seem that way to me."

The men at the table stirred at his words. Martellus glared at them to silence them, then nodded. "Some of the garrison have been transferred west, to Torunn. Thus we are short-handed."

"How many? On whose orders?"

"On the orders of King Lofantyr himself. Twelve thousand will be left here for the defence of the dyke, no more."

"Then the dyke will fall."

"I do not intend to let it fall, Ensign."

"You have refugees crawling all over the fortress. If the Merduks chanced upon this place it would not last an hour."

"There has been confusion, what with the transfers to the

west. It is coming under control." Martellus appeared faintly irritated. "Our scouts inform us that the Merduk main body is still in Aekir, though they have light troops out skirmishing a scant league away from here. We have time and to spare; it will be weeks yet ere the main enemy body begins to move. My orders are to get as many of Aekir's refugees away to the west as possible before cutting the bridges. Now, tell me. What is the enemy strength?"

Corfe hesitated. "Since the siege, they may be left with some hundred and fifty thousand."

The officers glanced at one another. Such an army had never been seen before, never imagined.

"How many did they have before the siege began?" one asked harshly.

"A quarter of a million, maybe. We cut them down like straw, but they kept coming. I know that many were also sent back to guard the supply routes over the mountains, but the first snows will be in the passes of the Thurians now. I cannot see how they will keep supplied through the winter."

"I can," Martellus said. "Duke Comorin of Kardikia says they are building boats by the hundred on the Ostian river. That will be their new supply route, and it will remain open through the winter. Their advance will continue."

Martellus bent over the table and examined a map of the land between the Searil and the Ostian rivers.

"Show me the line of their advance," he said to Corfe.

Corfe got up, but then something occurred to him. "Has Macrobius been seen yet, or his body found?"

"The High Pontiff? Why, no. He died in Aekir."

"Are you sure? Did anyone see him killed?"

"His palace burned, and just about every priest who was in the city was put to the sword. I have it from civilians and clerics who were there. I do not think the Merduks could have overlooked someone of his eminence."

"But Mogen had him locked in a storeroom in the palace to stop him fleeing the city."

Martellus stared, incredulous. "Are you serious?"

"It was a rumour in the city just before its fall. The Knights Militant almost left Mogen's command over it. Would you know the High Pontiff if you saw him?"

Martellus became exasperated. "I suppose so. I have supped at the same table as him a few times. Why?"

"Then you must send men over to the eastern bank. You will find an old man there near the barbican who lacks eyes, and a young monk with an injured face."

"What about them?"

"I think the old man may be Macrobius."

THIRTEEN

CHARIBON. The oldest monastery in the world, home of the Inceptine Order.

It stood on the shores of the Sea of Tor in the north-west foothills of the wild Cimbric Mountains. Surrounded by the Kingdom of Almark, it was nevertheless autonomous, as Aekir had been, and was governed by the elders of the Church and their head, the High Pontiff.

Some seven thousand clerics lived and worked here, the majority of them in Inceptine black though there were some in the brown of the Antillians and others in the warm saffron of the Mercurians. Very few indeed were robed in the ordinary, undyed wool of the ascetic missionaries, the Friars Mendicant.

Here resided the greatest libraries in Normannia, now those in Aekir were no more, and here were the chief barracks and training grounds of the Knights Militant. They had a citadel of their own higher up in the hills beside Charibon, and there some eight thousand of them were quartered. Usually there were several times that number on hand, but most of them were in the east or had been dispatched to the various Ramusian monarchies to aid in the struggle against heresy. Two thousand were even now riding west, to Hebrion.

Down in the complex of the monastery itself there were the famed Long Cloisters of Charibon, walked by fifteen generations of clerics, roofed over by cedar imported from the Levangore and floored with basalt blocks hewn out of the once-volcanic Cimbrics.

Radiating out from the square of the cloisters and the rich gardens they enclosed were the other structures of the monastery, built in massive stone and roofed with slate from the quarries in the nearby Narian Hills. No humble thatch here.

But the Cathedral of the Saint towered over and dominated the rest. Its outline defined the skyline of Charibon, made it recognizable from leagues away in the hills. A huge, three-sided tower with a horn of granite at each corner formed the apex of the triangle that was the rest of the cathedral. It was the classic Ramusian shape, reminiscent of the Praying Hands but on a scale vaster than anyone had ever envisaged. Only Aekirians might sniff at the cathedral of Charibon, comparing it to their own Carcasson, of which it was a copy.

But Carcasson was no more.

The monastery sprawled out from the twin foci of cloisters and cathedral, the original pure design of the place lost in a welter of later building. There were schools and dormitories, cells of contemplation, gardens restful on the eye and conducive to contemplative thought. Most of the theories which had shaped the Ramusian religion had sprung from here as their authors looked out on the fountain-rich gardens or the green hills beyond.

There were also kitchens and workshops, smithies and tanneries, and, of course, the famed printing presses of the Inceptines. Charibon had its own lands and herds and crops, for there was a secular side to it as well as the spiritual. A town had sprung up around the swelling monastery complexes and a fishing village on the lake's western shores kept the monks supplied with freshwater halibut, mackerel and even turtle on fast days. Charibon was a self-sufficient little kingdom whose chief exports were the books that the presses ceaselessly turned out and the faith that the Inceptines promulgated and the Knights Militant enforced.

The monastery had been sacked a hundred and fifty years before by a confederation of the savage Cimbric tribes. There had been a war then, with troops from Almark and Torunna sending expeditions into the mountains' interior along with contingents of the Knights. The tribes had eventually been crushed and brought into the Ramusian fold, finally completing the task which the Fimbrians had attempted and failed to accomplish some four centuries earlier. Since then, a dozen tercios of Almarkan troops had also been stationed at Charibon, even as the Torunnans had garrisoned Aekir further east. Charibon was a jewel, a light to be kept burning no matter how dark the night—especially as the brightness that had been Aekir was now extinguished.

ALBREC squinted into the cold, eye-watering wind, looking for all the world like a short-sighted vole peering from its burrow at the close of winter. This high in the hills the winters were bitter, snow lying for four months in the cloisters and the inland sea growing fringes of ice along its shores. His cell then would be like a small cube of gelid air in the mornings, and he would have to break the ice in his washing bowl before spluttering at the coldness of the water on his pointed face.

He wore a habit of Antillian brown, much worn, and the Saint symbol at his breast was of mere wood, carved by himself in the dim, candlelit nights. Though all were clerics alike here in Charibon, some were of a higher order than others. Some indeed were of aristocratic background, the younger sons of noble families whose fathers had nothing to give in the way of inheritance. So they became Inceptines, a different kind of noble. For the commoners, however, there was only the Antillians, the Mercurians, or if one was of a zealous turn of mind, and hardy to boot, the Friars Mendicant.

Albrec's father had been a fisherman from the shores of northern Almark. A dour man, from a hard country. He had never quite forgiven his son's fear of the open sea, or his ineptness with the nets and the tiller. Albrec had attached himself to a small monastery of Antillians from a nearby village, and found a place where he was not reviled or beaten, where the work was hard but not frightening as the days on an open boat had been frightening. And where his natural curiosity and inherent stubbornness could be put to good use.

He worked in the library of St. Garaso, his hand not being apt for the rigour of the presses or the finer of the illustrating that went on in the scriptorium. He lived in a dusty, half-subterranean world of books and manuscripts, old scrolls and parchment and vellum. He loved it, and could lay his hands on any tome in the entire library within a few minutes.

It was because of his labyrinthine knowledge of the shelves and chests and stacks that he was kept on as assistant librarian, and in return he was allowed to read anything he chose, which for him was a reward beyond price. There were levels to the library which were rarely visited, ancient archives and forgotten cupboards, their contents mouldering away in dust and silence. Albrec made it his mission in life to explore them all.

He had been here for thirteen years, his eyesight progressively worsening and his shoulders becoming more bowed with every book he squinted over. And yet he knew he had not yet unearthed one-tenth of the riches contained in the library.

There were scrolls there from the time of the Fimbrian Hegemony, works which he spent days coaxing open with sweet oil and a blunt knife. Most of them were dismissed by Brother Commodius, the senior librarian, as secular rubbish, or even heresy. Some had been burned, horrifying Albrec. After that he had shown no more of his unearthed treasures to the other brothers, but had hoarded them secretly. Books should not be burned, he believed, no matter what they contained. To him all books were sacred, fragments of the minds of the past, thoughts from men long gone to their graves. Such things should be preserved.

And so Albrec hid the more controversial of his finds, thus unintentionally beginning a private library of his own, a library of works which, had his spiritual superiors discovered them, would have consigned him to the flames in their company.

THIS morning he was staring out of one of the library's rare windows to the hills beyond. His Excellency the Prelate of Hebrion was expected to arrive today to join the three other Prelates who were lodged in Charibon already. The entire monastery was abuzz with gossip and speculation. There were rumours that since Macrobius was dead, God have mercy on his soul, the Prelates were meeting to choose a new High Pontiff. Others said there was heresy brewing in the western kingdoms, sorcerers willing to take advantage of the confused state of the Ramusian monarchies in the wake of Aekir's fall. This synod would be the beginnings of a crusade, it was said, a holy war to rid the west both of its enemies within and the Merduks who bayed at the gate.

Momentous times, Albrec thought a little nervously. He had always considered Charibon as a retreat of sorts, isolated as it was up here in the hills; but he saw now that it was becoming one of the hubs upon which the world turned. He was not sure if the feeling thrilled or frightened him. All he asked for was the peace to continue his reading undisturbed, to remain in his dusty, candlelit kingdom in the depths of the library.

"Gathering wool again, Brother?" a voice drawled casually.

Albrec backed away from the window hurriedly. His addresser was in rich Inceptine black, and the symbol clinking at his breast shone with gold.

"Oh, it's you, Avila. Don't do that! I thought you were Commodius."

The other cleric, a handsome young man with the pale, spare visage of a nobleman, laughed.

"Don't worry, Albrec. He's closeted with the rest of the worthies in the Vicar-General's quarters. I doubt if you'll be seeing him today."

Albrec blinked. He had an armful of books which he was cradling as tenderly as a young mother might her first child. They shifted in his grasp and he gave a grunt of dismay as they began to topple. But Avila caught them and set them to rights.

"Come, Albrec. Lay down those dead tomes for a while. Walk in the cloisters with me and watch the arrival of Himerius of Hebrion."

"He's here, then?"

"A patrol has reported his party to be approaching. You can lock the library after you—no one will be needing it for the next few hours. I think half of Charibon is outside indulging their curiosity."

"All right."

It was true that the library was deserted. The cavernous place resounded to their voices and the patient dripping of the ancient water-clock in a corner. They turned the triple locks of the massive door behind them—it was always a source of pride to Albrec, a pride that he immediately chastised himself for, that he carried on his person the keys to one of the great libraries of the world—and, tucking their hands in their habits, they journeyed out into the cold clearness of the day.

"What is it about this Hebrian Prelate that has the monastery in such a fuss?" Albrec asked irritably. The broad corridors they traversed were crammed with fast-walking, gabbling monks. Everyone, from novices to friars, seemed to be on the move today, and twice they had to stop and bow to an Inceptine monsignore.

"Don't you know, Albrec? By the Saints, you spend so much time with your head buried in the spines of books that you let the events of the real world roll over you like water."

"Books are real, too," Albrec said obstinately. It was an old argument. "They tell of what happened in the world, its history and its composition. That is real."

"But this is happening *now*, Albrec, and we are part of it. Great events are afoot, and we are lucky enough to be alive to see them happen."

Avila's eyes were shining, and Albrec looked at him with a curious mixture of affection, exasperation and awe. Avila was a younger son of the Dampiers of Perigraine. He had gone into the Inceptines as a matter of course, and no doubt his rise in the order would be meteoric. He had charisma, energy and was devastatingly attractive. Albrec was never sure how the two of them had become friends. It had something to do with the ideas they pummelled each other with, the arguments that they flung back and forth like balls between them. Half a dozen novices were hopelessly in love with Avila, but Albrec was sure that the young noble was not even aware of them. There was a curious innocence about him which had survived the rough and tumble of his first years here. On the other hand, no one could play the Inceptine game better than he. Albrec could not help but feel that his friend was wasted here. Avila should have been a leader of men, an officer in his country's army, instead of a cleric tucked away in the hills.

"Tell me, then, what I should know in my ignorance," Albrec said.

"This Himerius is the champion of the Inceptines at the moment. Hebrion has a young and irreligious king on the throne, one who has scant respect for the Church, I am told, and who regularly consorts with wizards. Abrusio has become a haven for all sorts of heretics, foreigners and sorcerers. Himerius has instigated a purge of the city and is coming here to try to persuade the other Prelates to do likewise."

Albrec screwed up his pointed nose. "I don't like it. Everyone is panicked after Aekir. It smells like politics to me."

"Of course it does! My dear fellow, *the Church is leaderless*. Macrobius is dead and we no longer have a High Pontiff. This Himerius is establishing his credentials as soon as he can, putting himself forward as the sort of strong leader that the Church needs at a time like this—one not afraid to cross swords with kings. Everyone is already talking of him as Macrobius' successor."

"Everyone except his fellow Prelates, I take it."

"Oh, naturally! There will be deals done, though, with the Vicar-General brokering the whole thing. He is barred of course from the Pontiffship by virtue of his present office, but I do not doubt that he will have another Inceptine at the Church's head in a short while."

"Over a century, it has been, since we have had a non-Inceptine High Pontiff," Albrec said, stroking his brown Antillian habit reflectively. "And of all the Prelates, only Merion of Astarac is not an Inceptine, but an Antillian like myself."

"The Ravens have always run things their way," Avila said cheerfully. "It'll never be any different."

They walked out of the cloisters and began toiling up the cobbled streets of the town that formed the fringes of the monastery. The buildings here were tall, leaning over the road, and the streets were clean. The entire place had been tidied up for the Synod on the orders of the Vicar-General.

Clerics clogged the streets, climbing higher so as to be the first to catch sight of the man who was favourite for the Pontiffship. Avila helped Albrec along as the little monk puffed and sweated up the hill. Their breath clouded around them in the cold air, and they could see the snow on the higher slopes above them.

"There," Avila said, satisfied.

They stood on the ridge that curled protectively about the south-west of Charibon. The slope around them was black with people, religious and lay alike. They could stare down and see the entire, beautiful profile of Charibon with its towers and spires kindled by the autumn sunlight, and the inland sea of Tor glittering off to their right.

"I see him," Avila said.

Albrec squinted. "Where?"

"Not there, you ninny, along the northern road. He's coming by way of Almark, remember. See the escort of Knights? There must be close on two hundred of them. Himerius will be in the second coach, the one flying the scarlet Hebrian flag. They're certainly putting on a show for him. I'd say he had the Pontiffship in the palm of his hand already."

One of their neighbors, a hard-faced priest in the plain robe of a Friar Mendicant, turned at Avila's words.

"What's that you say? Himerius as Pontiff?"

"Why yes, Brother. That seems to me to be the way of it."

"And you have looked deeply into these matters, have you?"

Avila's face seemed to stiffen. It was with his full aristocratic hauteur that he replied, "I have a mind. I can examine the evidence and form an opinion as well as the next man."

The Friar Mendicant smiled, then nodded to the approaching cavalcade. "If yon Prelate assumes the High Pontiffship you may no longer be permitted the luxury of an opinion, lad. And many innocent folk will no longer possess the luxury of life. I doubt if that was the way of the Blessed Ramusio when he was on this earth, but it is the way of your brother Inceptines these days, with their Knights Militant, their purges and their pyres. Where in the *Book of Deeds* does it say you must murder your fellow man if he differs from you? Inceptines! You are God's gorecrows, flapping round the pyres you have created."

The grey-clad Friar turned at that and stumped off, elbowing his way roughly through the gathering throng. Avila and Albrec stared after him, speechless.

"He's mad," Albrec said at last. "The Friars are always an eccentric lot, but he's lost his mind entirely."

Avila stared down the hillside to where the Prelate of Hebrion's retinue was thundering along the muddy northern road, raising a spray of water as it came.

"Is he? I cannot ever remember a tale of Ramusio destroying someone who did not believe in him. Maybe he is right."

"He struck down the demon-possessed women of Gebrar," Albrec pointed out.

"Yes," Avila said absently, "there is that." Then he grinned suddenly with his accustomed good humour. "Which is another reason why clerics do not marry. Women have too many demons in them! I believe all clerics have mothers, though."

"Hush, Avila. Someone will hear."

"Someone will hear, yes. And what if they do, Albrec? What would happen? What if they chanced upon that cache of books you have saved? Do you ever wonder what would happen if they did? We had a mage on my father's staff when I was a boy. He used to do tricks with light and water, and no one could heal a broken limb faster than he. He became my tutor. Is that the sort of man the Church wants to destroy? Why?"

"For the sake of the Saint, Avila, will you be quiet? You'll get us into all manner of trouble."

"But what manner?" Avila asked. "What manner, Albrec? When does a conversation, an idea, lead to the pyre? What must one do to earn such a death?"

"Oh shut up, Avila. I won't argue with you, not here and now." Albrec looked round with increasing nervousness. Some of the nearby clerics were turning to listen to Avila's voice.

Avila smiled again. "All right, Brother. We'll chase this hare later. Maybe Brother Mensio can help us out."

Albrec said nothing. Avila loved to carry a conversation to the edge of things—to the limits of orthodoxy. It was worrying. Albrec sometimes thought that the gap between what Avila believed and what he said was widening and even he, the nobleman's friend, could not say for sure just how deep was the gulf between what appeared to be and what was in the younger man's mind.

The Prelate's cavalcade splashed by, one pale hand waving graciously from the depths of the coach at the assembled crowd. Then it was gone. There was a feeling of anticlimax.

"He could at least have got out and given us his blessing," a monk next to them grumbled.

Avila slapped the man on the back. "That *was* his blessing, Brother! Didn't you see his fingers tracing the Sign of the Saint as he galloped past? A swift blessing, it's true, but none the worse for that."

The monk, an Inceptine novice with the white hood of a first-year student, beamed broadly.

"So I've been blessed by the future Pontiff of the world.

Thanks, Brother. I'd never have noticed. You have good eyes."

"And a lively imagination," Albrec muttered while he and Avila made their way back down into Charibon. The bells of the cathedral were tolling the third hour and the flocks of monks were returning to their respective colleges for the morning meal. Albrec's stomach gave a premonitory twinge at the thought.

"Why do you do such things?" he asked his friend.

"You are strangely snappish this morning, Brother. Why do I do it? Because it pleases me, and it brightened that novice's day. By tomorrow the tale will be round his college how Himerius endowed them with his personal blessing, much good may it do them."

"Avila, I do believe you are in danger of becoming a cynic."

"Maybe. Sometimes I think that every man who wears this black habit must be either a pious fanatic or a cold-blooded schemer."

"Or a nobleman's younger son. There are a lot of those, don't forget."

Avila grinned at his diminutive friend. "Come, Antillian. Will you dine with the noblemen's sons this morning? If anyone points a finger at your mud-coloured habit I'll say you're a scholar come to use our library. And our refectory is renowned, as you well know."

"I know. All right. So long as you fend off the antics of the novices. I'm in no mood for a bread fight this morning."

The two of them picked a path down the cobbled streets into the monastery proper, the tall Inceptine and the plump little Antillian. No one looking at the unlikely pair could have guessed that between them they would one day change the course of the world.

THE bells of the cathedral tolled the hours of Charibon away. The inhabitants of the monastery-city said their devotions, ate their meals and read their offices in fast mumbles, but in the splendidly appointed quarters of the Vicar-General a more select company sat at their ease and sipped the Candelarian wine that had come with the meal. They had pushed their chairs back from the long table, said their thanks to God for the bounty which had presented itself before them and were now enjoying the fire burning in the huge hearth to one side.

Five men, the most powerful religious leaders in the world.

At the head of the table sat the Vicar-General of the Inceptine Order, Betanza of Astarac, formerly a duke of that kingdom. He had found his vocation late in life, helped, some said, by the sea-rovers who had destroyed his fief in a lightning raid one summer thirty years ago. He was a big, powerful man edging into corpulence, with a ruddy face and a pate that would have been bald even had it not been tonsured. The Saint symbol that hung from his neck was of white gold inset with pearls and tiny rubies. He was fingering it absently as he stared into the candlelit depths of his wine.

The other men represented four kingdoms. Merion of Astarac was not yet present, delayed, it was believed, by early snowstorms in the passes of the Malvennor Mountains, but Heyn of Torunna was there, as were Escriban of Perigraine and Marat of Almark. And seated at the foot of the table, delicately drinking the last of his wine, was Himerius of Hebrion whose arrival this morning had caused such commotion throughout the monastery.

All the men present were Inceptines and all had served their novitiate in this very monastery. For all except Betanza, it was the home of their youth and held fond memories, but their faces were grave now, even disgruntled.

"I cannot let go any more of the Knights," Betanza said with the weary air of a man repeating himself. "They are needed where they are."

"You have thousands of them on the hill, sitting on their hands," Heyn of Torunna said. He was a thin, black-bearded man. He looked ill, so dark were the circles under his eyes and the hollows at his temples.

"They are our only reserve. Charibon cannot be left defenceless. What if the tribes grow restive?"

"The tribes!" Heyn scoffed. "They did not stop you sending two thousand men to Hebrion to do Brother Himerius's policing for him. Are there *tribes* in Hebrion, or Merduks at the gate?"

The Hebrian Prelate raised his eyebrows slightly at that, but otherwise maintained an aloof, patrician air that irritated his colleagues intensely.

"Lofantyr needs men, needs them desperately. Even five

thousand would be a boon at this time," Heyn went on dog-gedly.

"And yet he is withdrawing troops from Ormann Dyke," Himerius said mildly. "Is he so confident in the dyke's im-pregnability?"

"Torunn must be adequately garrisoned in case the dyke falls," Heyn said.

"God forbid!" said Marat of Almark.

"Really, Brothers," Betanza said. "We are not here to argue politics, but to debate the spiritual needs of the time that is upon us. It is for the kings of the world to be the buckler of the faith. We are merely guides."

"But—" Heyn began.

"And the resources of the Church surely should be reserved for the needs of the Church. We have been free enough with our help so far. How many thousands of the Knights perished in Aekir? No, there are other issues at hand here which are every bit as important as the defence of the western fortresses."

Escriban of Perigraine, a long, languid man who would have looked more at home in court brocade than a monk's habit, laughed shortly.

"My dear Betanza, if you are referring to the High Pontiff-ship, then surely there is nothing to decide. If the acclaim of your own monks is anything to go by, then our esteemed Brother Himerius already has the position in his lap."

The men around the table scowled. Even Himerius had the grace to look embarrassed.

"The High Pontiffship is decided by the votes of the five Prelates of the Ramusian monarchies and the Colleges of Bish-ops under them. Nothing else," Betanza said, his red face growing redder. "We will discuss it at the proper time, and pray for God's guidance in this, the most important of deci-sions. Besides, our number is not complete. Brother Merion of Astarac has yet to join us."

"Your countryman, the Antillian—of course. I meant no of-fence," Escriban said smoothly. "What way will he vote, do you think?"

Betanza glowered. "Brother Escriban, as referee and over-seer of these proceedings I advise you to take a more respon-sible tone."

"What proceedings? My dear friend, we are only colleagues

in the Church talking over dinner. The Synod is not even convened as yet."

The men around the table knew that. They also knew that the real business of the Synod would probably be resolved before it even began. Merion was a nonentity, a non-Inceptine, but if the Prelates were evenly divided his vote would be decisive. He could not be ignored.

"How did he ever become a Prelate anyway?" Marat muttered. "A man of no family and from another order."

"King Mark thinks the world of him. He was the only Astaran candidate put forward," Betanza said. "The College of Bishops had little choice."

"They order these things better in Almark," Marat said. He was stockily built, with a huge white beard that coursed down over his broad chest and belly. His homeland, Almark, had been the last land to be conquered by the Fimbrians before their Hegemony ended, yet it was widely seen as the most conservative of the Five Kingdoms.

"What of these purges our learned colleague has instigated in Hebrion?" Heyn asked, rubbing his sunken temples with bone-white fingers. "Are we to make them a continent-wide phenomenon, or are they merely a local problem?"

Himerius was studying his crystal goblet, his bird-of-prey features revealing nothing. He knew they were waiting for his word. For all their bluster and confidence, he realized that they looked to him at the moment; he was the only one among them who had dared to cross the wishes of his king.

He put down the glass and paused to make sure he had their attention.

"The situation in Hebrion is grave, Brothers. In its way it is every bit as grave as the crisis in the east." The firelight flickered off his wonderfully aquiline nose. He had the features of a Fimbrian emperor, and knew it.

"Abrusio is a colourful city, perched as it is on the edge of the Western Ocean. Ships call there from every part of Normannia, both Ramusian and Merduk. The population of the place is a hybrid, a conglomeration of the dregs of a hundred other cities. And in such a soil, Brothers, heresy takes root easily.

"The King of Hebrion is a young man. He had a great father, Bleyn the Pious whose name you all know, but the son is not hewn out of the same wood. He had a wizard as a tutor in his youth, scorning the wisdom of his Inceptine teachers and as a result he lacks a certain . . . respect for the authority and the traditions of the Church."

Escriban of Perigraine grinned. "You mean he's his own man."

"I mean nothing of the sort," Himerius snapped, suddenly peevish. "I mean that if he is left to do as he will the Church's influence in Hebrion may be irrevocably damaged, and then the Saint knows what flotsam and jetsam from the corners of the world will take root in Abrusio. I have acted to prevent this, seeking to cleanse the city and eventually the kingdom, but my sources tell me that the moment I left the place the scale of the purge was reduced, no doubt on the orders of the King."

"Nothing like a few burnings to bring them flocking to the Church on their knees," Marat of Almark said gruffly. "You did right, Brother."

"Thank you. At any rate, dear colleagues, I mean to bring the whole affair up at the Synod once it is convened. Abeleyn of Hebrion must be taught not to flout the authority of the Church."

"What do you mean to do, excommunicate him?" Heyn of Torunna asked incredulously.

"Let us say that the threat of excommunication is sometimes as effective as the act itself."

"You forget one thing, Brother," Betanza said, his fingers playing restlessly with his Saint symbol. "Only the High Pontiff has the authority to excommunicate—or otherwise chastise—an anointed Ramusian king. As mere Prelate, you cannot touch him."

"All the more reason for choosing the new Pontiff as soon as possible," Himerius said, unperturbed.

There was a silence as the others digested this.

"Is this really the time to be picking arguments with kings?" Heyn asked at last. "Are there not enough crises facing the west without adding more?"

"This is the best time," Himerius said. "The prestige of the Church has been badly damaged by the fall of Macrobius, of Aekir and the loss of the army of Knights Militant there. We *must* regain the initiative, use our influence as a coherent body and prove to the west that we are still the ultimate authority on the continent."

"Do we let Ormann Dyke fall, then, in order to prove how powerful we are?" Escriban asked.

"If we do, then later generations will abhor our names—and rightly so," Heyn said hotly.

"There is no reason that the dyke should fall," Himerius said, "but it is the responsibility of Torunna, not of the Church."

Heyn stood up at that, scraping back his chair. His black habit flapped around his thin form as he put his back to the fire, his eyes smouldering like the gledes at its heart.

"This talk of *responsibility* . . . the west has a responsibility to aid Torunna at this time. If the Merduks take the dyke, then Torunn itself will almost certainly fall and the heathens will have no other barrier to their advance save the heights of the Cimbrics. And what if they turn north, skirting the mountains? Then it will be our precious Charibon next in line. Will it be our *responsibility* then to defend it—or should we wait until the Merduk tide is lapping at the gates of Abrusio?"

"You are excited, Brother," Betanza said soothingly. "And with reason. It cannot be easy for you."

"Yes. I'll bet Lofantyr has all but got the thumbscrews on you, Heyn," Escriban said. "What did you promise him before you came here? An army of the Knights? The Lancers of Perigraine? Or perhaps the Cuirassiers of Almark."

Heyn scowled. His face was like a bearded skull in the firelight.

"Not all of us see life as one big joke, Escriban," he said venomously.

Betanza thumped a large hand on the table, setting the glasses dancing and startling them all.

"*Enough*! We did not assemble here to trade insults with one another. We are the elders of the Church, the inheritors of the tradition of Ramusio himself. There will be no pettiness. We cannot afford the time for it."

"Agreed," old Marat said into his white beard. "It seems to me there are two issues confronting us at this time, Brothers. First, the High Pontiffship. It must be decided before anything else, for it affects everything. And secondly, these purges which our Hebrian brother has instigated and wishes to see extended. Do we want to see them across the Five Kingdoms? Personally, I'm in favour of them. The common folk of the world are like cattle; they need to feel the drover's stick once in a while."

"Merion of Astarac is one of your cattle, Marat," said Escriban. "He will not vote for a continent-wide pogrom, I'll tell you now."

"He is only one man, and there are five of us." Marat glanced about the table, and then smiled. He looked like a benevolent patriarch, but his eyes held no humour. "Good," he said.

Heyn remained by the fire, isolated. At last he said:

"Torunna has not the resources to undertake a purge at the moment. We will need outside help."

Betanza nodded, his bald head shining. "But of course, Brother. I am sure I can let you have a sizeable contingent of the Knights to aid God's work in your beleaguered prelacy."

"Six thousand?"

"Five."

"Very well."

Himerius drained the last of his wine, looking like a hawk which had just stooped on a fat pigeon. "It is good to have these things out in the open, to talk them over with friends, amicably, without rancour." His eyes met Betanza's. He nodded imperceptibly.

Escriban of Perigraine chuckled.

"What about the Pontiffship?" Betanza asked. "Who here wishes to stand?"

"Oh, please, Brother Betanza," Escriban said with feigned shock. "Must you be so blunt?"

Another silence, more profound this time. In accepting Himerius' proposals the decision had more or less been made, but no one wanted to voice what they all knew.

"I will stand, if God will grant me the strength," Himerius said at last, a little annoyed that no one had publicly urged him to.

Betanza sighed. "So be it. This is entirely informal, of course, but I must ask you, Brothers, if there are any objections to Brother Himerius' candidature."

Still, no one spoke. Heyn turned away to face the fire.

"Will no one else put themselves forward?" Betanza waited

a moment and then shrugged. "Well, we have a candidate to put to the Synod. It remains to be seen what the College of Bishops makes of it."

But they all knew that the Bishops voted with their respective Prelates. The High Pontiffship of the western world had effectively been decided: by five men in a firelit room over dinner.

FOURTEEN

AUTUMN in the Malvennor Mountains. Already the snow had begun to block the higher passes, and from the vast peaks streamers and banners of white were being billowed out by the freshening wind.

Abeleyn pulled the fur of his collar tighter around his throat and stared up at the high land to the east and north. The Malvennors were fifteen thousand feet above sea level, and even here, on the snow-pocked hills at their knees, the air was sharp and thin and the guides had warned the party of the dangers of mountain sickness and snow blindness.

He was five weeks out of Abrusio, on his way to the Conclave of Kings at Vol Ephrir in Perigraine. His ship had made a rapid passage across the Fimbrian Gulf, docking at the breakaway Fimbrian city of Narbukir, then he had gone aboard a river boat for the laborious journey up the Arcolm river, taking to horses when the Arcolm was no longer navigable. He could see the river now, a narrow stream running and foaming through the icicle-dripping rocks off to one side. Further up in the mountains it was said that a man might bestride it if he had long legs. Hard to believe that down on the gulf its mouth formed an estuary fully three leagues wide.

The rest of the party were still below, labouring up the steep slopes towards him. He had a tolerably large escort: two hundred Hebrian arquebusiers and swordsmen and eighty heavy cavalry armed with lances and paired matchlock pistols. Then there were the muleteers of the pack-train, the cooks, the grooms, the smiths and the score of other servants who made up his travelling household. All told, some four hundred men accompanied the King of Hebrion across the Malvennor Mountains; a modest enough show. Only a king would ever be allowed to take such a force into a foreign country. It was part and parcel of the dignity of monarchs.

"We'll camp here, and attempt the pass in the morning," the King said to his chief steward.

The man bowed in the saddle and then wrenched his horse around to begin the job of setting up camp.

The King sat relaxed in the saddle and watched the ungainly straggling groups of men and animals gradually coalesce on the slope below him. The horses were finding it heavy going. If the snow grew much deeper—and it would—then they would all be afoot, hauling their mounts behind them. The snows had come early this year, and there was a bitter wind winnowing the high peaks. The baking heat of Abrusio seemed like a dream.

"Is it here you hope to meet up with King Mark, sire?" a woman's voice asked.

"Hereabouts." The King turned to regard the hooded lady who sat her palfrey behind him. The fine-stepping horse was feeling the cold; it was not the best of mounts for a journey such as this. "I hope you have good walking boots with you, lady. That nag of yours will drop in its tracks ere we've put another ten leagues behind us."

The lady Jemilla threw back her hood. Her dark hair was bound up in circled braids around her head, held in place with pearl-topped pins. Two larger pearls shone like little moons in her earlobes. Her eyes sparkled in the snow-light.

"The walk will do me good. I am putting on weight."

Abeleyn grinned. If so, he had not noticed. He looked down the hillside. His staff were erecting the huge hide tents, and he could see the dull flicker of a fire. His toes were numb in his furlined boots and his breath was whipped away from his lips, but he did not immediately ride down to the warmth of the fires. Rather he gazed south, along the line of the moun-

tains to where Astarac loomed blue with distance on the southern side of the Arcolm river. If truth be told, they were in
Astarac now, for the Arcolm had always been the traditional
boundary between Astarac and Fimbria. But up in the mountains such technicalities were irrelevant. Shepherds herded
their goats from one kingdom to another without formalities,
as they always had. Up here the niceties of borders and diplomacy seemed like a faraway farce to be played out in the
palaces of the world.

"When will he arrive, do you think?" Jemilla asked.

She was becoming a little familiar of late. He must watch
that.

"Soon I hope, lady, soon. But he will be here no quicker
for our watching. Come, let us warm ourselves and give our
poor mounts a rest." He kicked his horse into motion down
the icy slope.

Jemilla did not follow him at once. She sat her shivering
steed and stared at the King's retreating back. One gloved hand
felt her stomach tentatively, and for a moment her face became
as hard as glass. Then she followed her king and lover down
to the growing bustle of the camp, and the fires that were
burning orange and yellow against the snow.

THE wind had blown up into a gale. Abeleyn held his hands
out to the glowing brazier—they would be running out of
coal soon—and listened to the snowstorm that had come upon
them with the swooping in of night. Perhaps he should have
taken the sea route, south-east through the Malacar Straits, but
then he would have needed a small fleet as escort. To the
corsairs, a Hebrian king would have been too tempting a target
to let by unmolested, despite—or perhaps because of—the
longstanding accommodations they had had with the Hebrian
crown.

And besides, he needed this chance to talk openly with King
Mark before the intrigue of the conclave swallowed them all.

Something struck the side of the tent, seemingly propelled
by the wind. It scrabbled there for a moment, and the steward
came in from the adjoining extension. There was the clatter of
plates from in there; they were clearing the remains of dinner.

"Was there something, sire? I thought I heard—"

"It was nothing, Cabran. Dismiss the servants, will you? They can finish in the morning."

The steward bowed, then left for the spacious extension, clapping his hands at the serving maids. Abeleyn rose and let slip the heavy hide curtain that shut out their noise.

"Sire." It was the bodyguard at the entrance. "We've something here. It struck the tent, and you told us to look out for—"

"Yes," Abeleyn snapped. "Bring it here, and then let no others enter."

The tent flap was thrown back and a heavily cloaked and armoured man thrust his way in, admitting a gust of snow and chill air. He had something in his hands, which he left on the low cot at a nod from Abeleyn.

"Thank you, Merco. Have you men a decent fire out there?"

"Good enough, sire. We switch round every hour." The man's voice was muffled in the folds of cloak he had wrapped round his face.

"Very well. That will be all, then."

The man bowed and left. The snow he had let in began to melt on the thick hide of the tent's floor.

"Well, Golophin?" Abeleyn said. He bent over the ice-encrusted gyrfalcon that crouched on the furs of the cot and gently wiped its feathers. The yellow inhuman eyes glared at him. The beak opened, and the voice of the old wizard said:

"Well met, my lord."

"Is the bird drunk, that he crashes into my tent?"

"The bird is exhausted, lad. This damn snowstorm almost put paid to him for good. You will have a fine time forcing the pass if this keeps up."

"I know. What word of King Mark?"

"He is only hours away. He travels with a smaller party than you. Perhaps his ideas as to the dignity of kings differ."

Abeleyn smiled, stroking the bird's feathers. "Perhaps. Well, old man, what news have you for me this time?"

"Momentous news, my boy. I have had the bird monitor Charibon as you requested. He has just come from there. I thought the flight over the mountains would kill him, but he had the east wind on his tail so he made good time in the end.

"You have to know, I suppose. The Synod convened eight days ago. Our good Himerius has been elected High Pontiff of the Five Kingdoms."

Abeleyn's hand went very still on the water-beaded plumage of the savage bird. "So they did it. They actually elected that slaughter-mongering wolf-livered bastard."

"Guard your words, sire. You speak of the spiritual head of the Ramusian world."

"By the blood of the Saints! Did no one object, Golophin?"

"Merion did, but he's an Antillian of low birth, and thus an outsider. I had thought Heyn of Torunna would also, but he must have been bought off somehow. No doubt Himerius is even now doling out rewards to the faithful who voted him into office."

"And the purges. I take it they will be extended continent-wide."

"Yes, lad. A Pontifical bull is expected within a few weeks. It is a black day for the Dweomer-folk, and for the west."

Abeleyn's face was as white as bone in the scarlet shadow of the tent.

"I will not allow it. The kings will not allow it. I will put it to the conclave that we cannot tolerate this interference in the day-to-day running of the state. These people are our subjects; whether the Church considers them heretics or no."

"Careful, lad. There is talk of excommunication in the air at Charibon, and Himerius has the power to issue a bull against you. A heretic king has no right to rule in the eyes of the world."

"Damn them," Abeleyn said through clenched teeth. "Is there nothing an anointed king can do in his kingdom without these God-cursed Ravens meddling in it?"

"It is the Inceptine game, sire. They have been playing it for centuries."

"I will speak to Mark of it. He is a moderate like me. We may not sway Lofantyr of Torunna, for he needs the Knights Militant too badly at the moment, or Haukir of Almark—he is too old, too set in his ways. Cadamost of Perigraine, though. He may be open to reason; he has always struck me as an amenable sort of fellow. What news from the dyke, Golophin? Does it hold?"

"Shahr Baraz's army is finding the passage of the Western Road difficult. The main body has begun to move at last and there is skirmishing at the dyke itself, but so far there has been no major assault. This is old news, sire, gleaned from a colleague of mine. The bird has been too busy in Charibon to have a closer look at the east."

"Of course."

"There is a rumour, though, from Ormann Dyke."

"What? What of it?"

"It is rumoured that Macrobius was not slain in Aekir's fall, that he is alive. As I say, it is a rumour, no more."

"Macrobius alive? No, it's impossible, Golophin! Torunnan wishful thinking."

"Do you want me to look into it, sire?"

Abeleyn paused. "No. I need your feathered alter ego back at Charibon. I must be up to date with developments there when the conclave is assembled. There is no time to chase will-o'-the-wisps in the east."

"Very well, sire."

There was a silence. The gyrfalcon struggled to its taloned feet and shook its wings, spraying water over Abeleyn.

"Will the bird stay here tonight, Golophin?"

"If you please, sire. He needs a rest, and King Mark is on the right route to find you in the morning. I congratulate you on your navigating."

"I spend my life navigating, Golophin, trying to keep the ship of state from foundering."

"Then beware of shoals, my King. They are approaching by the score. Have you heard anything from Fimbria?"

Abeleyn rubbed his eyes, suddenly weary. "Yes. Narbukir is sending an envoy to the conclave. He travels with us, though he wants to remain as low-key as possible. From Fimbria proper there has been no reply to my emissary as yet. I do not honestly expect one, Golophin."

"Do not give up hope, sire. The Fimbrians may yet be the answer to some of our problems. They have never loved the Church; they blame it for their downfall. They would be a powerful ally if the worst happened and Hebrion went its own way."

"You mean if its king were excommunicated and it became an outlawed kingdom, beyond the pale of the Ramusian monarchies?"

"That is a picture I would not care to regard too closely, sire."

"Nor I. I am tired, Golophin, and your magnificent bird

seems a little the worse for wear. Maybe we'll both sleep now. I have a perch ready, if it does not object to roosting on the end of a king's bed."

"He—and I—would be honoured, sire."

"My lord King." It was the steward's voice, coming from the other side of the hide partition.

"Yes, Cabran, what is it?"

"The lady Jemilla wonders if you would receive her, sire."

Abeleyn frowned. "No, Cabran. Tell her I am not to be disturbed until morning."

"Yes, sire."

"And Cabran—I am to be wakened the moment King Mark's party is sighted."

"As you wish, sire. Good night."

Some kings and princes had body servants to undress them and prepare them for bed, but Abeleyn preferred to perform those functions himself. He reached under the low cot for the chamber-pot and pissed into it gratefully.

"You brought Jemilla, then," the gyrfalcon said. Odd to hear Golophin's deep tones issue out of the harsh beak, as though the bird had the lips and lungs of a man.

Abeleyn shoved the steaming pot back under the cot. "Yes. What of it?"

"She has ambitions, that one."

"She will never be my queen, if that's what you're afraid of. She's much too old, and she was married before."

"I think she hopes, sire, in the way women do. Be careful of her. I do not think she is the kind of lady to be discarded lightly."

"*I* will worry about that, Golophin."

"And it is high time you were married yourself. You must be the most eligible bachelor in the Five Kingdoms."

"You sound like a mother goose fussing over her brood, Golophin. You know why I have not married. If I ally myself with one of the other monarchies through a state marriage then I alienate the others—"

"And Hebrion depends on the goodwill of all the kings for the trade that sustains her. I know the arguments, sire, but there is a new one now. You must bind Hebrion to another state if you intend to flout the holy writ of our new Pontiff; you cannot afford to let yourself be isolated. It is something you might bring up with King Mark when you meet."

"What schemes are you hatching now, Golophin?"

"Think of it, sire. An alliance between Astarac and Hebrion, and in between them the neutral state of Fimbria. That would be a bloc that even the Church would think twice before provoking. If you wish to shake free of the Church's authority then you should be thinking of the part of the continent that lies west of the Malvennor Mountains. The western states have always had a reputation for going their own way."

"If certain clerics heard your words, Golophin, you would be a heap of ashes at the foot of a blackened stake."

"If certain clerics saw this talking bird my end would be the same. I no longer have anything to lose and nor have you, sire. Think about what I have said, and if you have to bend a little to avoid becoming a heretic king, then so be it—but make sure that if you cannot bend far enough Hebrion is not left to stand alone."

Abeleyn yawned. "All right, I am convinced. Ah, this mountain air! It makes a man sleepy. Your bird looks shattered, Golophin."

"We both are. The powers of mages are not all they are rumoured to be. This night I feel as old and brittle as a dried leaf. This will be the last you hear from me in a while, Abeleyn. The old man needs his rest."

"So does the King," Abeleyn said, yawning again. "I'd best get some ere King Mark turns up on our doorstep." He lay back on the cot and the falcon flapped and hopped, screaming softly, until it perched on the wooden frame at his feet.

Abeleyn stared at the roof of the heavy tent. The whole structure was swaying and creaking in the wind that was blasting down from the mountains.

"Do you remember the *Blithe Spirit*, Golophin?"

The bird was silent. Abeleyn smiled, putting his hands behind his head.

"I remember the green depths of the Hebrian Sea, and the master pointing out over the ship's rail to where the water turned deeper; that colour, as dark as an old wine. The Great Western Ocean that marks the end of the world.

"We were putting about to steer a course for the Fimbrian Gulf, back to the world of men. I remember the loom of the

Hebros Mountains, like a thin line at the edge of sight. And the coast of Astarac with the shadows of the Malvennors. I remember the smell, Golophin. There is no other smell on earth like it. The smell of the open ocean, and the ship smells.

"Sometimes I wish I could have been a master mariner, carving my own road upon the surface of the world and leaving nothing but a wake of white water behind me. And nothing but a plank of Gabrionese oak between my soul and eternity . . ."

Abeleyn's eyes were closed. His breathing slowed.

"I wonder if Murad has found his fabled land in the west . . ." he murmured. His head tilted to one side.

The King slept.

KING Mark of Astarac and his entourage arrived just before dawn, having travelled through the night in the blinding snowstorm. When the Astaran monarch was shown into Abeleyn's tent his face was grey beneath its mask of ice and frozen snow, and his young man's beard had been frosted white.

Abeleyn had had to struggle up from a great depth, a lightless pit of slumber, but he shrugged off his tiredness and shouted commands at his retinue. Mark had barely two hundred men in his party, and they were taken into the Hebrian tents to save them the labour of erecting their own in the snow-thick gale that still howled about the peaks of the mountains. Servants ran to and fro like men possessed, lighting extra braziers and heaving around platters of food and drink for the cold-blasted men of Astarac. King Mark's bodyguards joined Abeleyn's at the tent entrance, the two groups eyeing each other somewhat askance until some enlightened soul produced a skin of barley spirit and passed it round.

Dressed in dry clothes and seated in front of a glaring brazier, King Mark's face became slowly human again. There was little ceremony between him and Abeleyn; the two men had spent much time together as boys, skylarking at past conclaves whilst their fathers helped decide the fate of the world. Mark had a white gap in one eyebrow where Abeleyn had split his forehead open with a lead-bladed sword. They had shared wenches and wine and were much of an age. Now they sat in Abeleyn's tent companionably enough, and sipped mulled ale

and listened to the gradually dying hubbub that the arrival of
the Astarans had produced in the Hebrian camp.

Mark nodded to the gyrfalcon that perched with closed eyes
on the end of Abeleyn's cot.

"That Golophin's, is it?"

"Aye. Both he and his master are sleeping. He'll be full of
life later, no doubt."

Mark grinned, showing strong, even teeth in his square face.

"Saffarac has an owl as his familiar. An owl—I ask you!
And of course he has it flying in the daytime with never a
thought, and the common folk who see it making the sign of
the Saint at the bad omen."

They laughed together, and Abeleyn poured out more of the
steaming ale for them both.

"You and your men seem to be in a degree of haste, cousin,"
he said. He and Mark were not related, but kings often used
the term, implying that all royalty were somehow akin to each
other.

"Indeed, and I'll tell you why. Do you travel with any clerics in your entourage, Abeleyn?"

Abeleyn sipped his ale, grimacing at the heat of it. "Nary a
one. I refused every Raven I was offered."

"I thought as much. I'd best warn you then that I have one
here clinging to my coattails. He was foisted on me by the
College of Bishops, who were outraged at the thought of an
Astaran king travelling without a priest to shrive him of his
sins every so often."

"An Inceptine?"

"Of course. Just because I was able to get Merion the Antillian elected Prelate doesn't mean I get my way in all affairs
ecclesiastical. No, he's a spy, no doubt about it. It's as well
that Golophin is not with you, but I wouldn't let anyone catch
you talking to your bird if I were you, cousin. What used to
be seen as honest thaumaturgy is being transformed into something entirely different in the eyes of the Church."

"This doesn't explain your haste."

"Doesn't it? We've been pushing as hard as this ever since
we left Cartigella; the old crow is near to dropping. With a
little luck he'll lose himself in a snowdrift once we get into
the mountains proper, and we'll be well rid of his prying
beak."

They both roared with laughter.

"Has Saffarac's owl brought you any word of what is going on in the east?" Abeleyn asked when the mirth had faded. Mark's face grew sombre.

"Some word, yes. The Merduk army has stalled, it seems, bogged down by the weather, and Martellus has been sending out reconnaissances in force under the old cavalryman, Ranafast. There has been a good deal of skirmishing, but the Torunnans cannot commit themselves to any large-scale action beyond the Searil. They have not the men. Lofantyr has drawn off all but twelve thousand of the dyke's garrison, the Saints know why."

"He is afraid for his capital. Are there no generals left in Torunna to advise him?"

"The best one, Mogen, died at Aekir and Martellus commands the dyke. There is no one else at that level left in the country. Torunna is bled almost dry."

"Aye, they've been the bulwark of the west for too long, perhaps. Have you heard anything of a rumour concerning Macrobius?"

"That he is alive? Yes, I've heard. My guess is it's a tale set about by Martellus to put some heart into his men. As far as I know there's nothing behind it, but I do know that an old blind man has been paraded before the garrison as the High Pontiff. What the worthies in Charibon will make of that I cannot say. Martellus may be running a fine line on one side of excommunication with his holy impostor."

"Unless—" Abeleyn began.

Mark glanced at him. "No, I cannot believe it. Not one Ramusian of any rank escaped the wreck of Aekir. I cannot conceive that they somehow missed the most important man of all. He would have been the first they would have sought out."

"Of course, of course. What a blessing it would be for the west, though . . ."

"I take it you're not happy with your fellow Hebrian as High Pontiff."

"He means to excommunicate me, I think, if he cannot geld me first. This is one of the reasons I have asked you to meet me here, cousin."

Mark sat back on his camp chair looking satisfied.

"Aha! I wondered when you'd get round to it."

Abeleyn stared into the steam-wreathed depths of his ale flagon, his dark brows drawn together.

"Golophin's falcon was giving me the old man's advice last night, and it concurred with what I was thinking myself. This is a bad time, Mark—like the chaos of the world when the empire of the Fimbrians began to fall apart, or when the Merduks first invaded, or in the Religious Wars when Ramusio's faith was spread through the west with fire and sword. And I think this time may be the worst of the lot.

"It is not just the Merduks. Theirs is an outside threat, which I believe the west can see off if we cease our squabbling. No, it runs deeper than that. It is the very faith we all believe in, and the men who are the custodians of that faith. They have become princes in their own right, and they are hankering after kingdoms to rule. I tell you—I truly believe, and Golophin does too—that the Inceptines are intent on ruling, and if we let them they will make the monarchs of Normannia into mere ciphers, and they will write their rule in letters of fire and blood clear across the continent."

King Mark was listening intently, but he had an uneasy expression on his face. Abeleyn continued:

"The Inceptines need their wings clipped, and it must be done now or in the very near future. They have trodden on the authority of the rightful rulers of the kingdoms, and they have reduced the other Ramusian religious orders to the level of servants. With Aekir's fall, they have become not less powerful but more so, because of the fear the city's fall has generated in the west. Macrobius was a moderate, Inceptine though he was, but Himerius of Hebrion is a fanatic. He is determined to harness that fear, to be a priest-emperor."

"Oh come now, Abeleyn—"

But the Hebrian King held up a hand. "The contest has already begun. There are two thousand Knights Militant riding towards Hebrion even as we speak. When they arrive, they will instigate a purge the likes of which the west has not seen for centuries. And they wish to do the same in Astarac, in Perigraine, in Almark, even in besieged Torunna. Himerius' insanities are now Church policy, and we can either stand back and let the Ravens do as they will in our kingdoms, or we can stop them.

"And how do we stop them? Do you wish to be excommunicated, Abeleyn, Hebrion labelled a heretic kingdom, shunned by the other monarchies of the west?"

"Hebrion may not have to stand alone," Abeleyn said quietly.

Mark stared at him for a moment, then laughed shortly and stood up. He threw his flagon aside and started pacing up and down on the soft tent floor.

"I know what you are asking, and I tell you I want no part of it."

"Will you hear me out before you start refusing me?" Abeleyn asked irritably.

"What is it you envisage? Astarac and Hebrion standing alone outside the Ramusian world, cut off from the other kingdoms, ostracized? The rest of the Ramusian lands would have to mount a crusade to bring us back within the fold—and this in the midst of an eastern war which may be the climax to Merduk expansion. You are mad, Abeleyn. Such a plan would rip the west apart. I will have no part of it."

"For the Saint's sake, sit down, will you? And listen. Astarac and Hebrion would not be alone."

Mark sat, still visibly sceptical.

"Think, man. What is to the east of Hebrion and the north of Astarac? Fimbria. Fimbria, whose empire fell largely because of the Ramusian religion and the conversions of the Inceptines. The Fimbrians may be believers in the Saint now, but they have no love for the Church. And no alliance would lightly seek to force an armament through their electorates; it would be the one thing guaranteed to reunite them and have the Fimbrian tercios at war again."

"So we have Fimbria as a buffer. But there is always the sea route, Abeleyn. You of all people should know that."

"The four major sea powers of the world are Hebrion, Astarac, Gabrion and the Sea-Merduks."

"And the Macassian corsairs."

"True. And none of them has any love for the Church either. A crusading fleet would have to sail through the Malacar Straits, or detour to the south of Gabrion. The Sea-Merduks would attack any Ramusian naval armament in their waters, as would the corsairs. The Gabrionese would not be happy either. And what was left of it after those nations had mauled it could easily be taken care of by our combined navies."

Mark shook his head. "Ramusian versus Ramusian on a huge scale. I don't like it. It is not right, especially at this time."

"It won't happen, for the reasons I have outlined to you and for others besides."

"Tell me the others, then," Mark said wearily.

"I believe that if we can reinforce Torunna sufficiently then we will nullify Lofantyr's reliance on the Knights Militant. Perigraine may well follow the lead of Torunna and Almark will then be isolated, even if it has the support of Finnmark and the northern duchies. What will the Church do—excommunicate half the monarchs of Normannia? I think not. The power of the Inceptines will be broken, and we can promote another order in their place. The Antillians, perhaps."

Mark chuckled. "Divide and conquer? But what you are advocating could very well lead to a religious schism of the west. Almark is virtually governed by the Inceptines, and their influence runs deep in Perigraine also. Those bastions will not be easy to reduce."

Abeleyn flapped a hand casually. "Haukir of Almark is an old man. He will not last for ever. And Cadamost of Perigraine is a lightweight, easily swayed."

Mark was silent for a moment, then said: "How much of this do you intend to outline to the other kings at the conclave?"

"Very little. But I do want to go to the conclave with one or two weapons in my belt."

"Such as?" asked Mark, though he already knew.

"Such as a formal alliance between Hebrion and Astarac."

"And how do you propose to formalize it?"

"By marrying your sister."

The two kings stared at one another, wary, gauging. Finally a grin broke out on Mark's broad face.

"So the mighty tree is felled at last. Abeleyn the Bachelor King will finally consent to share his bed with a wife. She is not pretty, my sister."

"If she brings the friendship of a kingdom with her she can be as plain as a frog for all I care. What say you, Mark?"

The Astaran king shook his head ruefully.

"You are a cunning dog, Abeleyn, to sweeten the bitterness

of your pill thus. You know that half the kings in the west seek an alliance with Hebrion for the trade privileges it would bring, and now you throw it in my lap. But at what a cost!"

"I also have a certain influence with the corsairs who infest your southern coast," Abeleyn remarked.

"Oh, I know! Many's the Astaran cargo that has ended up on the wharves of Abrusio. You'd help curtail their depredations on your brother-in-law's ships, then?"

"Perhaps."

"An alliance. Where would it end, Abeleyn? I can see what you are doing—forming a trading block in the west of the continent that can remain self-supporting even if it becomes outcast from the rest of the Five Kingdoms. Even if it means increased trade with the Sea-Merduks. And you will hold this over the heads of the other kings like a cleaver over the neck of a lamb. Yet it is not lambs we are dealing with, cousin, but wolves."

"Which is why we must move quickly, and with sufficient might to force the issue. If you and I can go to the conclave already allied and say to the other kings, 'Look, this is the way things will be,' they should be startled enough to pay some attention to our ideas. And if you can promise help to Torunna also, why then I think we have them."

"If I can promise help?"

"Why, yes. You are closer to the dyke than I. You could have the place reinforced within two months by land or half that by sea, if you had a mind to."

"And if the place is still standing by that time."

"True. But the gesture is everything. Lofantyr will be grateful, and will not have to be so reliant on the soldiery of the Church. He will be his own man again."

"You mean he will be *our* man."

Abeleyn smiled. "Perhaps," he said again.

"My sister's dowry may yet cost me my throne," Mark muttered.

"Will you agree, then? Think of the opportunities, Mark! Our combined fleets would be irresistible. We might even clear Macassar of the corsairs entirely and make it into Rovenan again, your lost province."

"Don't seek to convince me with pipe dreams, Abeleyn. I must think about this."

"Do not take too long."

"My advisers will throw themselves into fits when the news gets back to the court."

"Not necessarily. All they need to know is that you have finally succeeded in wooing Hebrion. There should be no trouble from that quarter so long as they do not know the whole story."

Mark contemplated Abeleyn's face. "We have been friends for a long time, you and I, insofar as monarchs can ever be friends. I pray to the Saints that I do not let that friendship cloud my thinking now. I like you, Abeleyn. It is our mutual esteem that has brought an end to the endless raiding and rivalry that plagued our two kingdoms from time immemorial. But I tell you this as Astarac's king: if you play me false, or if I find that you intend to use Astarac as Hebrion's workhorse, then I will annul our alliance in the blink of an eye, and I will be in the first rank of those who bay for your blood."

"I would do likewise, were I Astarac's king," Abeleyn said gently.

"So be it." Mark stood up and held out a brawny hand.

Abeleyn rose also and took it, face grave. Mark topped him by half a head, but he did not feel the smaller man.

"Come," said Mark. "Let us sniff the air. My head is full of the fumes of ale and coal."

They slipped out of the tent together, the bodyguards at the entrance snapping to attention as they appeared. Their fire had burned down low and the men were stamping their feet and flapping their arms. Mark and Abeleyn dismissed them and stood alone. As one, they walked out to the edge of the camp where the ground fell away in a gentle curve of white to the lower land below. They trudged through knee-deep snow, bound by some mutual arrangement, until they could hear the tiny rill and trickle of water. The Arcolm river. When they found it, they each stood on one side: one man in Astarac, the other in Narboskan Fimbria.

The sun was beginning to top the mountains so the Malvennors were a huge soundless silhouette of shadow. Behind them the sky was brightening and glowing a delicate lilac, whilst over the highest of the peaks wisps of cloud caught fire from the sun and blazed in a glory of saffron and gold.

"Our path will be a hard one," Mark said quietly.

"Aye. But men have trod it before, and no doubt will again. And these mountains will see other sunrises, other kings making bargains in their shadow. It is the way of the world."

"Abeleyn, the Philosopher King," Mark said with gentle mockery.

Abeleyn grinned, but when he spoke again his voice was serious.

"We have the luck or the misfortune to be part of the forces which shape the fate of the world, Mark. We have a conversation over a flagon of ale and lo! History is changed. Sometimes I think about it."

He fumbled in his fur-lined robes and produced a small silver flask. He unscrewed the top, which transformed into two tiny, gleaming cups.

"Here. We'll seal our history shaping with a little wine."

"I hope it's good," Mark said. "We must toast the alliance of Astarac and Hebrion in the finest you possess."

"Good enough."

They raised their cups to each other and drank, two kings sealing a bargain, whilst above them the sun broke out over the peaks of the mountains and bathed them both in blood.

FIFTEEN

28th day of Forlion, year of the Saint 551.

    Wind NNW, backing. Light airs. Course due west with the wind on the starboard bow. Two knots.

    Sighted North Cape at two bells in the first dog-watch on this, the seventh day out of Abrusio harbour. At three bells the lead found white sand at forty fathoms. Changed course to due west, remaining on the same latitude. Bespoke a Brenn Isle herrin yawl and purchased three hundredweight of fish. Hands employed about the ship. Brother Ortelius preached a sermon in the afternoon watch and afterward the soldiers had small-arms practice. First Mate Billerand ran out the guns in the last dog-watch and called all hands for gunnery practice. Gunner reported to me that number two larboard gun is honeycombed.

Hawkwood laid down his quill and stretched his arms behind him until the muscles cracked. If he looked up he could see out of the stern windows to where the wake of the ship was faintly phosphorescent in the dimming light of the evening. There was very little swell; they had been plagued by light winds since leaving Hebrion and had not made good time, but he was pleased with the performance of the crew and of the ship herself. Though inclined to be sluggish with the extra cargo on board, the *Osprey* could still eat the wind out of any other carrack of her tonnage. Hawkwood was convinced it was because of her peculiar design, which he had supervised himself. Her fore- and sterncastles were lower than in other ships of her class, which meant they took less of the wind, and they were structures built as an integral part of the main hull, not tacked on afterwards. There were drawbacks, of course. There was less space on board, and she might be more vulnerable to boarding; but his crews knew their gunnery. The ship's culverins would riddle any enemy vessel long before she drew close enough to board.

The *Grace* was a different matter. Haukal had had to take in canvas to avoid outpacing the carrack entirely, though Hawkwood knew he chafed at the slow progress and longed to break out his whole store of lateen sails and plough ahead. At this moment the caravel was under main course alone, bobbing along some four cables to starboard. This beam wind suited her admirably, though she had yards enough down in her hold to transform her into a square-rigged ship should the wind veer round and come from right aft.

Little chance of that. They would be sailing close to the wind in more ways than one for nearly all of this voyage, if the word of long-dead Tyrenius Cobrian was to be believed.

Well, they had hit upon North Cape, as pretty a sighting as could be wished for. All Hawkwood had to do in theory was steer due west until he bumped into the Western Continent. It sounded simple, but there were the winds to take into account, ocean currents, storms or doldrums. He and Haukal both took sightings of the North Star every night with their cross-staffs and compared notes afterwards, but Hawkwood still felt that the ships were sailing in the dark. True, he had the baldly summarized sailing instructions that Murad had copied out of the old rutter for him, but he needed more. He needed to read the account of the *Cartigellan Faulcon's* crossing. He admitted to himself that he needed reassurance, the account of another seaman's accomplishment of what he was attempting to do. He also knew that Murad was concealing something, something to do with the fate of the earlier voyage. The knowledge maddened him.

He stood up from his desk, long accustomed to the slight roll and pitch of the ship, and extinguished the single candle which lit his cabin. Fire was one of the most dreaded accidents aboard ship, and the use of naked flame was carefully regulated. Only in the galley was any cooking permitted, and only on the forecastle could the soldiers and sailors smoke their pipes. There were sea lanterns hanging in serried rows in the crowded filth of the gundeck for the passengers' comfort, but these were the responsibility of the master-at-arms and his mates. The kegs which contained the powder both for the ship's guns and the soldiers' arquebuses were stored below the waterline in a tinlined room so that the rats might not gnaw at them, and no naked light was permitted in there. A tiny pane of double glass allowed the powder store to be illuminated from outside, and only the gunner had access to the interior.

And what a hullabaloo that had caused! Soldiers! They had moaned and bitched about not being able to get at their ammunition quickly enough, about not being able to smoke their pipes in the comfort of their hammocks, about not being able to prepare their own food in their own messes as they were used to. And Murad had not helped. He had insisted that his food and that of his officers be prepared separately from the men's and served at a different time, doubling the workload of the ship's cook. And the delicacies he had laid in by way of private stores! There were fully two tons of foodstuff in the hold that were for the exclusive consumption of Murad and his two officers. It beggared belief. And those damn horses! One was dead already, having gone mad in its cramped stall and thrashed about until it had broken its leg. That aristocratic young ensign, Sequero, had almost been in tears as he had cut its throat. The sailors had jointed the animal and salted down the meat despite the protestations of the soldiers. The cooper had barrelled it and placed it in the hold. Those same soldiers might be glad of it ere they saw land again.

Hawkwood made his unlit way out of his cabin, stepping over the storm sill with the grace of habit and exiting the companionway to enter the fresh air of the evening. He ran up the ladder to the quarterdeck where Velasca, the second mate, had the watch. The hourglass ran out, the ship's boy turned it, then stepped forward to the break of the deck and rang the ship's bell twice. Two bells in the last dog-watch, or the seventh hour after the zenith to a landsman.

"All quiet, Velasca?"

"Aye, sir. There are a few souls puking over the larboard rail, but most of 'em are below preparing for dinner."

Hawkwood nodded. Even in the failing light he could make out the wisps of smoke from the galley chimney drifting off to leeward.

Velasca cleared his throat. "I've had a deputation from the soldiers come to see me this watch, sir."

"Another one? What did they want this time?"

"They don't like the idea of a priest berthing in the forecastle with the common sailors, sir. They think he should be aft with the officers."

"There's no room aft, unless he cares to sling his hammock in my chartroom. No, we didn't ask for a Raven on board so he must make the best of it. Trust an Inceptine to put the common soldiers up to intercede for him."

"Oh, they say he hasn't said a word, sir. He seems to be a kindly enough sort of fellow for one of his order. They took it upon themselves to ask."

"Well they can take it upon themselves to keep their mouths shut, or go through their own officers. The running of the ship is difficult enough as it is without playing runaround with the assigned quarters."

"Yes, sir."

"How's the wind?"

"Light as a baby's fart, sir. Still nor'-nor'-west, though it's showing signs of backing to nor'-west."

"I hope not. We're close-hauled enough as it is. I'll take the watch now if you like, Velasca. I'm as restless as a springtime bear. Get yourself below and grab some food."

"Aye, sir, thanks. Shall I have the cook send something up?"

"No, I'll survive."

Velasca left the deck, Hawkwood having relieved him an hour early.

The carrack sailed on as the first stars came out to brighten the sky. There would be a moon later on; it was near the full, but the wind was fitful and wayward. The *Osprey* was under courses and topsails, the courses bonneted, but Hawkwood guessed she was making less than three knots. A peaceful eve-

ning, though. He could hear the growing hubbub from below-
decks as the passengers assembled for the evening meal, and
light poured out in shafts from the gunports. They kept them
open most of the time these nights, for ventilation.

He heard the clink of glass and laughter from the officers'
cabins below his feet: Murad entertaining again. The scar-
faced nobleman had even invited Ortelius, the last-minute Inceptine, to dinner a few times. Primarily, Hawkwood thought,
to interrogate him as to his reasons for joining the ship. Someone high up in the Inceptines of Abrusio had ordered him to,
that was clear, but so far Ortelius had deflected all Murad's
enquiries.

He was being watched. Turning, Hawkwood caught Mateo,
the ship's boy, staring at him. He frowned and Mateo looked
away hurriedly. The boy's voice was breaking; soon he would
be a man. He no longer held any temptation for Hawkwood,
not with the sneering Murad and an Inceptine on board. No
doubt the lad was hurt by Hawkwood's curt treatment of him,
but he would get over it.

Unwillingly Hawkwood found himself thinking of Jemilla,
her white skin and raven-dark hair, her wildcat passions. She
was a king's plaything now, not for the likes of himself any
more. He wondered if King Abeleyn of Hebrion had scratches
on his back under his regal robes. The world was a strange
place sometimes.

He paced his way to the weather rail, and stood there gazing
out on the even swell of the quiet sea whilst the breeze fanned
his face and pushed at the towering canvas above his head.

"YOU'RE not waiting on the high table tonight, then?" Bardolin asked as Griella joined him at the swaying, rope-
suspended table.

The girl sat on the sea chest next to him. Her colour was
up, and her coppery hair clung to her forehead in wires and
tails.

"No. Mara said she would do it for me. I can't stick the
thought of it tonight."

Bardolin said nothing. Around them the hubbub of the gundeck was like a curtain of noise. In between the dull gleam of
the long guns, hanging tables had been let down from the
ceiling (what was the nautical term, deckhead?) and around

each of these a motley crowd of figures jostled and elbowed for space. Each table seated six, and one person from each took it in turns to bring the food for the table down the length of the deck from the steaming galley.

This was the first night Bardolin had seen it as full as this; most of the passengers seemed to be getting over their seasickness, especially as the weather was mild and the ship's movement not too severe. They were an odd mix. He could see men in fine robes, some of whom he recognized as figures at the Hebrian court, and ladies in brocade and linen—even here clinging to their past status—but the majority looked like well-to-do merchants or small artisans with nothing remarkable about them. There had as yet been no manifestation of power, and he did not know if there might be a weather-worker on board to speed the passage of the ships. Probably the presence of the Inceptine had put the captain off from enquiring.

Neither did he know if there was another full-blooded mage on board, for he had as yet seen no other familiars in evidence and his own imp was asleep in the bosom of his robe. He and Golophin were not, of course, the only mages in Abrusio; Bardolin was personally acquainted with another half-dozen. But he saw none that he knew here, and wondered if Golophin had had other plans for them.

The air was heavy and thick, hanging around the brutal great guns and the laden tables. Bardolin could smell the aroma of the cooking pork, heavy with grease and salt, and around that the sweat of close-packed humanity. Underlying these was a faint stink of vomit and ordure. Not all the passengers possessed the necessary spirit to crouch out on the beakhead of the ship and perform their necessary functions there, with the warm sea lapping at their arse. And there had been those who had surrendered to seasickness a mite more violently than they had expected. The deck would have to be washed out, or *swabbed down*, but that was the sailors' job.

Oh, such a rich web woven by unknown forces! They were not a ship sailing serenely across a placid ocean, they were a fly caught quivering in a vast spider's web. And that nobleman, Murad, he was one of the spinners of the web, along with Golophin and the King of Hebrion.

But not Hawkwood, the captain. He and Murad loathed each other, that was plain. Bardolin got the impression that their good captain was about as enthusiastic for the voyage as the majority of his passengers were. He must know their destination; it might be worth talking to him, or to Billerand.

"HE has invited that Raven to his table yet again," Griella was saying between gulped mouthfuls of the tough pork and hard biscuit.

"Who, Murad?" Bardolin marshalled his thoughts hurriedly. Griella had a light in her eye that he did not like. He had already cursed himself a score of times for bringing her with him on this voyage. And yet—and yet . . .

"Yes. He means to ply him with brandy once more and find out who ordered him to take ship with us. But Ortelius is as slippery as an eel. He smiles and smiles and says nothing of import, just mouths saintly platitudes that no one can disagree with. There is something about him I truly do not like."

"Naturally enough. He's an Inceptine, child. There is nothing strange about your dislike of him."

"No, it is something more. I feel I know him, but I cannot think how."

Bardolin sighed. He was no longer hungry. His stomach had been used to such rough fare in his youth; it had grown dainty with age. And this was the good stuff. Later in the voyage their meat would be wormy and their bread full of weevils, while the water would be as thick as soup. He had endured it once before, on a Hebrian troop transport. He was not looking forward to undergoing such a diet again.

I've become soft, he thought.

"Don't worry about the damned Inceptine, girl," he said. "He cannot touch you here, unless he means to take on all the passengers of the ship by himself."

But Griella was not listening. Her fingers had curled into claws around her meat knife.

"Murad will ask for me again tonight, Bardolin. I cannot put him off much longer without—without something happening."

She was staring into her wooden platter as though its contents were the stuff of an augury. Bardolin leaned close to her.

"I beg you, Griella, commit no violence aboard this ship. Do not. Do not let your emotions overcome your reason, and do not lift a finger against him. He is a nobleman. He would be within his rights to slay you out of hand."

Griella grinned without humour. Her teeth were strong and very white, the lips almost purple against them.

"He might find that difficult."

"You might kill him." Bardolin's voice had dropped. It was almost inaudible in the clatter about them. "But even with the change upon you, you would find it hard to kill all the soldiers on this ship, and the sailors, and the passengers who would stand against you. And once your nature is revealed, Griella, you are lost, so for the Saint's sake rein in your temper, no matter what happens."

She kissed him on the mouth without warning, so hard that he felt the imprint of the teeth behind her lips. He felt his face flush with blood and the immediate stir of warmth in his groin. The imp moved restlessly in the breast of his robe.

"Why did you do that?" he asked her when she drew back. He was uncomfortably aware of the erection throbbing in his breeches.

"Because you wanted me to. You have wanted me to this long time, even if you did not know it."

He could not answer her.

"It's all right, Bardolin. I don't mind. I love you, you see. You are like a father and a brother and a friend to me."

She stroked the stubble of his ruddy cheek.

"You are right, though. Everyone knows you are my guardian. Were I to refuse him, I might be damning you along with myself and I would never do that." She smiled as sunnily as a child. Only her eyes mocked the image. He could see the beast in them, forever biding its time.

Bardolin took her hand, heedless of the stares they were attracting from their neighbours at the table.

"Hold fast, Griella, no matter what happens. Hold fast to that part of yourself that is not the animal; then you can beat it down; you can defeat it."

She blinked. "Why would I want to do that?" Then she flashed a feral grin at him and rose, her hand slipping out from under his. "I must go. Mara expects me to help her clear up. Dear Bardolin, don't look so worried! I know what I have to do—for your sake as well as mine."

Bardolin watched her slim, straight back as it moved down

the gundeck and was finally lost in the crowd. His face was
profoundly troubled, and the imp was trembling like a leaf
against the slick sweat on his chest.

"MORE brandy for the good cleric there, girl. Don't be
shy with the stuff!"

Murad was smiling, his scar a wriggling pink furrow down
one side of his face. When the girl Mara bent to pour the
brandy he slid a hand under her robe, up the satin-smooth back
of her leg. She twitched like a horse with a fly settling on it,
but did not move away. He tweaked the soft flesh where the
buttock swelled out at the top of her thigh. Then she straightened as if nothing were amiss and moved away. Di Souza was
red in the face with glee, but Sequero looked merely disdain-
ful. Murad smiled at him and raised his glass so the aristocratic
young man had to follow suit.

The four of them were seated around a table which ran fore
and aft along the line of the keel. At Murad's back were the
stern windows which he shared with the captain's cabin on
the other side of the thin bulkhead. The eastern sky was black,
but there was a glimmer from the ship's wake as if foamed
and churned behind them. They could see the level of wine in
the decanters arrayed about the table tilt slightly with the carrack's roll, but it was so slight as to be hardly noticeable.

Sequero was still out of sorts at the death of one of his
beloved broodmares. A good thing they had shipped two more
than originally planned. He was not a natural shipboard companion, was Ensign Hernan Sequero. He hated the cheek-by-
jowl promiscuity, the awkward hammocks, the continual
stench, and especially the stubborn independence of the mariners, who looked to their own officers alone and obeyed the
order of no soldier. It was an inversion of the natural order of
things. His plight had provided Murad with endless private
amusement in the week they had been at sea.

Di Souza, on the other hand, seemed to relish the entire
experience. His prowess with an arquebus had won him the
respect of soldiers and sailors alike, and his low birth seemed
to have inured him to the indignities of life aboard ship. He
could laugh when shitting from the ship's head, whilst Murad
suspected that Sequero performed his own functions in the
depths of the hold rather than let his men see their officer

hanging barearsed over the sea. Murad himself had a pot, emptied daily by one of his two cabin servants.

He studied the amber depths of his brandy in the light of the table lanterns. Fimbrian, casked in the time of his great-grandfather. And here he was wasting it on a low-born buffoon, a cleric and a tight-arsed minor noble. Well, it oiled the tongues. It let the evening slip along pleasantly enough. But it did not help loosen the lips of the damned Raven, Ortelius.

The girl, Mara, retrieved the dinner dishes and the silver cutlery that glittered the length of the table. They had dined on potted meat, freshly killed chicken, fish caught that morning and fruit from the orchards of Galiapeno. Now they sipped their brandy, cracked walnuts and popped black olives into their mouths. There was little conversation. The two junior officers did not like to speak without being spoken to first whilst at their superior officer's table, and the Inceptine seemed to value silence as much as his own discretion.

Murad would have to invite Hawkwood to dinner one night along with the Raven, and then watch the sparks fly. By the looks of things there would be little else in the way of amusement this voyage, and he would have to be inventive if he were not to expire of boredom before they made landfall in the west.

He caught the girl looking at him and stared back blandly until her eyes darted away. She had a pleasant peasant-brown face surrounded by a mass of dark curls, and her body was stocky and strong but not overly exciting. She had shared his hanging cot ever since leaving Abrusio, but she was not the one he was truly hungering for. That short-haired, snapping-eyed wench named Griella; she was the one he wanted. It would be diverting to break her in, and he was curious to see what kind of shape hid under those boyish clothes she wore. She hated him too, which was even better. Where was she tonight? Her absence irritated him, which was one of the reasons for the fear in the other girl's eyes.

"A capital brandy," Ortelius said in the silence. "You keep a good cellar even while afloat, Lord Murad."

Murad inclined his head. "There are certain luxuries which are not in fact luxuries, but more . . . accessories of rank. We may not need them, but they serve to remind us of who we are."

Ortelius nodded gravely. "Just so long as we do not find we cannot do without them."

"You have precious few luxuries with you on this voyage, I fear," Murad said sympathetically, though inwardly he was seething at the cleric's implication.

"Yes. I came aboard in some haste, I am afraid. But it is no matter. I may not have the austere habits of a Friar Mendicant, but it will do me no harm to forgo some of the prerequisites of my rank for a time. Such things bring us closer to God." He tossed back the last of his brandy.

"Of course, admirable," Murad said absently. He was searching for an opening, a chink in the Inceptine's bland manner. He saw Sequero and di Souza exchange glances; they knew the nightly game had started again.

"Well, we are in your spiritual charge, Father Ortelius. I am sure I speak for all the soldiers and mariners and common folk aboard when I say we shall rest easier knowing that you are here to shrive us of our sins and to watch over our moral welfare. But tell me: what do you think of the worthy crews who maintain these ships, or indeed of the passengers with whom you have taken ship?"

Ortelius looked at him, his normally urbane countenance twisting with what seemed like a spot of wariness.

"I'm not sure I follow you, my son."

"Oh come now, Father! Surely you must have noticed that half of Hawkwood's crew have faces as black as apes. They are heathens—Merduks!"

"Are you sure, my son?" Ortelius had stopped playing with his empty glass and was watching Murad closely, like a fencer waiting for the change of balance that heralded a thrust.

"Why, yes! Some of them are black worshippers of the evil prophet Ahrimuz."

"Then I must do my humble best to show them the true and righteous path to the Company of the Saints," Ortelius said sweetly.

But Murad went on as if the priest had not spoken.

"And the passengers, Father. Do you know who they are? I'll tell you. They are the dregs of our society. They are sorcerers, herbalists, oldwives and even, God save us, mages. Didn't you know?"

"I—I may have heard something to that effect."

"Indeed, the very type of folk that the Inceptines have so industriously been ridding Abrusio of for these past weeks. Yet now you take ship with them, you sleep in their midst, and you administer to their so-called spiritual needs. Forgive me for saying so, Father, but I find it difficult to comprehend why a man like you should have taken it upon himself to associate with such fellow travellers. We know the vocation of the Friars Mendicant is to proselytize and convert, to spread the news of the Visions of the First Saint, but surely the Inceptines are rather loftier in the Church's hierarchy."

Murad let the unspoken question hang in the air.

"We go where we are sent, Lord Murad. We are all servants, we wearers of the black robe."

"Ah, so you were *sent* to join us?"

"No. I have used that word clumsily. You must excuse me."

"Either you were sent or you were not, Father. Do have some more brandy, by the way."

Murad poured the cleric more of the Fimbrian whilst his two ensigns looked on like spectators at a gladiatorial contest. Sequero seemed amused and fascinated, but Murad was surprised to see a look of downright terror on di Souza's face.

"Are you all right, Valdan?" he asked at once. "A touch of seasickness, perhaps?"

The straw-haired officer shook his head. He was like a man going to the gallows.

"As I was saying," Murad said smoothly, turning to the cleric, "either you were *sent*, Father, or you came of your own accord. Or someone asked you to join our company."

Here he stared back at di Souza, reading the young man's suffused face and letting his last sentence hang in the air.

"I asked him to come!" di Souza blurted out. "It was me, sir—my idea alone. The soldiers wanted a chaplain. I asked Father Ortelius. I thought I did right, sir, upon mine honour!"

Murad glanced around the table. Ortelius was delicately wiping his lips with a napkin, eyes cast down and countenance serene once again. Sequero's face was wooden, as if he feared to be associated with di Souza's guilt by his proximity to his brother officer.

Murad laughed. "Well, why did you not say so?" He stood up. "I am sorry to have tried your patience thus these last few days, Father. Please forgive me." And he bent to kiss the priest's knuckle.

Ortelius beamed. "That is quite all right, my son."

"And with this revelation I am afraid I must end our delightful evening, gentlemen. I would like to retire. Good night, Father. I hope you have a pleasant sleep. Sequero, good evening. You will see Father Ortelius to his hammock, I am sure. Ensign di Souza, stay behind a moment, if you please."

When the other two had left di Souza sat stiffly in his chair with his hands in his lap.

"Talk to me, Ensign," Murad said softly.

The younger man's slab-like face was shining with sweat. His skin was red with wine and heat, contrasting vividly with his yellow hair.

"The men did not like the idea of sailing without a chaplain, as I said once before to you sir, I think."

"Did Mensurado put you up to this?" Murad interrupted.

"No, sir! It was my idea alone." Had di Souza placed the blame on his sergeant, Mensurado, Murad would have been forced to have the man strappadoed, or perhaps shot. And Mensurado was the most experienced soldier on the ship.

"How well do you know this Ortelius?"

Di Souza's eyes flickered up and met Murad's steady glare for a second. He seemed to shrink in his chair.

"Not well, sir. I know he was once on the staff of the Prelate of Hebrion, and is well thought of in the order."

"And why should such a distinguished cleric take ship with an expedition into the unknown and with such travelling companions, eh?"

Di Souza shrugged helplessly. "He is a priest. It is his job. When he shrove me before we took ship he seemed to know about the voyage. He asked if I was at ease at the thought of undertaking it with no spiritual guide. I was not, sir—I tell the truth. He volunteered to come, but I thought he was only trying to comfort my wretched soul. I did not think he truly meant what he said."

"You have a lot to learn, Valdan," Murad said. "Ortelius is a spy in the pay of Himerius the Prelate of Hebrion. He has come along to see what the King is up to, commissioning this expedition, and with such passengers. But no matter. I know him now for what he is, and can deal with him accordingly."

"Sir! You're not going to—"

"Shut up, Valdan. You are a stupid young fool. I could have you stripped of rank and put in irons for the rest of the voyage for what you have taken upon yourself to do. But I need you. I will tell you one thing you had best remember, though."

Murad leaned close until he could smell the brandy on his subordinate's breath.

"Your loyalty will be to *me*, and no one else. Not to the Church, not to a priest, not to your own mother. You will look to me for everything. If you do not your career is over, and mayhap your life as well. Do I make myself clear?"

"Yes," di Souza croaked.

Murad smiled. "I am glad you understand. You are dismissed."

The ensign got up out of his chair like an arthritic man, saluted and then bolted out of the door. Murad sat down in his own chair and propped his feet on the table. He turned his head to stare out aft at the ship's wake. No sign of land. The Hebrionese were already out of sight, which meant they were at last truly in the Great Western Ocean.

And no one can touch us, Murad thought. Not kings, not priests, not the machinations of government. Until one of these ships returns, we are alone and no one can find us.

He remembered the log of Tyrenius Cobrian, the dark story of slaughter and madness that it told, and felt a chill of unease.

"Wine!" he called loudly.

When he turned back from his contemplation of the stern windows he found that the wine was already on the table, glowing as red as blood in its decanter with one remaining table lantern burning behind it.

The girl, Griella. She stood in the shadows. He knew her by the absurd breeches she wore, the bob of hair. And the peculiar shine of her eyes which always reminded him of a beast's seen by torchlight.

Murad was momentarily startled by her silent presence; he had not heard a sound. He poured himself some of the luminous wine.

"Come into the light, girl. I won't bite you."

She moved forward, and her eyes became human again. She regarded him with a detached interest that never failed to infuriate him. He had to bed her, impress his presence and superiority upon her. Her skin had a kind of light about it, emphasized by the lantern. In the neck of her shirt he could see the swell of one slight breast, that curve of light and shadow.

"Take off my boots," he said brusquely.

She did as she was bidden, kneeling before him and slipping the long sea boots off his legs with a strength that surprised him. He could see down the neck of her shirt. He sipped wine steadily.

"You will share my bed tonight," he said.

She stared at him.

"There will be no excuses. The blood will have stopped by now, and if it has not I care not. Stand up."

She did so.

"Why do you not speak? Have you nothing to say? A few nights ago you were as livid as a cat. Have you reconciled yourself to your newfound station? Speak to me!"

Griella watched him, a small smile turning up one corner of her mouth.

"You are a noble," she said. "On this ship your word is the law. I have no choice."

"That's right," he sneered. "Has your ageing guardian been talking some sense into your pretty little head, then?"

"Yes, he has."

"A wise man, obviously." Why did he feel that she was getting the better of him, that she was secretly laughing at him? He wanted to kiss that smile off her ripe young mouth, bruise it away with his teeth.

"Remove your clothes," he said. He drank more wine. His heartbeat was beginning to become an audible thing, hammering in his temples.

She slipped her shirt off over her head, then unfastened her belt and let her breeches slip to the deck. As she stood before him naked he distinctly heard the ship's bell being struck eight times. Eight bells in the first watch. Midnight. It was like a warning.

Murad stood up, towering over her. She was golden in the lantern light before his shadow covered her. He brushed her nipples and heard the breath sucked down her throat. He grinned, happy at having punctured her weird composure. Then he bent his head and crushed his mouth on hers.

• • •

AFTERWARDS, he remembered how slight she had seemed in his arms, how slim and hard and alive. She was taut with muscle, every nerve jumping on the surface of her skin.

She had been virgin, too, but had not cried out as he entered her, merely flinching for a second. He remembered the hot, liquid sensation, the way he pressed her down into the blankets and bit at her neck and shoulder, her breasts. She had lain quiet under him until something kindled her. Unwillingly she had moved and begun to make small sounds. Then the coupling had transformed into a battle, a fight for mastery. Joined together, their bodies had struggled against one another until her scream had rung out and she had scissored her legs about him and wept furiously in the darkness. They had slept after that, spent, their bodies glued together by sweat and the fluid of their exertions. It had been strangely peaceful, like the truce after two armies had battled each other into exhaustion.

He had woken in the dark hour before the dawn—or thought he had. He could not breathe. He was suffocating in a baking, furnace heat and his lungs were being constricted by a crippling weight. Something huge and heavy was lying atop him, pinioning his limbs. He had opened his eyes, feeling hot breath on his face, and had seen two yellow lights regarding him from six inches away. The cold gleam of teeth. A vague impression of two horn-like ears arcing up from a broad, black-furred skull. And the paralysing heat and weight of it on his body.

He had passed out, or the dream had faded. He woke later, after sunrise, with a scream on his lips—but found himself alone in the gently swaying cot, sunlight streaming in the stern windows, a patch of blood on the blankets. He drew in shuddering breaths. A dream or nightmare, nothing more. It could be nothing more.

He swung off the cot on to rubber legs. The ship was rolling more heavily, the bow rising and falling. He could see white-topped waves breaking in the swell beyond the windows.

It took the last pint in the wine decanter to quell the trembling in his hands, to wipe out the horror of the dream. When it had faded all he could remember was the taut joy of her under him, the unwilling surrender. Strangely, he did not feel triumphant at the memory, but quickened, somehow invigorated.

By the time he had broken his fast, he had forgotten the vision of the night entirely. Too much brandy and wine, perhaps. All he could think of was the slim girl and her bright eyes, the taut joy of her under him.

He hungered for more.

SIXTEEN

THE Merduk army was on the move.

It had taken time; far too much time, Shahr Baraz thought. Aekir had damaged them more than they had cared to admit at the time, but now many of their losses had been made good. Fresh troops had been sent through the Thurian passes before the snows closed them for the winter, and Maghreb, Sultan of Danrimir, had sent fifty elephants and eight thousand of his personal guard to join the taking of Ormann Dyke. It was a gesture as much as anything else, with the inevitable political ramifications behind it. The other sultans had sat up quickly when Aekir had fallen, and soon the scramble for the spoils would begin. Shahr Baraz had heard camp rumours that ancient Nalbeni, not to be outdone by its northern rival, had commissioned a fleet of troop transports to cross the Kardian Sea and fall on the southern coastal cities of Torunna. That snippet made him smile. With luck, it had already reached the ears of the Torunnan king and might make him detach troops from the north.

Shahr Baraz had no illusions as to the difficulty of the task before him. He had maps of the fortress complex, made by the troopers of the countless armed reconnaissances he had sent west. The Fimbrians had first built the dyke, and as with every-

thing they constructed it had been built to last. His distant
ancestors had attacked it once, way back in the mists of tribal
memory when it had marked the boundary of the Fimbrian
Empire. They had died in their screaming thousands, it was
said, and their bodies had filled to the brim the dyke itself.

But that was then. This was now. One of the reasons the
Merduk advance had been so slow to recommence after the
fall of Aekir was because he had had his engineers at work
day and night. The results of their labour had been dismantled
and loaded on to gargantuan waggons, each pulled by four
elephants. Now he had everything he needed: siege-towers,
catapults, ballistae. And boats. Many boats.

He sat on his horse on a low muddy hill with a gaggle of
staff officers about him and his bodyguard in silent ranks on
the slope below. He watched his army trudging past.

Outriders on the flanks, squadrons of light cavalry armed
with lances and wearing only leather *cuir boulli*, something
they had picked up from the Ramusians. Then the main vanguard, a picked force of the *Hraibadar*, the shock-troops who
specialized in assaults, breachings and, if necessary, last
stands. Their ranks were thinner than they had been—so many
had fallen at Aekir that he was pressed to field more than ten
regiments of them, scarcely twelve thousand men.

Trundling through their ranks were the dotted bulk of elephants. Only a score of them travelled with the van, and each
pulled a train of light waggons loaded with provisions. The
vanguard was Shahr Baraz's most mobile force, and his most
hard-hitting. It would spearhead the final assault, once he had
softened the dyke up a little.

At the rear of the van, a brigade of heavy cavalry, what the
Ramusians called *cuirassiers*. They were known as *Ferinai* to
his own people, who had specialized in their use for generations. They wore chainmail reinforced with glittering plates of
steel, and their faces were covered by tall helms. In addition
to their swords they each carried a pair of matchlock pistols,
a recent innovation that the *Ferinai* had accepted only with
much grumbling. These were the best troops that Shahr Baraz
possessed; his own bodyguard had been picked mainly from
their ranks. They were professional soldiers, unlike the majority of the army, and their general was as niggardly with them
as a miser with his gold.

The van passed by, almost twenty thousand strong, and as Shahr Baraz calmed his restless horse, the main body came up. Here the discipline was not so rigid. Men waved and cheered at him as they marched past and he nodded curtly in reply. These were the *Minhraib*, the common footsoldiers who when not at war were small farmers, tradesmen, peasants or laborers. A hundred thousand strong, they marched in a column whose head was fifty men wide, and it extended for over three and a half miles. It would take an hour and a half at least for them to pass by their general in their entirety. The sight of them made Shahr Baraz stiffen, and he raised his old eyes to heaven in a moment's prayer, thanking his God and his Prophet that he had been given the chance to see this, to command this: the largest army ever fielded by an eastern sultanate. Its like had not been seen on the continent since the terrible wars of the Ramusians, when they had fought among themselves to bring down the Fimbrian Hegemony.

He would not wait to view the rearguard or the siege train; they were seven miles down the road. When the van went into camp that night, the rearguard would be ten miles behind them. Such was the logistical nightmare of moving an army this size across country.

Still, he had the Ostian river now. Already the first barges had come downstream from Ostrabar and the supplies were building up on the burnt wharves of Aekir's riverfront. Incredible, the amount of supplies an army of this size needed. The elephants alone required eighty tons of forage daily.

"Have you spoken to the chief of engineers about the road?" he asked an aide crisply.

The aide started in the saddle. The old man's eyes had seemed so vacant, so far away, that he had thought his general was in some sort of tired daze.

"Yes, Khedive. The materials are already on the road. Once the army is in position about the dyke, the work will go on apace. We have rounded up some thirty thousand head of labour from the countryside. The new road will, the engineer tells me, be finished in sixteen days. And it will bear the elephant waggons."

"Excellent," Shahr Baraz said, and stroked the silver-white moustache that fell past his chin in two tusk-like lengths. His black eyes glittered between their almond-shaped lids.

"Read me again that dispatch from Jaffan at the dyke."

The aide fumbled in a saddlebag and produced a piece of parchment. He squinted at it intently for a moment, making the old man's eyes narrow with humour. Officers had to learn to read and write before being seconded to his staff. For many it was an arcane chore that did not come naturally.

"He says," the aide reported haltingly, "that . . . that the refugees are all across the river and encamped about the fortress, but the—the bridges have not yet been cut. Ramusian forces are making sorties east of the river, harrying his troops. He wants more men." Finished, the aide blinked rapidly, relief on his face.

"He will have sixscore thousand of them in his lap soon enough," Shahr Baraz said casually, his eyes still fixed on the unending files of men and horses and waggons that were moving west. "I want another dispatch sent to Jaffan," he went on, ignoring the sudden rustle of paper and scratch of quill. "The usual greetings, et cetera.

"Your orders are changed. You are to cease the harrying of Ramusian forces east of the river and concentrate on reconnaissance of the enemy position. You will send squadrons to north and south of the dyke looking for fords or possible bridging points. The eastern bank will be reconnoitered for at least ten leagues on either side of the dyke. At the same time you will, using whatever means necessary, ascertain the strength of the fortress garrison and find out how many men have been detached for service further west. You will also confirm or deny the constant rumour I have been hearing that the head of the Ramusian Church did not die in Aekir but is alive and well in Ormann Dyke.

"May the Prophet Ahrimuz watch over you in your endeavours and the enlightenment of the true faith constantly illuminate your path. I and my forces will relieve you within a week. Shahr Baraz, High Khedive of the Armies of the Sultanate of Ostrabar. Et cetera . . . Did you get that, Ormun?"

The aide was scribbling frantically, using his broad pommel as a writing desk.

"Yes, Khedive."

"Good. Get it off to the dyke at once."

Ormun galloped away as soon as Shahr Baraz had inscribed

his flowing signature on the parchment with elaborate flourishes of the quill.

"An enthusiastic young man," he noted to Mughal, one of his senior officers.

The other man nodded, the horsehair plume atop his helm bobbing as he did. "You are a legend of sorts to them, the young men."

"Surely not."

"But yes, old friend. They call you *'the terrible old man,'* even at court."

Shahr Baraz allowed himself one of his rare grins. "Am I so terrible?"

"Only to your enemies."

"I have seen eighty-three winters upon the face of the world, Mughal. This will be my last campaign. If I am spared, I will make a pilgrimage to the land of my fathers and see the open steppes of Kambaksk one last time ere I die."

"The Khedive of Ostrabar, mightiest warleader the east has ever seen, in a felt hut eating yoghurt. Those days are done, Ibim Baraz." Mughal used the general's personal name as he was entitled to, being a close friend.

"Yes, they are done. And the old *Hraib*, the warrior's code of conduct, is gone too. Who out of this current generation remembers it? A different code rules our lives: the code of expediency. I believe that if I conclude this campaign successfully and do not step down, I may be forced to."

"Who by? Who would do—?"

"Our Sultan, of course, may the Prophet watch over him. He thinks me too soft on the Ramusians."

"He should have been at Aekir," Mughal said grimly.

"Yes, but he thinks I let the refugees escape out of chivalry, some outmoded sense of the *Hraib's* rules of conduct. Which I did. But there were sound tactical reasons also."

"I know that. Any soldier with sense can see it," Mughal said.

"Yes, but he is not a true soldier—he never has been, at heart. He is a ruler, a far more subtle thing. And he resents my popularity with the army. It might be best for me were I to quietly disappear once Ormann Dyke falls. I have no wish to taste poison in my bread, or be knifed in my sleep."

Mughal shook his head wonderingly. "The world is a strange place, Khedive."

"Only as strange as the hearts of men make it," Shahr Baraz retorted. "I am constantly harried by orders from Orkhan. I must advance, advance, advance. I am allowed no time to consolidate. I must assault the dyke at once. I do not like being hurried, Mughal."

"The Sultan is impatient. Since you gave him Aekir he thinks you can work miracles."

"Perhaps, but I do not appreciate meddling. I am to launch an assault on the dyke as soon as sufficient troops have come up. I am not allowed to probe the Torunnan flanks because of the time it will waste. I am to throw my men at this fortress as though they were the waves of the sea assaulting a rock."

Mughal frowned. "Do you have doubts about this campaign, Khedive?"

"I am not my own man since Aekir, my friend. Aurungzeb, may the sun shine on him, has appointed *commissioners* to oversee my movements. And to make sure I take my Sultan's tactical advice. If I do not attack and take the dyke speedily enough to suit them I have a feeling there will be another general commanding this army."

"I cannot believe that."

"That is because you—and I—are not creatures of the court, Mughal. I have taken Aekir, accomplished the impossible. Everything that follows is easy. So thinks Aurungzeb."

"But not you."

"Not I. I believe this dyke may give us more trouble even than Aekir, but my opinion does not count for much in Orkhan these days. The would-be generals are already lining up at court to fill my shoes."

"The dyke will fall," Mughal said, "and in no time. It cannot resist this army—nothing can. Their John Mogen is dead, and they have no general alive of his calibre, not even this Martellus."

"I hope you are right. Perhaps I am getting too old; perhaps Aurungzeb is right. I see things with an old man's caution, not the optimism of youth."

"Ask the troops if they would prefer the optimism or the caution. They pay for our mistakes with their blood. Sometimes even sultans forget that."

"Hush, my friend, it is not good to say such things where there are ears to hear. Come, let us ride to the camp. My tents have been set up and there is good wine waiting. A glass or two may sweeten our outlook."

The banner-bright knot of officers and mounted bodyguards took off towards the west, scattering clods of mud from the hooves of their horses. And all the while, the Merduk host continued its march upon the face of the land like a huge, integral beast crawling infinitesimally across the earth, as unstoppable as the approach of night.

HERIA was in his dreams again, and her screams brought him bolt upright in the narrow bunk, as they always did. Corfe pressed his hands against his eyes until the lights spangled in the darkness there and the vision was gone. She was dead. She was beyond that. It was not happening.

He looked up at the narrow windows high above his head. A faint light was turning the black sky into velvet blue. It would be dawn soon. No point in lying back and trying to burrow down into sleep again. Another day had begun.

He pulled on his boots, yawning. Around him other sleepers snored and tossed and grumbled on their rickety beds. He was in one of the great warehouses which surrounded the citadel in the southern end of Ormann Dyke, but many of the warehouses, built to house the provisions of the garrison, were empty and had been turned into dormitories so that the least hardy of the refugees might sleep out of the rain.

But he was a refugee no longer. He wore the old blood and bruises again, an ensign's sash under his belt and a set of heavy half-armour under his bed. He had been attached to Pieter Martellus' staff as a kind of adviser. That was promotion of a sort, and the thought made his mouth twist into a bitter smile.

He hauled on the armour and made his clinking way out to one of the battlements to sniff the air and see what the day had in store.

Dawn. The sun was rising steadily into an unsullied sky. If he turned his back to the light in the east he could almost make out the white line on the horizon that was the Cimbric Range, eighty leagues to the south-west. Beyond the Cimbrics was Perigraine, beyond Perigraine the Malvennor Mountains, beyond them Fimbria and finally the Hebrian Sea. Normannia, the Land of the Faith as the clerics had sometimes called it. It did not seem so large when one thought of it like that, when a man might fancy he saw clear across the Kingdom of Torunna at a glance one morning in the early dawn.

He brought his gaze closer to home, staring down on the sun-kindled length of the Searil river and the sprawling expanse of the fortress that ran alongside it. Miles of wall and dyke and stockade and artillery-proof revetments. The walls zigzagged so that the gunners might criss-cross the approaches with converging fire were any enemy to cross the Searil and assault the dyke itself. They looked strange, unnatural in the growing light of the morning, and the sharp-angled towers that broke their length every three hundred yards seemed like monuments to the fallen from some lost, titanic battle.

To the east, across the Searil, the eastern barbican lay on the land like a dark star. Its walls were flung out in sharp points and within them the fires of the Aekirian refugees were beginning to flicker and stipple the shadows there. Behind it the bridge barbican, a collection of walls and towers less strong and high, guarded the approach to the main bridge, and on the other side of the Searil was the island, so-called because it was surrounded by the river on the east and the dyke to the west. Another miniature fortress rose there, connecting the Searil bridge with the main crossing of the dyke. There were two other, smaller bridges of rickety wood, easily demolished, which crossed the dyke to north and south of the main bridge. These were to aid the deployment of sorties or to let the defenders of the island retreat on a broad front were it to be overwhelmed.

To the west of the dyke was the fortress proper. The Long Walls stretched for a league between the crags and cliffs of the ridges that hemmed in the Searil north and south. The citadel on which Corfe stood was built on an out-thrust crag on one of those ridges. In it Martellus had his headquarters. A general standing here would have a view of the entire battlefield and could move his men like pieces on a gaming board, watching them march and countermarch under his feet.

Finally, further west, beyond the buildings and complexes of the fortress, the dark shadow of the main refugee camp covered the land, a mist rising from it like the body heat of a slumbering animal. Almost two hundred thousand people were encamped there, even though thousands had been leaving day by day to trek further west. Martellus had managed to round up a motley force of four thousand volunteers from among the younger men of the multitude, but they were untrained and dispirited. He would not place much reliance on them.

One man for every foot of wall to be defended, the military manuals said. Though one man would actually occupy a yard of wall, the second would act as a reserve and the third would be set aside for a possible sortie force. Martellus had not the numbers to afford those luxuries.

Three thousand men in the eastern barbican. Two thousand manning the island. Four thousand manning the Long Walls. One thousand in the citadel. Two thousand set aside for a possible sortie. The four thousand civilian volunteers were in readiness behind the western walls. They would be fed on to the battlements as soon as the assault began to eat defenders.

It was impossible. Ormann Dyke was widely recognized as the strongest fortress in the world, but it needed to be garrisoned adequately. What they had here was a skeleton, a caretaker force, no more. With a general like Shahr Baraz commanding the attackers, there could be little doubt about the outcome of the forthcoming battle.

But this time, Corfe thought to himself, I will not run away. I will go down with the dyke, doing my duty as I ought to have done at Aekir.

CORFE broke his fast in one of the refectories, a meagre meal of army biscuit, hard cheese and watered beer. There were no problems with the dyke's supply lines—the route to Torunn was still open—but Martellus was also having to feed the refugees as well as he could. It was, Corfe considered, the reason why so many of them remained in the environs of the fortress. Had he been in command he would have stopped doling out rations to them days ago and sent them packing, but then he no longer responded to the same impulses as he had before Aekir's fall. Martellus the Lion was a man of compassion, despite his hard exterior.

As well for me he is, Corfe thought. The other officers would as soon as hung me on the spot for desertion.

He joined his general on the Long Walls, where he was

standing amid a knot of staff officers and aides, all of them in
half-armour, all looking east to the Searil and the land beyond.

There was a table littered with maps and lists, stones weighing down the parchment against the breeze. It was a fine morning, and sunlight was gilding the old stone of the battlements
and casting long shadows from their far sides. It caught the
many puddles that were strewn about the land and lit them up
like coins.

"There," Martellus said, pointing out beyond the river.

Corfe stared. He could see a line of horsemen coming down
the slopes of one of the further hills, pennons snapping and
outriders out to flanks and rear. Perhaps two hundred of them.

"The insolent dog," one of the other officers said hotly.

"Yes. He is happy to ride around under our very noses. A
flamboyant character, this Merduk commander. But this is only
a scouting force. Light cavalry, you see? Not a glint of plate
or mail among them, and unarmoured horses. He is here to
take a look at us."

There was a hollow boom that startled the morning, a puff
of white smoke from the eastern barbican, and a moment later
the eruption of a fiery flower on the hillside below the
horsemen. They halted. Martellus was grinning like a cat sighting the mouse.

"That's young Andruw. He was always a restless dog."

"Shall we assemble a sortie and chase them away?" one of
the officers asked.

"Yes. I've no wish to make their intelligence-gathering easy.
Tell Ranafast to saddle up two squadrons, no more. And see
if he can take some prisoners. We need information as much
as they."

"I'll tell him," Corfe said at once, and before anyone could
respond he ran down from the battlements.

Ranafast was commander of the five hundred cavalry that
the garrison possessed. A quarter of an hour after Corfe
reached him they were riding out of the eastern barbican at
the head of two squadrons: eightscore men in half-armour
carrying lances and matchlock pistols. They were mounted on
the barrel-chested Torunnan warhorses that were most often
black or dark bay in colour, much larger than the beasts of the
Merduk horsemen who preferred the smaller ponies of the
steppes and mountains for their light cavalry.

The two squadrons shook out into line abreast, cheered on by the occupants of the eastern barbican, and thundered up the slopes beyond the river at a fast, bone-shaking trot.

It had been a long time since Corfe had been on a horse. He had originally been a heavy cavalryman in the days before the Merduk siege of Aekir had rendered the city's cavalry superfluous. It took him back to his former life to be part of a moving squadron again, the lance pennons of the troopers whipping about his head.

"Stick close to me, Ensign," Ranafast shouted. He was an emaciated-looking, oldish man whose hawk-like face was now almost entirely hidden by the Torunnan horse helm.

"Out matchlocks!" the cavalry commander ordered, and the lances were settled in their saddle and stirrup sockets. The men drew the already smoking pistols from their saddle holsters.

"East, lads! Close in on them first. Make sure we get the range."

The line of horsemen advanced steadily, the horses labouring a bit to fight the gradient. Ribbons of powder-smoke eddied downhill in countless lines from the glowing slow-match of the pistols. The Merduk cavalry seemed to be somewhat disordered. Knots of them rode this way and that as though uncertain as to their course of action.

The Torunnans clattered and thumped closer, heavy men on heavy horses, a mass of iron and muscle. Ranafast raised his voice.

"Bugler, sound the charge!"

The bugler raised the short instrument to his lips and blew a seven-note blast that rose until it had the hair on the back of Corfe's neck rising with it. The squadrons quickened into a canter.

Up on the hilltop the Merduks were still milling around with what looked to Corfe to be inexplicable confusion until he heard the booms over the noise of the Torunnan advance, and caught sight of the shellbursts which were peppering the slopes behind the enemy. The gunners in the fortress had the Merduks' range and were deliberately overshooting, keeping the fast-moving horsemen from fleeing the approach of the Torunnan cavalry.

Corfe drew his sabre, possessing no lance or pistols, and leant low in the saddle to avoid the wicked Merduk lances.

They were at the hilltop. The Merduks were streaming away in disorder, the ground littered with smoking holes, dead horses, crawling men. The fort gunners were walking the barrage away eastwards, following their flight.

And then the Torunnans were upon them. The cannon had held back the enemy long enough for the heavier horses to close. The Torunnans fired their matchlocks, a great noise and smoke and riot of spouting flame, and then they were at full gallop, lances out and levelled.

There was no sense of impact, no rolling crash. The Torunnans melted into the rear of the fleeing Merduks and began spearing them from behind. Corfe picked a man on an injured horse, galloped up past him and took off most of his head with one satisfying, brutal blow of his sabre. He laughed aloud, searching for more quarry, but his horse was already tiring. He managed to slash the hindquarters of a fleeing Merduk pony, and then hack its rider from the saddle, but when he looked around again he saw that the Torunnan squadrons were over the hill. The fortress was out of sight and the cavalry was widely scattered, every man absorbed in his private pursuit. Ranafast and his bugler had halted and were blowing the *re-form* but the excited men on blown horses were slow to respond. It was the first chance many of them had had to inflict damage on the enemy in weeks, and they had made the most of it.

A line of Merduk cavalry, five hundred strong, came boiling up over the crest of the next hill.

"Saint's blood!" Corfe breathed.

The furthest out of the pursuing Torunnans were engulfed in small groups as the Merduk line came on at an easy canter. The bugler was blowing the *retreat* frantically and dots of horsemen were turning and fleeing back the way they had come.

"A fucking ambush!" Ranafast was yelling. He had lost his helm and looked almost demented with rage.

"If we get back over the hill the gunners in the fort can cover our retreat," Corfe told him.

"We won't make it—not as a body. It's every man for himself. Get you on back to the river, Ensign. This is not your fight."

Corfe bridled. "It's mine as much as anyone else's!"

"Then save your hide so you can fight again. There's no shame in running away from this battle."

They gathered up what they could of the two squadrons and fought a rearguard action back up the slope they had galloped down a few minutes before. Luckily the Merduks did not possess firearms, so the Torunnans were able to turn in the saddle and loosen off a volley from their pistols every so often to rattle the enemy and stall his pursuit. As soon as Ormann Dyke was in sight once more, they galloped in earnest for the eastern gate whilst the gunners opened up on the Merduk cavalry behind them. It had been a close thing, and Ranafast brought back scarcely a hundred men through the gate, a loss the dyke could ill afford. As soon as the Merduks saw that the Torunnan cavalry were back within the walls of the dyke they called off the pursuit and retreated out of cannon range.

Ranafast and Corfe dismounted once they had clattered across the two bridges to the Long Walls. The surviving Torunnans were subdued, made thoughtful by their narrow escape.

"Well, now we know the strength of the enemy scout force," Ranafast growled. "Caught like a green first-campaigner, damn it. What's your name, Ensign?"

"Corfe."

"Part of Martellus' staff, are you? Well, if ever you want back in the saddle, let me know. You did all right out there, and I'm short of officers." Then the cavalry commander stumped off, leading his lathered horse. Corfe stared after him.

T HE leonine Martellus bent his knee and kissed the old man's ring reverently.

"Your Holiness."

Macrobius inclined his head absently. They covered his ragged and empty eyesockets with a snow-white band of linen these days, so that he looked like a venerable blind-man's-buff player. Or a hostage. But he was dressed in robes of lustrous black, and a Saint's symbol of silver inset with lapis lazuli hung on his breast. His ring had been Martellus' own, a gift from the Prelate of Torunna before the general had set out for the dyke. Perhaps there had been an element of prescience in the gift, because it fitted the High Pontiff's bony finger almost as well as it had Martellus."

"They tell me there was a battle today," Macrobius said.

"A skirmish merely. The Merduks managed to stage an ambush of sorts. We came off worst, it's true, but no great damage was done. Your erstwhile bodyguard Corfe did well."

Macrobius' head lifted. "Ah, I am glad, but I never doubted that he would not. My other companion, Brother Ribeiro, died today, General."

"I am sorry to hear it."

"The infection had settled in the very bones of his face. I gave him his last absolution. He died raving, but I pray his soul will take itself swiftly to the Company of the Saints."

"Undoubtedly," Martellus said stoutly. "But I have something else I would discuss with you, Your Holiness."

"My public appearances, or lack of them."

Martellus seemed put out. "Why, yes. You must understand the situation, Holiness. The Merduks are finally closing in. Our intelligence puts their vanguard scarcely eight leagues away and, as you know, the skirmishes with their light troops go on daily. The men need something to hearten them, to raise their spirits. They know you are alive and in the fortress and that is to the good, but if you were to appear before them, preach a sermon and give them your blessing, it would be a wonderful thing for their morale. How could they not fight well, knowing they were safeguarding the representative of Ramusio on earth?"

"They knew that at Aekir," Macrobius said harshly. "It did not help them."

Martellus stifled his exasperation. His pale eyes flashed in the hirsute countenance.

"I command an army outnumbered by more than ten to one, yet they remain here at the dyke despite the knowledge that it would take a miracle to withstand the storm that is upon us. In less than a week we will see a host to our front whose size has not even been imagined since the days of the Religious Wars. A host with one great victory already under its belt. If I cannot give my men something to believe in, to hope for— no matter how intangible—we'd be as well to abandon Ormann Dyke here and now."

"Do you really believe that I can provide that thing they need to believe in, my son?" Macrobius asked. "I, who played the coward at Aekir?"

"That story is almost unknown here. All they know is that by some miracle you escaped the ruin of the Holy City and are here, with them. You have evidenced no desire to go south to Torunn or west to Charibon. You have chosen to remain here. That in itself is heartening for them."

"I could not play the coward again," Macrobius said. "If the dyke falls, I fall with it."

"Then help it stand! Appear before them. Give them your blessing, I beg you."

Eyeless though he was, Macrobius seemed to be studying the earnest soldier before him.

"I am not worthy of the station any more, General," he said softly. "Were I to give the men a Pontiff's blessing, it would be false. In my heart my faith wavers. I am no longer fit for this high office."

Martellus leapt up and began striding about the simply furnished apartments that were Macrobius' quarters in the citadel.

"Old man, I'll be blunt. I don't give a damn about your theological haverings. I care about my men and the fate of my country. This fortress is the gateway to the west. If it falls it will take a generation to push the Merduk back to the Ostian river, if we ever can. You will get up on the speakers' dais tomorrow and you will address my men, and you will put heart in them even if it means perjuring yourself. The greater good will be served, don't you see? After this battle is over you can do whatever you like, if you still live; but for now you will do this thing for me."

Macrobius smiled gently. "You are a blunt man, General. I applaud your concern for your men."

"Then you will do as I ask?"

"No, but I will do as you demand. I cannot promise a rousing oration, an uplifting sermon. My own soul stands sadly in need of uplifting these days, but I will bless these worthy men, these soldiers of Ramusio. They deserve at least that."

"They do," Martellus echoed heartily. "It's not every soldier can go into battle with the blessing of the High Pontiff upon him."

"If you are so very sure I am yet High Pontiff, my son."

Martellus frowned. "What do you mean?"

"It has been some weeks since my disappearance. A Synod of the Prelates will have been convened, and if they have not received word of my abrupt reappearance, they may well have chosen a new Pontiff already, as is their right and duty."

Martellus flapped one large hand. "Messengers have been sent both to Torunn and Charibon. Rest your mind on that score, Your Holiness. The whole world should know by now that Macrobius the Third lives and is well in the fortress of Ormann Dyke."

THE address of the High Pontiff to the assembled troops took place the next day in the marshalling yards of the fortress. The garrison knelt as one, their ranks swelled by thousands upon thousands of refugees who had come to look upon the most important survivor of Aekir. They saw an old man with a white bandage where his eyes had been, and bowed their heads to receive his blessing. There was silence throughout the fortress for a few moments as Macrobius made the Sign of the Saint over the crowds and prayed to Ramusio and the Company of Saints for victory in the forthcoming ordeal.

Scant hours later, the lead elements of the Merduk army came into view on the hills overlooking Ormann Dyke.

Corfe was there on the parapets of the eastern barbican along with Martellus and a collection of senior officers. They saw the enemy van spread out with smooth discipline, the long lines of elephant-drawn drays in their midst and regiments of heavy cavalry—the famed *Ferinai*—spread out on the flanks. Horsehair standards were lifted by the wind and on a knoll overlooking the deployment of the army Corfe could see a group of horsemen thick with standards and banners. Shahr Baraz himself and his generals.

"Those are the *Hraibadar*," Corfe told Martellus. "They spearhead the assaults. Sometimes the *Ferinai* dismount and aid them, for they are heavily armoured also. They are the only troops who are issued wholesale with firearms. The rest make do with crossbows."

"How far behind the van should the main body be?" asked Martellus.

"The main levy moves more slowly, keeping pace with the baggage and siege trains. They are probably three or four miles back down the road. They will be here by nightfall."

"He keeps his men well out of culverin range," Andruw,

the young ordnance officer in charge of the barbican's heavy guns said, disgruntled.

"His light cavalry found out their ranges for him in that skirmish the other day," Martellus said. "He will not have to waste good troops by inching forward to test those ranges. A thoughtful man, this Shahr Baraz. Ensign, what kind of siege works did he use before Aekir?"

"Fairly standard. His guns in six-weapon batteries protected by gabion-strengthed revetments. A ditch and ramp surmounted by a stockade with many sally-ports. And a rearward stockade in case of any attempt to raise the siege."

"No need for him to worry about that here," someone said darkly.

"How long did he spend in preparation before the first assault?" Martellus asked, ignoring the comment.

"Three weeks. But this was Aekir, remember, a vast city."

"I remember, Ensign. What about mines, siege towers and the like?"

"We countermined, and he gave up on that. He used enormous siege towers a hundred feet high and with five or six tercios in each. And heavy onagers to break down the gates. That's how he forced entry to the eastern bastion: a bombardment of both guns and onagers accompanied by a ladder-borne assault."

"He must have lost thousands," someone said incredulously.

"He did," Corfe went on, his eyes never leaving the group of Merduk horsemen that looked down on the rest out in the hills. "But he could afford to. He lost maybe eight or nine thousand in every assault, but we lost heavily too."

"Attrition then," Martellus said grimly. "If he cannot be subtle, he will simply attack head on. He may find it difficult here, with the dyke and the river to cross."

"I think he will assault with little preparation," Corfe informed them. "He knows our strength by now, and he has lost much time in the passage of the Western Road. I think he will come at us with everything he has as soon as his host is assembled. He will want to be in possession of the dyke before the worst of winter."

"Ho, the grand strategist," one of the senior officers said. "Someone after your job there, General."

Martellus the Lion grinned, but there was little humour in

the gesture. His canines were too long, the set of his face too cat-like.

"Corfe is the only one of us who has experienced a full-scale Merduk assault at first hand. He has a right to air his views."

There were some dark murmurings.

"Did the Aekir garrison sortie?" Martellus asked Corfe.

"In the beginning, yes. They harassed the enemy while he dug his siege lines, but there was always a large counterattack ready to be launched—mainly by *Ferinai*. We lost so many men in the sorties and they did so little damage that in the end Mogen gave up on them. We concentrated on counter-battery work, and mining. They are not so skilful with their heavy guns as we are, but they had more of them. We counted eighty-two six-gun batteries around the city."

"Sweet Saints!" Andruw the gunner exclaimed. "Here at the dyke we have less than sixty pieces, light and heavy, and we thought we were overgunned!"

"What about mortars?" Martellus asked. Everyone hated the huge, squat weapons that could throw a heavy shell almost vertically into the air. They rendered the stoutest protecting wall useless, firing over it.

"None. At least they used none at Aekir. They are too heavy, perhaps, to bring over the Thurians."

"That is something at least," Martellus conceded. "Direct-fire weapons only, so we will be able to rely on the thickness of our walls and the refugee camps cannot be bombarded while the wall stands."

"They should be herded out of the defences at once," Corfe blurted out. "It is madness to have a crowd of civilians in the fortress at a time like this."

Martellus blinked. "Among those civilians are would-be nurses and healers, powder and shot carriers, fire-fighters, labourers and perhaps a few more soldiers. I will not cast them out wholesale before seeing what I can get out of them."

"So that's why you have tolerated their presence for so long."

"Tomorrow they will be given orders to march west once more, except for those who are willing to place themselves in the aforementioned categories. I am willing to take help from any quarter, Ensign." Martellus' senior officers did not look too pleased at the news, but no one dared say anything.

"Yes, sir."

The group of men stared out at the deploying Merduk army again. The elephants looked like richly painted towers moving among the press of soldiers and horses, and the huge, many-wheeled wains they pulled were being unloaded with brisk efficiency. More of the animals were advancing with heavy-wheeled culverins behind them, drawing them up in batteries, and Merduk engineers were hurrying hither and thither marking out the hillsides with white ribbon and marker-flags. For fully three miles to their front, the hills were covered with men and animals and waggons. It was as if someone had kicked open a termite mound and the inhabitants had come pouring out searching for their tormentor.

"He will attack in the morning," Martellus said with cold certainty. "We can expect the first assault with the dawn. He will feel his way at first, feeding in his lesser troops as they come up. And the first blow will be here, on the eastern barbican."

"I'd have thought he'd at least spend a day or two setting up camp," one gruff officer said.

"No, Isak. That is what he expects us to think. I agree with our young strategist here. Shahr Baraz will hit us at once, to knock us off balance. If he can take the barbican in that first assault, then so much the better. But the Merduks love armed reconnaissances; this will be one such. He will watch our defence and the way we respond to his attack, and he will note our weaknesses and our strengths. When he knows those, he will commit his best troops and attempt to wipe us off the face of the earth in one massive assault."

Martellus paused and smiled. "That is how I see it, gentlemen. Ensign, you seem to have a head on your shoulders. I hereby promote you to haptman. Remain here in the barbican and stay close to Andruw. I want a full report on the first assault, so don't get yourself killed."

Corfe found it unexpectedly difficult to speak. He nodded at the tall, feline-swift general.

The senior officers left the parapet. Corfe remained behind with Andruw, a man not much older than himself. Short hair the colour of old brass, and two dancing blue eyes. They shook hands.

"To us the honour of first blood, then, in this petty struggle," Andruw said cheerfully. "Come below with me, Haptman, and we'll celebrate your promotion with a bottle of Gaderian. If our esteemed general is right, there'll be little time for drinking after today."

SEVENTEEN

12th day of Midorion, year of the Saint 551.

Wind nor'-nor'-east by north on the starboard quar-ter, veering and strengthening. White-tops and six-foot swell. Course due west at seven knots, though we are making leeway I estimate at one league in twelve.

Now three weeks out of Abrusio, by dead-reckoning some 268 leagues west of North Cape in the Hebrionese. Aevil Matusian, common soldier, lost overboard in the forenoon watch, washed out of the beakhead by a green sea. May the Saints preserve his soul. Father Ortelius preached in the afternoon watch. In the first dog-watch I had hands send up extra preventer-stays and bring in the ship's boats. Shipped hawse bags over the cable-holes and tarpaulins over all the hatches. Dirty weather on the way. The Grace of God is drawing ahead despite all Haukal does. Lost sight of her in the first dog-watch. I pray that both our vessels may survive the storm I feel is coming.

There was so much that the bald entries in the ship's log could not convey, Hawkwood thought, as he stood on the quarterdeck of the *Osprey* with his arm wrapped round the mizzen backstay.

They could not get across the mood of a ship's company, the indefinable tensions and comradeships that pulled it together or apart. Every ship had a personality of its own—it was one of the reasons that he loved his willing, striving carrack as she breasted the white-flecked ocean and slipped ever further westwards into the unknown. But every ship's company also had a personality of its own once it had been at sea for a while, and it was this which occupied his thoughts.

Bad feeling on board. The sailors and the soldiers seemed to have divided into the equivalent of two armed camps. It had started with the damned Inceptine, Ortelius. He had complained to Hawkwood that though the soldiers attended his sermons regularly—even the officers—the sailors did not, but went about their business as though he were not there. Hawkwood had tried to explain to him that the sailors had their work to do, that the running of the ship could not stop for a sermon and that those mariners not on duty were seizing four hours of well-earned rest—the most they ever had at one time, because of the watch system. Ortelius could not see the point, however. He had ended up calling Hawkwood impious, lacking in respect for the cloth. And all this at Murad's dinnertable whilst the scar-faced nobleman looked on in obvious amusement.

There were other things. Some of the sailors had gone to several of the passengers on board for cures to minor ailments—rope-burns, chilblains and the like, and the oldwives had been happy to cure them with the Dweomer they possessed. Friendships had sprung up between sailors and passengers as a result; after all, a large proportion of the crew were, so to speak, in the same boat as the Dweomer-folk: frowned upon by the Church and the authorities. Again Ortelius had protested, and this time Murad had backed him up, more out of devilry than for any real motive, Hawkwood suspected. No good could come to a ship which tolerated the use of Dweomer on board, the priest had said. And sailors being the superstitious lot they were, it had cast a pall over the entire crew. For many of them, however, the Ramusian faith was just another brand of Dweomer, and they did not stop their fraternization with the passengers.

There was a weather-worker aboard, Billerand had informed Hawkwood, one of those rare Dweomer-folk who could influence the wind. He was a mousy little man named Pernicus and had offered his services to the ship's master, but Hawkwood had not dared to use his abilities. There was enough trouble with the priest and the soldiery already. And besides, now that the wind had veered and was screaming in over the quarter, the ship was sailing more freely. They were logging over twenty-five leagues a day, no mean feat for an overloaded carrack. If, God forbid, the *Osprey* found herself on a lee shore, then Hawkwood would not hesitate to call on Pernicus' services, but for now he felt it was better to let well alone.

Especially considering what had happened today—that damned stupid soldier having a shit in the beakhead while the waves were breaking over the forecastle. He had been washed out of his perch by a foaming green sea, and they could not heave-to to pick him up, not with a quartering wind roaring over the side. Murad had been furious, especially when he had learned how many ribald jokes the incident had given rise to in the crew's quarters.

There was a change about the lean nobleman that Hawkwood could not quite define. He gave fewer dinners and left the drilling of the soldiers to his ensigns. He spent much of the time in his cabin. It was impossible to keep a secret on board a ship less than thirty yards long, and Hawkwood knew that Murad had taken two young girls from among the passengers to his bed. Apart from anything else, the noises coming through the bulkhead that separated their cabins were confirmation enough of that. But he had heard the soldiers' gossip: that Murad was somehow enamoured of one of the girls. Certainly, the man had all the symptoms of one lost in love, if one believed the bards. He was snappish, distracted, and his already pale face was as white as bone. Dark rings were spreading like stains below his eyes and when he compressed his thin lips it was possible to see the very shape of the teeth behind them.

A packet of spray came aboard and drenched Hawkwood's shoulders but he hardly noticed. The wind was still freshening and there was an ugly cross-sea getting up. The waves were running contrary to the direction of the wind and streamers of spray were tearing off them like smoke. The ship staggered slightly as she hit one of them; she was rolling as well as pitching now. No doubt the gundeck was covered with prostrate, puking passengers.

Billerand hauled himself up the ladder to the quarterdeck and staggered over to his captain.

"We'll have to take in topsails if this keeps up!" he shouted over the rising wind.

Hawkwood nodded, looking overhead to where the topsails were bellying out as tight as drumskins. The masts were creaking and complaining, but he thought they would hold for a time yet. He wanted to make the most of this glorious speed; he reckoned the carrack was tearing along at nine knots at least—nine long sea miles further west with every two turns of the glass.

"There's a bucketful on the way, too," Billerand said, glancing at the lowering sky. The clouds had thickened and darkened until they were great rolling masses of heavy vapour that seemed to be tumbling along just above the mastheads. It might have been raining already; they could not tell because of the spray that was being hurled through the air by the wind and the swift cleavage of the ship's passage.

"Rouse out the watch," Hawkwood said to him. "Get one of the spare topsails out across the waist. If we have a downpour I'd like to try and save some of it."

"Aye, sir," Billerand said, and wove his way back across the pitching quarterdeck.

The watch were prised from their sheltered corners by Billerand's hoarse shouts and a sail was brought out of the locker below. The seamen made it fast across the waist just as the clouds broke open above their heads. Within a minute, the ship was engulfed in a torrential downpour of warm rain, so thick it was hard to breathe. It struck the deck with hammer-force and rebounded up again. The sail filled up almost at once, and the sailors began filling small kegs and casks from it. Noisome water, polluted by the tar and shakings on the sail itself, but they might be glad of it some day soon, and if they were not it could be used to soak clothes made harsh and rasping by being washed in seawater.

The wind picked up as the crew were unfastening the sail and sent it flapping and booming across the waist like some huge, frightened bird. The ship gave a lurch, staggering Hawkwood at his station. He looked over the side to see that the waves were transforming themselves into vast, slate-grey monsters with fringes of roaring foam at their tops. The *Osprey* was plunging into a great water-sided abyss every few seconds, then rising up and up and up the side of the next wave, the green seas choking her forecastle and pouring in a torrent all the way down her waist. And the light failed. The clouds seemed to close in overhead, bringing on an early twilight. The storm Hawkwood had expected and feared was almost upon them.

"All hands!" Hawkwood roared above the screaming wind. "All hands on deck!"

The order was echoed down in the waist by Billerand, thigh-deep in coursing water. They had the sail in a bundle and were dragging it below-decks. A forgotten keg rolled back and forth in the scuppers, crashing off the upper-deck guns. Hawkwood fought his way over to the hatch in the quarterdeck that opened on the tiller-deck below.

"Tiller there! How does she handle?"

The men were choked with the water that was rushing aft, struggling to contain the manic wrenchings of the tiller.

"She's a point off, sir! We need more hands here."

"You shall have them. Rig relieving tackles as soon as you are able, and bring her round to larboard three points. We have to get her before the wind."

"Aye, sir!"

Men were pouring out of the companionways, looking for orders.

"All hands to reduce sail!" Hawkwood shouted. "Take in those topsails, lads. Billerand, I want four more men on the tiller. Velasca, send a party below-decks to make sure the guns are bowsed up tight. I don't want any of them coming loose."

The crew splintered into fragments, each intent on his duty. Soon the rigging was black with men climbing the shrouds to the topmasts. Hawkwood squinted through the rain and the flying spray, trying to make out how much strain the topmasts were taking. He would put the ship before the wind and scud along under bare poles. It would mean they would lose leagues of their westering and be blown to the south-west, off their latitude, but that could not be helped.

A tearing rip, as violent as the crack of a gun. The foretopsail had split from top to bottom. A moment later the two halves were blasted out of their bolt-holes and were flying in rags from the yard. Hawkwood cursed.

A man who was nothing but a screaming dark blur plunged from the rigging and vanished into the heaving turmoil of the sea.

"Man overboard!" someone yelled, uselessly. There was no way they could heave-to to pick someone up, not in this wind. For the men on the yards, a foot put wrong would mean instant death.

The men eased themselves out on the topsail yards, leaning over to grasp fistful after fistful of the madly billowing canvas. The masts themselves were describing great arcs as the ship plunged and came up again, one moment flattening the sailor's bellies against the wood of the yards, the next threatening to fling them clear of the ship and into the murderous, cliff-like waves.

The wind picked up further. It became a scream in the rigging and the spray hitting Hawkwood's face seemed as solid as sand. The ship's head came round slowly as the men on the tiller brought her to larboard, trying to put the wind behind them. Hawkwood shouted down into the waist:

"You there! Mateo, get aft and make sure the deadlights are shipped in the great cabins."

"Aye, sir." The boy disappeared.

They would have to shutter the stern windows or else a following sea might burst through them, flooding the aft portion of the ship. Hawkwood railed at himself. So many things he had left undone. He had not expected the onset of the storm to be so sudden.

The waves around seemed almost as high as the mastheads, sliding mountains of water determined to swamp the carrack as though she were a rowing boat. The pitching of the ship staggered even Hawkwood's sea-legs, and he had to grasp the quarterdeck rail to steady himself. They had the topsails in now, and men were inching back down the shrouds a few feet at a time, clinging to the rough hemp with all the strength they possessed.

"Lifelines, Billerand!" Hawkwood shouted. "Get them rigged fore and aft."

The burly first mate went to and fro in the waist, shouting

in men's ears. The noise of the wind was such that it was hard to make himself heard.

She was still coming round. This was the most dangerous part. For a few minutes the carrack would be broadside on to the wind and if a wave hit her then she might well capsize and take them all to the bottom.

Hawkwood wiped the spray out of his eyes and saw what he had dreaded—a glassy cliff of water roaring directly at the ship's side. He leaned down to the tiller-deck hatch.

"Hard a-port!" he screamed.

The men below threw their weight on the length of the tiller, fighting the seas that swirled around the ship's rudder. Too slowly. The wave was going to hit.

"Sweet Ramusio, his blessed Saints," Hawkwood breathed in the instant before the great wave struck the ship broadside-on.

The *Osprey* was still turning to port when the enormous shock ran clear through the hull. Hawkwood saw the wave break on the starboard side and then keep going, engulfing the entire waist with water, swirling up to the quarterdeck rail where he stood. One of the ship's boats was battered loose and went over the side, a man clinging to it and screaming soundlessly in that chaos of wind and water. He saw Billerand swept clear across the deck and smashed into the larboard rail like a leaf caught in a gale. Other men clung to the guns with the water foaming about their heads, their legs swept out behind them. But even as Hawkwood watched the wave caught one of the guns and tore it loose from the side, sending the ton of metal careering across the waist, devastation in its wake. The gun went over the larboard side, shattering the rail and tearing a hole in the ship's upper hull. Even above the roaring torrent of the water, Hawkwood thought he could hear the rending timbers shriek, as though the carrack were crying out in her maimed agony.

They were almost swamped. Hawkwood could feel the sluggishness of the carrack, as though she were doubly ballasted with water. The deck began to cant under his feet like the sloping roof of a house.

There was a tearing crack from above. An instant later the main topmast went by the board, the entire mast with its spars and yards and cordage coming crashing down on the larboard

side. Blocks and tackle and fragments of shattered wood were
hurled down round Hawkwood's ears. Something thudded into
the side of his head and knocked him off his feet. He slid
along the sloping deck and ended up in the lee scuppers, entangled with rope. The falling mast had crashed through the
sterncastle and was hanging over the side, dragging the carrack
further over. He was dimly aware that he could hear horses
screaming somewhere down in the belly of the ship, a wailing
like a multitude in pain. He shook his head, blood pouring
down across his eyes and temples, and reached for one of the
axes which were stowed on the decks. He began to swing at
the mass of broken wood and tangled cordage that was threatening to pull the ship over on to her side.

"Axemen here!" he shrieked. "Get this thing cut away or
it'll take us all with it!"

Men were labouring up out of the foaming chaos of the
waist with boarding axes in their hands. He saw Velasca there,
but no sign of Billerand.

They began chopping at the fallen topmast like men possessed. The carrack rose on the breast of another gargantuan
swell of water, tilting ever further. She would capsize with the
next wave.

The topmast shifted as they hacked at it. Then there was a
cracking and wrenching of wood, audible above the wind and
the roaring waves and the sharp concussions of the biting axes.
The mass of wreckage moved, tilted, and then slithered over
the ship's side into the sea, taking a fiferail with it.

The carrack, freed of the unbalancing weight, began to right
herself. The deck became momentarily horizontal again. Then
it began to slant once more, but from fore to aft this time. She
had turned. The ship was before the wind. Hawkwood looked
aft over the taffrail and saw the next wave, like a looming
mountain, rear up over the stern as if it meant to crush them
out of existence. But the ship rose higher and higher as the
bulk of water slid under the hull, lifting the carrack into the
air. Then they were descending again—thank God for the high
sterncastle to prevent them being pooped—and the ship was
behaving like a rational thing once more, riding the huge
waves like a child's toy.

"Velasca!" Hawkwood called, wiping blood out of his eyes.
"See to the foremast backstays. I think the topmast destroyed

one. We don't want the foremast going as well." He glanced around. "Where's Billerand?"

"Took him below," one of the men said. "Had his shoulder broke."

"All right, then. Velasca, you are acting first mate. Phipio, second mate." Hawkwood looked at the battered wreckage, the shattered rails, the stump of the mainmast like an amputated limb. "The ship is badly hurt, lads. She'll swim, but only with our help. Phipio, get a party down below to check for leaks, and have men working on the pumps as soon as you can. Velasca, I want all other hands sending up extra stays. We can't get the topmasts down, not in this, so we'll have to try and strengthen the masts. This is no passing squall. We're in for a long run."

The crowd of men split up. Hawkwood left them to their work for the moment—Velasca was a competent seaman—clambered down the broken remnants of the ladders to the waist and entered the companionway to the aft part of the ship.

The heaving of the carrack threw him against one bulkhead and then another, and there was water swirling in the companionway, washing around his calves. He made his way to the tiller-house where six men were battling to bring the tiller under control as it fought their grip in the monstrous battering of the waves.

"What's our course, lads?" he shouted. Even here the wind was deafening, and there was also the creaking and groaning of the carrack's hull. The ship was moaning like a thing in pain, and there was the horse still neighing madly somewhere below and people wailing on the gundeck. But that was not his problem now.

"Sou'-sou'-west, sir, directly before the wind," one of the struggling helmsmen answered.

"Very well, keep her thus. I'll try and have you relieved at the turn of the watch, but you may be in for a long spell."

Masudi, the senior helmsman and an ex-corsair, gave a grin that was as brilliant as chalk in his dark face.

"Don't you worry about us, sir. You keep the old girl swimming and we'll keep her on course."

Hawkwood grinned back, suddenly cheered, then bent over the binnacle. The compass was housed in a glass case, and to one side within it a small oil lamp burned so the helmsmen might see the compass needle at all times of the day or night. It was one of Hawkwood's own inventions, and he had been inordinately proud of it. As he bent over the yellow-lit glass his blood fell upon it, becoming shining ruby like wine with candlelight behind it. He wiped the glass clean irritably. Sou'-sou'-west all right, and with this storm his dead-reckoning was shot to pieces. They were going to be far off course when this thing blew itself out, and if they wanted to get back on their old latitude they would have to beat for weeks into the teeth of the wind: an agonizing, snail's-pace labour.

He swore viciously and fluently under his breath, and then straightened. How was the *Grace of God* faring? Had Haukal been caught as unprepared as he? The caravel was a sound, weatherly little vessel, but he knew for a fact that it had never before encountered seas as high as these.

He waved to the helmsmen and left the tiller-house, lurching with the dip and rise of the ship. He slid down a ladder and then kept going forward until he was through into the gundeck. There he halted, looking up the long length of the ship.

The place was a shambles. The sailors had lashed the guns tight so they were crouched up against the gunports like great, chained beasts, and in between them a mass of humanity cowered and writhed in a foot of water that came surging up and down the deck with every dip of the carrack's bow. Hawkwood saw bodies floating face-down in the water, the pathetic rag-tag possessions of the passengers drifting and abandoned. There was a collective wailing of women while men cursed. The lanterns had been put out, which was just as well. The deck resembled the dark, fevered nightmare of a visionary hermit, a picture of some subterranean hell.

Someone staggered over to him and took his arm.

"Well, Captain, are we sinking yet?"

There was no panic in the voice, perhaps even a kind of irony. In the almost dark Hawkwood thought he could make out a roughly broken nose, short-cropped hair, the square carriage of a soldier.

"Are you Bardolin, the girl Griella's guardian?"

"Aye."

"Well, we've no fear of sinking, though it was touch and go for a moment or two there. This storm may last some time so you had best get the passengers to make themselves as comfortable as they can."

The man Bardolin glanced back down the heaving length of the gundeck.

"How many hours do you think it will last?"

"Hours? More than that, it'll be. We're in for a blow of some days, if I'm any judge. I'll try and get the ship's cook to serve out some food as soon as we have things more settled. It'll be cold, mind. There will be no galley fires lit whilst the storm lasts."

He could see the dismay, instantly mastered, on the older man's face.

"Do you need any help?" Bardolin asked.

Hawkwood smiled. "No, this is a job for mariners alone. You see to your own people. Calm them down and make them more comfortable. As I say, this storm will last a while."

"Have you seen Griella? Is she all right?" Bardolin demanded.

"She'll be with Lord Murad, I expect."

As soon as he had said the words Hawkwood wished he had not. Bardolin's face had become like stone, his eyes two shards of winking glass.

"Thank you, Captain. I'll see what I can do here."

"One more thing." Hawkwood laid a hand on Bardolin's arm as he turned away. "The weather-worker, Pernicus. We may need him in the days to come. How is he?"

"Prostrate with fear and seasickness, but otherwise he is hale."

"Good. Look after him for me."

"Our ship's chaplain will not be happy at the thought of a Dweomer-propelled vessel."

"You let me worry about the Raven," Hawkwood growled and, slapping Bardolin on the arm, he left the gundeck with real relief.

Deeper he went, into the bowels of the ship. The *Osprey* was a roomy vessel, despite her lower than usual sterncastle. Below the gundeck was the main hold, and below that again the bilge. The hold itself was divided up into large compartments. One for the cable tiers, where the anchor cables were coiled down, one for the water and provisions, a small cubbyhole that was the powder store and then the newly created

compartment that housed the damned horses and other livestock.

There was water everywhere, dripping from the deckhead
above, sloshing around his feet, trickling down the sides of the
hull. Hawkwood found himself a ship's lantern and fought it
alight after a few aggravating minutes of fumbling in the dark
with damp tinder. Then he made his way deeper below.

Here it was possible to hear more clearly the sound of the
hull itself. The wood of the carrack's timbers was creaking
and groaning with every pitch of her beakhead, and the sound
of the wind was muted. The horses had gone silent, which was
a blessing of sorts. Hawkwood wondered if any of them had
survived.

He found a working party of mariners sent down by Velasca
to secure the cargo. There was four feet of water in the hold,
and the men were labouring waist-deep among the jumbled
casks and sacks and boxes, lashing down anything that had
come loose in the carrack's wild battle with the monster
waves.

"How much water is she making?" Hawkwood asked their
leader, a master's mate named Mihal, Gabrionese like himself.

"Maybe a foot with every two turns of the glass, sir. Most
of it came down from above with those green seas we shipped,
but her timbers are strained, too, and there's some coming in
at the seams."

"Show me."

Mihal took him to the side of the hull, and there Hawkwood
could see the timbers of the ship's side quivering and twisting.
Every time the carrack moved with the waves, the timbers
opened a little and more water forced itself in.

"We're not holed anywhere?"

"Not so far as I can see, sir. I've had men in the cable tiers
and in the stockpens aft—a bloody mess down there, by the
by. No, she's just taking the strain, is all, but I hope Velasca
has strong men on the pumps."

"Report to him when you've finished here, Mihal. The pump
crews and the helmsmen will need relieving soon."

"Aye, sir."

Hawkwood moved on, wading through the cold water. He
struggled aft against the movement of the ship and passed

through the bulkhead hatch that separated the hold from the stockpens nearer the stern.

Lanterns here, the terrified bleating of a few sheep, straw and dung turning the water into a kind of soup. Animal corpses were bobbing and drifting. Hawkwood approached the group of men who were working there in leather gambesons—soldiers, then, not members of his crew.

"Who's that?" a voice snapped.

"The Captain. Is that you, Sequero?"

"Hawkwood. Yes, it's me."

Hawkwood saw the pale ovals of faces in the lantern light, the shining flanks of a horse.

"How bad is it?"

Sequero splashed towards him. "What kind of ship's master are you, Hawkwood? No one was told to secure the horses, and then the ship went on its damned side. They never had a chance. Why could you not have warned my people?"

Sequero was standing before him, filthy and dripping. Something had laid open his forehead so that a flap of skin glistened there, but the blood had slowed to an ooze. The ensign's eyes were bright with fury.

"We had no time," Hawkwood said hotly. "As it was we almost lost the ship, and I've lost some of my men putting her to rights. We had no time to worry about your damned horses."

He thought for a second that Sequero was going to fly at him and tensed into a crouch, but then the ensign sagged, obviously worn out.

"I am no sailor. I cannot say whether you are in the right of it or not. Will the ship survive?"

"Probably. How many did you lose?"

"One of the stallions and another mare. They broke their legs when the ship went to one side."

"What about the other livestock?"

Sequero shrugged. It was not his concern.

"Well, get what stock have survived and secure them in their stalls. Lash them to the pens if you have to. This could be a long blow." Hawkwood was beginning to feel like a parrot, repeating his litany to everyone he met.

Sequero nodded dully.

"What about the soldiers? How are they faring?"

"Drunk, most of them. Some of the older ones have been

saving their wine rations. They thought they were going to die, and so decided to drown whilst drunk."

Hawkwood laughed. "I've heard of worse ideas. What of Lord Murad?"

"What of him? He's closeted with his peasant whore as usual."

A violent lurch of the ship pitched them both into the stinking water. They struggled out of it spitting and cursing.

"Are you sure this thing won't sink, Captain?" Sequero sneered.

But Hawkwood was already retracing his steps forward. Time to get back on deck and take up his proper place. He was blind down here.

IT had become a little lighter and the clouds seemed to have lifted above the level of the mastheads. The seas were just as mountainous though, great hills of water with troughs a quarter of a mile apart and crests as high as the carrack's topmasts. They were running before the wind now, and the waves were rising around the ship's stern, lifting her high into the air and then passing under her, leaving her almost becalmed in their lee. There seemed to be little danger of her being pooped, thanks to her construction, and would have to ride the storm out, letting it blow them where it willed.

Velasca had had hawsers sent up to the mastheads and there were men working in the tops, struggling to secure them. Others were double lashing the upper-deck guns and the two ship's boats that had survived, though the passage of the runaway gun had smashed chunks out of both their sides. And to both larboard and starboard thick jets of white water were spewing out of the pumps as men bent up and down over them, trying to lighten the ship.

"Tiller there!" Hawkwood shouted down the hatch. "How's she steering?"

"Easier, sir," Masudi called back. "But the men are tiring."

"Mihal and his mess will be up to relieve you soon. Steady as she goes, Masudi."

"Aye, sir."

For hour after hour the carrack rode the vast waves and careered before the wind roughly south-west, away off their course and into seas unknown even to Tyrenius Cobrian. Despite the fact that the yards were bare, her speed was very great as she was shunted forward on the shining backs of the enormous breakers.

The watch changed. Exhausted seamen were relieved by others scarcely less exhausted, but the hands remained on deck for hour after hour, pumping, splicing, repairing or simply remaining in readiness for the next crisis.

It grew colder. When Hawkwood estimated that their storm-driven run had taken them some forty leagues off course the balminess in the air vanished and the water took on a grey, chill aspect in the sunless dawn of the next day. All that day they continued to run before the wind, eating bread and raw salt pork when they could, feeling the salt in their clothing rasp their saturated skin and continuing the unending repairs.

After a second night and a second day they began to feel that they had never been warm or dry, and had never really known sleep before. They lost another man off one of the yards who had slackened his grip out of sheer weariness, and they threw overboard the bodies of three passengers who had died of the injuries sustained in the first, savage squall. And they continued south-west across the titanic, illimitable Western Ocean, like a stick of wood adrift in a millrace with a knot of frenzied ants clinging to it. There was nothing else to do.

EIGHTEEN

THEY came with the dawn, as Martellus had said they would. Had it not been for the vigilance of the pickets they might have swarmed up to the very walls, so sudden was their onset; for the Merduks had elected to forgo a preliminary bombardment, preferring to gamble on achieving surprise. But the watching sentries set light to the signal rockets and flares, and suddenly the eastern barbican and the river were lit up with smoking red lights that described bright parabolas across the lightening sky and illuminated the bristling phalanxes of advancing troops below.

The garrison of the barbican rushed out to their stations. All along the walls, slow-match was lit and set to one side, men shouldered their arquebuses and powder and shot-carriers hurried up to the parapets with their vital loads.

The Merduk host, discovered, came on with a mighty roar, a rush of shouting and thumping feet that set the hair crawling on Corfe's head. Once again, he beheld the teeming mass of a Merduk army assaulting walls, like a seaweed-thick tide lapping at a cliff face.

The sun was coming up. More powder rockets were launched, this time to help the gunners aim their culverins. The swarming mob of Merduks was perhaps two hundred yards from the walls when Andruw stabbed the slow-match into the touch-hole of the first cannon.

It jumped back with a roar and an exploding fog of smoke. At the signal, the other big guns of the fortress began to bark out also until the entire barbican was a massive reeking smoke cloud stabbed through and through with red and yellow flame.

Corfe was able to see the result of the first few salvoes before the smoke hid the advancing hordes. The Torunnans were using delayed-fuse shells that exploded in midair and scattered jagged metal in a deadly radius beneath them. He saw swathes of the enemy fall or be tossed into the air and ripped to pieces, like crops flattened by an invisible wind. Then they came on again, dressing their broken lines and screaming their hoarse battlecries. There were hundreds of ladders in their midst, carried shoulder-high.

"What of their numbers, Corfe?" Andruw shouted. "What do you make them?"

How to set a figure to that broiling mass of humanity? But Corfe was a soldier, a professional. His mind played with figures in his head.

"Nine or ten thousand in the first wave," he shouted back, the smoke aching his throat already. "But that's just the first wave."

Andruw grinned out of a blackened face. "Plenty for everyone then."

They were at the foot of the walls now, a roaring multitude horned with scaling ladders and baying like animals. The rising sun lit up the further hills, shafted through the billowing powder smoke and made something ethereal and beautiful out of it, the defenders seeming to be flat silhouettes in the fiery reek. The gunners of the lighter pieces depressed their guns to maximum and began firing down into the packed masses below, whilst the arquebusiers were holding fire, waiting for Andruw's order.

Scaling ladders thumping against the battlements. Grapnels, ropes and a shower of crossbow bolts that knocked down half a dozen men in Corfe's vision alone. The ladders began to quiver as the enemy climbed up them.

"Hold your fire, arquebusiers!" Andruw shouted. A few nervous men were already letting loose.

Faces at the top of the ladders, black as fiends from hell.

"Fire!"

A rippling series of explosions as two thousand arquebuses went off almost as one. Many ladders crashed back down in the press below, unbalanced by the death throes of the men at their tops. Others remained, and more of the enemy continued their climb.

"Fork-men, to the front!" the order went out, and Torunnans came forward bearing objects shaped like long-handled pitchforks. Two or three of the defenders would push these against the scaling ladders and send them out in a slow, graceful arc, packed with men, to swing down into red ruin in the massed ranks at the foot of the walls.

The assault paused, checked. The noise of men shouting and shrieking, the boom of cannon and crack of arquebus were deafening.

"Have they no strategy at all?" Andruw was asking Corfe. "They're like a ram butting a gate. Do they reckon nothing of casualties?"

"They don't have to," Corfe told him. "Remember what Martellus said? Attrition. They are losing men by the thousand, we by the score. But they can afford to lose their thousands. They are as numberless as the sand of a beach."

They stood near the gate that was the main entrance to this part of the fortress. The sun was rising rapidly and a rosy-gold light was playing over the scene. They could see through gaps in the smoke to where fresh forces were already being marshalled on the hills beyond. The Merduk guns were being brought into play now, but they were firing high. Most of their shots seemed to be falling into the Searil, raising fountains of white, shattered water.

"So they use explosive shells, too," Andruw said, surprised.

It was something the Ramusians had invented only twenty years ago.

"Yes, and incendiaries. I hope we have enough firefighters."

"Fire is the last thing we have to worry about. Here they come again."

A fresh surge at the foot of the walls. Crossbow bolts came clinking and cracking against the battlements in a dark hail. Men fell screaming from the catwalks.

Another assault, the ladders lifted up and thrown down once

more. The ground at the bottom of the fortifications was piled with corpses and wreckage.

"I don't like it," Corfe said. "This is too easy."

"Too easy!"

"Yes. There is no thought behind these assaults. I think they are a cover for something else. Even Shahr Baraz does not throw his men's lives away for no gain."

There was an earth-shuddering concussion that seemed to come from beneath their very feet. Almost the entire gatehouse was enveloped in thick smoke through which flame speared and flapped.

"They've blown the gate!" Andruw cried.

"I'll see to it. Stay here. They'll make another assault to cover the breaching party."

Corfe ran down the wide stairs to the courtyards and squares below. Torunnan soldiers and refugee civilians were running about carrying powder, shot, wounded men, match and water. He seized on a group of a dozen who possessed arquebuses and led them into the shadow of the gatehouse.

There in the arch a fierce fire was burning, and the massive gates were askew on their hinges, white scars marking the shattered wood. Already the Merduk engineers were swarming through the gaps and a hundred more were clustered behind them. It was like watching dark maggots writhing in a wound.

"Present pieces!" Corfe yelled to his motley command, and the arquebuses were levelled.

"Give fire!"

The volley flung back a score of Merduks who were clambering through the wrecked gates.

"Out swords. Follow me!" Corfe cried, and led the Torunnans at a run.

They stepped over wriggling, maimed men and began slashing and hewing in the burning gloom of the arch like things possessed. In a few moments there were no Merduks left alive inside the gatehouse, and those trying to force their way through the battered portals had limbs and heads lopped off by the defenders.

The fire spread. Corfe was dimly aware of men with water buckets. He hacked the fingers off a hand that was pulling at the broken gate. Then someone was tugging him away.

"The murder-holes! They're going to use them. Out of the gateway!"

He allowed himself to be hauled away, half blind with sweat and smoke. The Torunnans fell back.

Immediately the Merduks were squirming through the gates again. In seconds a score of them were on the inside and more of their fellows were joining them by the moment.

"Now!" a voice yelled somewhere.

A golden torrent poured down on the hapless Merduks from holes in the ceiling of the gatehouse. It was not liquid, but as soon as it struck the men below they screamed horribly, tearing at their armour and dropping their swords. They flailed around in agony for long minutes whilst their comrades halted outside, watching in helpless fury.

"What is it?" Corfe asked. "It looks like—"

"Sand," he was told by a grinning soldier. "Heated sand. It gets inside the armour and fries them to a cinder. More economical than lead, wouldn't you say?"

"Make way, there!" A gunnery officer and a horde of blackened figures were man-hauling two broad-muzzled falcons into position before the gate. As the torrent of sand faltered the Merduks outside began clambering inside again with what seemed to Corfe to be arrant stupidity or maniac courage.

The falcons went off. Loaded with scrap metal, they did the remains of the gates little damage, but the Merduks in the archway were blown to shreds. Blood and fragments of flesh, bone and viscera plastered the interior of the archway.

"They're falling back!" someone yelled.

It was true. The attack on the gate was being abandoned for the moment. The Merduks were drawing away.

"Keep these pieces posted here, and get engineers to work on these gates," Corfe commanded the gunnery officer, not caring what his rank might be. "I'll send men down from the wall to reinforce you as soon as I can."

Without waiting for a reply, he ran for the catwalk stairs to rejoin the men on the battlements.

Another assault—the cover for the breaching party—had just been thrown back. Men were reloading the cannons frantically, charging their arquebuses, doctoring minor wounds. The dead were tossed off the parapet like sacks; time for the solemnities later.

Andruw's sabre was bloody and his eyes startlingly white in a filthy face. "What about the gate?"

"It's holding, for the moment. They're persistent bastards. I'll give them that. We sent half a hundred of them to join their prophet before they drew back."

Andruw laughed heartily. "By sweet Ramusio's blessed blood, they'll not walk over us without a stumble or two. Was it as tight as this at Aekir, Corfe?"

Corfe turned away, face flat and ugly.

"It was different," he said.

MARTELLUS watched the failure of the assault from his station on the heights of the citadel. His officers were clustered about him, grave but somehow jubilant. The Merduk host was drawing back like a snarling dog that has been struck on the muzzle. All over the eastern barbican on the far side of the river a vast turmoil of rising smoke shifted and eddied, shot through with flame. Even here, over a mile away, it was possible to hear the hoarse roar of a multitude in extremity, a formless, surf-like sound that served as background to the rolling thunder of the guns.

"He's lost thousands," one of the senior officers was saying. "What is he thinking of, to throw troops bare-handed against prepared fortifications like that?"

A messenger arrived from the eastern bank, his face grimed and his chest heaving. Martellus read the dispatch with thin lips, then dismissed him.

"The gate is damaged. We would have lost it, were it not for the efforts of my new aide. Andruw puts his own casualties at less than three hundred."

Some of the other officers grinned and stamped. Others looked merely thoughtful. They eyed the retreat of the attacking Merduk regiments—orderly despite the barrage that the Torunnan guns were laying down—then their gazes moved up the hillsides, to where the main host was encamped in its teeming thousands and the Merduk batteries squatted silent and ominous.

"He's playing with us," someone said. "He could have continued that attack all day, and not blinked an eye at the casualties."

"Yes," Martellus said. The early light filled his eyes with

tawny fire and made a glitter out of the white lines in his hair. "This was an armed reconnaissance, no more, as I said it would be. He now knows the location of our guns and the dispositions of the eastern garrison. Tomorrow he will attack again, but this time it will not be a sudden rush, unsupported and ill-disciplined. Tomorrow we will see Shahr Baraz assault in earnest."

HUNDREDS of miles away to the west. Follow the Terrin river northwards to where the gap between the Cimbric Mountains and the Thurians opens out. Pass over the glittering Sea of Tor with its dark fleets of fishing boats and its straggling coastal towns. There, in the foothills of the western Cimbrics, see the majestic profile of Charibon, where the bells of the cathedral are tolling for Vespers and the evening air is thickening into an early night in the shadow of the towering peaks.

In the apartments that had been made over to the new High Pontiff Himerius, the great man himself and Betanza, Vicar-General of the Inceptine Order sat alone, the attending clerics dismissed. The muddy, travel-worn man who had been with them minutes before had been led away to a well-earned bath and bed.

"Well?" Betanza asked.

Himerius' eyes were hooded, his face a maze of crannied bone dominated by the eagle nose. As High Pontiff he wore robes of rich purple, the only man in the world entitled to do so unless the Fimbrian emperors were to come again.

"Absurd nonsense, all of it."

"Are you so sure, Holiness?"

"Of course! Macrobius died in Aekir. Do you think the Merduks would have missed such a prize? This eyeless fellow is an impostor. The general at the dyke, this Martellus, he has obviously circulated this story in order to raise the morale of his troops. I cannot say I blame the man entirely—he must be under enormous pressure—but this really is inexcusable. If he survives the attack on the dyke I will see to it that he is brought before a religious court on charges of heresy."

Betanza sat back in his thickly upholstered chair. They were both by the massive fireplace, and broad logs were burning merrily on the hearth, the only light in the tall-ceilinged room.

"According to this messenger," Betanza said carefully, "Torunn was informed also. Eighteen days he says it took to get here, and four dead horses. Torunn will have had the news for nigh on a fortnight."

"So? We will send our own messengers denying the validity of the man's claim. It is too absurd, Betanza."

The Vicar-General's high-coloured face was dark as he leaned back out of the firelight.

"How can you be so sure that Macrobius is dead?" he asked.

Himerius' eyes glittered. "*He is dead*. Let there be no question about it. I am High Pontiff, and no Torunnan captain of arms will gainsay me."

"What are you going to do?"

Himerius steepled his fingers together before his face.

"We will send out riders at once—tonight—to every court in Normannia—all the Five monarchies. They will bear a Pontifical bull in which I will denounce this impostor and the man who is behind him—this Martellus, the Lion of Ormann Dyke."

Himerius smiled.

"I will also send a private letter to King Lofantyr of Torunna, expressing my outrage at this heretical occurrence and telling him of my reluctance to commit our Knights Militant to the defence of his kingdom whilst that same kingdom harbours a pretender to my own position, an affront against the Holy Office I occupy, a stink in the nostrils of God."

"So you will withhold the troops you promised Brother Heyn," Betanza said. He sounded tired.

"Yes. Until this thing is dealt with Torunna shall receive no material aid from the Church."

"And Ormann Dyke?"

"What of it?"

"The dyke needs those men, Holiness. Without them it will surely fall."

"Then so be it. Its commander should have thought of that before he started elevating blind old men to the position of High Pontiff."

Betanza was silent. As the Knights Militant were quartered in Charibon they were nominally under the command of the head of the Inceptine Order. But never in living memory had a Vicar-General flouted the wishes of his Pontiff.

"The men are already on the march," Betanza said. "They must be halfway to Torunna by now."

"Then recall them," Himerius snapped. "Torunna shall receive nothing from me until it extirpates this impostor."

"I beg you to consider, Holiness . . . What if this man is who he says he is?"

"Impossible, I tell you. Are you questioning my judgement, Brother?"

"No. It is just that I do not want you to make a mistake."

"I am directly inspired by the Blessed Saint, as his representative on earth. Trust me. I know."

"By rights we should reassemble the Synod and put this to the convened Colleges and Prelates."

"They're happily trekking homewards by now. It would waste too much time. They will be informed in due course. What is the matter with you, Brother Betanza? Do you doubt the word of your Pontiff?"

One of the powers inherent in the Pontifical office was the nomination or removal of the Vicar-General of the Inceptines. Betanza looked his superior in the eye.

"Of course not, Holiness. I only seek to cover every contingency."

"I am glad to hear it. It is always better when the Vicar-General and the Pontiff have a good working relationship. It can be disastrous if they do not. Think of old Baliaeus."

Baliaeus had been a Pontiff of the last century who had quarrelled with his Vicar-General, removed the man from office and assumed the position himself in addition to his Pontiffship. The event had scandalized the entire Ramusian world, but none had attempted to reinstate the unfortunate head of the Inceptines. The man had died a reclusive hermit in a cell up in the Cimbrics.

"But you are no Baliaeus, Holiness," Betanza said, smiling.

"I am not. Old friend, we have worked too hard and striven too long to see what we laboured for torn away from us."

"Indeed." So if Himerius went, Betanza went. That much was clear at least.

"In any case," Himerius went on suavely, "we may be worrying over nothing. You have said yourself that the dyke must fall. If it does, the impostor will fall with it and all those who believe in him there. Our problems will be at an end."

Betanza stared at him, open-mouthed.

"That will do, my lord Vicar-General. Have the scribes sent to me when you leave. I will dictate the dispatches this evening. We must strike whilst the iron is hot."

Betanza got up, bowed and kissed his Pontiff's ring. He left the room without another word.

Brother Rogien was waiting for him as he exited. He strode along the wide corridors of Charibon with Rogien silent at his side. He could hear Vespers being sung from half a dozen college chapels and smell the enticing aromas from the kitchens of the monastery.

Rogien was an older man, broad-shouldered and stooped, with hair as white and fine as the down on a day-old chick. He was Betanza's deputy, experienced in the ways of Inceptine intrigue.

"He will not even investigate it!" Betanza raged at last, striding along at a swift, angry pace.

"What did you think, that he would tamely lie down and accept it?" Rogien asked caustically. "All his life he has coveted the position he now occupies. He is more powerful than any king. It is not a thing to be abandoned lightly."

"But the way he goes about it! He will recall the Knights promised to Torunna; he will alienate Heyn and the Torunnan king. He will gladly see Ormann Dyke fall rather than risk his own position!"

"So? We knew that was what would happen."

"I have been a soldier of sorts, Rogien. I commanded men in my youth and maybe that gives me a different outlook. But I tell you that this man will see the west riven by fire and ruin if he thinks it will advance his own cause one jot."

"You have attached yourself to him," Rogien said implacably. "His fortunes are yours. You worked with him to gain the Pontiffship; he helped vote you into your position. You cannot turn around now and forsake him. It will ruin you."

"Yes, I know!"

They reached the Vicar-General's quarters, dismissed the Knights at the door and went inside, lighting candles as they did so.

"You would never have become head of the order were it not for him," Rogien went on. "Your age and your late vocation counted against you. It was Himerius' lobbying that swung the Colleges. You are his creature, Betanza."

The Vicar-General poured himself wine from a crystal decanter, made the Sign of the Saint with a clenched fist and
drank the wine at a gulp.

"Yes, his creature. Is that what they will say in the history
books? That Betanza stood by whilst his Pontiff brought down
the west? Can the man be so blinkered that he is unable to see
what he is doing? By all means, denounce the impostor; but
withhold the Torunnan reinforcements as well? That smacks
of paranoia."

Rogien shrugged. "He is willing to take no risks. He knows
it will bring Lofantyr to heel quicker than anything else. And
you have to admit it would look odd were the High Pontiff to
send troops to bolster the garrison of a fortress which has
raised up a rival High Pontiff."

"Yes, there is that, I suppose." Betanza smiled wryly and
poured his colleague and himself more wine. "Mayhap I am
losing my skill at the Inceptine game."

"You bring to it the wisdom of a man who has not worn a
black habit his whole life. You were a nobleman once, a lay-
leader. But that is in the past. If you are to survive and to
prosper, you must learn to think wholly as an Inceptine. The
order must retain its pre-eminence. Let the kings worry about
the defence of the west; it is their province. We must concern
ourselves with the spiritual welfare of the Ramusian world—
and what would happen to it were there to be two Pontiffs?
Chaos, anarchy, a schism that might take years to heal. Think
on that, Brother."

Betanza regarded his subordinate with sour humour.

"I think sometimes that you would be better off sitting in
my chair and I in a soldier's harness before Ormann Dyke,
Rogien."

"As you are Himerius' creature, I am yours, lord."

"Yes," the Vicar-General said quietly. "You are."

He threw back his wine. "Send a half-dozen of our quickest
scribes to the High Pontiff's chambers. He will be wanting to
dictate his dispatches at once. And warn off a squad of our
dispatch-riders to be ready for a long journey."

Rogien bowed. "Will there be anything else? Shall I have
your meal sent up, or will you eat in hall?"

"I am not hungry. I must be alone for a while. I must think, and pray. That will be all, Rogien."

"Very well, my lord." The older man left.

Betanza moved to the window and threw back the heavy shutters. A keen air smelling of snow wafted into the dim room. He could see where the majestic Cimbrics loomed right at the shores of the Sea of Tor, the last light of the sun touching their white peaks while the rest of the world was sinking into shadow. Eighteen days the messenger had been on the road. The dyke had most likely already fallen and his worries were academic. The largest army yet seen could be even now resuming its march westwards, and he remained here splitting hairs with an egocentric Churchman.

He smiled. What Inceptine was not egocentric, ambitious, imperious? Even the novices behaved like princes when they walked the streets of the fisher villages.

It would cause trouble. He could feel it in his bones. It was not just the Merduk war; there were other straws in the wind tonight. The Conclave of Kings would be convening very soon; he would know more then. He had his informants in place.

A time of change was approaching. Attitudes were shifting, not just among the common people but among kings and princes. Himerius already had the aspect of a man on the defensive. But perhaps his efforts would be no more effectual than the efforts of those few unfortunates who were fighting and dying along the Searil River at this very moment. The mood of the age could not be turned around by a few ambitious men, even ones as powerful as the High Pontiff.

He wondered if Macrobius were truly alive. There was little chance of it, of course, and the likeliest explanation for the dispatch they had received that afternoon was the one proffered by Himerius. But if the impostor were the old Pontiff, Betanza doubted very much whether Himerius would step down. There would be a schism: two Pontiffs, a divided Ramusian continent with the Merduks baying at its borders. Such a scenario did not bear thinking about.

He left the window, shutting out the cold air and the sunset-tinted mountains. Then he knelt on the stone floor and began to pray.

NINETEEN

A N unending expanse of ocean, blue as the cerulean vault
which arced down to meet it, unbroken on every horizon.
Limitless as the space between stars.

And on that unruffled ocean a minuscule speck, a tiny piece
of flotsam overlooked by the elements. A ship, and the souls
contained within its wooden walls.

T HE *Osprey* was becalmed. After three days and nights the
storm had veered off to the north-west, having had its
diversion and driven the carrack uncounted leagues off her
course. Then the wind had died, leaving the sea as glassily
calm as the water in a millpond on a still summer's day. The
ship's company had watched the black towering banners of
the storm billow off into the distance, taking the darkness and
the cold with them, and they had been left with an eerie silence, an absence of noise that they could not quite account
for until they remembered the absence of the wind.

The ship was a battered hulk, a relic of the proud vessel
which had sailed out of Abrusio harbour a scant month before.
The main topmast had gone, and its passing had torn chunks
out of the larboard sterncastle. The gun that had been
wrenched overboard had also ripped a hole in the ship's side

so that the carrack looked as though some immense monster had been chewing on it. Rags and loose ends of rigging dangled everywhere and the normally smooth lines of the ropes which formed the rigging itself were bunched and untidy after being knotted and spliced countless times throughout the storm.

The ship was floating in a greasy pool of her own filth. Around the hull floated human waste and detritus, fragments of wood and hemp, and even the bloated corpses of a pair of sheep. The miasma of the stagnant surroundings stank out the ship along with the familiar reek of her bilge, now somewhat sluiced out by the tons of seawater the ship had made and pumped away throughout the tempest. The ship's boats were full of holes so the crew could not even tow the carrack out of the area. And the heat battered down relentlessly from a sun that seemed made of beaten brass. The pitch bubbled in the seams and, as the upper deck dried, so the planking opened and let water drip down through the ship, soaking everything. The ship's company became accustomed to finding mould and strange fungi sprouting in the unlikeliest of dark corners throughout the carrack.

19th day of Midorion, year of the Saint 551.

Flat calm. The fourth day with no wind. The ship is still in the doldrums. By my estimate we have been blown some one hundred and eighty leagues off our course to the south-west or sou'-sou'-west. From cross-staff observations I believe that we are on the approximate latitude of Gabrion, but my calculations must needs be largely guesswork. In the middle of the worst of the storm the glass was neglected for almost half a watch, and so our timings must begin anew and dead-reckoning becomes ever more unreliable.

There is only one recourse that I can see to help us make up our lost northing, and that is Pernicus, the weather-worker. If he can be prevailed upon to conjure up a favourable wind then we may yet make landfall ere the winter storms begin. But I know what prejudices such a line of action would evoke. I must talk to the man Bardolin, who seems to have become a spokesman of sorts for the passengers since the storm, and, of course,

Murad. But I will be damned to the bottom if I will
endanger my ship any further for the religious fanati-
cism of a cursed Raven whom no one wanted on this
ship in the first place.

Hawkwood looked over what he had written and then, cursing under his breath, he scored out the last sentence heavily
and retrimmed his quill.

Ortelius will surely see reason. It may be a choice be-
tween utilizing the abilities of the weather-worker or, at
best, extending the voyage by a good two months. At
worst it could mean our deaths.
Crew employed about the ship on repairs. We will be
swaying up a new topmast in the first dog-watch, and
then working on the ship's boats. I must report the
deaths of Rad Misson, Essen Maratas and Heirun Ja-
para, all able seamen. May the Company of the Saints
find a place for their benighted souls, and may the
Prophet Ahrimuz welcome Heirun to his garden.
Four men, including First Mate Billerand, confined to
their hammocks with injuries sustained in the storm. Ve-
lasca Ormino acting first mate for the duration.
I must report also the deaths of three passengers, who
were consigned to the sea during the storm itself. They
were Geraldina Durado, Ohen Durado and Cabrallo
Schema. May God have mercy on their souls. Brother
Ortelius today conducted a ceremony to mark their pass-
ing and preached a sermon about the consequences of
heresy and disbelief.

"The bastard," Hawkwood said aloud.

Of Haukal and The Grace of God *there is no sign. I*
cannot believe that such a well-found ship under such
a captain could have foundered, even in the blow that
we went through.

Unless, Hawkwood thought with that persistent hollow feeling in his stomach, they had been pooped and broached-to
whilst running before those enormous waves. The *Grace's*

stern was not as high as the carrack's, and a wave might have overwhelmed her whilst Haukal had been putting her before the wind. And those lateen yards were less handy than the square-rigged ones of the carrack. Frequently sail was taken in by lowering the yards to the deck, and in such a sea there might not have been time to do that.

He had a man in the foretop round the clock, and from up there the lookout could survey at least seven leagues in any direction, despite the haze that was beginning to cloud the horizon with the growing heat. There was just no telling.

Hawkwood looked up from his desk. Beyond the stern windows he could see the glittering, unmoving sea, and the darkness on the northern horizon that was the last of the storm. The windows were open to try and get some air circulating, but it was a fruitless gesture. The heat and the stench were hanging in the throats of every soul on the ship, and the hold was a shattering wooden oven, humid as the jungles of Macassar. He must get the animals out of there for a while, and rig up a wind sail to get some air below-decks. If there were any wind to fill it.

There was a knock at the cabin door.

"Enter."

He was startled to see Ortelius the Inceptine standing there when he turned.

"Captain, do you have a moment?"

He was half inclined to say "no," but he merely nodded and gestured to the stool behind the door. He closed the ship's log, feeling absurdly shifty as he did so.

The cleric pulled out the stool and sat down. He was obviously uncomfortable with the low perch.

"What is it you would say to me, Father? I cannot give you long, I am afraid. We'll be swaying up the new topmast in a few minutes."

Ortelius had lost weight. His cheeks seemed to have sunk in on themselves and the channels at the corners of his nose were as deep as scars.

"It is the voyage, my son."

"What of it?" Hawkwood asked, surprised.

"It is cursed. It is an offense against God and the Holy Saint. The smaller vessel is already lost and soon this one will be also if we do not turn back and set sail for the lands that are lit by the light of the Faith."

"Now wait a moment—" Hawkwood began hotly.

"I know you are Gabrionese, Captain, not from one of the five Ramusian bastions that are the Monarchies of God, but I say this to you: if you have any piety about you whatsoever, you will heed my words and turn the ship around."

Hawkwood could have sworn that the man was sincere—more, that he was genuinely afraid. The sweat was pouring off him in drops as big as pearls, and his chin quivered. There was an odd glitter to his eyes that somehow made Hawkwood uneasy, as though they had something lurking behind them. For an instant he was inclined to agree with the distressed priest, but then he dismissed the notion and shook his head.

"Father, what reasons can you give for this, beyond the usual disquiet of a landsman at being far out to sea? It affects all of us at one time or another—the absence of land on any horizon, the limitless appearance of the ocean. But you will grow used to it, believe me. And there is no reason to think the caravel is lost. It is as fine a vessel as this one, and I'll be surprised if we ever have to weather a worse storm than the last in our crossing of the Western Ocean."

"Even if we are upon it when winter comes?" the Inceptine asked. He had one hand white-knuckled round his Saint's symbol.

"What makes you think we will still be at sea by then?" Hawkwood asked lightly.

"We have been blown far off our course. Any fool can see that. Can you even tell us where we are, Captain? Could any man? It could be we will be sailing until our provisions run out." His hand tightened further on the symbol at his breast until Hawkwood fancied he could hear the fine gold creak. "And we will thirst or starve to death, becoming a floating graveyard upon this accursed sea. I tell you, Captain, it is rank impiety to suppose that any man can cross the Western Ocean. It is a border of the world set there by the hand of God, and no man may breach it."

Here he looked away, and Hawkwood could have sworn that the priest knew these words were false.

"I cannot authorize the abandonment of the voyage," Hawkwood said in measured tones, hiding the exasperation he felt.

"For it is not I who bears the ultimate responsibility. While the ship floats and is in a condition to carry on, the broader decisions are left to Lord Murad. I can only override him if I feel that my technical knowledge renders my decisions more valid than his. The ship *can* go on, once we have made our repairs, so the decision to turn back is not mine to make, but Murad's. So you see, Father, you have come to the wrong man."

Let Murad muzzle this priest, not I, he was thinking. The pious dastard thinks of me as common scum, to obey the orders of the Church nobility without question. Well, I will not disabuse him of that notion. Let him go to Murad for his refusal. He may take it more easily from one of his station.

"I see," the priest said, bowing his head so that Hawkwood might not see his eyes.

They could hear the shouts of the sailors out on deck, the creak of rope and squeak of pulleys. The crew must have been hauling the new topmast out of the hold. Hawkwood chafed to be away, but the Inceptine continued to sit with his head bowed.

"Father—" Hawkwood began.

"I tell you there is a curse on this ship and those aboard her!" the priest blurted out. "We will leave our bones upon her decks ere we ever sight any mythical Western Continent!"

"Calm down, man! Making wild claims like these will help no one. Do you want to panic the passengers?"

"The passengers!" Ortelius spat. "Dweomer-folk! The world would be better rid of them. Do they even know where they are headed? They are like cattle being driven to the slaughter!"

With that he leapt up off his stool and, throwing open the cabin door, launched out into the companionway. He barked his shin on the storm sill and went sprawling, then gathered himself up and billowed off, out to the glaring brightness of the deck. Hawkwood stared after his black flapping form in wonder and disquiet. He had the strangest idea that the Inceptine knew more of the ship's destination than he did himself.

"The old Raven is going mad," he said, slamming the bulkhead door and laughing a little uneasily.

Another knock at the just-closed door, but before Hawkwood could say anything it had opened and Murad was standing there.

"I heard," the nobleman said.

"Thin bulkheads. There are few secrets on board ship," Hawkwood said, annoyed.

"Just as well. Forewarned is forearmed, as they say." Murad perched on the edge of Hawkwood's desk nonchalantly. He had taken off his leathers and was in a loose linen shirt and breeches. A scabbarded poniard hung from his belt.

"Do you believe him?" Murad asked.

"No. Seamen may be superstitious, but they are not fools."

"Will we be at sea through the winter then, trying to regain our course?"

"Not necessarily," Hawkwood admitted. Murad looked terrible. They all did in the aftermath of the storm. Most of the crew were like badly animated zombies, but Murad was as lean as a well-gnawed bone and there were muddy puddles under his eyes, red lines breaking across his corneas. He was like a man who had forgotten how to sleep.

"There is a weather-worker on board. I suppose you've heard."

"The soldiers speak of it."

"Well, we have two choices. Either we whistle for a wind and then try beating north-west, which according to Tyrenius' rutter—or what you have allowed me to read of it—would be right into the teeth of the prevailing north-westerlies."

"What would that mean?" Murad snapped.

"It would mean extra months at sea. Half-rations, the loss of your remaining horses. Probably the deaths of the weakest passengers."

"And the other alternative?"

"We ask the weather-worker to utilize his skills."

"His sorcery," Murad sneered.

"Whatever. And he blows us back on course as easy as you please."

"Have you sailed with a weather-worker before, Hawkwood?"

"Only once, in the Levangore. The Merduks employ them in their galley squadrons to bring down calms when they are attacking sailing ships. The one I met was chief pilot in the port of Alcaras in Calmar. Their magic works, Murad."

"Their magic, yes." The nobleman seemed deep in thought. "Do you realize that Ortelius is a spy, sent to observe the voyage for his master the Prelate of Hebrion?"

"The thought had crossed my mind."

"It will be bad enough that our crew are half-Merduk and our passengers a parcel of sorcerers. Now we are to use sorcery to propel the very ship itself."

"Surely the voyage comes under the King's protection. The Prelate would not dare—"

"It is the colony I am thinking of. It is a new Hebrian province we will be seeking to establish in the west, Hawkwood, but if the Prelate of Hebrion sets his face against it, it may become simply a place of exile for undesirables."

Hawkwood laughed at that. "I can see it now: Murad, lord of witches and thieves."

"And Hawkwood, admiral of prison hulks," Murad countered.

They glared at one another, tension sizzling in the air between them.

"It is your decision to make," Hawkwood said stiffly at last. "But as master of the *Osprey* I feel bound to tell you that if we do not use sorcery to fill our sails then we will be drinking our own piss ere we sight land."

"I will think on it a while," Murad told him, and moved towards the door.

"One more thing," Hawkwood said, feeling reckless.

"Yes?"

"That fellow Bardolin. He asked me to have a word with you about the girl Griella."

Murad spun on his heel. "What about her?"

"I suppose he wants you to leave her alone. Perhaps she does not relish your attentions, my lord."

Before Hawkwood could even flinch, Murad's poniard was naked and shining at his throat.

"My affairs of the heart are not a basis for discussion, Captain, at any time."

Hawkwood's eyes were aflame. "The passengers are my responsibility, along with the running of the ship."

"What's the matter, Captain? Are you jealous? Have you lost your taste for boys, perhaps?"

The poniard broke the skin.

"I do not hold with rape, Murad," Hawkwood said steadily.

"Bardolin is rumoured to be a mage, not a man to cross lightly."

"Neither am I, Captain." The blade left Hawkwood's throat, was scabbarded again. "Find this weather-worker, and let him ply his trade," Murad said casually. "We can't let a man like our good priest end up drinking his own piss."

"What will you tell him?"

"Nothing. He is worn-looking, don't you think? Maybe he has a streak of madness in him induced by the strain of the past days. It would be a shame were something to happen to him ere we sight land."

Hawkwood said nothing, but rubbed his throat where the poniard tip had pricked it.

PERNICUS was a small man, red-haired and weak-eyed. His nose was long enough to overhang his upper lip and he was as pale as parchment, a bruise on his high forehead lingering evidence of the passage of the storm.

He stood on the quarterdeck as though it were the scaffold, licking dry lips and glancing at Hawkwood and Murad like a dog searching for its master. Hawkwood smiled reassuringly at him.

"Come, Master Pernicus. Show us your skill."

The waist was crowded with people. Most of the passengers had learned of what was happening and had dragged themselves out of the fetid gundeck. Bardolin was there, as stern as a sergeant-at-arms, and beside him was Griella. Most of the ship's crew were in the shrouds or were standing ready at the lifts and braces, waiting to trim the yards when the wind appeared. Soldiers lined the forecastle and the gangways, slow-match lit and sending ribands of smoke out to hang in the limpid air. Sequero and di Souza had their swords drawn.

But at the forefront of them all, at the foot of the quarterdeck ladder, stood Ortelius, his eyes fixed on the diminutive weather-worker above. His face was skull-like in the harsh sunlight, his eyes two deep glitters in sunken sockets.

"Get to it, man!" Murad barked impatiently. Pernicus jumped like a frog, and there was a rattle of laughter from the soldiers on the forecastle. Then silence again as the two ensigns glared round and sergeant Mensurado administered a discreet kick. The sails flapped idly overhead and the ship was motionless under the blazing sun, like an insect impaled upon a pin. Pernicus closed his eyes.

Minutes went past, and the soldiers stirred restlessly. Three bells in the afternoon watch was struck, the ship's bell as loud as a gunshot in the quiet. Pernicus' lips moved silently.

The main topsail swayed and flapped once, twice. Hawkwood thought he felt the faintest zephyr on his cheek, though it might have been his hopeful imagination. Pernicus spoke at last, in a choked murmur:

"It is hard. There is nothing to work with for leagues, but I think I have found it. Yes. I think it will do."

"It had better," Murad said in a low, ominous voice.

The sun was unrelenting. It baked the decks and made tar drip from the rigging on to those below, spotting the painfully bright armour of the soldiers. Finally Pernicus sighed and rubbed his eyes. He turned to face Hawkwood.

"I have done it, Captain. You shall have your wind. It is on its way."

Then he left the quarterdeck, gaped at by those who had never seen a weather-worker perform before, and went below.

"Is that it?" Murad snapped. "I'll have the little mountebank flogged up and down the ship."

"Wait," Hawkwood said.

"Nothing happened, Captain."

"Wait, damn you!"

The crowd in the waist was already dispersing, buzzing with talk. The soldiers were filing down off the gangways, beating out their slow-match on the ship's rail and guffawing at their own jokes. Ortelius remained motionless, as did Bardolin.

A breeze ruffled Hawkwood's hair and made the sails crack and fill.

"Ready, lads!" he called to the crew, who were waiting patiently at their stations.

The light faded. The ship's company looked up as one to see outrider clouds moving across the face of the sun. The surface of the sea to the south-east of the ship wrinkled like folded silk.

"Here she comes. Steady on the braces. Tiller there, course nor'-nor'-west."

"Aye, sir."

The breeze strengthened, and suddenly the sails were full

and straining, the masts creaking as they took the strain. The
carrack tilted and her bow dipped as the wind took her on the
stern. She began to move, slowly at first and then picking up
speed.

"Brace that foresail round, you damned fools! You're spilling the wind. Velasca, more men to the foremast. And set
bonnets on the courses."

"Aye, sir!"

"We're moving!" someone shouted from the waist, and as
the carrack began to slide swiftly through the water the passengers broke out into laughter and cheers. "Good old Pernicus!"

"Leadsman to the forechains!" Hawkwood shouted, grinning. "Let's see what she's doing."

The carrack was alive again, no longer the stranded, battered
creature she had been in the past days. Hawkwood experienced
a jet of sheer joy as he felt the ship stirring under his feet and
saw her wake beginning to foam astern.

"So we have our wind," Murad said, sounding a little be-
mused. "I have never seen anything like it, I must say."

"I have," said Brother Ortelius. He had climbed up to the
quarterdeck, his face like granite. "May God forgive you
both—and that wretched creature of Dweomer—for what you
have done here today."

"Easy, Father—" Hawkwood began.

"Brother Ortelius," Murad said coldly, "you will kindly re-
frain from making comments which might be construed as
detrimental to the morale of the ship's company. If you have
opinions you may seek to air them in private with either myself
or the captain; otherwise you will keep them to yourself. You
are not well, obviously. I would not like to have to confine a
man of your dignity to his hammock, but I will if need be.
Good day, sir."

Ortelius looked as though a blood vessel might burst. His
face went scarlet and his mouth worked soundlessly. Some of
Hawkwood's crew turned aside to hide their exultant smiles.

"You cannot muzzle me, sir," Ortelius said at last, dripping
venom. "I am a noble of the Church, subject to no authority
save my spiritual superiors. I answer to them and to no one
else."

"You answer to me and to Captain Hawkwood as long as

you are aboard this ship. Ours is the ultimate responsibility, and the ultimate authority. Priest or no, if I hear you have been preaching any more superstitious claptrap I'll have you put in irons in the bilge. Now go below, sir, before I do something I may regret."

"You have already done that, sir, believe me," Ortelius hissed out of a mottled countenance. His eyes glittered like a snake and he made the Sign of the Saint as though flinging a curse at the lean nobleman.

"I said go below. Or will I have a pair of soldiers escort you?"

The black-garbed priest left the quarterdeck. There was a hoot of laughter, quickly smothered, from one of the sailors on the yards.

"That may not have been wise," Hawkwood said quietly.

"Indeed. But by all the saints in God's heaven, Hawkwood, I enjoyed it. Those black vultures think they have the world in their pocket; it is good to disabuse them of the notion now and again." Murad was smiling, and for a moment Hawkwood almost liked him; he knew he could never have stood up to the Inceptine in the same manner. No matter how much he hated the Ravens, their authority was deeply ingrained in his mind, as it was in the mind of every commoner. Perhaps one had to be a noble to see the man behind the symbol.

"There is something I cannot account for, though," Murad said thoughtfully.

"What is that?"

"Ortelius. He was angry, yes; furious, even. But I could have sworn his outrage was founded on more than that. On fear. It is strange. Inexplicable."

"I think he knows more than he seems to," Hawkwood said in a low voice. As one, he and Murad moved to the larboard rail to be out of earshot of the crew.

"My thought also," the scarred nobleman agreed.

"You're sure he was sent by the Prelate of Hebrion?"

"Almost, yes. I have not encountered him before, though, and I know most of the clerics who hang about Abeleyn's court and the Prelate's."

"There is no clue as to his background?"

"Oh, he'll be a scion of some minor noble family—the Inceptines always are. There will probably be a plum post or other waiting for him in return for his services on the voyage."

"You do not seem too concerned about what he may report back to the Church in Abrusio."

Murad stared at Hawkwood, face expressionless. "There are many long leagues of sailing before us yet, Captain, and an unknown continent awaiting our feet. Many things could happen before any of us sees Hebrion once more. Hazardous things. Dangerous things."

"You cannot do that, Murad! He is a priest."

"He is a man, and his blood is the same colour as my own. When he chose to set his will against mine he fixed his own fate. There is nothing more to be said."

Murad's matter-of-fact tone chilled Hawkwood. He had seen battle, ship-to-ship actions with the corsairs where blood had washed the decks and men had been mangled by shot and blade, but this cold, calculated dismissal of another man's life unsettled him. He wondered what he would have to do to earn the same treatment from the scheming nobleman.

He left the larboard rail and stood at the break of the quarterdeck, wishing to put distance between himself and Murad. The carrack was flying along and spray was coming aboard to cool his brow. The third of the leadsmen, the one stationed by the taffrail, was holding the dripping, knotted rope with the thick faggot of wood fastened to the end.

"Six knots, sir, and she's still gathering way!"

Hawkwood forced himself to respond to the leadsman's gaiety, though whatever joy he had in the ship's progress had been dampened by Murad.

"Try her again, Borim. See if she won't get up to eight when the bonnets are on."

"Aye, sir!"

Murad left the quarterdeck without another word. Hawkwood watched him go, knowing that the nobleman was plotting murder on his ship.

BARDOLIN leaned on the forecastle rail and stared down into the breaking foam of the carrack's bow. They were clipping along at a wonderful rate and the cool moving air was like a benison after the unmoving furnace of the doldrums.

The soldiers had hauled the remaining horses up out of the waist hatches and were exercising them, leading them round and round the deck. The poor brutes were covered in sores and their ribs stood out like the hoops on a barrel. Bardolin wondered if they would ever live to set foot on the new continent that awaited them in the west.

A good man, that Pernicus. It had been Bardolin who had convinced him to use his powers and call in a wind. He was below now, concentrating. There were few suitable systems of air in the region, and he was having constantly to maintain the one that propelled the ship. Usually a weather-worker selected a suitable system nearby and manoeuvred it into a position where it could do his work for him, but here Pernicus was having to keep at it to make sure the sorcerous wind did not fade away.

A desolate ocean, this. They were too far from land to sight any birds, and the only sealife Bardolin had glimpsed were a few shoals of wingfish flitting over the surface of the waves. He had seen a deep-sea jellyfish, too, which the sailors called devil's toadstools. This one had been twenty feet across, trailing tentacles half as long as the ship and glowing down in the dimmer water as it pulsed its obscure way through the depths.

The imp chirruped with excitement. It was peeking out of his robe, its eyes shining as it watched the water break under the keel and felt the swift breeze of the ship's passage. It was growing steadily more restless at having to keep out of sight. The only time Bardolin set it free was in the night, when it hunted rats up and down the ship.

He had wondered about sending it into Murad's cabin, to observe him and Griella, but the very thought had shamed him.

As though conjured up by his preoccupations, Griella appeared at his side. She leant on the rail beside him and scratched the ear of the imp, which gurgled with pleasure.

"We have our wind, then," she said.

"So it would seem."

"How long can Pernicus keep it going?"

"Some days. By then we should have picked up one of the prevailing winds beyond the area of the doldrums."

"You're beginning to sound like a sailor, Bardolin. You'll be talking of decks and companionways and ports next . . . Why have you been avoiding me?"

"I have not," Bardolin said, keeping his gaze anchored in the leaping waves.

"Are you jealous of the nobleman?"

The mage said nothing.

"I thought I told you: I sleep with him to protect us. His word is law, remember? I could not refuse."

"I know that," Bardolin said testily. "I am not your keeper in any case."

"You *are* jealous."

"I am afraid."

"Of what? That he might make me his duchess? I think not."

"It is common knowledge amongst the crew and the soldiers that he is . . . besotted with you. And I look at his face every day, and see the changes being wrought in it. What are you doing, Griella?"

She smiled. "I think I give him bad dreams."

"You are playing with a hot coal. You will get burned."

"I know what it is I do. I make him pay for his nobility."

"Take care, child. If you are discovered for what you are, your life is forfeit—especially with that rabid priest on board. And even the Dweomer-folk have no love for shifters. You would be alone."

"Alone, Bardolin? Would you not stand by me?"

The mage sighed heavily. "You know I would, though much good it would do us."

"But you don't like killing. How would you defend me?" she asked playfully.

"Enough, Griella. I am not in the mood for your games." He paused, then, hating himself, asked: "Do you *like* going to his bed?"

She tossed her head. "Perhaps, sometimes. I am in a position of power, Bardolin, for the first time in my life. He loves me." She laughed, and the imp grinned at her until the corners of its mouth reached its long ears.

"He will be viceroy of this colony we are to found in the west, and he loves me."

"It sounds as though you *do* expect to be a duchess."

"I will be something, not just a peasant girl with the black disease. I will be something more, duchess or no."

"I spoke to the captain about you."

"What?" She was aghast. "Why? What did you say?"

Bardolin's voice grew savage. "At that time I thought you were not so willing to be bedded by this man. I asked the captain to intercede. He did, but he tells me that Murad would hear none of it."

Griella giggled. "I have him in thrall, the poor man."

"No good will come of it, girl. Leave it."

"No. You are like a mother hen clucking over an egg, Bardolin. Leave off me." There was a touch of violence in her voice. Bardolin turned and looked into her face.

It was almost four bells in the last dog-watch, and the sky was darkening. Already the lanterns at the stern and mastheads had been lit in the hope that the other ship would see them and the little fleet would be reunited. Griella's face was a livid oval in the failing light and her tawny hair seemed sable-dark. But her eyes had a shine to them, a luminosity that Bardolin did not like.

"Dusk and dawn, they are the two hardest times, are they not?" he asked quietly. "Traditionally the time of the hunt. The longer we are at sea, Griella, the harder it will become to control. Do not let your tormenting of this man get out of hand, or the change will be upon you ere you know it."

"I can control it," she said, and her voice seemed deeper than it had been.

"Yes. But one time, in the last light of the day or in the dark hour before the dawn, it will get the better of you. The beast seeks always to be free, but you must not let it out, Griella."

She turned her face away from him. Four bells rang out, and the watch changed, a crowd of sailors coming up yawning from below-decks, those on duty leaving their posts for the swaying hammocks below.

"I am not a child any more, Bardolin. I do not need your advice. I sought to help you."

"Help yourself first," he said.

"I will. I can make my own way."

Without looking at him again she left the forecastle. He watched her small, upright figure traverse the waist—the sailors knew better than to molest her now—and enter the sterncastle where the officers' cabins were.

Bardolin resumed his watching of the waters whilst the imp cheeped interrogatively from his breast. It was hungry, and wanted to be off on its nightly search for rats.

"Soon, my little comrade, soon," he soothed it.

He leaned on the rail and watched the sun sink down slowly into the Western Ocean, a great saffron disc touched with a burning wrack of cloud. It gave the sea on the western horizon the aspect of just-spilled blood.

The carrack forged on willingly, propelled by the sorcerous wind. Her sails were pyramids of rose-tinted canvas in the last light of the sunset and the lanterns about her gleamed like earthbound stars. The ship was alone on the face of the waters; as far as any man might see, there was no other speck of life moving under the gleam of the rising moon.

TWENTY

ORMANN Dyke.

The tumbling thunder of the bombardment went on relentlessly, but they had grown used to it and no longer commented upon it.

"We are more or less blind to what goes on over the brow of the nearest hill," Martellus told his assembled officers. "I have sent out three different scouting missions, but none has returned. The Merduks' security is excellent. All we know therefore is what we see: a minimum of siegeworks, the deployment of the batteries to the front—"

"And a hive of activity to the rear," old Isak finished.

"Just so. The eastern barbican has taken a pasting, and the gunnery battle is all but over. He will assault very soon."

"How many guns do we have still firing across the river?" one man asked.

"Less than half a dozen, and those are the masked ones that Andruw has been saving for the end."

"We cannot let the eastern side of the bridge go without a struggle," one officer said.

"I agree." Martellus looked round at his fellow Torunnans. The engineers have been working through the night. They have planted charges under the remaining supports. The Searil bridge can be blown in a matter of moments, but first I want to bloody their nose again. I want them to assault the barbican."

"What's left of it," someone murmured.

Three days had passed since the first, headlong assault of the Merduk army. In those three days there had, contrary to Martellus' prediction, been no direct attack on the eastern fortifications. Instead Shahr Baraz had brought up his heavy guns, emplaced them behind stout revetments and begun an artillery duel with the guns in the eastern barbican. He had lost heavily in men and material in the first deployment, but once his pieces were secure the more numerous Merduk heavy culverins had begun to pound the Torunnan fort on the eastern bank to rubble. The bombardment had continued unabated for thirty-six hours. Most of Andruw's guns were silenced, and the eastern barbican was holed and breached in several places. Only a scratch garrison remained there. The rest had been withdrawn back over the river to the island, that long strip of land between the river and the dyke.

"The heavy charges are in place. When they occupy the eastern fort they are in for a shock, but we must make them occupy it—we must make them pay for it. And to do that we must keep troops there, to tempt them in," Martellus said relentlessly.

"Who commands this forlorn hope?" an officer asked.

"Young Corfe, my aide, the one who was at Aekir. Andruw will have his hands full directing the remaining artillery. The rest of the skeleton garrison is under Corfe."

"Let us hope he will not turn tail like he did at Aekir," someone muttered.

Martellus' eyes turned that pale, inhuman shade which always silenced his subordinates.

"He will do his duty."

JAN Baffarin, the chief engineer, came scuttling like a crab through the low-ceilinged bomb-proof towards Corfe and Andruw.

"We've repaired the powder lines. There should be no problem now."

He was shouting without realizing it, as they all had been for the past day and night. The huge tumult of the bombardment overhead had ceased to seem unusual and was now part of the accepted order of things.

The bomb-proof was large, low and massively buttressed. Five hundred men crouched within it as the shell and shot rained down on the fortress above their heads. Dust and fragments of loose stone came drifting down when there was a particularly close hit, and the air seemed to shake and shimmer in the light of the shuddering oil lamps. "The Catacombs" the troops had wryly labelled their shelter, and it seemed apt. All around the bodies of men sprawled and lolled, some asleep despite the unending noise and vibration. They looked like the aftermath of the plague, a scene from some febrile nightmare.

Corfe roused himself from the concussed stupor he had been in.

"What of the guns?"

"The casemates are intact, but Saint's love, those are the heaviest calibre shells I've ever seen. The gatehouse is a pile of rubble, and the walls are in pieces. They don't have to attack. If they keep this up they'll reduce Ormann Dyke to powder without ever setting foot in it."

Andruw shook his head. "They can't have the ammunition and powder, not with their supply line as long as it is. I'll wager a good bottle of Candelarian that they're running low right now. This bombardment is for show as much as anything else. They want to stun us into surrender, perhaps."

A particularly close explosion made them wince and duck instinctively. The granite ceiling seemed to groan under the assault.

"Some show," Baffarin said dubiously.

"Your men know the drill," Corfe said. "As soon as the rearguard is across the bridge you touch off the charges, both on the bridge itself and in the barbican. We'll send the whole damn lot of them flying into the Thurians. There's a show for you."

The engineer chuckled.

The bombardment stopped.

There were a few tardy detonations from late-falling shells, and then a silence came down which was so profound that Corfe was alarmed, for a second believing that he had gone deaf. Someone coughed, and the noise seemed abnormally loud in the sudden stillness. The sleeping men began rousing themselves, staring around and shaking each other.

"On your feet!" Corfe shouted. "Gunners to your pieces, arquebusiers to your stations. They're on their way, lads!"

The catacombs dissolved into a shadowy chaos of moving men. Baffarin grasped Corfe's arm.

"See you on the other side of the river," he said, and then was gone.

THE devastation was awe-inspiring. The eastern barbican was like a castle of sand which had been undermined by the tide. There were yawning gaps in the walls, mounds of stone and rubble everywhere, burning timber crackling and shimmering in the dust-laden air. Corfe's meagre command fanned out to their prearranged positions whilst Andruw's gunners began wheeling the surviving culverins into firing positions.

Corfe clambered up the ruin of the gatehouse and surveyed the Merduk dispositions. Their batteries were smoke-shrouded, though a cold breeze from the north was shredding the powder fog moment by moment. He glimpsed great bodies of men on the move, elephants, regiments of horsemen and lumbering, heavy-laden waggons. The hills were crawling with orderly and disorderly movement.

A gun went off, as flat as a hand-clap after the thunder of the heavy-calibre cannons, and a sort of shudder went through the columns behind the smoke. They began to move, and soon it was possible to make out three armies marching towards the line of the river. One was aimed at the ruin of the barbican, the other two to the north and south, their goal apparently the Searil River itself. They were oddly burdened, and waggons rolled along in their midst, hauled by elephants.

The five hundred Torunnans who were the barbican's last defenders spread out along the tattered battlements, their arquebuses levelled. Their orders were to make a demonstration, to draw as many of the enemy as possible into the fortifications and then withdraw slowly, finally escaping over the Searil bridge. It would be a difficult thing to control, this fighting retreat. Corfe felt no fear at the thought of the coming assault or the possibility of injury and death, but he was mortally afraid of making a hash of things. These five hundred were his command, his first since the fall of Aekir; and he knew he was still regarded by many of his fellow Torunnans as the man who had deserted John Mogen. He was coldly determined to do well today.

The warmth of the sun was bright and welcome. Men wriggled fingers in their ears to let out the ringing aftermath of the artillery, then sighted down their weapons at the advancing enemy.

"Easy!" Corfe called out. "Wait till I give the word."

A gun barked from one of the upper casemates, and a second later a blossom of blasted earth appeared on the slope before the Merduk formations. Andruw testing the range.

They came on at a slow walk, the high-sided waggons trundling in their midst. The northern and southern hosts had more of these elephant-drawn vehicles than the one which was aimed at the barbican. Corfe strained his eyes to make out the strange loads, then whistled.

"Boats!" The waggons were loaded with shallow-hulled, puntlike craft piled one on top of the other. They were going to try and cross the Searil to north and south whilst engaging the garrison on the east bank at the same time.

"They'll be lucky," a nearby soldier said, and spat over the battered wall. "The Searil's swollen after the rain. It's running along like a bolting horse. I hope they have strong arms, or they'll be washed all the way down to the Kardian."

There was a spatter of brief laughter along the ramparts.

Andruw's guns began to sing out one by one. The young gunnery officer had kept his five most accurate pieces this side of the river, and was adjusting their traverse and elevation personally. They began to lob explosive shells into the forefront of the central enemy formation, blasting them into red ruin. Corfe saw an elephant lifted half off its feet as a shell exploded squarely under it. Another hit one of the high-laden wains and sent slivers of deadly wood spraying like spears through its escort. There was confusion, men milling about, panic-stricken beasts trampling and trumpeting madly. The Torunnans watched with a high sense of glee, happy to be repaying the Merduks in kind for the relentless bombardment of the past days.

But the ranks reformed, and the Merduks came on again faster, loping along at a brisk trot, leaving the waggons behind. Corfe could see that the lead elements of these men were in shining half-armour and mail. They were the *Hraibadar*, the shock-troops of Shahr Baraz.

The formation splintered and spread out so that the shell-bursts took a lesser toll. As they jogged ever closer Corfe rapped out orders, pitching his voice to carry over the rippling booms of the Torunnan artillery.

"Ready your pieces!"

The men fitted the smouldering slow-match into the wheel-locks of their arquebuses.

"Present your pieces!"

He raised his sabre. He could see individual faces in the ranks of the approaching enemy, horsehair plumes, panting mouths underneath the tall helms.

He swept his sabre down. "Give fire!"

The walls erupted in a line of smoke and flame as nigh on five hundred arquebuses went off in a single volley. The enemy, scarcely a hundred yards away, were thrown back as if by a sudden gale of wind. The front ranks dissolved into a mass of wriggling, crawling men, and those behind faltered a moment, then came on again.

"Reload!" Corfe shouted. It was Andruw's turn now.

The five guns of the remaining Torunnan battery waited until the Merduks were within fifty yards, and then fired as one. They were loaded with deadly canister: hollow cans of thin metal containing thousands of arquebus bullets. Five jets of smoke spurted out, and the Merduks were flattened once more in a dreadful slaughter.

The smoke was too thick for aiming. Corfe shouted at the top of his voice, waving his sabre: "Back off the walls! Second position, lads! Back on me!"

The Torunnans ran down from the ruined battlements and formed a swift two-deep line below. Their sergeants and ensigns pushed them into position and then stood ready.

The gunners were leaving their pieces, having spiked the touch-holes. Corfe saw Andruw there, laughing as he ran. When the last artillerymen were behind the line of arquebusiers he gave the order.

"Ready your pieces!"

A line of figures pouring through the gaps in the walls now, hundreds of them, screaming as they came.

"Front rank, present your pieces!"

Thirty yards away. Could they be stopped? It seemed impossible.

"Give fire!"

A shattering volley that hid the enemy in clouds of dark smoke.

"First rank, fall back. Second rank, give fire!"

The first rank were running back through the fortress to the bridge, where Baffarin and his engineers waited. It would be very close.

The second volley staggered the smoke, flattened more of the oncoming enemy, but Corfe's men were falling now for the Merduks had arquebusiers up on the battlements firing blindly into the Torunnan ranks.

A shrieking line of figures issued out of the powder cloud like friends catapulted out of hell.

A few weapons were fired, a ragged volley. And then it was hand-to-hand down the line. The arquebusiers dropped their weapons and drew their sabres, if they had time. Others flailed about them with the butts of their firearms.

Corfe gutted a howling Merduk, swept the heavy sabre across the face of another, punched the spiked hilt into the jaw of a third.

"Fall back! Fall back to the bridge!"

They were being overwhelmed. The enemy was pouring in—thousands of them, perhaps. All across the rubble-strewn and pitted drill square Corfe saw his line dissolve into knots and groups of isolated men as the Merduks punched into it. Those who could were retreating; others went down under the flashing scimitars still swinging their weapons.

He clanged aside a scimitar, elbowed the man off-balance, thrust at another, then spun round at the first man and slashed open his arm. They were all around him. He whirled and hacked and thrust without conscious volition. The knot broke apart. There was space again, a moving turmoil of figures running past, shouting; there was flashing murder every instant and so much blood it seemed some other element spilling everywhere.

Someone was pulling frantically at his arm. He swung round and almost decapitated Andruw. The gunner officer had a slash across his face which had left a flap of flesh hanging over one eye.

"Time to go, Corfe. We can't hold them any longer."

"How many at the bridge?"

"Enough. You've done your duty, so come. They're preparing to blow the charges."

Corfe allowed himself to be tugged away and followed Andruw's lead out of the fortress, calling the last of his men with him as he went.

The bridge was standing on a few stone supports. The rest had been chiselled and blasted away. Baffarin was there, grinning. "Glad to see you, Haptman. We thought you had got lost. You're among the last."

Corfe and Andruw ran across the long, empty bridge. The lead elements of the enemy were a scant fifty yards behind, and arquebus balls were kicking up splinters of stone around their feet as they made the western bank. The survivors of Corfe's command were crouched there among the revetments of the island. Those who still possessed their firearms were firing methodically into the press of the advancing enemy. As they saw Corfe and Andruw a hoarse cheer went up.

Baffarin's engineers were touching off ribbons of bound rags with slow-match. A culverin was firing canister across the bridge, stalling the Merduk advance. Corfe sank to his knees in the shelter of the earthworks behind the bridge, chest heaving. He felt as though someone had lit a fire inside his armour and the black metal seemed insufferably heavy, though when running he had not even noticed its weight.

"Only a few seconds now," Baffarin said. He was still grinning, but there was no humour on his face; it was like a rictus. Sweat carved runnels down his black temples.

Then the charges went off.

Not a noise, just a flash, an immense . . . impression. A sense of a huge happening that the brain could not quite grasp. Corfe felt the air sucked out of his lungs. He shut his eyes and buried his face in his arms, but he heard the secondary explosions distantly, as though he were separated from them by thick glass. Then there was the rain of rubble and wood and more terrible things falling all around him. Something heavy clanged off his backplate. Something else hit his hand as it gripped the back of his head, hard enough to numb. Rolling concussions, a swift-moving thunder. Water raining, men moaning. The echoes of the detonations reverberated off the face of the hills, faceted thunder, at last dwindling.

Corfe looked up. The bridge was gone, and the very earth seemed changed. Of the eastern barbican, that great, high-walled fortress, there was little left. Only stumps and mounds of smoking stone amid a huge series of craters. The catacombs laid bare to the sky. Fire flickering—the smell of powder and blood and broken soil, a reek heavier and more solid than any he had ever experienced before, even at Aekir.

"Holy God!" Andruw said beside him.

The slopes leading down to the site of the barbican were black with men, some alive and cowering, others turned into corpses. It was as if they had simultaneously experienced a vision, witnessed an apparition of their prophet, perhaps. The carcasses of elephants lay like outcrops of grey rock, except where they had been mutilated into something else. The entire battlefield seemed frozen in shock.

"I'll bet they heard that in Torunn," Baffarin said, the end of the slow-match still gripped in an ivory-knuckled hand.

"I'll bet they heard it in fucking Hebrion," a nearby trooper said, and there were automatic chuckles, empty humour. They were too shocked.

The air clicked in Corfe's throat. He found his voice, and surprised himself with its steadiness.

"Who have we got here? Tove, Marsen, good. Get the men spread out along the earthworks. I want weapons primed. Ridal, get you to the citadel and report to Martellus. Tell him—tell him the eastern barbican and bridge are blown—"

"In case he hadn't noticed," someone put in.

"—And tell him I have some . . ." He glanced around. Sweet Saints in heaven! So few? "I have some tenscore men at my disposal."

The survivors of Corfe's first command busied themselves carrying out his orders.

"They're fighting along the river," someone said, standing and peering to the north. The boom of artillery and crackle of arquebus fire had shattered the momentary silence.

"That's their fight. We've a job to do here," Corfe said harshly. Then he sat down quickly with his back to a revetment, lest his rubber legs turn traitor and buckle under him.

●　　●　　●

MARTELLUS watched the climax of the battle from his usual vantage point on the heights of the citadel. Not for him the hurly-burly of trying to command his men from the thick of things. John Mogen had been the man for that. No, he liked to stand back and study the layout of the developing conflict, base his decisions on logic and the dispatches that he received minute by minute, borne by grimed and bloody couriers. A general could direct things best from afar, distanced from the shouting turmoil of his battle. Some men, it was true, could command an army whilst fighting almost in the front rank, but they were rare geniuses. Inevitably Mogen came to mind again.

The roar of the explosion was a distant echo of thunder rolling back and forth between hills ever further away. A huge plume of smoke rose up from the centre of the battlefield where the eastern barbican had once been. The assault had been blunted there, perhaps even crippled. Young Corfe had done a good job. He was someone to watch, despite the cloud hanging over his past.

But to north and south of the smoke two fresh Merduk formations, each perhaps twenty-five thousand strong, had closed on the river. The artillery on the Long Walls and the island had peppered their ranks unceasingly with shells, but they came on regardless. Now they were unloading the flat puntlike boats from the elephant wains and preparing to brave the foaming current of the swollen Searil River.

Once they cross the river in force, Martellus thought, it is only a matter of time. We may destroy them in their thousands as they cross the dyke, but cross it they will. The river is our best defence, at least while it is running this full.

He turned to an aide.

"Is Ranafast standing ready with the sortie force?"

"Yes, sir."

"Then go to him. Give him my compliments and tell him he is to take his command out to the island at once. He can also strip the walls of every fourth man except for gunners, and all are to be arquebus-armed. He is to contest the crossing of the river. Is that clear?"

"Yes, sir."

A scribe nearby had been scrawling furiously. The written order was entrusted to the aide after Martellus had flashed his signature across it, and then the aide was gone, running down to the Long Walls.

There was not much time for Ranafast to scratch together his command and get into position. Martellus cursed himself. Why had he never envisaged a mass boat crossing? They had been busy, the Merduk engineers, in the weeks they had been stalled at Aekir.

The first of the boats were already being shoved down the eastern bank and into the water. They were massive, crude affairs, propelled by the paddles of their passengers. Fourscore men at least manned each one, and Martellus counted over a hundred of them lining the eastern bank like southern river lizards basking in a tropical sun. Shellbursts were sprouting up in their midst like momentary fungi, shattering boats, sending men flying, panicking the elephants.

The Searil was three hundred yards across at the dyke, a wide brown river that was churning wild and white in many places and was thick with debris from its headwaters. No easy task to paddle across it at the best of times. To do it under shellfire, though . . . These men excited Martellus' admiration even as he plotted their destruction.

The first wave was setting out. To north and south of the ruined bridge the Searil suddenly became thick with the large, flat boats, like a stream clogged with autumn leaves near its banks.

A thunder of hooves, and Ranafast was leading his horsemen—the vanguard of his command—across the dyke bridges to the island. A column of marching men followed on after the cavalry. With luck, there would be over seven thousand on the western bank to contest the crossing, supported by artillery from the walls.

And yet when he looked at the size, the teeming numbers, of those who clogged the eastern bank, Martellus could not help but feel despair. For miles the edge of the Searil was crawling with enemy soldiers, boats, elephants, horses and waggons. And that was only the assaulting force. On the hills beyond the reserves, the cavalry, the artillery, the countless camp-followers darkened the face of the land like some vast blight. It was inconceivable that the collective will of such a multitude should be thwarted.

And yet he must do it—he *would* do it. He would defy the

gloom-mongers and amateur generals and all the rest. He would hold this fortress to his last breath, and he would bleed the Merduk armies white upon it.

Globes of smoke, tiny with distance, appeared along the length of the walls. After a few seconds the boom of the cannon salvoes came drifting up to the citadel, and soon the guns of the citadel itself were firing. The noise was everywhere, together with the blood-quickening smell of gunpowder.

White fountains of exploding water began to burst amid the Merduk boats. Martellus could make out the men in the craft straining like maniacs at their paddles, but remaining in time. They had their heads bowed and shoulders hunched forward as though they were braving a heavy shower of rain. Martellus had seen the same position assumed by most men advancing against heavy fire; it was a kind of instinct.

One, two, then three of the boats were struck in quick succession as the Torunnan artillery began to range in on their targets. Martellus had the best gunners in the world here at the dyke, and now they were fulfilling his faith in them.

The men in the shattered boats sank out of sight at once, weighed down by armour. Even had they worn none, they had no chance in the rushing current.

Ranafast was deploying his men along the western bank whilst his own shells whistled over his head. He had a couple of galloper-guns with him also. But the men were spread perilously thin, and Martellus could see now that the central Merduk column was staging an attack on Corfe's position, manhandling boats amid the debris of the bridge, all the time under heavy fire from Corfe's surviving command and the other defenders who were posted there. Ranafast should see the danger, though.

Sure enough, the cavalry commander brought his two light guns down to Corfe's position, and soon they were barking canister at close range into the Merduks trying to cross there. An ugly little fight, but the main struggle was still going on along the flanks.

The waterborne Merduks were in trouble. More boats were being struck by Torunnan shells, and when these did not sink at once they began to roar downstream like sticks caught in a millrace, crashing into their fellows and sending them downriver in their turn. Soon there were scores of boats whirling and drifting in the middle of the river, wreckage and bodies bobbing up and down, the geysers of shellbursts exploding everywhere.

Some boats reached the western bank, only to receive a hail of arquebus bullets. Their complements straggled ashore to be cut down by Ranafast's men. A tidemark of bodies built up there on the western bank while the Torunnans reloaded methodically and fired volley after volley into the wretches floundering ashore.

The battle had quickly degenerated into a one-sided slaughter. Signal guns began to sound from the Merduk lines calling off the attack, and those on the eastern bank halted as they were about to push a fresh wave of craft into the water. The unfortunates already on the river tried to come about and retrace their course, but it was impossible in that maelstrom of shot, shell and white water. They perished almost to a man.

The assault ground to a bloody and fruitless halt. Some of the Merduks remained on the edge of the river to try and help those labouring in the water, but most began a sullen retreat to their camps on the hillsides above. And all the while, Torunnan artillery lobbed vindictive and jubilant shells at their retreating backs. The attack had not just failed; it had been destroyed before it could even start.

"I want another battery of gallopers detached from the walls and sent to Corfe's position," Martellus said crisply. "Send him another three tercios also; he is closest to the enemy. He must hold the island."

An aide ran off with the order. Martellus' brother officers were laughing and grinning, scarcely able to believe their eyes.

For miles along the line of the river powder smoke hung in the air in thick clouds, and strewn along both banks was the wreck of an army. Men, boats, animals, weapons. It was awesome to behold. They dotted the land like the fallen fruit in an untended orchard, and the river itself was thick with boats half awash, a few figures clinging desperately to the wreckage. They were coursing downstream out of sight, helpless.

"He's lost ten thousand at least," old Isak was saying. "And some of his best troops, too. Sweet Saints, I've never seen carnage like it. He throws away his men as though they were chaff."

"He miscalculated," Martellus said. "Had the river been less full, he would have been at the dyke by now. This attack was intended to see him to the very walls on which we stand. Its repulse will give him pause for thought, but let us not forget that he still has fifty thousand men on those hills who have not yet been under fire. He will try again."

"Then the same thing will happen again," Isak said stubbornly.

"Possibly. We have exhausted our surprises, I think. Now he knows what we have and will be searching his mind for openings, gaps in our defences."

"He cannot mean to assault again for a while, not after that debacle."

"Perhaps not, but do not underestimate Shahr Baraz. He was profligate with his men's lives at Aekir because of the prize that was at stake. I had thought he would be more careful here, if only because of the natural strength of the dyke. It may be that someone in higher authority is urging him on into less well-judged assaults. But we cannot become overconfident. We must look to our flanks. After today he will be probing the upper and lower stretches of the Searil, looking for a crossing point."

"He won't find one. The Searil is running as fast as a riptide and apart from here, at the dyke, the banks are treacherous, mostly cliffs and gorges."

"We know that, but he does not." Martellus sagged suddenly. "I think we have won, for the moment. There will be no more headlong assaults. We have gained a breathing space. It is now up to the kings of the world to aid us. The Saints know we deserve some help after the defence we have made."

"Young Corfe did well."

"Yes, he did. I intend to give him a larger command. He is able enough for it, and he and Andruw work well together."

A few desultory cannon shots spurted out from the Torunnan lines, but a calm was descending over the Searil valley. As though by common consent, the armies had broken off from each other. The Merduks rescued the pathetically few survivors of the river assault without further molestation and loaded them on carts to be driven back within the confines of the camps. A few abandoned boats burned merrily on the eastern bank. The guns fell silent.

•   •   •

THE indaba of officers had broken up less than an hour before, and Shahr Baraz was alone in the darkened tent. It was as sparsely furnished as a monk's cell. There was a low wooden cot strewn with army blankets, a folding desk piled with papers, a chair and some stands for the lamps.

And one other thing. The old general set it on the desk and drew the curtain from around it. A small cage. Something inside it chittered and flapped irritably.

"Well, Goleg," Shahr Baraz said in a low voice. He tapped the bars of the cage and regarded its occupant with weary disgust.

"Ha! Man's flesh is too tough for Goleg. Wants a child, a young, sweet thing just out of the cradle."

"Summon your master. I must make my report."

"I want sweet flesh!"

"Do as you are told, abomination, or I'll leave you to rot in that cage."

Two tiny dots of light blinked malevolently from the shadows behind the bars. Two minuscule clawed hands gripped them and shook the metal.

"I know you. You are too old. Soon you will be carrion for Goleg."

"Summon your master."

The two lights dimmed. There was a momentary quiet, broken only by the camp noises outside, the neighing of horses in the cavalry lines. Shahr Baraz sat as if graven in stone.

At last a deep voice said: "Well, General?"

"I must make my report, Orkh. Relay me to the Sultan."

"Good tidings, I trust."

"That is for him to judge."

"Did the assault fail, then?"

"It failed. I would speak to my ruler. No doubt you will be able to eavesdrop."

"Indeed. My little creatures all answer to me—but you and Aurungzeb know that, of course." Another pause. "He is busy with one of his new concubines, the raven-haired Ramusian beauty. Ah, she is exquisite. I envy him. Here he is, my Khedive. The luck of the Prophet be with you."

And with that mild blasphemy, Orkh's voice died. Aurungzeb's impatient tones echoed through the tent in its place.

"Shahr Baraz, my Khedive! General of generals! I am afire. Tell me quickly. What happened?"

"The assault failed, Majesty."

"*What?* How? How did this happen?"

The old soldier seemed to stiffen in his chair, as though anticipating a blow.

"The attack was hasty, ill-judged and ill-prepared. We took the eastern barbican of the fortress, but it was mined and I lost two thousand men when the Ramusians touched it off. The river, also, was flowing too fast for our boats to make a swift crossing. They were cut to pieces whilst still in the water. Those who made it to the western bank died under the muzzles of Torunnan guns."

"How many?"

"We lost some six thousand of the *Hraibadar*—half of those who remained—and another five thousand of the levy."

"And the—the enemy?"

"I doubt he lost more than a thousand."

The Sultan's voice, when it came again, had changed; the shock had gone and it was as hard as Thurian granite.

"You said the attack was ill-judged. Explain yourself."

"Majesty, if you will remember, I did not want to make this assault. I asked you for more time, time to throw up siegeworks, to look over our options more thoroughly—"

"Time! You have had time. You dawdled in Aekir for weeks. You would have done the same here had I not enjoined you to hasten. This is a paltry place. You said yourself the garrison is less than twenty thousand strong. This is not Aekir, Shahr Baraz. The army should be able to roll over it like an elephant stepping on a frog."

"It is the strongest fortification I have ever seen, including the walls of Aekir," Shahr Baraz said. "I cannot throw my army at it as if it were the log hut of some bandit chieftain. This campaign could prove as difficult as the last—"

"It could if the famed Khedive of *my* army—*my* army, General—has lost his zest for campaigning."

Baraz's face hardened. "I attacked on your orders, and against my own judgement. That mistake has cost us eleven thousand men dead or too maimed ever to fight again. I will not repeat that mistake."

"How dare you speak to me thus? I am your Sultan, old

man. You will obey me or I will find someone else who will."

"So be it, my Sultan. But I will be a party to no more amateur strategy. You can either replace me or leave me to conduct this campaign unhindered. Yours is the choice, and the responsibility."

A long silence. The homunculus' eyes blinked in the shadow of its cage. Shahr Baraz was impassive. I am too old for diplomacy, he thought. I will end what I have always been—a soldier. But I will not see my men slaughtered in my name. Let them know who ordered the attack. Let them see how their Sultan values their lives.

"My friend," Aurungzeb said finally, and his voice was as smooth as melted chocolate. "We have both spoken hastily. Our concern for the men and our country does us credit, but it leads us into passionate utterances which might later be regretted."

"I agree, Majesty."

"So I will give you another opportunity to prove your loyalty to my house, a loyalty which has never faltered since the days of my grandsire. You will renew the attack on Ormann Dyke at once, and with all the forces at your disposal. You will overwhelm the dyke and then push on south to the Torunnan capital."

"I regret that I cannot comply with your wishes, Majesty."

"Wishes? Who is talking about wishes? You will obey my *orders*, old man."

"I regret that I cannot."

"And why not?"

"Because to do so would wreck this army from top to bottom, and I will not permit that."

"Eyes of the Prophet! Will you defy me?"

"Yes, Majesty."

"Consider yourself my Khedive no longer, then. As the Lord of Victories rules in Paradise, I have suffered your ancient insolence for the last time! Hand over your command to Mughal. He can expect orders from me in writing—and a new Khedive!"

"And I, Majesty?"

"You? Consider yourself under arrest, Shahr Baraz. You will await the arrival of my officers from Orkhan."

"Is that all?"

"By the Lord of Battles, yes—that is all!"

"Fare thee well then, Majesty," Shahr Baraz said calmly. He stood, lifted the cage with its monstrous occupant, and then dashed it to the ground. The homunculus screamed, and in its scream Shahr Baraz heard the agony of Orkh, its sorcerous master. Smiling grimly, he stamped his booted foot on the structure, crunching metal and bone in a morass of ichor and foul-stinking flesh. Then he clapped his hands for his attendants.

"Take this abomination away and burn it," he said, and they flinched from the fire in his eyes.

TWENTY-ONE

I T was a scream that brought Murad bolt upright in his hanging cot. He remained stock-still, listening. Nothing but the
creak of the ship's timbers, the lap of the water against the
hull, the tiny thumps and slaps that were part of being at sea.
Nothing.

A dream. He relaxed, lying down again. The girl had disappeared as she always did, and she had left him with a hideous dream—as she always did. The same dream. He preferred
to put it out of his mind.

But could not. She was a witch, that was clear—otherwise
she would not be a passenger aboard this ship. Maybe she was
the man Bardolin's apprentice. He was a wizard of sorts. No
doubt she was putting a black spell on him, perhaps ensnaring
him with some kind of love magic.

But he doubted it. Their love-making was too real, too solid
and genuine to be the product of any spell. It was almost as
though she had been dry tinder waiting for a spark. She came
to life in his arms, and their coupling was like a nightly battle,
a duel for mastery. He had her mastered, he was sure of that.
Smiling up at the deckhead he relived the satisfaction of plunging into her and feeling her body heave up in answer. She was
a delightful little animal. He would find a position for her when

the colony was established, keep her by him. He could never marry her—the idea was absurd enough to make him chuckle aloud—but he would see her decently provided for.

He must keep her. He needed her. He craved that nightly battle, and wondered sometimes if any other woman would interest him again.

Why did she always leave just before the dawn? And that old man—what was she to him? Not a lover, surely.

His mouth tightened and he clenched his fists on the coverlet.

She is mine, he thought. I will allow her to have no others. *I must keep her.*

But the dreams: they came every night, and every night they were the same. That suffocating heat, the weight and prickling fur of the beast on top of him. Those eyes regarding him with unblinking malevolence. What could it mean?

He was always tired these days, always weary. He had been a fool to put down the Inceptine like that—the man would have to die now. He was too powerful an enemy. Abeleyn would see the necessity of it.

He rubbed the dark orbits of his eyes, feeling as though he could never entirely grind the tiredness out of them. He wanted her here, warm and writhing in his arms. For a second the intensity of that desire unnerved him.

He sat up again. There was something strange about the ship, something he had to consider for a moment before realizing. Then it struck him.

The carrack was no longer moving.

He leapt from the hanging cot so that it swung and banged against the bulkhead, pulled on his clothes hurriedly and grabbed the rapier with its baldric. As he reached the door, it was knocked on loudly. He yanked it open to find the ship's boy, Mateo, standing there with a white face.

"Captain Hawkwood's compliments, sir, and he asks would you join him in the hold? There is something you ought to see."

"What is it? Why have we stopped moving?"

"He said to . . . You have to see, sir." The boy looked as though he was about to be sick.

"Lead on then, damn you. It had better be important."

•   •   •

THE whole ship was astir, the passengers milling on the gundeck and soldiers posted at every hatch and companionway with their slow-match lit and swords drawn. In their journey into the bowels of the carrack Murad ran into a prowling Sergeant Mensurado.

"Sergeant, by whose orders are these sentries posted?"

"Ensign Sequero, sir. He's down in the hold. We've orders to let none but the ship's officers pass."

Murad was about to ask him what had happened, but that would reflect poorly on his own grasp of the situation. He merely nodded and said, "Carry on, then," and followed Mateo down the dark hatches towards the hold.

Some water washing about among the high stacks of casks and crates and sacks. Rats skipping underfoot. It was pitch black but for the small hand lantern Mateo carried, but as they came through one of the compartment bulkheads Murad saw another clot of light flickering ahead and men gathered in a knot within its radiance.

"Lord Murad," Hawkwood said, straightening from a crouch. Sequero was there, and di Souza, and the injured first mate, Billerand, his arm strapped to his side and his face puffed with pain.

They drew back, and he saw the shape lying in the water, the dark gleam of blood and viscera, the limbs contorted beyond life.

"Who is it?"

"Pernicus. Billerand found him half a glass ago."

"I was mooching around," the mustachioed first mate said, "checking the cargo. It's all I'm up to these days."

Murad knelt and examined the corpse. Pernicus' eyes were wide open, the mouth agape in a last scream.

Had he heard it? Or had that been part of his dream?

The man's neck had been almost entirely bitten through; Murad could see the clammy tube of the windpipe, the ragged ends of arteries, a white-shard of vertebra.

Lower down the intestines had spilled out like a coil of greasy rope. There were chunks missing from the body. The marks of teeth were plain to see.

"Sweet Ramusio!" Murad whispered. "What did this?"

"A beast of some kind," Hawkwood said firmly. "Something came down here in the middle watch—one of the crew thought he glimpsed it. Pernicus liked to work his magic from the hold because it was more peaceful than the gundeck or the waist. It came down here after him."

"Did the man say what it was like?" Murad asked.

"Big and black. That's all he could say. He thought he had imagined it. There is nothing like that aboard the ship."

A dream or nightmare of a great, black-furred weight atop him. Could it have been real?

Murad mastered his confusion and straightened up out of the foul water.

"Is it still aboard, do you think?"

"I don't know. I want a thorough search of the ship. If whatever did this is on board, we'll find it and kill it."

Murad remembered the log of the *Cartigellan Faulcon*. It could not be. The same thing could not be happening again. Such things were not possible.

"I have sent for the mage, Bardolin. He may be able to enlighten us," Hawkwood added.

"Do the passengers know what has happened?"

"They know Pernicus is dead. I could not stop that from leaking out, what with the loss of the wind, and all. But they don't know the manner of his death."

"Keep it that way. We don't want a panic on board."

The four of them stood round the corpse in silence for a moment. It occurred to all of them in the same instant that the beast could be here with them now, lurking among the shadows. Di Souza was shifting uneasily, his drawn sword winking in the lantern light.

"Someone's coming," he said. Another globe of light was approaching and two men were clambering over the cargo towards them.

"That's far enough, Masudi!" Hawkwood called. "Go back. Bardolin, you come forward alone."

The mage splashed towards him, and they could make out Masudi's lantern growing smaller as he returned the way he had come.

"Well, gentlemen," Bardolin began, and bent to the corpse much as Murad had done.

"Well, Mage?" Murad asked coolly, having regained his poise.

Bardolin's face was as pale as Mateo's had been. "When did this happen?"

"Sometime before the dawn, we think," Billerand told him gruffly. "I found him here, as he lies."

"What did it?" Murad demanded.

The mage turned the limbs, examining the lacerated flesh with an intensity that was disturbing to the more squeamish among them. Sequero looked away.

"How were the horses last night?" Bardolin asked.

Sequero frowned. "A bit restless. They took a long time to quieten down."

"They smelled it," the mage said. He got to his feet with a low groan.

"Smelled what?" Murad demanded impatiently. "What did this, Bardolin? What manner of beast? It was not a man, that's plain."

Bardolin seemed reluctant to speak. He was staring at the mangled corpse with his face as grim as a gravestone.

"It was not a man, and yet it was. It was both, and neither."

"What gibberish is this?"

"It was a werewolf, Lord Murad. There is a shape-shifter aboard this ship."

"Saint's preserve us!" di Souza said into the shocked silence.

"Are you sure?" Hawkwood asked.

"Yes, Captain. I have seen such wounds before." Bardolin seemed downcast and strangely bitter, Murad thought. And not as shocked as he ought to be.

"So it is not just an animal," Hawkwood was saying. "It changes back and forth. It could be anyone, any one of the ship's company."

"Yes, Captain."

"What are we to do?" di Souza asked plaintively.

No one answered him.

"Speak to us, Mage," Murad grated. "What can we do to find the beast and kill it?"

"There is nothing you can do, Lord Murad."

"What do you mean?"

"It will be wearing its human face again now. We will simply have to be watchful, to wait for it to strike again."

"What kind of plan is that?" Sequero snapped. "Are we cattle, to wait for the slaughter?"

"Yes, Lord Sequero, we are. That is exactly what we are to this thing."

"Is there no way of telling who is the werewolf?" Billerand asked.

"Not that I know of. We will simply have to be vigilant, and there are certain precautions we can take also."

"Meanwhile we are becalmed once more," Hawkwood said. "Pernicus' wind died with him. The ship is in the doldrums again."

They stood in silence, looking down at the wreck of the weather-worker.

"I do not think this a chance murder," Bardolin said eventually. "Pernicus was singled out for slaughter. Whatever other motives this thing has, it does not want this expedition to reach the west."

"It is rational then, even when in beast form?" Hawkwood asked, startled.

"Oh, yes. Werewolves retain the identity of their human form. It is just that their . . . impulses are naked, uncontrollable."

"Bardolin, Captain, I wish to confer with you both in my cabin," Murad said abruptly. "Ensigns, between you you will dispose of Pernicus' body. Make sure no one else sees it. The man was murdered, that is all the rest of the folk aboard need to know. Sequero, keep the guards posted on every hatch leading down into the hold. It may still be down here."

"Have you any iron balls for the arquebuses?" Bardolin asked.

"No, we use lead. Why?"

"Iron and silver are what harm it most. Even the steel of your sword will do but little damage. Best get some iron bullets moulded as fast as you can."

"I'll get the ship's smith on to it," Billerand said.

They left Sequero and di Souza to their grisly work and made their way back up through the ship.

"Are you sure you should be out of your hammock?" Hawkwood asked Billerand. The first mate was groaning and puffing as he progressed up the companionways.

"It'll take more than a few cracked bones to keep me from

my duty, Captain. And besides, I have a feeling that soon we'll be needing all the ship's officers we can get."

"Aye. See the gunner, Billerand. I want every man issued with a weapon. Arquebuses, boarding axes, cutlasses, anything. If anyone gets overly curious, spin them a tale of pirates."

Billerand grinned ferociously under his shaggy moustache. "And won't they wish it were true!"

"You'd best beat to quarters as well, to complete the picture. If we can make everyone think the danger we face is external, human, then there's less chance of a panic."

"Let slip that there's some kind of spy on board," Bardolin put in, "and that is who murdered Pernicus."

Murad laughed sourly. "There *is* a spy on board."

H AWKWOOD, Bardolin and Murad assembled in the nobleman's cabin, whilst behind them the ship went into an uproar. The decks were filled with thunder as the guns were run out, the sailors issued with arms and the passengers shepherded into spare corners. It would be easy for Murad's officers to quietly splash Pernicus' body over the side in the turmoil.

"Have a seat, gentlemen," Murad said sombrely, gesturing to the cot and the stool that were spare. The heat was beginning to build up below-decks now that the wind had dropped, and their faces were shining with sweat. But Murad did not open the stern windows.

"The noise will cover our conversation," he said, jerking a thumb at the din beyond the cabin. "Just as well."

He opened a desk drawer and brought out an oilskin-wrapped package. It was rectangular, the covering much worn. He unwrapped it and revealed a thick, battered book.

"The rutter," Hawkwood breathed.

"Yes. I have deemed it time to reveal its contents to you, Captain, and to you, Bardolin, since I feel you probably have an expertise in these matters."

"I don't understand," the mage said. The imp squirmed in his robe, but went unnoticed.

"We are not the first expedition to search for the Western Continent. There was one—in fact there were two—who went

before us, and both ended in disaster; the second because the
ship had a werewolf on board."

There was a pause. The racket and clamour of the carrack
went on heedlessly outside.

"I was never informed of this," Hawkwood said coldly.

"I did not think it necessary, but I do now with things the
way they are. It would seem that western expeditions have a
way of coming to grief that is similar."

"Explain, please," Bardolin said. Sweat was trickling down
his temples and dripping off his battered nose.

Briefly, Murad informed them both of the fate of the *Cartigellan Faulcon*, over a century before. He also told them of
the references in the rutter to an even earlier voyage west, one
undertaken by a group of mages fleeing persecution in the
Ramusian kingdoms.

"The information is fragmentary, and obscure, but I have
tried to glean what I can from it," he said. "What disturbs me
are the similarities between the three voyages. Werewolves,
Dweomerfolk. Murders on board ship."

"And ultimate disaster," Hawkwood added. "We should turn
back for Abrusio, get the boats out and tow the ship's head
into a wind. That Inceptine is right: this voyage is cursed."

Murad brought a fist down on the desk with a startling
thump. Dust rose from the pages of the ancient book.

"There will be no turning back. Whatever demon has taken
ship with us wants precisely that. You heard what Bardolin
said. Someone or something has been sabotaging westward
voyages for three centuries or more. I intend to find out why."

"Do you think the Western Continent is inhabited then?"
Bardolin enquired.

"Yes, I do."

"What about the *Grace of God*?" Hawkwood asked suddenly. "Could her disappearance be the result of some kind of
sabotage also?"

"Perhaps. Who can say?"

Hawkwood cursed bitterly.

"If the caravel is lost, Captain, don't you want to find out
how or why? And who it was that destroyed your ship and
killed your crew?" Murad's voice was low, but as hard as frost.

"Not at the expense of this ship and the lives of her company," Hawkwood said.

"That may not be necessary, if we are vigilant enough. We have been warned by the fate of the previous ships; we need not go the same way."

"Then how do we track this thing down? You heard Bardolin—there is no telling which man on this ship is the shifter."

"Perhaps the priest can tell. I have heard it rumoured that the clergy can somehow sniff out these things."

"No," Bardolin put in quickly. "That is a fallacy. The only way to weed out a shifter is to wait until it changes and be ready for it."

"What makes it change?" Hawkwood asked. "You said it was rational after a fashion, even in its beast form."

"Yes. And I also said it is impulsive, uncontrollable. But if we turn back it will, I believe, have got what it wants and may not find the need to shift again. On the other hand, if we announce that we are sticking to our course it may feel forced to persuade us otherwise."

"Excellent," Murad said. "There you are, Captain. We must continue westwards if we want to hunt this thing out into the open."

"Continue westwards!" Hawkwood laughed. "We are not continuing anywhere at the moment. The sails are as slack as a beggar's purse. The ship is becalmed."

"There must be something we can do," Murad said irritably. "Bardolin, you are supposed to be a mage. Can't you whistle up a wind?"

"A mage is master of only four of the Seven Disciplines," Bardolin replied. "Weather-working is not one of mine."

"What about the other passengers? They're mages and witches to a man, else they would not be here. Surely one of them could do something?"

Bardolin smiled wryly. "Pernicus was the only one gifted in that particular field. Perhaps you should ask Brother Ortelius to pray for a wind, my lord."

"Do not be insolent," Murad snapped.

"I only point out that the dregs of Ramusian society have suddenly become sought-after in a crisis."

"Only because one of those dregs jeopardizes the entire ship's safety with his own accursed brand of hellish sorcery," Murad said icily. "Set a thief to catch a thief, it is said."

Bardolin's eyes glinted in his old-soldier face. "I will catch your thief for you, then, but I will not do it for nothing."

"Aha! Here's the rub. And what would you like in way of payment, Mage?"

"I will let you know that at the appropriate time. For now, let us just say that you will owe me a favour."

"The damn thing isn't caught yet," Hawkwood said quietly. "Worry about obligations after we have its head on a pike."

"Well said, Captain," Murad agreed. "And here"—he threw the rutter into Hawkwood's lap—"peruse that at your leisure. It may be of use."

"I doubt it. We are far off our course, Murad. The rutter is no longer any use to me. From now on, unless we regain our former latitude—which is well-nigh impossible without a Dweomer wind—we are sailing uncharted seas. From what you have told me, it seems that the *Faulcon* never came this far south. My intent now is to set a course due west, parallel to our old one. There is no point in trying to beat up towards our former latitude."

"What if we miss the Western Continent altogether and sail to the south of it?" Murad asked.

"If it is even half the size of Normannia it will be there on this latitude. In any case, to try and sail back north would be almost suicidal, as I told you before we enlisted Pernicus' services."

Murad shrugged. "It is all one to me, so long as we sight land in the end and are in a fit state to walk ashore."

"Let me worry about that. Your concern is this beast that haunts the ship."

B Y the end of the morning watch the guns had been run back in and the rumour had circulated round the ship like a fast-spreading pestilence: Pernicus had been murdered by a stowaway spy, and the murderer lurked aboard, unknown. The carrack began to take on some of the aspects of a besieged fortress, with soldiers everywhere asking people their business, the crew armed and the ship's officers barking orders left and right. The patched-up boats were swung out from the yardarms and crews of sailors began hauling the carrack westwards, out of the doldrums; a killing labour in the stock-still heat of the day.

In the midst of the militant uneasiness the last of the storm's damage was rectified and the ship began to look more like her old self, with new timber about the sterncastle and waist and new cable sent up to the tops. But the sails remained flaccid and empty, and the surface of the sea was as obstinately flat as the surface of a green mirror, whilst the sun glared down out of a cloudless sky.

It was in the foretop that Bardolin and Griella finally found the peace to speak without being overheard. They sat in the low-walled platform with the bulk of the topmast at their backs and a spider tracery of rigging all about them.

Still red-faced from clambering up the shrouds in this heat, Bardolin released the imp. With a squeak of pleasure it darted around the top, gazing down at the deck far below and peering out at the haze-dim horizon.

"You've heard, I suppose?" Bardolin asked curtly.

"About Pernicus? Yes. Why would anyone have done such a thing? He was a harmless enough little man." Griella was dressed in her habitual breeches and a thin linen shirt that Bardolin suspected was a cast-off of Murad's. Fragments of lace clung to its neck and she had rolled the voluminous sleeves up to her elbows, exposing brown forearms with tiny golden hairs freckling them.

"He was killed by a shifter, Griella," the mage said in a flinthard voice.

The pale eyes widened until he could see the strange yellow-golden circle around the pupils. "Bardolin! Are you sure?"

"I have seen shifters kill before, remember."

She stared at him. Her mouth opened. Finally she said:

"But you don't think—you *do*! You think it was me!"

"Not you, but the beast that inhabits you."

The eyes flared; the yellow grew in them until they were scarcely human any longer. "We are the same, the beast and I, and I tell you that it was not I who slew Pernicus."

"Are you expecting me to believe there are two shifters on board this ship?"

"There must be, or else you are mistaken. Maybe someone killed him in such a way as to make it look as though it was done by a beast."

"I am not a fool, Griella. I warned you about this many times. Now it has happened."

"*I did not do it!* Please, Bardolin, you must believe me!"

The glow in the eyes had retreated and there was only the light of the pitiless sun setting the tears in them afire. She was a small girl again, tugging at his knee. The imp looked on, aghast.

"Why should I?" Bardolin said harshly, though he longed to take her in his arms, to say that he did, to make it all right.

"Is there nothing I can do to convince you?"

"What could you do, Griella?"

"I could let you see into my mind, the way you did before when I was about to change into the beast and you stopped me. You saw into me then, Bardolin. You can do it again."

"I—"

He was not so sure of himself now. He had thought to extract a confession from her, but he had not considered beyond that. He knew he would never have turned her over to Murad—there would have been some bargain made, some deal done. But now he no longer knew what to do.

Because he did believe her.

"Let me see your eyes, Griella. Look at me."

She tilted up her head obediently. The sun was behind him and his shadow fell upon her. He looked deep, deep into the sea-change of the eyes, and the top, the mast, the ship and the vast ocean disappeared.

A heartbeat, huge and regular. But as he listened the rhythm changed. It became erratic, slipping out of time. It took him a moment to realize that he was listening to two hearts beating not quite in tune with each other.

Pictures and images flickering like a shower of varicoloured leaves. He saw himself there, but shied away from that. He saw the ragged brown peaks of the Hebros Mountains that must have been her home. He saw swift, red-tinted images of wanton slaughter flitting past.

Too far back. He had gone too deep with his impatience. He must pull out a little.

The other heartbeat grew louder, drowning out the first. He thought he could feel the heat of the beast and the prickle of its harsh fur against his skin.

There! A ship upon a limitless ocean, and in the dark hours aboard a vision of white limbs intertwined, linen sheets in crumples of light and dark. An ecstatic, lean face he knew to be Murad's hovering over him in the night.

The beast again, very close this time. He felt its anger, its hunger. The unrelenting rage it felt at being confined.

Except it was not. It was free and lying beside the naked man in the swaying cot, the stout supporting ropes creaking under the weight. It wanted to kill, to rip the night apart with scarlet carnage. But did not. It lay beside the sleeping, nightmare-ridden nobleman and watched over him in the night.

It wanted to kill, but could not. There was something that prevented it, something the beast could not understand but could not disregard.

Nothing else. A few spangled images. Himself, the imp, the terrible glory of the storm. Nothing more. No memory of murder, not on the ship, not since Abrusio. She had told the truth.

Bardolin lingered a moment, peering round the tangled interstices of Griella's mind, noting the linkages here and there between the wolf and the woman, the areas where they were pulling apart, where control was weakest. He withdrew with a sense both of relief and of mourning. She did love Murad, in some perverse manner that even the beast could recognize. And in loving him, she was doing some violence to herself that Bardolin could not quite fathom.

She loved himself, old Bardolin, also—but not in the same way, not at all. He scourged himself for the unexpectedly acute sense of grief at the discovery.

The sun was beating down on them. Griella's eyes were glassy. He tapped her lightly on the cheek and she blinked, smiled.

"Well?"

"You told the truth," he said heavily.

"You don't sound too overjoyed."

"You may not have killed Pernicus, but you play a dangerous game with Murad, child."

"That is my business."

"All right, but it seems that the impossible is true: there is another shifter aboard the ship."

"Another shifter? How can that be?"

"I have no idea. You have not sensed anything, have you? You do not have any suspicions?"

"Why, no. I have never in my life met another sufferer of

the black disease, though folk said the Hebros were full of them."

"Then it seems there is nothing we can do until he chooses to reveal himself."

"Why would another shifter take ship with us?"

"To cause the abortion of the voyage, perhaps. That would be his motive for killing Pernicus. Murad told me something today which intrigues me. I must go down and consult my books."

"Tell me, Bardolin! What is going on?"

"I don't yet know myself. Keep your eyes open. And Griella: do not let the beast free for a while, not even in the privacy of Murad's cabin."

She flushed. "You saw that! You pried on us."

"I had no choice. The man is bad for you, child, and you for him. Remember that.

"I am not a child, Bardolin. You had best not treat me like one."

He stroked her satin cheek gently, fingers touching the tawny freckles there, the sun-brown skin.

"Do not think ill of me, Griella. I am an old man, and I worry about you."

"You are not so old, and I am sorry you worry." But her eyes were unrelenting.

Bardolin turned away and scooped up the watching imp.

"Come. Let us see if this not-so-old man can make his way down this labyrinth of ropes without cracking open his grey-haired skull on the deck."

THE carrack inched westwards painfully, towed by the labouring men in the ship's boats. They made scarcely two leagues a day, and the sailors became exhausted though the boat crews changed every hour. Hawkwood began to ration the water as though it were gold, and soldiers with iron bullets in their arquebuses guarded the water casks in the forward part of the hold day and night. The ship's company became subdued and apprehensive. Salt sores began to appear on everyone's bodies as the allowance of fresh water for washing was cut and the salt in garments began to abrade the skin. And still the sun blasted down out of a flawless sky, and in the clear green water below the keel the shadow of hanging weed grew longer as it built up on the carrack's hull.

The sailors trolled for fish to eke out the shipboard provisions. They hauled in herrin on their westward migration, wingfish, huge tub-bodied feluna, and sometimes the writhing, entangled sliminess of large octopuses, some of them almost big enough to swamp the smaller of the longboats.

Weed began to be sighted in matted expanses across the surface of the sea, and on the weed itself colonies of pink and scarlet crabs scuttled about seeking carrion. The weed beds stank to high heaven and were infested with sealice and other vermin. Inevitably some made their way aboard, and soon most of the ship's company had their share of irritating red bites and unwelcome itches on scalp and in groin.

In the dark of one middle watch a great glistening back rose like a birthing hill out of the sea alongside the carrack, and for half a glass it rose and sank there, a bulk that rivalled the ship in size. A long-necked head with a horny beak regarded the astonished ship's watch before diving below the surface again in a flurry of white foam. A knollback turtle. The sailors had heard of them in old maritime tales and legends. They were supposed to have been mistaken for islands by land-hungry mariners far from home. The crew made the Sign of the Saint at their breasts, and the next day Brother Ortelius' sermon was better attended than it had ever been before, affording the Inceptine a grim kind of pleasure. He called the voyage a flight in the face of God, and with Murad looking on declared that God's servants could not be muzzled by threats or fear. God's will would be done, in the end.

The same evening Hawkwood had two men flogged for questioning the orders of the ship's officers.

The men in the boats rowed on through the humid nights, watch on watch, their oars struggling through the stinking, matted weed with its population of crabs and mites. And on the gundeck the talk was turned to Pernicus' death and its possible author. Wild theories were hatched and did the rounds and it was all Bardolin could do to keep the Dweomer-folk calm. As it was, there were more manifestations of magic now. Some of the oldwives were able to purify small amounts of salt water whilst others worked to heal the salt sores everyone bore, and still more ignited white were-lights and left them

burning through the night for fear of what would creep about
the decks in the dark hours.

And then, eight tense, airless, back-breaking days after Pernicus had met his end, a wind came ruffling over the surface
of the undisturbed sea. A north-easter that gathered in strength
through the morning watch until the carrack's sails were drawing full again and the white foam broke beneath her bow. The
ship's company drew a collective sigh of relief as the wake
began to extend ever further behind her and she set her bow-
sprit squarely towards the west once more.

It was then that the killing began.

TWENTY-TWO

V OL Ephrir, capital of Perigraine. A city considered by
  many to be the most beautiful in the world.

It sat on an island in the midst of the mighty Ephron river.
Here, three hundred miles from its headwaters, the Ephron was
a glittering blue expanse of water over a mile wide. Ephrir
island was a long, low piece of land that curved with the me-
anders of the Ephron for almost three leagues. Centuries ago
the Fimbrians had walled it in against the constant flooding of
the river water and they had reared up an artificial hill a hundred feet high in its midst so that a citadel might be built there.
The city had grown around the fortress, fisher villages coa-
lescing into towns, merchant wharves taking up more and
more of the riverfront, fine houses and towers springing up in
the island's interior—until one day the entire island had been
built over, a sprawl of houses and villas and warehouses and
taverns and shops and markets with no discipline, no order. A
long-ago king of Perigraine had decreed that the city must be
better regulated. The fisher slums were demolished, the streets
widened and paved, the harbours rebuilt and dredged out to
accommodate the deep-bellied grain lighters that came upriver
from Candelaria.

The city had been reconstructed along the lines of an architectural ideal, and had become a marvel for most of the western world: the perfect city. And Vol Ephrir had never known war or been besieged, unlike many of the other Ramusian capitals.

There was something peculiarly innocent about the place, Abeleyn mused as he rode along its wide streets and inhaled the fragrance of its gardens. Perhaps it was the balminess of the climate. Although a man might look east and see the Cimbrics thirty leagues away, white with early snow, here in the Vale of Perigraine the air was neither warm nor cold. It could be bitter in the winter, but this slow slide into autumn suited the city, as did the millions of red and yellow leaves that floated in the city's ponds and upon the surface of the mighty Ephron, having fallen from the birch and maple woods that were flaming everywhere. The drifting leaves heightened the impression of quietude, for though Vol Ephrir was a busy, thriving place, it was nonetheless sedate, dignified. Somehow ornamental. The population of the place, at a quarter of a million, was almost as great as that of Abrusio, but there was something about Abeleyn's home city that was more frantic. Its teeming colour, perhaps, its vibrant cheek-by-jowl disorder. If Vol Ephrir was a dignified lady who welcomed guests with regal stateliness, then Abrusio was a bawdy old whore who opened her legs for the world.

King Abeleyn of Hebrion had been two days in the Perigrainian capital. Already he had been feasted by young King Cadamost and had tried his hand at hunting vareg, the vicious, tusked herbivore which haunted the riverside forests. Now he was impatient for the conclave to convene. The major rulers had arrived: himself and Mark of Astarac, their alliance a secret between the pair of them; white-haired, irascible Haukir of Almark, Inceptine advisers flapping around him like vultures eyeing a lame old warhorse; Skarpathin of Finnmark, a young man who had assumed his throne in rather murky, murderous circumstances; Duke Adamir of Gabrion, the very picture of a grizzled sea-dog; and Lofantyr of Torunna, looking harried and older than his thirty-two years.

There were others, of course. The dukes of the Border Fiefs were here: Gardiac, Tarber, and even isolated Kardikia had sent an envoy, though Duke Comorin could not come in person. Since the fall of Aekir, Kardikia was cut off from the rest of the Ramusian world; the only links it had with the other western powers now were by sea.

The Duke of Touron and the self-styled Prince of Fulk were present also, and in Abeleyn's own entourage, but not seated at the council table, was a representative of Narbukir, that Fimbrian electorate which had broken away from its fellows almost eighty years ago. The Narbukan envoy was to be revealed at the proper time. From the Fimbrian Electorates proper Abeleyn had had no news, no response to his overtures. He had expected as much, for all Golophin's optimism.

The rulers of the Ramusian kingdoms of the world were young men in the main. It seemed that a generation of older kings had relinquished their hold on power within a few years of each other, and the sons had taken their father's thrones whilst in their twenties or early thirties.

There were three Prelates present in the city also, newly arrived from the recent Synod at Charibon. Escriban of Perigraine, who was Prelate of the kingdom itself, Heyn of Torunna, who had spent hours closeted with King Lofantyr, and Merion of Astarac, who had spent the time likewise with Mark. Old Marat, the Prelate of Almark, had taken the quickest route home, but his monarch, Haukir, was so hemmed in by clerical advisers that he had probably deduced his presence unnecessary; so Abeleyn thought sourly.

The first meeting of the conclave was convened amid a buzz of rumour and speculation. There were reports that the first assaults on Ormann Dyke had taken place, and though part of the fortress complex had fallen the rest was standing, defying a Merduk horde half a million strong. Thanks to Golophin's gyrfalcon, Abeleyn was more accurately informed. Though it had taken place only days ago, and was almost a month's travel away, he knew of the failed river assault and the current enemy lethargy. He was at a loss to account for it, however.

But the miracle had been granted: the dyke still stood. It might be possible to reinforce it now. Five thousand Knights Militant were purportedly riding to the relief of the fortress from Charibon even as the kings took council in Vol Ephrir.

But there was another item of news which only Abeleyn and a few others were privy to. It had been confirmed that Macrobius was alive and well at the dyke, blinded but in possession of his senses. Himerius' elevation to the Pontiffship was therefore null and void. It was the best news Abeleyn had heard in weeks. He settled back in his leather-padded chair at the council table in the King's Hall of Vol Ephrir in a better mood than might otherwise be expected.

King Cadamost of Perigraine, as befitted his status as host, called the meeting to order.

The most powerful men in the western world were in a circular chamber in the highest tower of the palace. The floor upon which their chairs scraped was exquisitely mosaicked with the arms and flags of the Royal houses of Normannia. Tall windows of coloured glass tinted the flooding sunlight twenty feet above the heads of the assembled kings, and Perigrainian war banners hung limp from the rafters. There were no guards in the great chamber; they were posted on the staircases below. The round table at which everyone sat was littered with quills and papers. Those who disdained to read or write themselves had brought scribes along with them.

Courtesies were exchanged, greetings bandied about, protocol satisfied with an interminable series of speeches expressing the gratitude of the visiting kings to their host. As a matter of fact, hosting the conclave was no mean feat, even for the spacious city of Vol Ephrir. Every ruler present had brought several hundred retainers with him, and these had to be accommodated in a certain style, as did the monarchs themselves. Entertainments had to be laid on, banquets and tourneys to keep the crowned heads diverted when they were not in the council chamber, delicacies to whet their appetites, beer and wine and other liqueurs to help them relax. All in all, Abeleyn thought petulantly, Cadamost could have raised and equipped a sizeable army with the money he had spent playing the gracious host to his fellow monarchs. But that was the way the world worked.

Once the preliminaries were over, Cadamost rose from his seat to address the men about the table. They awaited his words with interest. Some of the seats among them were empty, and they were keen to know whether or not they would be filled, and by whom.

"This is a time of trial for the Ramusian states of the world," Cadamost said. He was a slim man of medium height, and he had the aspect of a scholar rather than that of a king. Some ocular complaint had ringed his eyes with red. He blinked painfully, but in compensation his voice was as musical as a bard's.

"In the past, conclaves have been called to deal with a crisis affecting the kingdoms and principalities of Normannia. They are convened to offer a place of arbitration and settlement. All the kingdoms represented here have at one time warred upon one another—and yet their monarchs sit now in peace beside each other, united by a common crisis, a foe who threatens us all.

"In the past there has been one power upon the continent that has always gone unrepresented at our meetings, and has refused to join in our councils. This power was once supreme across Normannia, but of late it has withdrawn into itself. It has become isolated, cut off from the concourse of normal diplomacy and international relations. I am glad to say that this state of affairs has changed. Only this morning, envoys arrived from that state. I ask you, my fellow rulers, to bid welcome to the envoys of Fimbria."

On cue, a pair of doors opened in the wall and two men stood there, dressed wholly in black.

"I bid you welcome, gentlemen," Cadamost said in his lilting voice.

The men marched into the chamber and took seats at the council table without a word. The doors boomed shut as if to emphasize the finality of their entrance.

"I give you Marshals Jonakait and Markus of Neyr and Gaderia, authorized in this instance to speak also for the electorates of Tulm and Amarlaine. In effect, they are the voice of Fimbria."

The other monarchs sat stunned, none more so than Abeleyn. His own envoys had returned empty-handed from the enigmatic Electors of Fimbria. But the four electorates had combined to send two representatives to the conclave. It was unprecedented. One of the reasons for the fall of the Fimbrian Hegemony had been the bitter rivalries between the electorates. What had caused this change of heart?

Cadamost looked rather smug. Regarded as a political lightweight by the other monarchs, he had nevertheless pulled off a massive diplomatic coup. Abeleyn glanced at the red-rimmed eyes, the unimpressive exterior of Perigraine's king. There was more to him than a singer's voice.

The Fimbrians sat impassively. They were square men, their hair shorn brutally short and their hollow-cheeked faces speaking of great physical endurance. They wore traditional Fimbrian black, the garb of all men of any rank in the electorates since the fall of their Hegemony and the death of the last emperor. Torunnan black and scarlet, the dress of Lofantyr, was a derivative of Fimbrian sable, and it was the Torunnans who had inherited the mantle of foremost military power upon the continent. But who knew how the Fimbrians would fare these days? Narbukan Fimbria, it was true, had opened itself to the outside world after the schism with the rest of the electorates, but as a result it was no longer seen as truly Fimbrian.

"We are here at the behest of two kings," Jonakait said. "We of the electorates recognize that the west is facing its greatest threat since the time of the Religious Wars. Fimbria, once the foremost power in the world, will no longer isolate itself from the normal run of diplomatic contact. I am here, authorized to enter into agreements and treaties with the other monarchs of Normannia, and authorized also to promise military aid if that is what is required."

"Why didn't your Electors come in person?" Lofantyr asked sharply, clearly resenting the "foremost power" bit.

Jonakait blinked. "Markus and I are authorized to act on their behalf. We have been invested with Electoral Imperium. We sit here as the de facto rulers of Fimbria, and are able to authorize any course of action we see fit."

Things had been changing in Fimbria then, and no one had even noticed, Abeleyn thought. The Electorates had somehow patched up their squabbles and acted in unison. He wondered just how much authority these two men truly possessed.

"Can you sanction the commitment of Fimbrian troops?" Lofantyr asked, his eagerness transparent.

"We can."

The Torunnan king leaned back. "You may be held to that promise, Marshal."

The Fimbrian shrugged ever so slightly.

Abeleyn wondered, though, who else among the men seated around the table would truly tolerate Fimbrian tercios on the march again across Normannia. He had thought himself open-minded, devoid of any prejudices springing from the past, but even he felt a cold shiver at the thought. The memories ran deep. No wonder many of the faces around the table looked outraged as well as astonished.

Cadamost took the floor again, striving to push the meeting past the sensational entrance of the two marshals.

"Urgent questions lie before us at this time, and it is imperative that the issues behind them be addressed. If the west is to have any kind of concerted policy towards the eastern crisis—and other happenings—then we must, as the heads of our nations, come to some decisions within the walls of this chamber."

"Do we work on the basis of rumours or of fact, cousin?" Haukir asked. His white beard bristled. It was said that he and his Prelate, Marat, were related, and more closely than might be supposed. The Almarkan Prelate, gossip had it, was born into the Royal house, but on the wrong side of the blanket. Certainly the two men were as similarly gruff and obstinate as to be twins.

"What do you mean, cousin?" Cadamost shot back.

"These rumours that Macrobius is alive and at Ormann Dyke, for instance. They must be quashed before they do harm."

"I agree," Abeleyn spoke up. "They should be thoroughly investigated, in case there is some germ of substance at their heart."

"Pieter Martellus at the dyke insists that Macrobius is there," Lofantyr said.

Haukir snorted. "Do you believe him? He's just trying to inject a little backbone into his garrison, is all."

"I have never heard that Torunnan soldiers lacked backbone," Lofantyr flared. "I thought perhaps their conduct at Aekir would have been testimony enough to their courage. My countrymen have been dying in their tens of thousands so that the kingdoms which shelter behind their bucklers might rest easy at night. So do not prate to me of *backbone,* cousin."

Bravo! Abeleyn thought gleefully as Haukir's face darkened and he began to sputter with wrath.

But Lofantyr was not yet done.

"It has been brought to my attention that the five thousand Knights Militant promised to my Prelate by the Vicar-General of the Inceptines have turned around in their march to the dyke and are retracing their steps to Charibon. So much for the help of the Church. Himerius takes the same line as you, Haukir: he condemns out of hand without waiting to hear the evidence for or against. Myself, I vow to keep an open mind. If Macrobius is truly alive, then surely it is a sign from God that the Merduk tide is on the turn. The news from the dyke confirms this."

Abeleyn shared a look with Mark of Astarac. So that was it. Lofantyr had found the strength to defy the new Pontiff because of the successes at the dyke. But also, Abeleyn suspected, because there were Fimbrian at the table making promises of troops. The Torunnan king did not feel he had to rely on Church forces any longer. Lofantyr was his own man again, and that was all to the good.

"Accusations and recriminations have no place at this assembly," Cadamost said, holding up a hand to forestall Haukir's explosion.

"Do we defy the Pontifical bull of the new spiritual leader of the Ramusian world, then?" Skarpathin of Finnmark asked easily, his killer's face creased by a sardonic smile.

Cadamost paused, and Abeleyn spoke quickly into the silence.

"The Pontiff may not be adequately informed. He acted as he thought best to prevent disorder, confusion—even schism— within the Church at this vital time. But though we can abide by the letter of the bull, I yet believe that we can conduct ourselves as just men, and await the result of further investigations with an open mind."

There were rumbles at this, but no open disagreement. Everyone knew that the Hebriate King and his one-time Prelate had always been at odds with one another. Haukir glared at Abeleyn suspiciously. He was the irreligious boy-king, the trickster. He must be up to something. Abeleyn kept his own face carefully bland.

Cadamost flicked a look of gratitude at Abeleyn. Clearly, his role of referee was a wearing one.

"The subjects for discussion have most of them been raised, then," he said. "This rumour of Macrobius' survival, the defence of Ormann Dyke and the other eastern marches, and the advent of our new colleagues, the Fimbrians."

"There are others, cousin," Mark of Astarac said.

"Such as?"

"Such as these damned burnings that have been going on in Hebrion and which seem set to be extended to every Ramusian state on the continent."

"That is an issue for the Church alone to decide," Haukir said.

"It is an infringement of the authority of the crown, and as such will be debated by this assembly," Abeleyn said. There was nothing of the boy about him now. His dark eyes flashed like glass catching the sun.

The other rulers stared at Mark and Abeleyn, sensing something there, some secret agreement. Time enough yet, though, before revealing the Hebro-Astaran Treaty of Alliance. Abeleyn and Mark had copies of it lurking in their suites, ready to be brought out at the right moment.

"Very well," Cadamost said. "The issue of the purges will be tabled also, though I do not see what lay rulers are able to do about it; it seems to me to be the Province of the Church alone."

"Let us say that I have my doubts as to the motives behind it," Abeleyn said.

"Are you questioning the judgement of the Holy Pontiff?" Lofantyr asked, ignoring the fact that he had done that very thing himself moments ago.

"He was not Pontiff when this decision was made. He was Prelate of Hebrion, and thus his actions come under the purlieu of the Hebriate crown."

"Lawyer's niceties!" Haukir snorted.

"Those lawyer's niceties may have some import if the case is brought before a Royal commission," Abeleyn said.

"You cannot put the High Pontiff on trial," Skarpathin of Finnmark said, a conservative despite his youth and the bloody steps he had taken to secure his throne.

"No, but perhaps he is not the High Pontiff, if Macrobius yet lives. Also the purges were initiated by a Prelate, not a Pontiff. We have yet to read a Pontifical bull extending them formally."

"I hear that two thousand of the Knights are almost on Hebrion's borders, cousin. That would not have anything to do with your haste to table this issue?" Haukir said, smiling unpleasantly.

"I rejoice that the resources of the Church are so lavished

on my kingdom, but like Lofantyr I think they could be better employed elsewhere."

"You need men to fight the Merduks, not words," Markus, the Fimbrian marshal said suddenly, his bluntness disconcerting. "You can no longer rely on the troops of the Church, that is plain. The Pontiff and his Prelates are playing their own game; they do not care about the fate of Ormann Dyke. They may even be glad to see it fall, if it rids them of this rival Pontiff at the same time."

It was unforgivable to speak the truth so openly. Isolation has atrophied any kind of diplomatic subtleties the Fimbrians might once have possessed, Abeleyn thought.

Haukir seemed to be on the verge of another explosion, but the Fimbrian continued speaking in his level, toneless voice.

"The Fimbrian Electorates have decided to put their forces at the disposal of the west. There are six hundred tercios under arms in Fimbir itself. These troops have been set aside for possible employment beyond the borders of the electorates. Any monarch who needs them may have them."

The table sat stunned in silence. Six hundred tercios! Over seventy thousand men. They had had a chimera in their midst and had not known it.

"Who will these tercios serve under?" Lofantyr asked.

"They will have their own officers, and any expeditionary force will be commanded by a Fimbrian marshal who will in turn accept orders from whichever ruler employs him."

"*Employs?*" Cadamost asked, his red eyes narrowing. "Tell me, Marshal, who will pay the wages of these soldiers?"

For the first time Markus looked less than impassive.

"Their costs will have to be met by the monarch they serve under, of course."

So that was it. The Fimbrians were killing two birds with the same stone. Now that the electorates had seemingly patched up their differences they no doubt had a wealth of unemployed soldiers on their hands. What to do with them, these peerless fighters? Farm them out to the other western states, relieve a no-doubt strained economy—and extend Fimbrian influence at the same time. The Fimbrian crutch might well transform into a club one day. It was a neat policy. Abeleyn wondered if Lofantyr were desperate enough to take the bait. Surely he must see the ramifications.

"I would speak to you privately after this day's meeting is concluded, Marshal," the Torunnan king said at last.

Markus bowed slightly, but not before Abeleyn had caught the gleam of triumph in his eye.

"THE damn fool!" Mark raged. "Can't he see what he is doing? The Fimbrians will put a leash about his throat and lead him around like a dog."

"He is in a tight corner," Abeleyn said, sipping his wine and rolling a black olive round and round the table to catch the sunlight. "He has been baulked of his reinforcements by the Church, so he must have men from somewhere. The Fimbrian intelligence service must be quite efficient. The timing of this offer is perfect."

"Do you think they hanker after empire again?"

"Of course. What else could have persuaded the electorates to cease their internal strife? My ploy of bringing the Narbukan envoy here has fallen flatter than a pricked bladder. It is strange. Golophin must have suspected that there was something afoot in Fimbria, for it was he who advised me to sound out the electorates. I do not think he imagined this, though, not in his wildest dreams."

"Or nightmares. Our alliance looks like pretty small beer compared with this news."

"On the contrary, Mark. It is more important than ever. Cadamost has come to some secret arrangement with the marshals, of that I am sure. They accepted his invitation, not mine. And Torunna needs troops. How does one get to Torunna from Fimbria? Via Perigraine! Cadamost has been playing a very deep game. Who would have believed him capable of that?"

They were seated at a roadside tavern in one of the main thoroughfares of the city. Waggons and carts trundled past unendingly, and around them was the red-gold shade of the turning trees, avenues of which lined almost every street in Vol Ephrir. Scarlet and amber leaves dotted the ground like a crunching carpet, and there was a cool breeze blowing. If they looked up, past the well-constructed buildings on the other side of the street, they could see the palace towers of Vol Ephrir shining white with marble. Abeleyn raised his glass to them and drank. It was Candelarian. Fully half of Candelaria's exports were to Perigraine.

"We must speak with Lofantyr," Abeleyn said. "He must be made to see what he is doing. We will not dissuade him from utilizing Fimbrian troops, but he must at least be frugal in their deployment. One good thing about this: it has secured his independence from the Church, and it may ensure the recognition of Macrobius as Pontiff once again. Lofantyr will back him all the way. He has nothing to lose and much to gain from a Pontiff who might well become a Torunnan puppet."

"If Himerius steps down," Mark said sombrely.

"A very interesting if, cousin. Who would support him if he did not? Almark, of course, and Finnmark—most of the Border Duchies."

"Peregraine, maybe."

"Maybe. I am all at sea when thinking of this kingdom. Cadamost has rattled me—most unpleasant."

A third person joined them at their table, appearing out of the throng of people who coursed up and down the street. She bowed to both kings and then drank some wine from Abeleyn's glass.

"My lady Jemilla," the Hebrian monarch said easily. "I trust you have been enjoying your trip about the city?"

"It is a wonderous place, sire, so different from our crowded old Abrusio. Like something from one of the old courtly tales."

"You look pale. Are you well?"

Jemilla was wearing a loose robe of deep scarlet encrusted with pearls and gold thread. Her dark hair was bound up on her head with more pearl-headed pins, and her face was as white as sea-scoured bone.

"Quite well, sire. I am a little tired, perhaps."

Mark ignored her. He had been rather scandalized by Abeleyn's bringing her to the conclave, especially since the Hebrian king was officially, if secretly, betrothed to his sister.

"You should keep out of the sun. It is very bright on the eye in this part of the world. There is no dust to blunt its passage."

"I am waiting for my barouche, sire. Will you walk me to the corner? My maids seem to have deserted me for the moment."

"By all means, my lady. Cousin, you will await my return?"

Mark flapped a hand affably enough and buried his nose in his glass.

"He doesn't like me," Jemilla said when they were out of earshot.

"He is attracted to you, but Mark is an austere sort of fellow at times. He loves his wife, and is prone to guilt."

"You and he behave like a pair of 'prentice ensigns out on the town. Have you no attendants with you?"

Abeleyn laughed. "My bodyguards—and Mark's—are very discreet, and Cadamost no doubt has people watching us also. You need not fear for my safety in Vol Ephrir. If anything happened here it would reflect badly on Perigraine's king."

Jemilla leaned on his arm. She was walking more slowly than her usual brisk pace.

"Is anything the matter, my lady?"

She leaned close to him, spoke into his ear.

"I am with child."

They halted in the street, curious folk glancing at the pair as they passed by.

"Are you sure?" Abeleyn asked in a voice gone toneless and cold.

"Yes, sire. It is yours. There has been no one else in the time we have been together."

Abeleyn stared at her. The bright sunlight brought out the lines at the corners of her eyes, accentuated the whiteness of her skin, the shadows under her cheekbones.

"You are not well, lady," he murmured.

"I can keep nothing down. It is a passing thing."

"Does anyone else know?"

"My maid will have guessed." Jemilla caressed her stomach through the thick, loose robe. "It is hardly noticeable as yet, but my flow has been—"

"All right, all right! I don't want to hear about your woman's mechanisms!" Like most men, Abeleyn knew little and cared less about that particular subject. It was bad luck to couple with a woman at that time, an offence against God. That was as far as he cared to enquire.

"You're sure it's mine, Jemilla?" he demanded in a low voice, taking her by the arms.

Her eyes filled with tears. "Yes, sire." She bent her head and began to sob quietly.

"Saint's teeth! Where is that blasted cart? Dry your eyes, woman, for God's sake!"

The covered carriage came trundling along the street and Abeleyn hailed it.

"Will you be all right?" he asked as he helped her inside. He had never seen her weep before and it disconcerted him.

"Yes, sire, I will be fine. But I cannot—I cannot perform the same services that I have undertaken up until now."

Abeleyn coloured. "Never mind that. We'll get you back to Hebrion by sea. You won't be climbing the Malvennors in your state. There are a few things I must arrange. You will be looked after, Jemilla."

"Sire, I have to say—I want to keep this child. I will not have it . . . disposed of."

Abeleyn stiffened. For a second he bore an uncanny resemblance to his severe, rigidly pious father.

"That is one notion that never entered my mind, Jemilla. As I said, you will be looked after, and the child also."

"Thank you, sire. I never doubted it."

He closed the door and the carriage sped away to the palace where she had a suite of her own. He followed its departure with a grim set to his mouth.

A bastard child, and not by some strumpet either. By a lady from a noble house. That could cause problems. He would have to be careful.

"Anything wrong?" Mark asked when Abeleyn rejoined him.

"No. Women's inquisitiveness. I sent her on her way."

"A handsome woman, if rather on the mature side."

"Yes. She's a widow."

"And nobly born," Mark noted unsmilingly.

Abeleyn gave him a piercing look. "Not nobly enough, cousin, believe me. Not nobly enough. Order some more wine, will you? I'm as dry as a summer lane."

IN the closed carriage, the lady Jemilla's face was bright and hard, the tears dried. The carriage was well-sprung, the motion easy, for which she was grateful. She had never borne a child full-term before. She was not entirely sure about what awaited her. But that was not important.

He had believed her—that was the main thing. What would he do now? What prospects had a bastard son of Hebrion's king? It remained to be seen. She did not like the way Abeleyn was so friendly with Mark of Astarac. As a bachelor he might secretly welcome a son, even one from the wrong side of the blanket, but were he to marry and make an Astaran princess his queen . . .

It was not Abeleyn's child, of course; it was Richard Hawkwood's. And it would be a boy—she could feel it in her marrow. But Hawkwood was no doubt dead by now, fathoms deep in the waters of some unending ocean. And even if he were not, he was not nobly born. He must never know that he had a son. No, this child of hers would grow up a king's son, and one day she would see that he claimed what he was owed. He would not be cheated of his birthright, and when he claimed it his mother would be there to guide him.

TWENTY-THREE

THEY found Billerand halfway through the middle watch, down in the cable tiers in the fore part of the hold. He had gone below to check on the eight-inch cables that served the anchors. The boy Mateo had been with him; of his body there was no trace. The soldiers said they had heard nothing.

A file of arquebusiers fired a volley as what remained of his corpse was slipped over the side in recognition of the soldier he had once been, then they went back to their posts, in fours now instead of pairs, and with lanterns burning throughout the hold to try and keep the shadows at bay.

Hawkwood and Murad spent what was left of the night drinking good brandy in the nobleman's quarters and racking their tired brains for something to do, some course of action that would help. Hawkwood even suggested asking Ortelius for aid, but Murad vetoed him. Bad enough that the priest seemed to be winning more and more influence among the soldiers and the sailors, but for the ship's officers to go running to him for help was intolerable.

Bardolin joined them, bad news written all over his face.

"Ortelius is addressing a meeting of sorts on the gundeck," he told them.

"The gundeck!" Murad exclaimed.

"Yes. It would seem he has made it his mission to win over the poor lost souls of the Dweomer-folk to his way of thinking. There are many of the soldiers there, and some of the mariners too."

"I'll get Sequero to break up their little party," Murad said, beginning to rise from his chair.

"No, Lord Murad, I beg you do not. It can only do harm. Most of your men are still at their posts, and the majority of your sailors, Captain, but I noticed one of your ship's officers, Velasca. He was there with the rest."

"Velasca?" Hawkwood exploded. "The mutinous dog!"

"It would seem," Murad drawled, "that our subordinates are evolving minds of their own. Have some brandy, Mage. And take that thing out of the front of your robe for the Saint's sake. I have seen familiars before."

Bardolin released the imp. It hopped on to the table and sniffed at the neck of the brandy decanter, then grinned as Murad chucked it gently under the chin.

"Good luck, an imp aboard ship," Hawkwood said quietly.

"Yes," Bardolin said. "I remember Billerand telling me once, back in Abrusio."

There was a heavy silence. Hawkwood downed his brandy as though it were water. "What have you found out?" he asked the wizard at last, eyes watering from the strong spirit.

"I have been doing some reading. On werewolves. My collection of thaumaturgical works is pitifully inadequate—my home was ransacked ere we left Hebrion—and I have had to be discreet in enquiring as to whether any of the other passengers have similar works in their possession, you understand. But according to what meagre researches I have been able to carry out, shifters do not like confinement of two kinds. Gregory of Touron reckons that the longer the man who is the shifter retains his human form, the more violent the actions of the beast once he transforms. Hence if shifters do not intend to run entirely amok once in animal form, they must change back and forth regularly, even if the beast form only lies motionless. It is like lancing a boil. The pus must be let out occasionally. The beast must breathe."

"What's the other form of confinement?" Murad asked impatiently.

"That is simple. Any prolonged period of incarceration in close quarters, such as a house, a cave—"

"Or a ship," Hawkwood interrupted.

"Just so, Captain."

"Brilliant," Murad said caustically, flourishing his glass. "What good do these priceless nuggets do us, old man?"

"They tell us that this shifter is suffering on two counts. First because he is in the confined space of a ship, and second because he cannot change back and forth with the frequency he might desire. And so the pressure builds up, and the frustration."

"You're hoping he will make a mistake, lose control," Hawkwood said.

"Yes. He has been very careful so far. He has murdered our weather-worker and left us becalmed, thinking perhaps that will be enough. But the wind has struck up again and still the ship is pointed west, so he strikes again—at a ship's officer this time. He is starting to sow the seeds of panic."

"They know it was a shifter that killed Pernicus," Murad said, his eyes two slits in his white-skinned face. "It's hard to say who are the most terrified, the soldiers or the passengers."

"He hopes to ignite a mutiny, perhaps," Hawkwood said thoughtfully.

"Yes. There is one other thing Gregory tells us, however. It is that the shifter who has recently killed is not sated—quite the reverse, in fact. Often he finds he must kill again and again, especially when he is in these confined conditions I have mentioned. He loses more control with every murder until in the end the rational part of him recedes and the mindless beast gains control."

"Which perhaps is what happened to the shifter aboard the *Faulcon*," Hawkwood put in.

"Yes, I am afraid so."

"The *Faulcon* did not carry a complement of Hebrian soldiers, nor arquebuses with iron bullets," Murad said stoutly. "No, this thing is becoming afraid, is my guess. If the wizard is correct then the shifter is beginning to succumb to his more bestial impulses. It may work to our advantage."

"And in the meantime we await another death?" Hawkwood asked.

"Yes, Captain, I think we do," Bardolin said.

"I don't think much of your strategy, Mage. It is like that of the sheep as the wolf closes in."

"I can think of nothing else."

"There is no mark, no sign by which the beasts can be recognized in human form?"

"Some old wives say there is something odd about the eyes. They are often strange-looking, not quite human."

"That's not much to go on."

"It is all I have."

"Where will he strike next, do you think?" Murad asked.

"I think it will be at what he perceives to be the centre of resistance and the source of authority. I think that next he will strike at one of those sitting about this table."

Murad and Hawkwood stared blankly at one another. Finally the scarred nobleman managed a strangled laugh.

"You have a sure way of ruining good brandy, Mage. It might be vinegar in my mouth."

"Be prepared," Bardolin insisted. "Do not let yourselves be found alone at any time, and always carry a weapon that will bite its black flesh."

T HE carrack sailed on with its twin cargoes of fear and discontent. Velasca, Hawkwood noted, was slow to obey orders and seemed perpetually ill at ease, even when the splendid north-easter continued steadily, breezing in over the starboard quarter and propelling the ship along at a good six knots. Two leagues run off with every two turns of the glass, one hundred and forty-four sea miles with every full day of sailing. And west, always due west. The carrack's beakhead bisected the sinking disc of every flaming sunset as though it meant to sail into its very heart. Hawkwood loved his ship more than ever then, as she responded to his attentions, his cajolings, his lashing on of sail after sail. She seemed unaffected by the feelings on board, and leapt over the waves like a willing horse scenting home in the air ahead.

2nd day of Endorion, year of the Saint 551.
    Wind north-east, fresh and steady. Course due west. Speed six knots with the breeze on the starboard quarter. Courses, topsails and bonnets.   .
    Six weeks out of Abrusio harbour, by my estimate over

eight hundred leagues west of North Cape in the He-
brionese, on the approximate latitude of Gabrion, which
we will follow until we find land in the west.

In the forenoon watch Lord Murad had three soldiers
strappadoed from the main yardarm for insubordina-
tion. As I write they are being attended on the gundeck
by Brother Ortelius and some of the oldwives aboard.
Strange bedfellows.

Hawkwood looked over the entry, frowning, then shrugged
as he sat and dipped his quill in the inkwell again.

In the five days since First Mate Billerand and Ship's
Boy Mateo were lost there have been no further deaths
on board, though the mood of the ship's company has
not improved. I have had words with Acting First Mate
Velasca; it seems he is not happy with our course and
the voyage as a whole. I told him that I expect to sight
land within three weeks, which seemed to improve his
temper and that of the crew. The soldiers, however, are
growing more restless by the day, and despite the efforts
of Murad's junior officers, they refuse to man their posts
down in the hold. There is something down there, they
say, and they will only guard working parties hauling
up provisions.

Billerand is sorely missed.

Hawkwood rubbed his tired eyes as the flickering table lantern played over the pages of his log. On the desk by the
lantern Bardolin's imp squatted cross-legged and watched the
scrawling quill with fascination. The little creature was covered with ink; it seemed to love daubing itself with it.

On a chair by the door of the cabin his master slumped,
asleep. The mage had an iron spike loosely gripped in one
hand and his head had fallen forward on to his chest. He was
snoring softly.

They had taken Bardolin's advice to heart. None of them
remained alone any more, especially at night.

If Hawkwood paused to listen, he could hear the creak and
groan of the ship's timbers, the rush and hiss of the sea as the
carrack's bow went up and down, the voices of men on the

deck above his head. And from the other side of the thin bulk-head, dark moans and thumps from Murad's cabin. He was not alone either. He had the girl in there with him, Griella.

It was late. Hawkwood felt he had neglected the log; he felt he should pad out the bald entries more fully, leave something for posterity perhaps. The thought made him smile wryly. Perhaps some fisherman might find it one day, grasped in his skeletal hand.

He looked again at the last sentence he had written, and his face fell.

Billerand is sorely missed.

Aye. He had not truly realized how much he had depended on the bald, mustachioed ex-soldier. He and Julius Albak had been the two indomitable pillars aboard ship. Good shipmates, fine friends.

Now they were both gone, Julius at the hands of the Incep-tines—they had killed him, no matter that it was a marine's arquebus which had stopped his heart—and Billerand under the muzzle of a werewolf. Hawkwood felt strangely alone. On him rested the entire responsibility for the expedition, espe-cially if the *Grace of God* had foundered, which he was be-ginning to believe had happened. He and he alone could point the *Osprey's* beakhead in the right direction.

The knowledge weighed on him sorely. He had told Velasca that three weeks would see landfall, but that had been a mere sop to the man's fear. Hawkwood had no idea how long they had to go before the fabled Western Continent would loom up out of the horizon.

He heard the ship's bell struck twice. Two bells in the mid-dle watch, an hour past midnight. He would take a last sniff of air up on deck, check the trim of the sails and then retire to his bunk.

He placed a sea cloak over the gently snoring Bardolin and went to the door. The imp chirruped wheedlingly at him and he turned.

"What is it, little one?"

With a bound, it launched itself off the desktop and landed on his shoulder. It nuzzled his ear, and he laughed.

"All right, then. You want some fresh air too?"

He left, reasoning that Bardolin would be all right for a moment or two, and climbed up to the quarterdeck. Mihal had

the watch, a good, steady fellow who was also Hawkwood's
countryman. Two soldiers, ostensibly on guard duty, leaned at
the break of the deck smoking pipes and spitting over the
ship's rail. Hawkwood scowled. Discipline had gone to the
wall these past days.

Mihal stared at the imp momentarily and then recited:

"Steady nor'-west, sir. Course due west under everything
she can bear."

"Good. You might want to furl the courses in a glass or
two. We don't want to run smack into the Western Continent
in the middle of the night."

"Aye, sir."

"Where's the rest of the watch?"

"On the forecastle, mostly. I've two men on the tiller. She's
steering easily enough."

"Very good, Mihal."

Hawkwood leaned on the windward rail gazing out at the
night sea. It was as dark as the ink on his desk. The sky was
almost clear, and great bands of speckled stars were arching
from horizon to horizon. Most he knew and had steered by for
twenty years. They were old friends, the only familiar things
on this unending ocean.

The imp made a noise, and he looked down into the waist
to see a black-robed figure disappearing into the sterncastle.
Ortelius, most likely. What would he want at this time of
night?

"Wake me if the wind shifts," he told Mihal, and made his
way back down the companionway.

The imp was whimpering and shifting around on his shoulder, clearly upset. He shushed it and then, stepping into the
deeper dark of the sterncastle, he knew something was wrong.

A golden bar of lantern light was coming from the door to
his cabin—but he had closed it after him.

He drew his dirk and pushed through the door quickly. Bardolin was still asleep in his chair but the sea cloak had fallen
to the floor. The imp hopped from Hawkwood's shoulder to
his master's, still chittering urgently.

The door was pushed shut behind Hawkwood.

He spun round and his mouth dropped with shock.

"Mateo!"

"Well met, Captain," the figure said with a ghastly smile.

The ship's boy was filthy and bloody, his hair crawling with lice and his nails long and black. His eyes had a light in them that made the hair on the back of Hawkwood's neck stand up like wire.

"Mateo, we thought you were dead!"

"Aye, and so did I, Captain." The voice which had been on the verge of breaking before he disappeared was as deep and full as a man's. "And didn't you wish I was dead—the bumboy you were so ashamed of having used? Didn't you, Captain? But I wasn't and I'm back again, different but the same."

"What in the world are you talking about, Mateo?" Hawkwood asked. The boy was circling like a prowling cat. Now he was between Hawkwood and the sleeping mage. The imp was frozen, utterly petrified. It eyed Mateo as though he were a fiend incarnate. Then the horrible thought occurred to Hawkwood.

"It was you," he breathed. "You are the werewolf. You killed Pernicus and Billerand." His voice shook as he said it. He wondered how many would hear his shout, how much time he would have.

Mateo grinned, and Hawkwood could see the lengthening canines, the black flush of hair that was breaking out like a rash down the sides of his face.

"Wrong, Captain, it was not me. It was my new master, a man who appreciates me as you never did."

"Your—? Who is he?"

"A man high up in his society, and high up in other things too. He has promised me much and given me much already. But I am tired of rats and what he gave me of Billerand. I want a fresh kill. You, whom I loved and who discarded me like a spent horse. You, Richard."

"Bardolin!" Hawkwood screamed in the same instant as Mateo launched himself at him.

MURAD sat up to find Griella awake beside him, her eyes shining in the dark, something strange about her profile. Another dream?

"I thought I—"

She shook her head and nodded towards the door of the cabin. Standing hunched in the doorway was a vast, black shape, its ears as tall as horns and its eyes two burning yellow lights. Around its feet in a puddle of shadow were a set of black robes.

"My Lord Murad," the beast said, its long teeth gleaming. "Time for you to die."

In the same moment, Murad heard Hawkwood scream out Bardolin's name on the other side of the partition. There was a thump and crash. The beast cocked its massive head.

"He has much to learn," it said, seemingly amused.

Then it leapt.

THE thing was on top of him, its fetid breath wreathing about his face. It was recognizable as Mateo, but the face was changing even as Hawkwood grappled with it, the nose broadening and pushing out into a snout. The eyes flared with saffron light and the heat of it made him choke.

It dipped its forming muzzle and bit deep.

Hawkwood shrieked in agony as the jaws met in his flesh. The dirk glanced off the thick fur that now covered the boy's body and slipped out of his nerveless hand. The pair of them rolled across the deck of the cabin, blood jetting from Hawkwood's mangled shoulder. They knocked against the table and it came down. Ink splattered them; the loose pages of the log flew about like pale birds and the table lantern crashed to the ground with a spatter of burning oil.

The heat, the awful heat. It was wholly beast-like now and it covered him like a choking carpet. He lay still, strength ebbing away with the thick ropes of blood that were pulsing out of his ripped veins.

"I love you, Richard," the werewolf said, its insane eyes glaring at him over its blood-soaked muzzle. The maw descended again.

Then it had thrown itself back off him, howling in agony and fury. The cabin was a thrashing, flickering chaos of shadows and flames. The wood of the deck and bulkhead were on fire, and the werewolf was wrenching a black spike out of its neck, still howling.

Bardolin stood there, the flames illuminating his face, filling the imp's eyes with light as it perched on his shoulder. Dimly Hawkwood was aware of other voices shouting in the ship, and a turmoil of snarling and violence on the other side of the bulkhead, Murad's voice raised in fear.

"Get you gone," Bardolin said quietly, almost conversation-ally, and he pointed one large hand at the writhing beast.

Blue fire left his fingers, crackled like lightning and sank into the black fur to disappear.

The werewolf shrieked. Its head snapped up and down. It retreated to where the flames were climbing the wall of the cabin and blue fire sparked out of its mouth. There was the smell of burning flesh.

Then the entire cabin wall disintegrated beside it.

Two huge black figures smashed clear through the bulkhead and fell on to the floor entangled in each other's arms. Hawkwood crawled feebly away from the flames and the thrashing beasts, slumping at the further wall. He watched the scene with utter amazement.

Murad was standing in the gap of the shattered partition wall with a long knife in his hand, whilst on the deck *three* were-wolves fought and howled amid the rising flames. Hawkwood saw one detach itself from the mêlée, azure light spurting from its eyes and nostrils. It hurled itself at the stern windows and they gave way, glass, frame, planking and all. It flew out into the dark night beyond and splashed into the carrack's foaming wake. There was a flash of aquamarine, so bright it dimmed the fire on board ship, and then a concussion that shook the entire stern and sent the sea into an insane turmoil of explo-sions and geysers brilliantly lit from below.

The entire aft end of the cabin was a gaping, blazing hole with two firelit silhouettes battling there, their fur on fire and their eyes glaring the same colour as the flames. The violence of their battle made the entire ship quiver and the blackened planking screeched and groaned under their clawed feet whilst their howls hurt Hawkwood's ears.

The cabin door was flung open to reveal Ensign Sequero, behind him a crowd of soldiers with smoking arquebuses. He stared blankly at the hellish scene for a second, then shouted a command. The soldiers levelled their weapons through the doorway.

"No!" Bardolin yelled.

A volley of shots, plumes of smoke and fire spurting from the weapons. Hawkwood saw fur lifted from the grappling beasts, blood erupting over the walls and deckhead.

One of the werewolves broke free and came roaring towards the soldiers, its fur blazing and gore spurting from its wounds.

It batted Sequero aside, wrenched an arquebus from a terrified soldier and clubbed another so brutally that the weapon's stock shattered. For a moment it seemed that it would succeed in getting away.

But then the second werewolf leapt on to its back. Hawkwood saw the thing's jaws sink deep into fur and flesh, then wrench free with a gobbet of bleeding meat between the teeth.

Someone hauled him out of the way. It was Murad. He dragged Hawkwood out of the cabin and into the companionway.

"Griella, it's Griella," he was saying. "She's one of them. She's a shifter too."

"The fire," Hawkwood croaked. "Put out the fire, or the ship is lost." But Murad had gone again.

There were more soldiers there, crowding the sterncastle, and then some sailors.

"Velasca!" Hawkwood managed to shout.

"Captain! What in the world—"

"The ship's afire. Leave the soldiers to their work and organize fire-fighting parties."

"Captain—your shoulder—"

"Do it, you insubordinate bastard, or I'll see you marooned!"

"Aye, sir." Velasca disappeared, chalk-faced.

Hawkwood heard Bardolin's voice raised in fury, telling the soldiers to hold fire. He struggled to his feet, his one working hand clutching the bloody mess of his shoulder. He could feel the ends of his collar-bone under his hands, and splinters of bone pricked his palm like needles.

"Sweet Ramusio," he groaned.

He staggered back into the wreck of the stern cabin, pushing aside the arquebusiers. The place was thick with smoke and the reek of blood and powder. The flickering radiance of the fire played about the deck and bulkheads.

Hawkwood sank down on the storm sill, light-headed but as yet not in much pain. He could no longer remain on his feet.

Men shouting, a shower of water coming down past the gaping hole in the stern of the ship, the flames eating into the precious wood. His poor *Osprey*.

Bardolin and Murad standing like statues, the nobleman's

iron knife dangling from one hand. The imp had buried its little face in its master's neck.

And lying amid the flames two hulking, broken shapes with the blood bubbling in their wounds and swathes of bare, blistered flesh shining where the fur had been burnt off.

One werewolf had a paw clutched to its chest much as Hawkwood nursed his shoulder. The black lips drew back from the teeth in a parody of a smile.

"Your iron has done for me, after all," it sneered. "Who'd have thought it? The maid a fellow sufferer. Little lady, we could have talked, you and I."

The other beast was barely conscious. It growled feebly, the light in its eyes becoming fainter moment by moment.

More water cascaded down from above. They had rigged the hand-pumps and were frenziedly pumping seawater over the burning ship.

"You will never find the west," the werewolf said to Hawkwood, whose eyes were stinging and blurred with smoke and pain. To him the beast that had been Ortelius was nothing but a looming shadow backlit by sputtering flames and brightly lit cascades of seawater. "Better for you and yours that you do not. There are things there best left alone by the men of Normannia. Turn your ship around if it remains afloat, Captain. I am only a messenger; there are others more powerful than I whose faces are set against you. You cannot survive."

The werewolf hauled itself with startling speed to its feet. At the fore end of the cabin the crowd by the door watched transfixed as it hurled itself, laughing, from the shattered stern and disappeared into the sea beyond.

A volley of shots followed it down into the water, stitching the sea with foam. It was gone.

"Griella," Murad groaned, and started forward into the fire. Bardolin stopped him.

"Better to let her burn," he said with great gentleness. "She cannot live."

The men watched as the shape in the flames became smaller and paler. The ears shrank, the fur withered away and the eyes dulled. In seconds there was a naked girl lying there in the fire, her body ravaged with terrible wounds. She turned her head to them before the end, and Hawkwood thought she smiled. Then her body blackened, as though some preserving forces had suddenly failed, and the flames were licking around a charred corpse.

Murad's face was as bleak as a skull.

"She saved my life. She did that for me. She loved me, Bardolin."

"Get more water in here," Hawkwood said calmly, "or we'll lose the ship. Do you hear me there? Don't just stand around."

Murad shot him a look of pure hatred and stormed out past the staring soldiers.

"The ship. You must save the ship," Hawkwood insisted, but the fire and the bulkheads and the faces were retreating down a soundless tunnel away from him. He could not hold the scene in focus. Men were coming and going, and he was being lifted. He thought Bardolin's face was close to his, lips moving soundlessly. But his tunnel continued to lengthen. Finally it grew so long that it blotted out the light, and all the pictures faded. The faces and the mounting pain dimmed with growing distance. He held on as long as he could, until he could hear the pumps sluicing water all around him. His poor ship.

Then the shadows swooped in on his tired mind, and bore it off with them to some howling place of darkness.

TWENTY-FOUR

"SHAHR Indun Johor," the vizier announced.

Aurungzeb the Golden waved a hand. "Send him in."

He kissed the nipple of the raven-haired Ramusian concubine one last time then threw a silk sheet over her naked limbs.

"You will remain," he said in her barbaric tongue, "but you will be a statue. Do you hear me?"

Heria nodded and bowed her head. He tugged the sheet up until she was entirely covered, then pulled his robe about him and sashed it tight. He thrust his plain-hilted dagger into the sash and when he looked up again Shahr Johor was there, kneeling with his eyes fixed floorwards.

"Up, up," he said impatiently, and gestured to a low stool while he himself took his place on a silk-upholstered divan by one wall.

They could hear the birds singing in the gardens beyond the seraglio, the bubble of water in the fountains. This room was one of the most private in the entire palace, where Aurungzeb perused the most exquisite of his treasures—such as the girl cowering on the bed by the other wall, the sheet that cloaked her quivering as she breathed. The chamber was thick-walled, isolated from the labyrinth of the rest of the complex. One might scream to the depths of one's lungs within its confines and yet go unheard.

"Do you know why you are here?" the Sultan of Ostrabar and Aekir asked.

Shahr Johor was a young man with a fine black beard and eyes as dark as polished ebony.

"Yes, Majesty."

"Good. What think you of your new appointment?"

"I shall try to fulfil your wishes and ambitions to the best extent of my abilities, Majesty. I am yours to command."

"That's right," the Sultan grunted emphatically. "Your predecessor, the esteemed Shahr Baraz, is unfortunately rendered infirm due to the weight of his years. A magnificent soldier, but I am told his faculties are not what they once were—hence our failure before this absurd Ramusian fortress. You will carry on where Baraz left off. You will take Ormann Dyke, but first you will reorganize the army. My sources report that it is somewhat demoralized. Winter is coming on, the Thurian passes are closed and your only supply line is the Ostian river. When you reach the dyke you will put the army into winter quarters, and attack again once the weather has improved. In the meantime the accursed Ramusians will have to contend with coastal raids from our new allies, the Sultanates of Nalbeni and Danrimir. They will be prevented from reinforcing the dyke, and you will storm it when the winter snows abate."

"Then I am not to attack at once, Majesty?"

"No. As I said, the army is in need of some . . . reorganization. This present campaign is over. You will see that communications between the camps and the supply depots in Aekir are improved. Baraz was building a road, I believe; one of the last of his more coherent plans. Everything must be made ready so that in the spring the army is ready to move again. The dyke will be crushed and you will march on Torunn. A fresh levy will be made available to you then. Have you any questions?"

Shahr Johor, new supreme commander of the Merduk armies of Ostrabar, hesitated a moment and then said:

"One question, Majesty. Why was I selected for this particular honour? Shahr Baraz's second-in-command Mughal is surely better qualified."

Aurungzeb's florid face darkened. His fingers toyed with the hilt of his dagger.

"Mughal has a certain absurd attachment to Shahr Baraz. It would not do to leave him in command. He is being transferred elsewhere, as are most of the previous staff officers. I want a new beginning. We have been shackled by the old *Hraib* for too long; the world is entering a new age, when such outdated codes are a hindrance rather than a help. You are young and you have studied the new modes of warfare. I want you to apply your knowledge to the coming campaigns. There is a shipment of forty thousand arquebuses travelling down the Ostian River even as we speak. You will equip the best troops with them, and train them in the tactics that the Torunnans have used against us in the past. We will no longer face firearms with steel and muscle and raw courage. War has become a scientific thing. You will be the first general of my people to wage it according to the new rules."

Shahr Johor flung himself to the floor.

"You honour me too much, my Sultan. My life is yours. I will send you the spoils of all the Ramusian kingdoms. The west shall be brought into the fold of the True Faith, if Ahrimuz wills it."

"He wills it," Aurungzeb said sharply. "And so do I. Do not forget that." He waved a hand. "You may go."

Shahr Johor backed away, bowing as he went. Aurungzeb stood motionless long after he had gone, then: "Sit up!" he said abruptly.

Heria straightened, the silk sliding like water from her shoulders.

"Raise your head."

She did so, staring at a point on the ornate ceiling.

Aurungzeb sidled over to her. He was as silent as a cat in his movements, despite being a big man on the edge of corpulence. His eyes drank her in. One brown ring-encrusted hand slid along her torso. She remained as motionless as marble, a lovely statue sculpted by some genius.

"I shall give you a name," the Sultan breathed. "You must have a name. I know. I shall call you Ahara. It is the old name for the wind that every year sweeps westward across the steppes of Kambaksk and Kurasan. My people followed that wind, and with them went the Faith. Ahara. Say it."

She stared at him dumbly. He cursed and began speaking in the halting Normannic that was the common language of the western kingdoms.

"Your name is Ahara. Say it."

"Ahara."

He grinned hugely, his teeth a white gleam in his beard.

"I will have you taught our tongue, Ahara. I want to hear you speak it to me on our wedding night."

Still her eyes revealed nothing. He laughed.

"I talk to myself, do I not? You Ramusians . . . You will have to be consecrated into the Prophet's worship, of course. And you are too thin, the marks of the journey are upon you yet. I will feed you up, put flesh on those bones of yours. You will bear me fine sons in the time to come, and they will spend so much time killing each other that their sire will be left in peace in his old age." He pulled the sheet up around her. "Wife number twenty-six, you will be. I should have had more, but I am an abstemious man."

He flung an arm out towards the doorway. "Go," he said in Normannic.

She scampered from the chamber, the silk billowing from her shoulders like a pair of wings. Her feet could be heard pattering on the marble and porphyry of the floors beyond. Aurungzeb smiled into the empty room. He was in a good mood. He had found himself a superb new wife—he would marry her, despite the inevitable objections. She was too rare a jewel to keep as a mere concubine.

And he had rid himself of that relic from the past, Shahr Baraz. The orders had gone out by special courier, a picked squad of the palace guard journeying with them to carry them out. Soon the old man's head would be carted towards Orkhan in a jar, pickled in vinegar. He had been a faithful servant, a superb soldier, but now that Aekir had fallen and the impossible had been achieved, he was no longer needed. And besides, he was growing dangerously insubordinate. Shahr Johor was different. He was forward-looking for one thing, and after the example of Baraz he would know better than to disobey his Sultan.

Aurungzeb lay back on the rumpled, sex-smelling bed.

A pity they would not take the dyke in the same campaigning season as they had taken Aekir. That would have been a feat indeed. But it was of no great import that they would have to wait out the winter. It would give him a chance to cement the new alliances with Nalbeni and Danrimir.

The Ramusians, he knew, mostly thought of the Seven Sultanates as one Merduk power-bloc, but the reality was different. There were rivalries and intrigues, even minor wars between this sultanate and that Danrimir was virtually an Ostrabarian client state, so closely tied to Orkhan had she become in the last months, but Nalbeni was a different matter.

The oldest of the Merduk countries, Nalbeni had been founded before even the Fimbrian-Hegemony had fallen. It was primarily a sea power and its capital, Nalben, was supposed to be the largest port in the world, save perhaps for Abrusio of Hebrion in the west. It did not trust this upstart state from the north of the Kardian Sea, so naturally had allied with it to keep a closer eye on its progress. It was a good way of insinuating Nalbenic diplomats into Aurungzeb's court. Diplomats with flapping ears and heavy purses. But such was the way of the world. Ostrabar needed Nalbeni to keep up the pressure on Torunna from a different direction, so that when Shahr Johor moved against the dyke in the spring he would not find it manned by all the armies of Torunna.

This war was not coming to a close; it was only beginning. Before I am done, Aurungzeb thought, I will have all the Seven Sultanates doing my bidding, and Merduk armies will be marching to the very brim of the Western Ocean. Charibon I will set afire, and its black priests I shall crucify by the thousands. Temples of the True Faith shall be reared up over the whole continent. If the Prophet wills it.

A shadow fell through the doorway. Aurungzeb sat up at once.

"Akran?"

"No, Sultan. It is I, Orkh."

"You were not announced."

"I was not seen."

The shadow glided into the room and was nothing more than that: an absence of light, a mere shape.

"What do you want?"

"To speak with you."

"Speak, then. And let me see you. I am sick of this ghost business."

"You might not like what you see, Sultan."

"Show yourself. I command it."

The shadow took on substance, another dimension. In a moment a man stood there in long dun-coloured robes. Or what had once been a man.

"Beard of the Prophet!" Aurungzeb breathed.

The thing smiled, and the lights that were its eyes became two glowing slots.

"Is this what happened to you when—?"

"When Baraz slew my homunculus? Yes. I was relaying your own voice through it, acting as a conductor; thus I could not defend myself against the . . . consequences until it was too late."

"But why has it done this to you?"

"The surge of power was like the explosion of a gun when the barrel is blocked. Something of the Dweomer that went into making the homunculus was blasted back through me, and I had no barriers up because of my role in the communication. It changed me. I am working on a remedy for the unfortunate effects."

"I see now why you haunt the palace like a shadow."

"I have no wish to frighten your concubines—especially one so delicious as just passed me in the corridor."

"What did you want, Orkh? I am meeting the Nalbenic ambassadors soon."

"I am your eyes and ears, Majesty, despite the malady which afflicts me. I have agents in every city in the west. It is partly because of my network of information gatherers that this sultanate has risen to the prominence it now enjoys. Is that not true?"

"There may be something in what you say," Aurungzeb admitted, scowling. He did not like to be reminded of his reliance on the sorcerer, or on anyone else for that matter.

"Well, I have a very interesting piece of information I would like to impart to you. It does not concern the present war, but an occurrence much further west in one of the Ramusian states."

"Go on."

"It seems there is a purge in progress in the kingdom of Hebrion, which seeks to rid the land of its exotic elements. I lost two of my best agents to their damned pyres, but the chief targets of the purge seem to be oldwives, herbalists, weather-workers, thaumaturgists and cantrimers—in short, anyone who has an inkling of the Dweomer."

"Interesting."

"My sources—those who survived—tell me, however, that this purge was initiated by the accursed Inceptines—the Black Priests of the west—and has not found favour with King Abeleyn."

"Why does he not command it stopped then?" Aurungzeb asked gruffly. "Is a king not King in his own land?"

"Not in the west, sire. Their Church has a great say in the running of every kingdom."

"Fools! What kind of rulers are they? But I interrupt. Continue, Orkh."

"Abeleyn hired a small fleet, I am told, filled it to the brim with fleeing sorcerers and the like and commissioned the fleet to sail west."

"To where? Hebrion is the westernmost kingdom of the world."

"Exactly, sire. To where? They did not touch upon any of the other Ramusian states as far as I know. It may be they made landfall in the Brenn Isles or the Hebrionese, but there are rumours flying round the Hebrian capital."

"Rumours of what?"

"It is said that the fleet sailed with a Royal warrant for the setting up of a new colony, and it carried in addition to its passengers and a complement of soldiers everything that might be needed when starting a settlement in a hitherto uninhabited land."

"Orkh! Are you saying—?"

"Yes, my Sultan. The Ramusians have discovered a land in the far west, somewhere in the Great Western Ocean, and they are claiming it for themselves."

Aurungzeb sank back on the bed. Orkh let his Sultan sit in silence for a few moments; he could see the wheels turning.

"How reliable is this information, Orkh?" the Sultan asked at last.

"I am not a peddler of hearsay, sire. My informants know that to feed me false news is the best way to ensure a swift end. The rumours have been investigated, and they have substance."

Another pause.

"We cannot let it be, of course," the Sultan said thoughtfully. "We must test the veracity of your rumours, and if they possess the substance you say they do we shall outfit our own expedition and stake our claim. But Ostrabar is not a sea power. We have no ships."

"Nalbeni?"

"I trust them less than I do Ramusians. No, this must be done further from home. The Sea-Merduks of Calmar. Yes. I will commission them to send a fleet into the west, commanded by my own officers of course."

"It will be expensive, my Sultan."

"After Aekir, my credit is good anywhere," Aurungzeb said with a chuckle. "You have agents in Alcaras. See to it, Orkh. I will select the officers of this expedition personally."

"As my Sultan wishes. I have one boon to ask of him, however."

"Ask! Your information merits reward."

"I wish to be included in this expedition. I wish to sail west."

Aurungzeb stared closely at the hideously inhuman face of his court mage. "I need you here."

"My apprentice Batak, whom you know, is well able to take my place, and he does not have the same disability that afflicts me."

"Are you seeking a cure in the west, or oblivion, Orkh?"

"A cure if I can find one—oblivion if I cannot."

"Very well. You shall sail with the expedition."

Orkh faded back into misty shadow as the vizier came into the room, bent low, eyes averted.

"My Sultan, the Nalbenic ambassadors are here. They await your inimitable presence."

Aurungzeb waved a hand. "I'll be there directly."

The vizier left, still bowed. Aurungzeb stared around the chamber.

"Orkh? Are you there, Orkh?" But there was no answer. The mage had gone.

THE first snows had come to the Searil valley. Shahr Baraz had felt them in his tired old bones before he had even thrown off the furs. His head ached. It had been too long since he had slept out under the stars like his forebears, the chieftains of the eastern steppes.

Mughal already had the fire going. It was almost colourless in the bright morning light and the snow glare. Melted slush sizzled around the burning wood.

"Winter arrives early this year," Mughal said.

Shahr Baraz climbed to his feet. Darkness danced at the corners of his vision until he blinked it away. He was almost eighty-four years old.

"Pass me the skin, Mughal. My blood needs some heat in it."

He drank three gulps of searing mare's-milk spirit, and his limbs stopped shuddering. Warmth again.

"I had a look over the hill as the sun came up," Mughal said. "They have pulled back the camps to the reverse slopes and are busy entrenching there."

"A winter camp," Shahr Baraz said. "Campaigning is finished for this year. Nothing else will happen until the spring."

"Jaffan's loyalty is to you, my Khedive."

"Jaffan will obey the orders of Orkhan or he will find his head atop a spear before too long. He will not be left in command for he was too close to me. No, another khedive will be sent out. I hope, though, that Jaffan will not suffer for letting two old men slip away into the night."

"Who will the new khedive be, you think?"

"Who knows? Some creature of Aurungzeb's who is more malleable than I. One who will put his own ambitions above the lives of his men. The Searil will flow scarlet ere we take that fortress, Mughal."

"But it will fall in the spring. It will fall. And where will we be then?"

"Eating yoghurt in a felt hut on the steppes."

Mughal guffawed, then bent his face to the fire and nudged the kettle into the flames. They would have steaming *kava* to warm them before they broke camp and continued their journey.

"Will you turn your back on it so easily?" he asked.

Shahr Baraz was silent for a long time.

"I am of the old *Hraib*," he said at last. "This war which we have begun will usher the world into a new age. Men like myself and John Mogen were not destined to be leaders in the times to come. The world has changed, and is changing yet. The Merduk people are no longer the fierce steppe horsemen of my youth; their blood is mixed with many who were once Ramusian, and the old nomadic times are only a memory.

"Even the way of the warrior itself is changing. Gunpowder counts for more than courage. Arquebus balls take no heed of rank. Honour counts for less and less. Soon generals will be artisans and engineers rather than soldiers, and war will be a thing of equations and mathematics. That is not the way I have waged it, or ever will.

"So yes: I will turn my back on it, Mughal. I will leave it to the younger men who come after me. I have seen a Merduk host march through the streets of Aekir; my place in the story is assured. I have that to take with me. Now I will ride east to the land of my fathers, there to see the limitless plains of Kambaksk and Kolchuk, the birthplace of our nation, and there I will leave my bones."

"I would come with you, if I may," Mughal said.

The terrible old man smiled beneath the twin tusks of his moustache.

"I would like that. A companion shortens a journey, it is said. And it will be a long journey."

"But it is the last journey," Mughal murmured, and poured steaming *kava* for them both.

TELL me what you see," Macrobius said.

They stood on the battlements of the citadel of Ormann Dyke, a cluster of officers and soldiers and one old man who was missing his eyes. Corfe stared out at the white, empty, snow-shrouded land beyond the flinty torrent of the Searil river.

"There is nothing there. The camps have been abandoned. Even the trenches and walls they delved and reared are hard to see under the snow; mere shadows running across the face of the hills. Here and there is the remnant of a tent, a strew of wreckage covered with snow. They have gone, Holiness."

"What is that smell on the air, then?"

"They gathered their dead under the terms of the burial truce, and burned them on a pyre in one of the further valleys. It is smoking yet, a hill of ashes."

"Where have they gone, Corfe? Where did that great host go to?"

Corfe looked at his commander. Martellus shrugged.

"They have retreated into winter camp, a league or more from the walls."

"Then they are defeated. The dyke is safe."

"For now, yes. They will be back in the spring, when the snows melt. But we will be ready for them. We will hurl them back beyond the Ostian river and cleanse Aekir once more."

The High Pontiff bent his ravaged head, his white hair flickering in the chill breeze. "Thanks to God and the Blessed Saint."

"And you, Your Holiness, have done your duty here and done it well," Martellus said. "It is time you left to take up your proper place."

"My proper place?" Macrobius said. "Perhaps. I am no longer sure. Has there been no word from Charibon?"

"No," Martellus lied. "King Lofantyr will be returning from Vol Ephrir very soon; it is best you are in Torunn to meet him. There will be much for you and he to discuss. Corfe will go with you. He is a colonel now; he has done well. He is the only Torunnan to have survived Aekir and he will be able to answer the King's questions."

"Are you so sure the Merduks will not attack again, General?"

"I am. They have abandoned their artillery emplacements and will have to fight to rehouse their batteries again. No— my scouts tell me that they are completing a great new road between here and Aekir for the passage of supplies. And they have small parties sniffing the upper and lower stretches of the Searil, searching for a way to outflank the Dyke. They will not find it. The Fimbrians did well to build their fortress here. The campaign is finished for this year. You will spend a more comfortable winter in Torunn than you would here, Holiness, and you will be of more service to us there."

"Meaning?" Macrobius asked.

"Meaning I want you and Corfe to work on King Lofantyr. The dyke must be reinforced ere the snow melts. The Merduks have been having command difficulties—one of the reasons we are still here. But come spring they will be at our throats again under a new general. So it is rumoured."

Macrobius started. "Is Shahr Baraz dead then?"

"Dead or replaced—it makes little difference. But the Ostian is reputed to be thick with supply barges, many of them carrying firearms. The tactics will be different when they come again, and we have lost the eastern barbican. We hang on here by a thread, despite the fools who are celebrating in the refugee camps—another subject that Corfe will bring up when he meets the King."

Macrobius smiled wryly, looked blindly at Corfe.

"You have come far, my friend, since we shared burnt turnip on the Western Road. You have become a man who consorts with kings and Pontiffs, and your star has not finished rising yet; I can feel it."

"You will have thirty of Ranafast's troopers to escort you," Martellus said, a little put out. "It is all we can spare, but it should be enough. The road south is still open, but you should leave as soon as you can."

"I travel in state no longer, General," Macrobius said. "All I own I wear on my back. I can go whenever you wish."

"It is time the world saw Macrobius again, and heard of the things that have been done here. We have done well, but it is only the first battle of a long war."

THE year was turning. Even in Vol Ephrir the balminess was vanishing from the air and the flaming trees were growing barer by the day. The Conclave of Kings ground on interminably as the land settled into an early winter, a bitter winter that was already rendering the mountains impassable. This dark season would be long and hard, harder still for those lands which were under the shadow of invasion and war.

The High Pontiff in Charibon, Himerius II, issued a Pontifical bull denouncing the old blind man rumoured to be Macrobius and housed in Ormann Dyke as an impostor and a heretic. His sponsor, the Torunnan general Pieter Martellus, who had successfully defended the dyke against the army of Shahr Baraz, was indicted on charges of heresy in his absence, and couriers were sent to Torunna to demand his removal and punishment.

A second bull authorized clerical authorities in the Five Ramusian Kingdoms of the West, as well as the duchies and principalities, to seize and detain any person or persons who were users of black magic, who were natives of a state not within the Ramusian fold or who publicly objected to the seizure of any of the above. These persons' property was to be considered confiscate and divided between the Church and the secular authorities of the region, and they were to be detained pending a Religious Trial.

At roughly the same time two thousand Knights Militant reached Abrusio in the Kingdom of Hebrion and were met by representatives of the Inceptine Order. The city of Abrusio was put under Theocratic Law and governed by a body of Inceptines and nobles answerable only to the High Pontiff and to the Hebrian king—who unfortunately was far away in Vol Ephrir. The first day of the new rule was marked by the burning of seven hundred and thirty people, thus emptying the catacombs for the influx of fresh heretics and foreigners the Knights were rounding up throughout the city and the kingdom beyond.

But the crisis that would do most to affect the shape of the world in the times to come occurred in Vol Ephrir, where the assembled kings met to discuss the bulls of Himerius and the dilemmas facing the west.

"To all appearances, we have two Pontiffs," Cadamost said simply. "That is a situation which cannot be allowed to continue. If it does, then anarchy will ensue."

"Anarchy is already alive and well throughout the Five Kingdoms, thanks to Himerius," Abeleyn snarled. He had been apprised of the situation in Hebrion by Golophin's gyrfalcon, and now he burned to be away, to take back his kingdom and halt the atrocities.

"You verge on the edge of heresy, cousin," Skarpathin of Finnmark said, smiling unpleasantly.

"I teeter on the abyss of common sense, whilst you fools dance arguments on the heads of pins. Can't you see what is happening? Himerius realizes he is the impostor—the wrongly elected High Pontiff—so he strikes first, stamping his authority across the continent in fire and blood—"

"And rightly so," said Haukir of Almark resoundingly. "It is time the Church governed with a strong hand. Macrobius, who is undoubtedly dead, was an old woman who let things slide. Himerius is the kind of man we need on the Pontifical throne: a man unafraid to act. A strong hand on the tiller."

"Spare me the eulogy, cousin," Abeleyn sneered. "Everyone knows that the Inceptines have had Almark in the pocket of their habits for years."

Haukir went white. "Even kings have limits," he said in an unusually subdued voice. "Even kings can transgress. Your words will condemn you, boy. Already the Church governs your capital. If you do not take care it will end up governing your kingdom and you will die an excommunicate."

"I will die my own man then, and not a puppet of power-hungry Ravens!" Abeleyn cried.

The chamber went silent, the heads of state appalled at this exchange. The Fimbrians, however, looked only distantly interested, as if this were nothing to do with them.

"I will not obey the bulls of Himerius," Abeleyn said in a calmer voice. "I do not recognize him as Pontiff, but call him impostor and usurper. The true Pontiff is Macrobius. I repudiate the authority of Charibon, based as it is on a falsehood, and I will not see my kingdom torn apart by avaricious murderers who happen to be in the guise of clerics!"

Cadamost started to speak, but Abeleyn quelled him with a look. He was on his feet now, and every eye in the room was turned to him. In the silence it was possible to hear the birds singing in the tallest of the trees that surrounded the palace towers.

"I hereby withdraw Hebrion from the company of Ramusian Kingdoms which recognize the Prelate Himerius as High Pontiff. His inhumane edicts I will ignore, his servants I will banish from my borders. I stand here and say to you: who else is with me in this thing? Who else recognizes Macrobius as the true head of the Church?"

There was a pause, and then Mark of Astarac stood up slowly, heavily. His reluctance was obvious, but he faced the other rulers squarely.

"Astarac is allied to Hebrion in this thing; Abeleyn is betrothed to my sister. I will stand by him. I also repudiate Himerius the usurper."

A buzz of talk swept the room. It was silenced by the scraping of another chair on the beautifully ornate floor.

Lofantyr of Torunna was on his feet.

"Torunna has stood alone against the threat from the east.

No succour have we had from any western state, and as Pontiff, Himerius has denied us the aid which is our right. I believe my general, Martellus the Lion of Ormann Dyke. Macrobius is alive and is Pontiff. I will stand with Hebrion and Astarac in this thing."

That was all. No one else stood up, no one else spoke. The Ramusian Kingdoms were irrevocably split down the middle, and the continent possessed two High Pontiffs, perhaps two Churches. The air in the chamber was pregnant with foreboding, a sense of the destiny of the moment.

Cadamost cleared his throat and when he spoke was as hoarse as a crow, his singer's voice crushed.

"I beg you, think of what you are doing. You lead three of the great kingdoms of the west. At a time when the enemy howls on our borders, we cannot afford to be riven apart like this. We cannot let the faith that sustains us be the weapon which cleaves our ranks apart."

"You are Heretics, all three of you," old Haukir said with scarcely concealed satisfaction. "No aid will you receive now, Lofantyr; you have signed the death warrant of your kingdom. And Hebrion and Astarac cannot stand alone against the other states of the west."

Abeleyn looked at them as they sat there: kings, dukes and princes. Almark and Perigraine, Finnmark and Candelaria, Tarber and Gardiac, Touron and Fulk. Even Gabrion, long known for its tradition of independence. But what of the two men in black who sat silent in their midst? What of the Fimbrians?

"Do the electorates have anything to say about this, or will they follow the lead of others?" he asked.

Marshal Jonakait raised his eyebrows slightly.

"Fimbria has never recognized the authority of any power outside its borders, including that of the Pontiff. We too are a Ramusian country, and the Inceptines live and work within our borders, but the electors are not bound by the bulls or edicts of the head of the Church."

Hope sprang up in Abeleyn. "Then your offer of troops still stands?"

Something like a smile crossed the marshal's hard face and then was gone.

"We will not contribute soldiers to any fellow-Ramusian

state which wars upon another, but we will make them available to fight the Merduks."

Cadamost started up. "You cannot! You will be aiding heretics whose souls are as damned as the Merduks' are!"

Jonakait shrugged. "Only in certain eyes. The struggle in the east takes precedence over all else in the eyes of our superiors. If others disagree, then they will have to make their arguments known and we will consider them. But no Fimbrian will be farmed out as a mercenary in a fratricidal religious war."

"That is absurd!" Haukir cried. "Not long ago you were promising troops to whoever wanted them. What is that if not farming your soldiers out as mercenaries?"

"Each and every case will be considered on its merits. I can promise no more."

The Fimbrians naturally could not commit themselves here and now. The west had split down the middle. In honour, the electorates would have to send troops to Lofantyr—he had already asked for them, Abeleyn knew that. But they would wait and see what happened before committing them anywhere else. No doubt the marshals were secretly hugging themselves with glee at the thought of a divided west, the Five Kingdoms at each other's throats. It augured well for any Fimbrian attempt to reestablish the Hegemony she had lost centuries before. But for the moment, more important was the fact that Lofantyr would have his reinforcements—though they would have a long journey ahead of them were they not to traverse Perigraine to reach Ormann Dyke.

The gamble had paid off. Mark and Lofantyr had played their roles well, but then Abeleyn had had them well-rehearsed in the days following the news from Charibon.

Haukir glared at the three renegade monarchs.

"I will personally see that the High Pontiff excommunicates you, and it will mean war—Ramusian versus Ramusian. May God forgive you for what you have done this day."

Abeleyn leaned forward on to the table. His eyes were like two black holes.

"What we have done today is lift our heads out of the Inceptine yoke that has been tightening on the throat of every land in the west for decades. We have delivered our kingdoms from the terror of the pyre."

"You have plunged the west into war at a time when she is already fighting for her life," Cadamost said.

"No," Lofantyr told him hotly. "Torunna is fighting for her life. My kingdom, my people—we are the ones who are dying on the frontier. You here know nothing of what we have suffered, and you have cared less. The true Pontiff resides in Ormann Dyke at the heart of the struggle to defend the west. He is not sitting in Charibon issuing edicts that will send thousands to the pyre. I tell you this: before I am done, I will see this Himerius burned on the same pyre he has already burned so many innocents upon."

There was a shocked stillness. The men sitting at the table had an air of disbelief about them, as though they could not quite credit what they had heard.

"Leave this city," Cadamost said finally, his face white as paper and his eyes two red-limned orbs. "Leave it as kings in due state, for once Charibon hears of this you will be beyond the Church and every right-thinking man's hand will be turned against you. Your anointed right to rule will be stripped from you and your kingdoms declared outlaw states. No orthodox ruler need fear retribution if he invades your borders. Our faces are turned against you. Go."

The three kings left their places and stood together. Before they started for the door, Abeleyn turned round one last time.

"It is Himerius we defy. We harbour no ill-will towards any other state or ruler—"

Haukir snorted derisively.

"—but if any seek to injure us without good cause, then I swear this to all of you: our armies will seek redress in the blood of your subjects, our fleets will make unending infernos of your coasts and we will show less pity to our foes than the blackest Merduk sultan. You will rue the day and hour you crossed swords with Hebrion, or Astarac, or Torunna. And so, gentlemen, we bid you good day."

The three young men, all kings, turned and left the chamber together. In the silence that followed, the Himerian kings, as they would come to be known, stared at the round table which had witnessed their conclave and the dissolution of the Five Kingdoms. The path of history had been set; all they could do now was follow it and pray to God and the blessed Ramusio for guidance on their journey.

TWENTY-FIVE

THE north-easter stayed with them, as steady and as welcome as the Hebrian trade. Hawkwood could feel the constant thrumming of its power on the ship as though it were acting on the marrow of his very bones. The *Osprey* was alive, afloat, running before the wind. His mind relaxed and wandered off to that other place once more.

HE was a boy again, at sea for the first time on the clumsy caravel which had been the first Hawkwood-owned ship. His father was there, shouting obscenities at the straining seamen, and the white spray was coming aboard in packets as the vessel ran before the wind on the peridot-green swells of the Levangore. If he looked aft he could see the pale, dust-coloured coast of Gabrion with the darker rises of forests among the inland hills; and to larboard were the first islands of the Malacar Archipelago, floating like insubstantial ghosts in the haze of heat that had settled on the horizon.

Up and down, up and down the bow of the caravel went, the green waves like shimmering walls looming up and retreating again, the gulls screeching and calling and dropping guano over the deck, the rigging straining and creaking in time to the working timbers of the ship, and the blessed wind they had harnessed bellying out the booming and flapping sails.

This, he had thought, is the *sea*. And he had never questioned his right to be on it; rather he had welcomed his craft as a man would his wife.

HAWKWOOD could not move. He was drenched in sweat and as immobile as a marble caryatid. There was an unfamiliar smell in his nostrils. Burning.

Avast shudder as the ships came together, their hulls crunching and colliding.

"Fire!" Hawkwood yelled, and along the deck the men whipped the smoking slow-match across the touch-holes of the guns. Like a rippling thunder they exploded in sequence, leaping back on their carriages like startled bulls. There was an enormous noise, unlike any other. Louder than a storm-surf striking a rocky shore or a tempest in the heights of the Hebros. The whole starboard side of the ship disappeared in smoke and fire. Only men's screams and the shrieking of the blasted timbers carried above the roar.

The corsairs fired their own broadside, the muzzles of their culverins touching the very side of the carrack. They elevated the muzzles so the shot plunged upwards through the deck. The air exploded, became full of jagged shards of wood which ripped men apart, flung them clear across the deck or tossed them overboard like gutted fish. Hawkwood clambered on to the starboard quarterdeck rail and raised the heavy cutlass above his head. "*Now*, lads, at them. Boarding parties away!"

And then he leapt on to the crowded slaughterhouse of the enemy ship.

"RICHARD!' she cried as he pushed into her, expending himself, driving her backbone into the stuffed softness of the bed. The sweat dripped off his face to land on her collarbone and trickled between her breasts. Jemilla grinned fiercely up at him, her body answering his, struggling against him. The sweat was a slick glue between them so their skins sucked and slid as they moved together and apart, like a ship breasting a heavy swell, the keel burying itself in each wave.

• • •

BUT the heat. His body was on fire, lying in a pool of liquid metal, every movement a torment, every pore oozing his life's fluid. The heat squeezed the water out of him until he was as dry and withered as the salted fish they had barrelled in the hold. If he moved he would crackle and creak and break apart into fragments as fine and desiccated as ash.

"Richard."

He opened his eyes.

Bardolin smiled. "So you have returned from your voyaging at last."

The ship moved about him, a lulling presence. He sensed that the wind was fine and steady on the quarter, a fresh breeze pushing them ever westwards. In the almost-quiet he heard the ship's bell struck three times, and the noise was incredibly comforting, like hearing the sound of a familiar voice.

He turned his face to one side and immediately the pain began, a molten glow that was centred deep in his right shoulder. He groaned involuntarily.

"Easy." The mage's strong fingers steadied his head, grasping his chin.

"The fire," he croaked.

"We got it under control. The ship is safe, Captain, and we are making good progress."

"Help me sit up."

"No. You—"

"Help me up!"

The pain came and went in sobbing waves, but he blinked and ground his teeth until it was a bearable presence, something he could live with.

Their surroundings were unfamiliar to him. A small cabin, with a culverin squatting against one wall.

"Where is this?"

"The gundeck. The carpenter rigged up some partitions for you. You needed the peace."

So. He recognized it now, but it was strangely silent, as though the deck were almost deserted. He could hear many feet thumping above his head, and voices murmuring.

"The fire. The stern cabin—"

"More or less patched up. Chips has been working like a man possessed. We have no new glass for the stern windows though, so they must be shuttered most of the time."

"The log. Bardolin, did the log survive?"

The mage looked grim. "No. It went in the fire, as did most of your charts and the old rutter."

"Griella?"

"She is at peace. I was wrong ever to bring her on this voyage, and yet she saved our lives, I think. Murad's, anyway. It is hard to know. A hard thing to have done."

"She loved him." It could have been question or statement.

"In her own way, yes. But no good would have come of it. They would have destroyed each other in the end and it is better, perhaps, that it has come about this way." The mage's arm, unexpectedly strong, steadied Hawkwood as he swayed. "Be careful, Captain. We don't want anything springing its seams again."

"Ortelius," Hawkwood was saying, ignoring him. "I can't believe it."

"Yes, who would have? An Inceptine cleric also a werewolf! That raises many questions, Captain, both for us on board ship and for the great and the good back home. I have this feeling that we have overlooked something, in our pride and our wisdom. There is something deep down in our society which we had not thought to find. Something abominable."

"Mateo, ere he changed, said his master was high in a society. I don't think he meant the one we know."

"We may find some answers in the west, I suppose. I do not see this as a voyage of discovery any longer, Captain, or an attempt at colonization. It is more of an armed reconnaissance. Murad concurs."

"The west. You think—?"

"That it is inhabited? Yes, but by what manner of men or beasts or both I know not."

Hawkwood swung his legs off the hanging cot. He could manage the pain now. It came and went like a tide. His right arm was strapped tightly to the side of his chest, unbalancing him.

"How bad is this?"

"The thing bit your collar-bone clean through, and mangled the ends of the bone. I have been cleaning the wound, removing the splinters. A couple of the oldwives have sat with me and kept wound-sickness at bay. It smells sweet enough and I think we have brought it off, but you will have a terrible scar and a lump, and your right arm will never be as strong again."

But I'm alive, Hawkwood thought. That is something. And my ship is afloat; that is something more.

He was wearing only a clout of linen about his loins and his legs seemed oddly pale to him, the feet a long distance away. He stared at them absently, and then a jet of fear thrilled him.

"Bardolin, the beast bit me. Does that mean I have its disease? Will I change?"

"The black disease is not contagious in the way people think. It is not carried in a bite."

"But Ortelius made a werewolf of Mateo."

"Yes. That intrigues me, I must admit. Fear not, Captain, whatever arcane and bloody initiation turned the ship's boy into a shifter was not practised on you. Men do not catch lycanthropy from a bite, no matter what the superstitions say. Gregory confirms it, and my old master, Golophin, believed it also. There is something more at work which we cannot yet understand."

Relieved somewhat, Hawkwood relaxed. "Why did he do it? Why did he do that to poor Mateo?"

"My guess is he needed help. He had seen how determined we were to continue west and was set on wiping out the three of us—you, Murad and I. To do that swiftly and in one swoop, he would need a fellow conspirator. He may also have been . . . lonely. Who knows? I cannot lay claim to any great insights into the souls of shifters, for all that I knew Griella better than most. There is a mystery in them that has to do with the relationship between the man—or the woman—and the beast." He halted and smiled wryly. "My apologies. I had not intended to confront you with a treatise."

"You knew—you knew what she was before ever she came aboard."

"I knew, may God forgive me. I was a little in love with her also, you see. I thought I could control her. I even had wild ideas of curing her. But that is done with. I will have it on my conscience."

"It's all right. It's over with anyway—for the best, maybe. Tell me, how long has it been since the fire and the rest? How long have I been on my back?"

"Eight days."

"Eight days! Sweet Saints in heaven! Help me to my feet, Bardolin. I must talk to Velasca. I must check our course."

Bardolin pushed him gently but inexorably back on to the cot.

"Velasca, it seems, knows how to sail due west, and the wind has been as steady as you please. I will send him down to you if you desire, but you are not going anywhere. Not for a while yet."

Hawkwood sank on to the blankets once more. His head was spinning.

"Very well. Send him down at once, and get someone to help me dress, will you? And send Chips, too. I want to talk to him about the repairs."

"All right, Captain. I'll get them down as soon as I may."

Bardolin left him, frowning.

Eight days. They might be within a sennight of reaching land, if Velasca had kept to his course. They were going to do it. Hawkwood could feel it in his mangled bones. He could feel the land, bulking somewhere on some unconscious horizon illuminated only by a mariner's intuition. It was there, and they were closing on it with every hour the carrack ploughed on before the kindly wind.

MURAD stood at the break of the quarterdeck with his officers on either side, his stance adjusting itself automatically to the roll of the ship. His long lank hair was flying free and he was dressed in his black riding leathers. His rapier hung scabbarded by his side. Though his face was white as chalk, the scar that furrowed one hollow cheek seemed to have been kindled by the wind into a blazing carmine and his eyes were as dark as sloes.

The waist was packed with people, the gangways lined with watching soldiers. Nearly all the ship's company were present for punishment.

"Carry on, Sequero," Murad said tonelessly.

Sequero stepped forward to the rail. "Sergeant Mensurado, bring the man forward."

There was a boil of activity in the waist. Mensurado and two other soldiers thrust through the throng with a fourth man whose hands were tied behind his back.

"Read the charges, Ensign."

Sequero called out in a clear voice so the assembled company could hear:

"Gabriello Habrar, you are charged that on the eleventh day of Endorion in the year of the Saint five hundred and fifty-one, you did in the forecastle of the carrack *Gabrian Osprey* utter remarks detrimental to the morale and determination of a crown-sponsored expedition and thus did revile and denigrate the authority of our commander and his lord, our sovereign King, Abeleyn of Hebrion and Imerdon."

Sequero paused and glanced at Murad. The lean nobleman nodded curtly.

"You are therefore sentenced to the strappado. Sergeant Mensurado, carry on. Drummer."

A harsh, dry drumming began as one of the soldiers started to ply the goatskin of his instrument. A sailor perched on the main yardarm let down a rope which Mensurado and his comrades fastened to the wrists of the accused man. The other end of the rope was thrown to the soldiers on the gangway.

Murad lifted a hand.

The bound man was hauled into the air by the wrists, his hands at a horrible angle up his back and his shoulder-blades protruding grotesquely. He screamed in agony, but the rasping drumroll smothered the sound. Then he dangled, kicking and twisting. After a few minutes the screaming stopped and he swayed on the end of the rope like a sack of meat, his eyes bulging, blood trickling from his bitten tongue.

"Cut him down," Murad ordered, and turned away from the sight to a contemplation of the carrack's wake. Sequero and di Souza went to him.

"I will have discipline," Murad said coldly. "You, gentlemen, have not been doing your job. The men are muttering and mutinous. I will have that out of them if I have to flog and strappado every last one of the dastards. Is that clear?"

Di Souza mumbled an agreement. Sequero did not speak, but his eyes were blazing.

"Have you something you wish to say, Ensign?" Murad demanded, turning on his aristocratic subordinate.

"Only that if you strappado every man in the tercio we'll have damned few fit to shoulder an arquebus when finally we hit land," Sequero said, not one whit intimidated by the snake-blank eyes of his superior officer.

Murad stared at him for a long moment, and the ensign blenched but stood his ground. Finally a smile twisted the older man's face.

"I would sooner have a maimed man who is loyal than a fit one who is not," he said quietly. "It would seem, Sequero, that you are developing some regard for your fellow men, scum from the bottom of the heap though they might be. Perhaps this voyage is teaching you the compassion of a commoner or a Mendicant Friar. If at any stage your burgeoning sympathy for the common soldiery interferes with your duty and your loyalty to your superior and your king, you will, I am sure, be the first to let me know."

Sequero said nothing, but he looked at his senior officer with open hatred. Murad smiled again, that dead, cold smile which was worse than an angry glare.

"You may go, both of you. See to Habrar, di Souza. Get one of these witches on board to have a look at him. Sequero, we will have small-arms practice this evening after the meal."

They both saluted, then turned on their heels and left the quarterdeck. The crowd in the waist was already dispersing, many black looks being thrown at the nobleman who lounged at the carrack's taffrail.

Murad did not care. He knew that his vision of a colony in the west governed by himself was a pipe-dream, morning mist to be burned away by the sun. Talking to Bardolin, he had found himself agreeing with the mage that there must be something in the west, something Ortelius had been charged to keep them from discovering. But by whom had he been charged? Either the shape-shifting cleric had been sent on his mission by a Ramusian monarch, which was unlikely—none of the western kings would willingly use both an Inceptine and a werewolf as an agent—or he was working for someone already in the west. Murad's undiscovered continent had already been claimed.

But by whom?

Werewolves. Shifters. Mages. He was sick to death of the lot of them. They made him shudder. And the memory of his dreams—what he had thought were dreams—still caused him to lie open-eyed and sweating in the night. He had shared a bed with the beast, had felt its heat and the baleful regard of its eyes.

He remembered Griella's body taut as cord under him, the tawny smoothness of her skin. And he turned his face to the carrack's wake once more so that none of the scum below might see the burning brightness that flooded his expressionless black eyes.

THE carrack was regularly running off sixty leagues a day, the north-easter propelling her along at a smooth seven knots. Four hundred and eighty leagues, perhaps, since Hawkwood had been confined to his bunk. They had travelled the distance from the southern Calmaric deserts to the far frozen north of Yazdegard; the extent of the known world. And still it seemed there was no sign of an end to the ocean.

The fire on board had caught the mizzen course and burned away the mizzen backstays and a fair portion of the shrouds. If a squall had hit them then they would have lost the mast, but the sea had been kind to them. The flames had been doused with Dweomer-pumped seawater, some of the sorcerers on board lifting hundred-gallon packets of the stuff out of the waves and dumping it over the mizzen, the quarterdeck and the stern. Whilst Hawkwood had been unconscious the repairs had gone on apace, and the carrack was whole again with only a few black charred scars to mark how close to disaster she had come. But as the carpenter informed Hawkwood that afternoon, they had used up the last of their timber stores to put right the damage and could now do no more. If the ship was damaged again they would have nothing to repair her with. They had no spare cordage or cable, either. It would be knotting and splicing until they made landfall.

Velasca made his report also. He had kept a tolerably legible log in the days he had conned the ship alone, but he was obviously relieved to have his captain conscious and clear-headed. He knew little of the nuances of navigation, being just about able to take a cross-staff reading and keep the ship on a compass bearing. As soon as he was able, Hawkwood was up on deck, taking sightings from the Pole Star and checking his deadreckoning over and over. He had a man in the forechains day and night with the deep-sea lead, sounding for the bottom, and he shortened sail at night despite the protests of Murad, who wanted them to tear along under every scrap of canvas the carrack possessed. He could not convince the nobleman of his own conviction that they were nearing land at last. It was a mariner's guess, something in the smell of the air, perhaps, or the appearance of the ocean, but Hawkwood was sure that the Western Continent was not far away.

O N the twentieth day of Endorion, nine days after Hawk-wood had woken to find Bardolin leaning over him, the leadsman in the forechains raised his voice into a strangled shout that made every man and woman on board look up. For days he had been chanting monotonously: "No bottom. No bottom here with this line." But now he yelled excitedly:

"Eighty fathoms! Eighty fathoms with this line!"

Hawkwood and Murad were on the quarterdeck, Hawkwood bending over the table they had brought up from below, writing laboriously and painfully with his left hand into his new log.

"Seventy-five! Seventy-five fathoms!" the leadsman called. And the ship was swept with a buzz of excited talk. The companionways thundered as passengers and soldiers clambered out on deck to see what was going on.

"Seventy fathoms! White sand and seashells in the lead!"

"Keep sounding!" Hawkwood bellowed forward. "All hands! All hands to shorten sail!"

Eight bells in the last dog-watch had just been struck and the watch had changed, but the whole ship's crew came scampering out into the waist and forecastle.

"Velasca!" Hawkwood roared over the soft thudding of feet and the rising babble. Topsails alone! Keep her braced round there!"

"Is it land?" Murad was asking, his eyes glittering. "Is that it? I can see nothing."

Hawkwood ignored him and peered up at the foretop where the lookout was stationed.

"In the foretop there! What do you see?"

There was a pause.

"Nothing but haze out to six or seven leagues, sir."

"Keep a good eye out, then."

"What is happening?" Murad demanded, his face puce with anger.

"We are on a shelving shore, Lord Murad," Hawkwood said calmly. "The sea is shallowing."

"Does that mean we are approaching landfall?"

"Possibly, yes."

"How far away is it?" Murad scanned the horizon as though he fully expected the Western Continent to pop up over it at that very second.

"I have no way of knowing, but we're shortening sail so we don't run full-tilt on to any reefs."

"Saints in heaven!" Murad said hoarsely. "It's really out there, isn't it?"

Hawkwood allowed himself to grin.

"Yes, Murad, it really is."

O N into the evening the carrack ran smoothly with the wind on her quarter and most of the ship's company on deck, their faces turned towards the west. When the first stars came out in the towering blue-black vault of the night sky the passengers retired below to eat, but Hawkwood kept both watches on deck, chewing salt pork and ship's biscuit. And the leadsman continued his chant from the forechains:

"Sixty fathoms. Sixty fathoms with this line."

There was a different quality to the air. The sailors could feel it. There was something more humid and cloying about it that was entirely at odds with the usual keen nature of the open sea, and Hawkwood thought he could smell something now; that growing smell like a breath of a summer garden. It was not far away.

"White foam! White foam dead ahead two cables!" the lookout screamed.

Hawkwood bent to call down the tiller-hatch. "Tiller there! Larboard by two points. West-sou'-west."

"Aye, sir."

The carrack moved smoothly round, the wind coming right aft now. The crew rushed to the braces to trim the yards. Hawkwood saw the white flicker and rush of foam breaking on black rocks off on the starboard side.

"Leadsman! What's our depth?"

There was a splash, a long waiting minute, then the leadsman declared, "Forty fathoms, sir, and white sand!"

"Take in topsails!" Hawkwood shouted.

The crew raced up the shrouds, bent over the topsail yards and began folding in the pale expanses of canvas. The ship lost speed.

"Why are we slowing down, Captain?" It was Murad, coming up the quarterdeck ladder almost at a run.

"Breakers ahead!" the lookout shrieked. "Starboard and larboard. Three cables from the bow!"

"God almighty!" Hawkwood exclaimed, startled. "Let go anchor!"

A seaman knocked loose the heavy sea anchor from the bows with the blow of a mallet. There was an enormous splash that lit up the black sea and the ship lost way, coming gradually to a full stop. She began to yaw as the wind pushed her stern around.

"Get a bower anchor out from the stern, Velasca," Hawkwood told his first mate. "And pray it holds in this ground."

He could see them himself: a broken line of white water barely visible off in the night and there was a new sound, the distant roar of surf. Hawkwood found he was trembling, his shoulder a scarlet flame of pain and the sweat sour and slick about him. But for the vigilance of the lookout, the ship would still be sailing towards the distant rocks.

"Is that it?" Murad asked in a breath, gazing out at the white foam which sliced open the darkness.

"Maybe. It might be a reef. We can't take any chances. I've dropped anchor. I don't like the ground, but there's no way I'm going any further in at night. We'll have to wait for daylight."

They both listened, watched. Hard to imagine what might be out there in the night; what manner of country lay beyond the humid darkness and the line of treacherous breakers.

"Stern anchor out and holding, sir," Velasca reported.

"Very good. Send down the larboard watch, and have the starboards haul the boats out over the side. They need a wetting, or they'll leak like sieves in the morning."

"Aye, sir."

Hawkwood stared out into the darkness, feeling the ship roll and pitch beneath his feet like a tethered animal bucking the halter. The heat of the night seemed more intense now, and he thought he saw the tiny bodies of insects flickering about the stern lantern. Not an isolated reef, then, but something more substantial. It was hard to believe after all this time that their destination was most likely out there in the darkness, under their lee.

He wondered what Haukal would have made of it, and for a moment pondered the disappearance of his other ship, the graceful little caravel and the good seamen who had manned her. Were they sailing still, on some distant latitude? Or were the fishes gnawing at their bones? He might never know.

Murad had gone. Hawkwood could hear the nobleman shouting orders down in the waist, calling for his officers and sergeants. He must have everything polished and shining; they would be claiming a new world for their king in the morning.

THAT last night, Hawkwood, Murad and Bardolin shared a bottle of Candelarian wine in the stern cabin, the shutters open to let in some air. A moth flew in the glassless windows and flapped about the table lantern like a thing entranced, and they, equally entranced, watched it avidly until it ventured too close to the flame and fell to the table, blackened. They let it lie there like some sort of mocking talisman, a promise of things to come, perhaps. And they toasted the voyage and whatever the morning might bring in the good wine, saving the last drops for a libation to be poured into the sea in a ritual far older than any vision of Ramusio's. They drank to those whose souls had been lost in their passage of the ocean and to whatever future might appear to them out of the sunrise.

In the morning the sun came up out of a belt of molten cloud, like the product of some vast furnace housed below the eastern horizon. Every member of the ship's company was on deck dressed in their best; Hawkwood was even wearing a sword. They could hear clearly the thunder of breaking surf, feel the damp, heavy air of the land. There were birds perched in the rigging, little dun sparrow-like creatures that twittered and sang with the rising of the sun. It was a sound that had the crew staring and smiling with wonder. Birdsong—something from a former life.

There was a mist, honeyed by the sunrise. The lookout in the foretop was the first man to be clear of it, and he yelled out to the depth of his lungs:

"Land ho! Abaft the starboard beam there—hills and trees. Great God!"

There was a spasm of cheering which Murad and his officers silenced. The mist thinned moment by moment.

And there it was. A green country of thick vegetation solidifying out of the veils of morning. Mountains rearing up into a clear sky, and the gathering sunrise gilding it.

"Man the boats," Hawkwood said hoarsely.

The crews of the two ship's boats that had survived scrambled down the ship's side, the soldiers clumsy with armour and weapons, the seamen agile as apes.

"Cast off!" Hawkwood shouted as soon as they were seated on the thwarts. There was no need to say anything else; all the crew had been well briefed, and Velasca knew his duty.

The lines were flung clear of the gunwales and the oars were lowered. The men began to row steadily, the exertion squeezing sweat out of their pores despite the youth of the morning. The ship grew smaller behind them.

There was a long gap in the breakers which would have accommodated the *Osprey* the night before, had there been the light to see it. The two boats powered through, lifted and tossed by the breaking waves. Within the reefs the water was calmer and they could see a ribbon of white sand fringing the unbroken curtain of jungle ahead.

"Captain!" one of the men cried. "Captain, look aft, on the landward side of the reef!"

Hawkwood and Murad turned as one to squint into the morning sun.

"I can't—" Murad began, and then was silent.

There on the westward side of the reef was the fragment of a ship. It was a beakhead part of a keel and a few other skeletal timbers. It looked as though the ship had run full tilt upon the reef, the fore part of the hull riding over it, the rest smashed away and sunk.

It was the *Grace of God*.

Men made the Sign of the Saint at their breasts, murmuring. Hawkwood's eyes were stinging as though in sympathy with his aching shoulder. To have come so far only to fail. So many good men.

"God have mercy on them," he murmured.

"Could any have survived?" Murad asked.

He shook his head slowly, studying the fragmented wreck and the booming surf, the jagged reef. It was sheer fluke that a portion of the ship had remained caught on the reef; it had been wedged there by the explosive force of the breakers. Only a miracle could have preserved those aboard.

"We are alone then," Murad said.

"We are alone," Hawkwood agreed.

The water shallowed. They could feel the heat of the land like a wall. The men raised their oars and a few seconds later the bottom of the boats kissed the sand.

Richard Hawkwood splashed out of the first boat, closely followed by Murad. Through the noise of the breakers out on the reef a glimmer of strange birdsong could be heard from the wall of jungle ahead.

They walked up out of the shallows and stood in hot white sand with the early sun heating their backs. The crews hauled the boats out of the water and stood panting. Soldiers held their arquebuses at the ready.

Murad turned to look at Hawkwood, and without a word they both began walking up the blazing beach, to where the jungle of the Western Continent gleamed dark and impenetrable before them.